Van Rijn

Sarah Emily Miano was born in Buffalo, NY, in 1974. Former chef, tour guide and private eye, she received an MA in Creative Writing from the University of East Anglia. *Encyclopædia of Snow*, her first novel, was published in the UK, Germany, Spain, Holland and Slovakia. As a work-in-progress, *Van Rijn* earned her an Arts Council Writers' Award in 2004. She lives in London.

Also by Sarah Emily Miano

Encyclopædia of Snow

SARAH EMILY MIANO

Van Rijn

PICADOR

First published 2006 by Picador

First published in paperback 2007 by Picador
an imprint of Pan Macmillan Ltd
Pan Macmillan, 20 New Wharf Road, London N1 9RR
Basingstoke and Oxford
Associated companies throughout the world
www.panmacmillan.com

ISBN 978-0-330-41181-3

A CIP catalogue record for this book is available from
the British Library.

Typeset by SetSystems Ltd, Saffron Walden, Essex
Printed and bound in Great Britain by
Mackays of Chatham plc, Chatham, Kent

Visit www.panmacmillan.com to read more about all our books
and to buy them. You will also find features, author interviews and
news of any author events, and you can sign up for e-newsletters
so that you're always first to hear about our new releases.

for Andrew Motion

'There's no art to find the mind's construction in the face.'

SHAKESPEARE, *Macbeth*, 1606

'But this is my fate and this is my misfortune; I can't help it; I have to follow him: we're from the same village, I've eaten his bread, I love him dearly, he's a grateful man, he gave me his donkeys, and more than anything else, I'm faithful; and so it's impossible for any thing to separate us except the man with the pick and shovel.'

MIGUEL DE CERVANTES, *Don Quixote*, 1615

'Proverbs are particularly attractive because of a certain mysterious quality, for while they appear to be one thing, in fact they are another. Experience teaches us that many things gain by not being completely seen, but veiled and concealed.'

JACOB CATS, 1627

'Force not your theme into narrow circuit, run not on with prolix trail in small matters to fill a thousand pages. To achieve success, let the picture you paint be simple in its tale.'

SIR THOMAS BROWNE, 1683

Contents

Contents

Dramatis Personæ

PIETER BLAEU, a dashing young writer, editor and translator of books

JOAN BLAEU, his father, an incorrigible geographer and publisher

PRINCE COSIMO DE' MEDICI, a strutting Florentine in feathers and furs

FRANCESCO FERRONI, his agent, a behemoth

REMBRANDT VAN RIJN, a master painter, dramatist, etcher and engraver

TITUS VAN RIJN, his son by birth, an art dealer, painter and sketcher of dogs

REBECCA WILLEMS, an old housekeeper, shrivelled in a skirt and apron, scowling

HARMEN GERRITSZ VAN RIJN, a maimed and blind miller, father to Rembrandt

CORNELIA 'NEELTGEN' VAN ZUYTBROUCK, his wife, a prophetess who forsakes herself for all others

JAN LIEVENS, an artist born with all his battles won, partner and friend to Rembrandt

CLARA DE GEEST, 'the fallen woman', a poet, daughter of the famous portrait painter Wybrand de Geest and Hendrickje Van Uylenburgh, both deceased

CONSTANTIJN HUYGENS, SIR, a lawyer, musician, athlete, diplomat, Protestant, poet and translator, secretary to the Stadhouder, patron to Rembrandt

CHRISTIAAN HUYGENS, his son, a mathematician and astronomer amongst the choicest wits in Christendom

CHRISTIAAN PORET, an apothecary and Aristotelian collector of rarities

HENDRICK VAN UYLENBURGH, a Polish Mennonite and art dealer who, appropriately, resembles a large sausage

PUSSY WILLOW, a hairy, pock-marked whore

SAMUEL VAN HOOGSTRATEN, a specialist in optical deceits, gossipmonger and former pupil to Rembrandt

ATHANASIUS KIRCHER, a Jesuit scientist and inventor, who once plunged into Mount Etna

PIETER LASTMAN, a painter of fiery histories, teacher to Rembrandt

SASKIA VAN UYLENBURGH, a Friesland girl, innocently beautiful like a well-bred cow, wife to Rembrandt

DR NICOLAES TULP, an anatomist

WILLEM BLAEU, a cartographer and collector of bird skulls, fish jaws, dragon bones, elephant teeth and possibly other things, grandfather to Pieter

RENÉ DESCARTES, a French philosopher living in the slaughterhouse district

THOMAS BROWNE, an English doctor of medicine, metaphysical scholar and admirer of curiosities scarce or never seen by any man now living

THE WOMAN WITH THE BIG BOSOM, a house with fortitude but sinking piles

GEERTJE DIRCX, a trumpeter's widow, dry nurse to Titus, wench to Rembrandt

JAN SIX, a wealthy poet and playwright, friend to Rembrandt

SAMUEL MENESSAH BEN ISRAEL, a rabbi, prophet and expert on the Kabbalah

HENDRICKJE STOFFELSDOCHTER JAGER, a sergeant's daughter from Bredevoort, maidservant and mistress to Rembrandt, mother of his child

CORNELIA VAN RIJN, the sweet, beautiful daughter of Rembrandt and Hendrickje

JORIS FONTEYN VAN DIEST, a dead criminal at the mercy of tweezers

BENEDICT D'ESPINOZA, a philosopher and black-cloaked heretic

THE OX, a slaughtered creature

MAGDALENA VAN LOO, a wealthy resident of the Gilded Scales, wife to Titus

THE GHOST, a deceased painter on his way to the Promised Land

Merchants, Soldiers, Blind Beggars, Harpies, Mongrels, Pancake Sellers, Fishermen, Traitors, Wood Nymphs, Angels, Predikants, Wafflewives, Cowards, Hurdy-Gurdy Players, Apparitions

Prologue

You might ask me how I came to write this strange story. Well, it began with a curiosity that seized my heart, mind and soul to the exclusion of everything else (*almost*, I should say, for there was a woman too), then I created it piece by piece in the way your eyes search a painting for its overall harmony, the one true image, by examining its dislocated parts.

It was not as simple as that, and at first, looking and leaving, returning and looking, I felt like a blind man grasping for handfuls of air (imagine old Tobit, fumbling for the door to meet his lost son). My tale – the one I had chosen to tell – had proportions that fled or fogged whenever I hastened to catch them. I realized, however, that I could alter my approach. Instead of trying to claw my way out of this foreign place, thereby ensnaring myself further, I could be content within, inside, where the darkness was formidable and the stillness most profound. Once my senses learnt to be patient, and grew accustomed to my surroundings, I began to see a glare filtering through the seemingly endless layers of greyish-green, a world beyond. Then I gently embraced whatever was there, however amorphous, and whatever I suspected to be there. Like a painter, I moulded these forms and images, coloured and recoloured them, reversed and forwarded them until they seemed recognizable to the eye.

Perhaps, in the end, I succeeded in creating a good likeness of my subject as if you had seen and known him yourself, but in the odd occurrence that anything remains nebulous, remember that the things unseen are everlasting, and *the light is shining in the darkness but the darkness does not overpower it.*

Pieter Blaeu
Amsterdam, 1672

And God Said

Look at her, my friend. Raise your eyes all around and see.
One might say she is an angel, but others a ghost.
How lies her path? Where can her name and her features be found?
Diving from the heavens, sprinting inside the flame,
a tint on the horizon, a dapple in the snow.

A day does not pass without her.

At dawn, she comes to collect you. She steals into your house and
stirs you from sleep, when you have forgotten who you are. She
lifts you from the oblivion of nightmares, chasing away all fear and
grief until you are filled with an indescribable happiness, a soft and
penetrating comfort that enfolds you like a blanket, warms your
bones, stings your temples and swells your breast.

Her holiness and beauty move you to tears.

There is ease and pride in your footsteps as they make their way
across the scorched land in search of the living waters, and you
follow her without hesitation, because who else is faithful and true?
Everything around you assumes its proper place as if revealed for
the first time. Newfound lines and peculiar shapes spring forth.

Long-forgotten faces and once-familiar objects return. Myriads of colours spread out before you,

> rising and falling,
>> streaming and wavering,
>>> rippling on and on . . .
>>>> (on and on . . .)

But before you proceed any further.
Blink your eyes, shut those lids down tight, and look again:
what once you saw you no longer see.

'Il Pittore Famoso'

Ferroni's fist, the size of a large continent, sank into the fog. With *one, two, three* insistent raps, he rattled the door planks and the rusty latch. An echo groaned over the frozen canal, empty of skaters in the early hour, roused the hovels on the filthy alleyways and recoiled to the stoop where the three of us waited, toes curling in boots. I stole under my cloak and took a stealthy swig of gin from my flask. The house was the colour of ash, hazy about the edges, with rickety shutters and a sloping roof. As bells tolled and minutes passed, the door seemed to be laughing at us while the windows stared slyly through webs of frost, reluctant to give up their secrets. After wiping the nearest pane with my glove, I pressed my nose to the icy glass and saw my own face, wearing the baffled curiosity of a child. Then a wooden stool, an oak press and several decrepit chairs bulged into view. Was Rembrandt van Rijn at home this morning? There was no glowing lamp or framed silhouette, not even the stealthy creak of a footstep, only a funereal stiffness that made me feel the room might moulder if ever I entered it. Perhaps, I thought, he would rise like a dead man from a vault.

The second man next to me was a pleasant distraction, strutting like a peacock in his feathers and furs, his appearance and movements so regal and winning they flared every nostril in the curious crowd – even the mongrels dared to sniff his sweet-smelling

groin. He was none other than His Highness Prince Cosimo de'
Medici, who, I suspected, had never set foot in a squalid lane or
kept such shadowy company, for his golden carriage was ready to
retreat should anyone, apart from the dogs, make one improper
gesture. By some stroke of Fate, I found myself in the role of his
escort, but little did I realize then that the following minutes would
alter my life, and most certainly not the previous week, when he
and his entourage rolled into our city and every citizen gathered to
greet them.

First, there was a series of triumphant trumpet blasts, and the
arquebusiers marched across the Dam Square, fluttering their blue
and white flags, then the governor stepped forward to announce
the great-grandson of Duke Ferdinand who had rumbled over the
Alps on his grand tour. With the clickety-clack of horses' hooves,
a train of coaches snaked into the courtyard, avoiding the crates of
goods outside the Weighing House, and rolled into the colonnaded
court. When the retinue halted before the seven arched doorways,
bathed in lemony light, all eyes focused on one carriage concealing the Prince. The onlookers stopped milling about and closed in
for a better view – lunging burghers, fishmongers, drunks, beggars,
soothsayers, women, children, poets, clerics, dogs and cats alike,
and me, the thin bookseller, who wriggled his way through cloaks
and skirts towards the front of the crowd as bells tolled across the
city.

Prince Cosimo stepped out of the coach in feathers and furs,
surrounded by his *cavalieri*: three secretaries, a treasurer, a confessor,
a physician and one Florentine merchant, Francesco Ferroni.
Citizens clapped, whistled and shrieked, 'Make way! Make way!'
as I danced from foot to foot, trying to catch a glimpse through the

knot of heads. Eventually a spyhole opened up between two tall hats, and what I saw was most unexpected: the Prince was a mere boy, delicate and spare, whose face and body could hardly compete with his oversized, boisterous costume. He carried himself with exaggerated refinement, his nose raised high in the air to catch a whiff of the rings of Saturn, and while one hand bade a theatrical welcome, the other stroked and fondled his fur collar as if it were a pet. A trio of men followed closely behind him, lifting the edges of his coat so it did not trail along the ground, though a red carpet led a path for him towards the Hall. As soon as he reached the members of the city council, one of which was my father, assembled in tidy rows on the stairs, they descended on him like vultures, hiding him from view.

My father, Joan Blaeu, was the man to blame for the nervous chill creeping up my spine, for without my consent he had volunteered me as Prince Cosimo's guide to Amsterdam painters. I was not a connoisseur even on the best of days, but I knew enough about paintings to make a satisfactory tour – and my father considered it as a chance for me (perhaps my final chance) to vindicate the family, no later than today. Now, here he was: tall, slim and impeccable, taking long steps from side to side, his coat buttoned up to his chin, his sleeves billowing outwards. His steely eyes scanned the crowd for me as he called out in a devilish voice: 'Pieter?'

I ducked behind a woman wearing a burdock-green hat with parrot's feathers.

'Pieter!'

When I peeked out again, another man, monstrous in form like a behemoth, had joined my father in the search: Ferroni. Although at a distance, I saw his face clearly – olive skin, vulgar wrinkles, misshapen lips and untamed brows – and felt his presence, nonsensically large, just as when I first met him a year ago on his visit to our foundry on the Bloemgracht. Ferroni was the other reason I found myself in this predicament: that day he had purchased two of our twelve-volume, French-edition Grand Atlases with 600 maps, for 450 guilders each. Several months later, when he requested a guide for Prince Cosimo, my father dared not refuse and offered up his eldest son. I could have easily resisted, I could have kicked my father in the shins and ran away; instead, my throat tightened as he raised a hand in the air and prepared to lower the shimmering blade.

To my dismay, the wind blew in from the harbour and lifted off the woman's hat to expose me behind her, crouching like a defecating dog. Ferroni spotted me first, and raising his arms, parted the crowd. He advanced toward me, a ship navigating tiny islands with a dinghy, my father, bobbing behind.

'The explorer has honoured us with his presence, I see.' When Ferroni smiled, his mouth opened wide enough for someone to crawl inside. I knew he could, without hesitation, chew me up and spit me out.

'I am not an explorer,' I said firmly, then feeling guilty, made a courteous bow.

Ferroni's hand clasped my shoulder and nearly toppled me. 'But you will be our guide?'

'Yes, sir, the itinerary is under control.'

He wiped his dripping nose. 'Your father tells me you are dependable.'

I met my father's niggling gaze. 'His Highness will be seeing the renowned marine painter, Willem van de Velde and also . . .'

'*Il pittore famoso?*'

'Well, if you mean Rembrandt van Rijn, then yes. I have sent word to his agent, his son Titus.'

Ferroni leered. 'The Prince believes he is the greatest of all European masters. How is he splashing on the paint these days?'

'Oh, his impasto is half-a-finger thick,' I said, recalling a rumour I had heard in the tavern. I was embarrassed to admit that most of my knowledge of the painter came from gossip, and mostly blasphemous at that.

He laughed. 'Van Hoogstraten says you can pick up one of his portraits by the nose.'

My eyes widened. 'Van Hoogstraten said that? He would know, I suppose.'

'What is he painting now?'

'Van Hoogstraten?'

'No, no, no,' He twirled his cloak. 'Rembrandt.'

'I don't know,' I replied, hoping that Rembrandt was not painting at all. There were plenty of stories about his uncertain temper: apparently, he would not give access to the most powerful monarch if he were at work. Besides, even if we managed to enter his house, I feared the Prince would be utterly disappointed in his latest paintings. The artist's reputation was not what it used to be; his style was long out of fashion, his fame greater than his excellence.

'Well, find out. We must get inside his workshop. MUST!' When Ferroni turned round, his hair, cut short, stood on end like a brush. Slow and heavy in his limbs, he forged his way through the crowd and towards the Prince.

My father thrust his face in mine, spitting through his teeth. 'You're incorrigible, Pieter. Don't disappoint me!' Then, tottering on his high heels, he followed in Ferroni's tempestuous wake.

Moments later, the three of us — Prince Cosimo, Ferroni and I — settled inside the golden carriage and departed from the city centre. As the wheels squelched through the thick mud on the path, alongside canals coming to life, my hopes bubbled forth: the Prince would be pleased if we found at least one picture for the Medici Palace, I thought, and perhaps I would finally do something to please my father, or even better, to achieve a place for myself. It seemed unlikely under the circumstances; Ferroni's gargantuan body spilled over the seat, thrusting me against the window and partially concealing me from the Prince who sat opposite us, his girlish hands folded across his silken lap, intimidating in this tiny space. When I peeked at him from behind Ferroni's shoulder, I was thankful that my knees were held together, or they would have been shaking wildly. The Prince's black hair gleamed with pomades underneath his hat, which boasted emeralds and turkey feathers pierced by tortoiseshell pins. A mole adorned his pale face near his nose, and spidery lashes framed his Medician wide eyes set in a vacant stare. From time to time he pulled out a handkerchief to wipe his cherry-red lips, but otherwise he remained fixed like a Florentine statue, making it difficult to guess what he was thinking. The silence between us was either ridiculous or historic, I thought.

As we headed down the expansive Herengracht with its handsome houses, I manage to free a hand and wipe the window with my sleeve. 'This wide canal was the starting point of our great expansion,' I said, 'a canal belt that was intended to resemble an onion but ended up as a half-onion. The aim was to make Amsterdam a perfect circular city, where people could live and work in the same area.'

'A residential paradise?' he asked. I nodded. He did not mention the end of the war against England, but remarked on the city's growth in trade, industry and the arts. I thought of Vondel: *Though it lies in ruins, the city will not tremble, it will rise again in greater glory out of ash and dirt.* He also acknowledged the beauty of our women with their deep cleavages. Realizing we were the same age, I smiled, and found myself loosening up as the carriage stopped in the Lauriergracht district, home to artists and dealers. When I said that Willem van de Velde was sure to have a few maritime scenes floating around his workshop, Cosimo laughed, a ringing sound that emerged in a stream of myrtle-scented breath.

Thank the Lord it was wintertime, I thought, after we stepped into the slimy street, for during the summer the canals reeked of garbage and afterbirth and danced with mosquitoes. Still, Ferroni and I had to shield the Prince from a crowd of onlookers – chattering, waving, pointing – as we walked the path towards our first sojourn. Van de Velde, a squat man with a beard of stiff bristles hiding his face, ushered us to his workshop, which resembled a secret den in the mountains. We feasted our eyes on pictures of herring buses with masts lowered and nets out; frigates on calm seas with furled topsails and shooting cannons; a man-of-war heeling in high winds; a flute carrying grain into the harbour, its anchor stowed. Alas, when Cosimo showed interest in the man-of-war, I rubbed my hands in triumph, but Van de

Velde told us it was not for sale. 'We must be off,' I said to my companions, 'if we want to see the great dealer, Gerrit van Uylenburgh.'

Gerrit was the son of Rembrandt's former business partner, and lived in a mansion previously owned by a pupil of Rembrandt's, Govert Flinck, who had died seven years previously. In his splendid showroom, a hazy light filtered down from the cathedral skylight to reveal his collection – busts of emperors, casts of antique marbles, coats of armour, and works by great masters from floor to ceiling. Gerrit, always interested in finding new talent, had discovered Gérard Lairesse from Liège. As we looked around, Gerrit told us the story: he had summoned Lairesse to Amsterdam, and in the presence of nobles and painters, had made him sit in front of a blank canvas to show his skill. Gerrit said to Lairesse, paint me a Nativity scene. Lairesse nodded, standing before the canvas, and surprised everyone by pulling out a fiddle to play a sprightly tune before getting to work. In the end, he had sketched the head of the Virgin, Joseph and a cow. Gerrit asked if we would like to see Lairesse's etchings, and after that delightful tale, we were keen to. Yet, in the end, Cosimo thought they were too graceful. Ferroni merely barked. I had one more chance.

Our carriage skirted the white landscape of the Nieuwe Dool-hof, with its wandering sailors, matrons, Turks and Jews, and rattled over the bricks of the humpbacked bridge to the Rosen-gracht. This was our final destination: the simple house once owned by playing-card maker Jacques van Leest, now deceased, where we hoped to find the artist Rembrandt, poor and suffering, living in the shadows like an owl.

As I said previously, Ferroni's fist sank into the fog.

Our toes curled in our boots.

The door seemed to be laughing at us.

I peeked through the window, and tried to convince myself it did not matter if nobody answered, until Ferroni whispered in my ear, 'If we don't get in, I'll make *hutsepot* of you!'

The door opened slowly, as if it were yawning, and a peculiar mustiness welled out to meet us. An ancient housekeeper stood under the archway, heavy-cheeked in a white cap, shrivelled in a skirt and apron, scowling. 'What is your business?'

I knew I should say something, but my mouth felt full of old stockings, so Ferroni uttered a polite greeting, introduced us and stated our intention.

The housekeeper nodded and stepped back. 'The master is engaged, but on account of the cold, you may enter.'

'We have an appointment,' Ferroni growled, raising a suspicious eyebrow at Cosimo. Was he blaming me? I had already written to Titus to notify him of our visit; it was not my fault if they were unprepared.

The servant rested a basket of laundry at her hip and motioned us inside. When we crossed the threshold into the fusty front room, a subterranean world hemmed in by peeling, stained walls, I saw on closer inspection that the stiff furniture was laden with dust and half-eaten by termites.

'You may wait here,' the old woman said, gesturing towards the cracked leather chairs. 'It's unlikely the master will see you, but I will notify him of your arrival.'

When she disappeared down the dark passage leading from the entry hall, I regretted having drained my flask, for I sensed something even more hideous lying beyond: the inhabitant of this ghastly cave. By means of the feeble light coming from the windows, I seized my chance to look at the paintings – some finished and hanging on the walls, some unfinished and stacked in the corner – but could only distinguish Rembrandt's works from the others because they were utterly different from anything I had ever seen. They were loaded down with pigment, shockingly lewd and crude! What could the Prince be thinking? It almost made me blush. There were landscapes, biblical scenes, histories and portraits – one of Rembrandt himself, one of a young boy who resembled him. Could this be Titus? Before I had a chance to inspect each picture closely – perhaps there would be time later – the maid returned and invited us in to what she referred to as their 'best room', the parlour.

'Oh, the parlour,' Ferroni muttered. 'But only on account of the cold weather!'

We advanced into a cold and deep darkness, for this larger room did not have the advantage of tall windows like the vestibule, and there were only two candles, brought in by the servant, while no fire burnt in the cavernous hearth. The 'best room' was spare to say the least: a bed with bolsters and straggling green curtains graced the back wall; an oak table sat in the middle of the room, and against the side wall, a couple of chairs. I counted four paintings here – uninteresting, Flemish ones.

The old woman took her leave again. Ferroni was restless, stumping over the floorboards and making them creak like the hulls of ships at anchor in the Zuiderzee. Cosimo, obviously annoyed after our unsuccessful morning, sat stiffly in a chair with his forearms settled on his thighs. While the house lay silent, my shadow seemed to be rooted to the floor. I thought of what to say to Rembrandt if he did arrive, then considered possible avenues of escape if things became unbearable. Minutes later, the side door opened a crack. I held my breath as a head peeked through the opening, a visage with intense black eyes.

Could this be Rembrandt van Rijn? No. The door opened fully and a handsome young man entered the room, his shoulder-length hair like a flame of fire. I was immediately drawn to his face, smooth and angelic, with a prominent nose, dark eyes under swollen lids and arching brows. He closed the door behind him, so I could no longer see the empty corridor.

'Titus van Rijn,' he said, bowing to the Prince. 'I represent my father Rembrandt.'

'Titus, let me intro—' I began, raising a finger.

'Thank the Lord!' Ferroni exclaimed, charging at Titus. 'We were all getting worried.'

'Titus,' I started again. 'Let me introduce Prince Cosimo de' Medici and his agent, Francesco Ferroni.'

Titus addressed the Prince directly. 'So kind of you to visit us, my lord.' He turned to Ferroni. 'There is nothing to worry about, sir. There are several pieces here you may be interested in . . .'

'They're for the Palace,' Ferroni grumbled.

'Oh?' Titus said with a grin, which surprised me because he already knew about the Medicis: I had told him myself in the letter. So he was bluffing, and I silently chuckled at his courage.

'What did you think,' Ferroni added, laughing, 'the Prince is here on a social visit?'

Ignoring him, Titus bowed again. 'Your Highness, we are

honoured.' He turned towards me and extended an ink-stained hand reminiscent of a notary's or a secretary's. 'You must be the publisher.'

'Y-yes,' I stuttered.

'What other workshops have you visited this morning?'

'First we saw Van de Velde and then some etchings by Lairesse . . .'

A half-cough, half-laugh sputtered from his throat before he declared in a loud voice: 'He comes nowhere near my father's work!'

His outburst ruffled my feathers, but those kind, sensitive eyes revealed that he was not angry, merely headstrong. It dawned on me that he was the one with real power in this situation, as his father's agent and keeper. Everyone in the city knew that Rembrandt was bankrupt: a once wealthy and successful man, he found himself his son's heir. I decided at once that I was going to like this Titus van Rijn.

He lit the lantern, and thrusting it into my hands, told us to stand at a distance. Then he took a painting from the corner, and after removing the green serge cloth, hung it on the wall at eye-level. It was a self-portrait, approximately three feet by two feet, with a muddy-brown background. The artist occupied the left part of the canvas, due to the angle at which he was poised, right shoulder forward. He wore a scarlet cloak spattered with red paint and a long scarf, hanging loosely. A wide-rimmed beret formed an ominous halo above his head, and arabesques of shadow fell on his stippled face. The deepest wrinkles were scrabbles and scratches as if cut with a needle. His lips, forming a slight smirk, seemed to be guarding a secret – not as an artist but as an old man. What was it? I wished I were older and wiser in order to understand this mystery, which could now be only an obscure, uneasy feeling that held me to the painting. My gaze became heavy, and I lost myself in his eyes, black and deep, though their soft solitude oppressed me.

I had seen the master's prints before, never a live painting, so I stepped forward to look closer. There existed one subject, himself, and no props, though there was an endless variety of elements. The canvas was covered with dark, earthen colours rising in bumps and curdles, sinking to pits and folds. At this range, the picture no longer revealed a man, but something like a tangled forest or a choppy sea. Indeed, the rumour was true: one could have picked it up by the nose! Although it was years ago, and I was too young to remember, Rembrandt had once been the most revered painter in the country, but his style had changed since then. I worried about the Prince's reaction – again, it almost made me blush – this was the very antipode to the preferred *fijnschilder* manner, the smooth and glossy ways of Gerard Dou and Gerard ter Borch, already part of his collection. Frankly, the portrait was knotty and murky.

'My father says to hang this piece in strong light, and to always view it AT A DISTANCE,' Titus said loudly.

My blood froze. Jumping back in shame, I stumbled over Ferroni's brutish foot.

He swatted the air, an attempt to blacken me out. 'You clumsy oaf!'

I straightened up and glanced over at Titus and the Prince, who pretended not to notice my lack of grace. Whispering into each other's hair, they resembled a pair of conspirators, in what I did not know.

Titus went on, 'Every picture has an optimum place from which it should be seen. At a shorter or greater distance, there is a blurred perception. The parts mingle and become confused.'

'That's just what we will do, then,' the Prince said.

'But even if one looks at a painting from the proper distance,' I blurted out, 'the eyes tend to stray and single out some aspect or another. And if one looks at a picture from other points of view, at various angles or distances, while it may appear changed, there is no difference in reality.'

Titus laughed. 'Speak with my father about that . . .'

Ferroni interrupted. 'We have to settle on a price.'

'Three hundred guilders,' Titus said.

'What? Two hundred,' Ferroni haggled.

'My father is asking three hundred, if you are interested.'

'Two hundred/fif . . .'

'Three hundred it is,' Cosimo declared, then shook Titus's hand.

The door burst open and banged against the wall. 'This is Rebecca, bringing the tea . . .' Titus announced.

But he was wrong – it was not the old servant at all – I knew that even before turning round, when a sinister penumbra spread across the wall and a sharp smell invaded the room. Instead, it was a most imposing figure, a man of such singular appearance that I would have screamed aloud had it not been for my good manners. He stood just inside the door, stout in proportion and almost posing, his thumbs tucked under a wide sash at his rounded belly. Draped over his broad shoulders was a ragged black cloak, and underneath it, a brown smock stained with paint – brushprints, handprints. Despite his age and poverty, he behaved like a man accustomed to the curiosity of others, and seemed to be waiting for one of us to say something or to welcome him, but there were no signs of movement, certainly not from me. With an instinctive fear, I stared in wonder at this fascinating creature. He had a bilious face of an elastic nature, ruddy jowls that sank into his neck, a many-lined forehead, a yellowed moustache protruding over his pursed upper lip, and a shiny farmer's nose that boldly asserted itself. A dry cloud of grey hair swallowed his brown beret and his eyebrows frowned over his bloodshot whites as his beady black eyes examined the room. This was Master Rembrandt: painter, etcher and engraver.

When he dragged himself inside, I was surprised to be so affected by his presence, which had nothing to do with his magnitude or the reputation that preceded him; rather, because he reminded me of an old comfortable chair whose seat and arms were coming apart in tangled and frayed bits of thread. He appeared to be a forsaken remnant of something that once existed in an extraordinary form, and now, though weathered and worn, remained dignified and resolute. I could not resist being drawn forward, seduced by all that was accursed and sombre about him: *Thus art as well brings forth the sons of darkness.* I thought, this is a man I am not only going to like, but will also love. Now that I have seen him, I have a great desire to know him and even to paint him, though I have no artistic ability and no vision to represent a man's humour or a convincing illusion of it. Perhaps, I thought — conscious of Rembrandt's eyes settling on me in a reverie — perhaps he will want to paint *me*, standing here in the candlelight. Could I be his next sitter: a man of substantial height — five feet, six inches tall — and of a slender build, distinguished and charming? What does he see? Soft curls of fair hair, wide blue eyes, high cheekbones, a pointed nose and cleft chin. Surely, he must . . .

I looked at him squarely and attempted to deliver a convincing performance as scholar (if only I had an open book or a classical bust!) by sucking in my chest to stand tall, sliding my hand into the front pocket of my coat. For a moment everything seemed possible, then the master turned away and the doubts crept in. Would he prefer, instead, a corpse cut down from the gallows and taken to his workshop in a sack? Most likely, I thought, casting my eyes modestly aside, for it must be necessary to suffer in order to be beautiful. Is it the Prince he wants? That would not be surprising — and he is welcome to him — all the better! Those chairs are too stiff to sit in for hours and days on end, anyway. Then, when I checked his face again, when I looked more properly, I realized I had been altogether presumptuous. Rembrandt was not gazing at me or at the Prince, but was focused on something else, lost in thought. And that's when I noticed it: the mirror on the wall. He was soaking up the light in the room, so it glowed on his face and bounced off the collar of his coat, leaving the rest of us in shadow.

Leyden, 1628

On The Moment of Conception

I make faces for the glass: draw in my cheeks, wriggle my eyebrows, puff out my nostrils, pucker my lips. My appearance constantly changes. A snarl, a grimace, a flinch, a smile — with teeth, without teeth — an exclamation of surprise! The light causes a shadow to fall across my brow and hides one side of my face. Now I will cover the mirror with a cloth and try to recall the image I have seen. It is not enough to create a reflection. I must paint myself from the mind.

On the table next to me, the necessary items:

a warming-tray

my palette and knife, caked with paint

pots of medium

a white stocking, holes in toe, for wiping

a jar of linseed oil, half empty

my brushes, made from the soft and fine hairs of squirrel or sable, the coarse and thick hairs of badger backs or oxen ears

& this tablet of black leather, bolted with a metal needle, where I will record my rules of art and life — the caprices of my restless brain — from this point forward. I will write it for myself as a companion to my pictures when I am numbered among the dead. I hope that someone may remember me, even in another time, as the greatest painter who ever lived.

The joiner has not completed my panels so I have decided to work on a spare piece of oak in the workshop. I found it lying in the corner with other scraps, where the plaster is coming off the wall. Rather small but without warp. My story, only the seed of an idea, will come alive in this tiny space.

I am reminded of a painting contest I attended last week, held on the Breestraat near the Town Hall. Accurse the jury for excluding me! Still, I watched the competition from early morning until dark. This is what I saw, as the three artists sat beside each other in the Square, facing their easels and working.

The first artist, a landscape painter from The Hague, named François Knibbergen, opted for a very sizeable canvas. As if without prior thought, he painted everything in an accomplished fashion. He depicted the sky, trees and greenery, rushing waterfalls, drifting clouds and rocky cliffs, letting his hand find its way out of habit. The second man, Jan van Goyen, a landscape painter from Leyden, took an entirely different approach. He covered his whole panel in a variegated manner, here light, there dark, using delicate touches. He created, effortlessly and in glorious detail, a pleasant village with a gateway, a landing stage and ships at sea carrying cargo and passengers. His eye guided his hand and mind in wisdom, as if by Fortuna.

Finally, there was Jan Porcellis, a marine painter recently arrived in our city, who initially appeared very tense. He sat quietly before he began, handling his brushes in a time-wasting manner. Once he started, his movements were languid and hesitant, so that everyone became impatient. Soon I realized he understood precisely what he was doing. He had been forming the entire picture in his mind before he started. By evening, his piece was extraordinary in its well-chosen naturalness, an image of the stormy sea like a work of Raphael. In the end, the connoisseurs gave the prize to Porcellis and dismissed the other two artists. The outcome proved that the correct procedure is to form the desired image in one's head before beginning.

So, imagine me now. I sit in a chair, facing the easel, my feet resting in the grooves on its bottom rung. Everything seems quiet. I am looking at my small panel but I see myself, in the corner, watching it. Such is the embryo of my idea. After the sun goes down, the light fades from my high window and the room grows wan and gloomy. At twenty-two, I am sound of body and in good heart. I close the shutters before I close my book.

Apelles and Protogenes: Jealousy vs Admiration

Gerrit has interrupted me again. Look at him prowling into my area of the workshop! This time, he wants to know how to keep the dust off his painting while it is drying. I tell him to use the Japanese umbrella, then send him into his corner. I won't ask him to prepare my pigments, because he tries my patience and works too slowly. Mr Shilly-shally, I call him.

I am diligently engaged in painting as quickly as possible, now Lievens is in The Hague, making a portrait of Sir Constantijn Huygens. For a few years, we have worked well together, Lievens and I, though lately we work better apart. He is the only one able to break my concentration, and sometimes I think he is a better painter. Lievens — a prodigy at the age of twelve; no one else can work such wonders in pigments, varnishes and oils.

When Apelles visited his rival, Protogenes, he found his workshop empty except for a large panel resting on his easel. There he painted a single fine line. Protogenes returned to see this brushstroke, and knew his visitor had been Apelles. So he drew another, even finer line exactly over the first one. When Apelles came again, he must have felt a mixture of jealousy and admiration — the same things I feel for Lievens. But Apelles was the true talent, for then he drew a third line, this time so fine that no other could compare. Protogenes was forced to admit defeat. He decided the panel should remain as it was, to be admired for its virtuosity.

If someone feels jealousy, his entire face responds: the eyebrows come together, the eyes grow wider, the mouth arches downwards, and the neck bulges or creases. When someone feels admiration, his face alters hardly at all. He may raise his brows, open his eyes more than ordinary, fix his pupil on the object of esteem or part his lips slightly. But not many of his features will change, as they do when he feels envy, for the heart is disturbed very little.

ACCOUNTS AT START OF YEAR

Fee from Gerard ... 100 guilders

To apothecary, colours ... 15 g.

Item, tankard of ale ... ½ stuiver

Item, loaf of rye ... 5 st.

Item, a jerkin ... 10 g.

Panels & supports ... 25 g.

An Introduction to the Painter

Today I am tired after sitting up late at night, drawing Mother by candlelight. She held the Great Book in her hands as she often does. When I sketch Father, he is usually wearing a skullcap, asleep in a chair by the fire. He injured his hands in an accident with a musket fifteen years ago, and now that he is blind, I suspect he will die soon. Moeder looks after him and prays constantly. I wish I had as much faith. She reminds me of the prophetess Anna or even Naomi, gleaning the barley fields.

This is not the reason I write this journal, but lately I feel a sense of urgency. Though I am young, I have advanced quickly in my art. There is much to record, and everything is bound to come out in a haphazard way. I should start with the distant well of my early life, however humble, so I can peer inside it as a man of old age. After all, there will only be my memories.

I live with my parents on the Weddesteeg — the old home of the gallows — a small alleyway facing the Rijn, which runs towards the dunes and the North Sea. Our house is like most others with its red-brick facade, tall leaded windows and steeply pitched roof. From my bedroom window, I see the White Gate tower opposite the city wall and the two windmills slowly turning their arms. The giants who guard our fortress in times of distress! When one of them was burnt down by those dirty Spaniards who besieged our city, my grandmother had it rebuilt immediately. Aside from the creaking of their wooden gears and axles, all is silent.

My life began here, in this industrial town with weaving mills and handsome canals, a famous university, a botanical garden, two Protestant churches and an eleventh-century keep called the Burcht. I was born on 15 July 1606, a lusty crying boy, the ninth of ten children to Harmen Gerritszoon and Cornelia 'Neeltgen' Willemsdochter van Zuytbrouck, the son of a miller and the daughter of a baker, both then Catholics. My parents called me Rembrandt with a d, though I sometimes forget to spell it that way; Harmenszoon — after my father; and Van Rijn — for the family mill, known as 'De Rijn', which grinds barley for malt. I do not like this name, Rembrandt, particularly because it is old-fashioned. When I have a son, he will be named for a hero, Samson or Apollo.

Four of my siblings have passed from this world. Two children were taken by the plague before I was born, and another died in infancy. We buried my sister Machtelt in the Pieterskerk three years ago. May God bless their souls! Adriaen was a cobbler until he married into a miller's family and became a miller. He lives on the Aalmarkt with his wife Lysbeth, his three children and my younger sister Lysbeth, who is of bad mental health. My brother Willem is a baker and lives on the Nieuwe Rijn. Cornelis has taken to running Father's mill for the last few years since my eldest brother, Gerrit, suffered an accident and mutilated his hands, making him unfit for service. With Father and Gerrit in such a poor state, I am determined to make the most of my hands. These blessed, strong, capable hands, the instruments of my soul and my sight ... I will protect them at all costs and thank God for them every day.

I turned to painting when I was fourteen, just after enrolling at Leyden University, because I realized during a lengthy lecture in Latin that my one natural inclination was to paint and draw. To invest my time in anything else would have seemed contrary to my nature, unless I became a great player on the stage. But I had an eye on my purse. There's a good guilder in making pictures! After leaving school, I pursued a career in art under the apprenticeship of Jacob Isaacsz van Swanenburg. I was a late beginner at that age, an amateur. Gerrit Dou, on the other hand, is already a stained-glass painter.

Swanenburg taught me about the proportions of the human figure, how to fashion the limbs in positions and actions according to their nature, how the sinews, bones and muscles work together. Soon enough, my forms no longer appeared wooden. He taught me perspective, which means drawing every object according to measure, because everything has a certain scale depending on its distance, whether near or far. Because I was born with a slight affliction in my right eye — it is weaker than the left one and tends to wander — when I first began drawing, my figures would often come out on the paper in reverse. Over time, the problem has corrected itself and I hardly notice it any more. If anything, my weakness has proved an advantage, allowing me a better sense of figures on a flat surface.

As a painting apprentice, I learnt how to plane down the bumps in a panel, to grind the pigments on a slab using a muller, to mix the primuersel and dead-colouring and prepare the basic pigments — lamp black, vermilion, ochres and umbers, verdigris — suspending them in linseed oil. We made white lead in thirty or forty clay pots, which were divided into two sections — one for lead, one for vinegar. First, we filled the pots and stacked them in the shed, then we heaped horse dung around them and sealed the door. Next, we waited. Ninety days later, the apprentices would gather round and draw straws to see who would have to re-open the shed. While the other boys dreaded that encounter, I could hardly contain my excitement about the magic working inside. So I always tried for the shortest straw. When I re-opened the shed, I walked into a thick, dead heat and the most awful stench of manure and sour vinegar. But my heart rejoiced when I discovered the cleanest white on the grey metal, formed in scales.

Since leaving Swanenburg's workshop, I have made it my aim to understand all the qualities and possibilities of my medium. An artist cannot work by intuition alone. He is an inventor but also a scientist. I will not hesitate to say, the pupil has surpassed his master.

Note: *Lievens owes you 2 stuivers or a new jar!!!!!*

Thoughts on Composition

Over the last few hours, I have been preparing the support for my latest painting. First, I cover the oak panel with glue made either from white sheepskin and kid leather, or parchment waste, which is even better, or from the clippings of rabbit skins, which possesses great strength. Fish glues are best avoided. After that layer dries, I brush on a yellowish, thick coat of chalk and glue mixture to create an even surface. Many painters pay too *little attention to this ground, though it has a great influence on the durability and action of the colours. The above-said shines through everywhere, either luminous and clear or dirty and greasy. Because it is tinted, rather than white, I can later organize light and shadow without distorting the cohesion of my painting. Next, my undercoating is a proportioned mixture of lead white, umber, red ochre and the accumulated remains of paint from my brushes. I lay down the colour with a brush, sweeping over large areas in a washed manner. It lies over the ground like a veil.*

My Idea has become a composition, and my draft is done in thin lines with the same mixture. I do not sketch on to a separate drawing tablet but directly on to the panel, because everything is preserved in my brain. (When artists paint a clever sketch, they seldom paint a picture equal to it!) I work in sections or planes, commencing with the background, moving gradually towards the foreground.

In my picture, you can now identify the outlines of the room — the door, the planked floor and the two walls. The left corner and the rear of the painting are already complete. There is the rotted, stained, crumbling brick wall, the two palettes hanging there, the worn grindstone and wooden table with pots of medium. The artist stands in the rear of his workshop with the table behind him. Whether the young artist is my pupil, Gerrit Dou, my partner, Jan Lievens, or even myself remains to be seen. As it stands, his face is a blur. I must come to know him.

My Workshop of Colours

The workshop is a dark place, lit by a small upper window, located on the first floor of the Lievenses' two-storey house. Though we have a cast-iron stove, the damp spreads through the room like a plague and collects in secret places. Over the months, it rusts the locks and hinges, penetrates the walls, floorboards, corners, ceiling and door. It loosens their surfaces, warps from within. I watch this continual transformation. One day the walls are smooth, the next they have a rough texture. Then, without warning, they erupt with blisters, bubbles and cracks. The plaster rises and clots, lumps and flakes like my paints, reflecting the light.

... Like my paints, which have been ground by Gerrit and mixed with a viscous oil, usually linseed or walnut. Using a slab, a muller and a clean horn, he begins with the light, transparent colours which require a great deal of oil. The dense, heavy colours require little. He grinds the pigments to the consistency of paste, so they stand up on the slab and do not run.

Now is my chance to give everything its proper tint and to set the contours of the forms. On my palette, a rainbow formation: vermilion near the thumb, a large portion of white lead then yellow ochre, red lake, brown earth pigments, lamp black. I mix them by setting down the simple colours, white and black, then blending in each of the others, one with one, two with two, and so on, until they cover the whole board. A palette must have good balance so as not to tire the arm. These are my old friends: greasy, smooth, sparkling mysteriously. Though I choose to use few, I get the utmost variety from them. The arrangement of these pigments must appeal to all the senses:

WHITE LEAD: *The greatest of all the whites (also made from chalk, feldspar, rice, zinc, fossilized sea creatures, alabaster, rock-crystal). Excellent opacity and a good dryer. The sum of all colours and compatible with each one.*

NAPLES YELLOW: *Corroded iron heated up. Found on the tiles of Babylon. Very heavy & dense, of exceptional covering power, needs little grinding and oil. Nothing can compare in beauty or quality.*

YELLOW OCHRE: *An earth colour, purest from France. Must be ground and washed. Offered in many tones and hues. Test for genuineness: when heated, turns red.*

VERMILION: *Mercury and melted sulphur, when mashed together, make a black clotted substance called moor. Heated in the oven, it gives off a bright red vapour that condenses on to the surface of a clay tablet. When ready, scrape off the vapour and grind. Very heavy pigment, covers well but only conditionally. Dries poorly.*

CARMINE: *Origin in the cochineal insect. The finest quality, known as nacarat, is very beautiful but very impermanent.*

ULTRAMARINE BLUE: *Made from lapis lazuli, expensive & very beautiful. First, make a dough of finely powdered lapis, resin, wax, gum and linseed oil, knead it for three days. To coax out the blue, put the dough into a bowl of lye or water, knead it with two sticks, squeezing for hours until saturated. Then separate the blue into a clean bowl, let it dry into a powder. The first pressing is best. Used as a thin glaze over a light base. (A less costly alternative is smalt, ground potash glass mixed with cobalt.)*

TERRE VERTE: *Malachite, a mineral found in copper mines, coarsely powdered or it comes out a dingy colour. Similar to ochre. Used in all techniques. The cool tones resemble unripe apples.*

VERDIGRIS: *Made by suspending copper over a bath of vinegar. After a few hours, the orange metal and red wine leave a green deposit.*

RAW UMBER: *A natural ochre, an excellent dryer, used in all techniques, requires much oil. A greenish tinge is especially valued. When heated, becomes a reddish brown.*

ASPHALTUM: *Bitumen, dries poorly, softens in higher temperatures, but when used as a glaze does no such damage. Lightproof, requires much oil.*

LAMP BLACK: *Soot freed from oil. Permanent.*

IVORY BLACK: *Prepared by charring bones from corpses, cattle horns, etc. in the absence of air. The purest & deepest. Requires oil but the best dryer.*

Oh, the smells of these mixtures! The oils, glues and emulsions are acidic enough to make one's head topple — especially if I forget to open the windows of the workshop. Lievens says the aromas turn my brain into a wretched bag of worms and incite my bad temper. I say there is no sense in becoming a painter if you do not love the odours, even if they make one's mind wander like a decapitated chicken. Besides, I can always recover my mood with a little bread and some gin.

How I Regulate My Life: A Son of Homer

An artist needs only a solid roof, a crust of bread, his easel, a box of colours and holy sunlight through the windows. I adorn myself with love, fear of God, obedience and perseverance. I drink moderately, eat at least twice a day, and protect my hands from such strains as heaving stones or carrying large objects, anything that would weary them. Yet a man paints with his mind as much as with his hands, so for the sake of prosperity, I also refrain from overindulging in the company of women. Oh, my dreams are often visited by the seamstress and her bulging bosom! To relax, I read Homer. For my education, I train myself in:

Medicine

History

Anatomy
Theatre
Philosophy
Geometry (not my best subject)
Natural Science

Friendship Between Painters

Someone hammers on the door, breaking the painter's trance. He hears scurried movements and muffled voices downstairs, then creaky footfalls on the narrow staircase. There is a sound of struggled breathing outside the workshop before another young painter, his rival, enters the room, carrying two leather cases, which he sets down on either side of him with a sigh. The rival has wild hay-coloured hair, a red aquiline nose and chestnut-coloured eyes. He hangs his soiled cloak on the wall peg, approaches the painter's chair and throws his reedy arms around him in an awkward embrace.

RVR: *Peeking out from behind his easel.* How was it?

JL: Couldn't have been better. Sir Constantijn is a good man. He treated me like a noble. His brother Maurits, too.

The rival collapses in an empty chair near the fire and stretches his long legs in front of him. Beneath his knee-length pantaloons, his stockings are a dingy grey. When he crosses one ankle over the other in an abrupt, ungraceful movement, dried mud crumbles from his boots on to the floor.

RVR: What was he like?

JL: Good but severe. Relentless, indeed! The entire time I was there he tried to convince me to travel to Italy.

RVR: That's none of his concern ... Was he harsh about your work?

JL: No, he loved the portrait. *Takes a handkerchief out of his pocket to blow his nose.* Where would we be without him, aye?

RVR: We? Why, did he mention me?

JL: Come to the tavern, and I'll tell you everything.

RVR: *Eyes the hazy light on his panel.* Later. It's ten o'clock in the morning. There's work to do. (*Aside*) Good news or bad news, why won't he just tell me now? I've been waiting on Huygens for months!

JL: Is it? *His eyes race from side to side.* It seems centuries since we've seen each other. What are you working on now?

RVR: Nothing important.

JL: *A laugh uncovers his teeth and his gums.* Why that face? Don't be such an ox. I want to see.

RVR: It's not finished yet.

JL: You always say that. Anyway, leave it to the gods for a few hours. *Glances about the room.* Do you have anything to eat around here?

RVR: There's a pot of porridge you can heat on the fire. Or if you don't want that, go down to the kitchen and find some leftover stew. But why are you asking me? It's *your* house.

JL: *Stands up and lets out a phlegmy cough.* Phew! The smell of turpentine in here is making me choke. Why are the windows closed?

RVR: When I need fresh air, I go for a stroll.

The rival walks over to unbolt the shutters, pushing each of them wide open. A steady breeze wafts into the room.

RVR: *Glares.* It wasn't that bad.

JL: *Stomach rumbles. Giving it a pat, he mutters.* I must eat something . . .

RVR: Didn't they feed you there?

JL: Did they ever, elaborate banquets every day!

RVR: Oh? What did they serve?

JL: Bird pie, roasted pike's tail, pasties of finches, calf's tongue tart and all variety of fruits and greens. You would have been amazed by the colour of the carrots, not yellow or even the usual orange, but a dark crimson-purple! I wanted to rush off immediately, so I could create this exact tone with my pigments. I didn't, of course, out of a sense of duty to the Orange, but perhaps now . . .

RVR: That's funny, a duty to the Orange.

JL: I hadn't thought of that. *Forces a laugh.*

RVR: You don't look as if you've gained a stitch.

The rival paces the room, doing everything by fits and starts. He fondles the canvases leaning against the back wall, fingers the clean brushes, which are set out on the worktable, leafs through an album of prints on the desk.

JL: The workshop is terribly neat. Has Gerrit been up to his tidy work again?

RVR: *Gruffly.* The same as ever, but do you have to rifle through my things?

JL: A good boy, that Gerrit. Where is he, by the way?

RVR: I told him to get outside today. He's doing sketches from nature.

JL: Were you losing concentration?

RVR: It has nothing to do with me. I've only noticed that Gerrit has the ability to work images out of himself, but lacks a proper sense of perception when painting from life.

JL: But all good work is done from memory, whether the scene is actually there or not.

RVR: True, but there is nothing in the mind that hasn't been previously received by the senses.

JL: *Smirks.* If you're a sensualist.

RVR: *Raising his voice.* Don't be so simple. Every painter must be able to comprehend nature in its entirety, which is only possible by at first being in its intimate presence. Otherwise, we would all be painting men with camels' humps . . .

JL: Look at Rubens! *Speaking over his shoulder as he moves towards the door.* He paints from the depths of himself, and carries invention and expression to the utmost limit.

RVR: Still, knowledge comes before intuition.

JL: Yes, well, I'll leave you to work now. Be ready in a few hours so we can set off . . .

RVR: (*Aside*) There is a thoughtful silence as the mirror shadows us. My friend stands tall and finger-thin. His slender waist is delicate, pinched with a sash, while my own belly is rounded and slack-muscled. His legs, slender and strong; my legs: flabby and stubby. Everything, I believe – even beauty – has been easy for him, as if he were born with all his battles won. He does not count those blessings, either. While there are infinite reasons why I hate this man – this is one of them – there are equally infinite reasons why I love him. Friendship is that way, I think, between painters.

Obstacles Incite Genius

The artist is becoming Lievens, wearing a floppy black hat, his greedy feet in black boots. He is mysterious, as he should be, but something is missing. He seems untouched by the divine fire. It is even worse, he has no soul! All this hard work for nothing. My throat tightens and my belly swells with anger. Why must I live this lonely, pious existence? What could be better than to soak myself in a crowded pub with brandywine and malt ale? Perhaps I should work on something else for a while. My Supper at Emmaus is still unfinished. The silhouette of Christ needs a good smudge, and the halo of light around him is too orange. I also want to add a lock of hair falling over his brow . . .

No, I must not do this: it would be fatal. Vasari tells me my virtù *needs thought, solitude and opportunity, so as not to lead my mind into error. You hear that? Solitude. I must do something else . . .*

Ha! I'll chew on this rind of cheese, then I'll take a shit. There is no better place to muse than on the chamber pot.

My young artist possesses a spark of determination, an ingenium, *but he does not merit respect as one esteemed in my trade. His genius is not authentic.*

If only those fat pigs in the marketplace weren't squealing to high heaven! What else?

Yes, I will adorn him in a regal blue smock with golden trimming, so he'll be fit for a Prince, perhaps even for his secretary, that gentleman in The Hague. I will be damned if Huygens is not impressed with my work!

This afternoon, I ask Gerrit to break from his own painting and pose for me. He stands in the corner, next to the grindstone, wearing the blue tabard. In a running movement his left hand is raised, holding a palette and some brushes to his chest. His pinkie curls round the maulstick. The lower part of his face — closed mouth, clenched chin — is bathed in bright light. But his floppy hat casts a shadow over his brow and upper cheek. His eyes are hollow.

I use a blue-grey colour, a mixture of white lead and ground charcoal, for his costume. The drapery shouldn't have many folds, but fall where nature makes it flow and harmonize with the resilience of the fibre, whether thin or thick, new or old, heavy or transparent. I make pleats in the fabric at his upper right arm while the rest of the sleeve, unbuttoned, hangs loose. The coat puckers in little lines at his waist, pinched with the sash; its two overlapping ends settle across his hip. I run a shadowy furrow along his middle, a darker shade from belly to ankle. Eventually, the drapery, with the folds running vertical down to the hem, suggests the fullness of his form. Yellow ochre, for the trimming of the collar, defines the curves of his shoulder and torso. With the same pigment, I paint a border on the bottom edge of the tabard.

While working Gerrit and I are silent, except when I express my opinions about his work (which I must do or he is bound to fail). His latest piece is a composition of Tobit and Anna after my own depictions. He treats his objects too precisely and attacks them with painstaking detail, I tell him. Though they must be executed with the height of skill, if the individual items are given too much interest they become isolated within the picture. The pieces overcrowd one another. Doesn't he see? He should aim for a unified composition. Also, he must use the light as a tool for his storytelling.

My Mind Is like a Stage

Good news, my old life is ending! A messenger has brought word that Huygens — secretary to the stadhouder, Prince Frederik Hendrik, and connoisseur of the superior arts — wants to see my recently finished biblical piece of Judas. Good news, because there is nothing left for me in Leyden, not if I am to become a burgher. Lievens, the portraitist and I, the historicist: two Protestant Rubenses, Huygens thinks.

Here is how I played Judas, on his knees, returning the pieces of silver ... With his hands clasped in woe, his eyes focus on the coins — all thirty of them — scattered on the wooden floor in front of the astonished Sadducees. One priest wears a rich vermilion cape and golden turban, another has bulging eyes and a gaping mouth. A sharp ray of light enters from the left *and shines on the Holy Book, then reflects off the metal Torah shield. The shadowy figure at the front is in silhouette. My room is a theatre and my mind is a stage. When I pull back the curtain, a scene is re-enacted there. Huygens has sent for me and I must go.*

While Rembrandt sat in the corner, taking laboured breaths from his pipe, I stood at the fireplace, pretending to polish my waistcoat buttons with a restless thumb, but my left eye was watching him: if only he would do something to reveal his character . . . until now, he seemed enveloped by an opaque cloud that my senses did not have the strength to penetrate. The only thing his aspect might suggest was impatience. Although he had been polite to us, more so than I expected, his glowing nose, clenched lips and fluttering moustache told me he was raging inwardly. Perhaps we had overstayed our welcome, I thought, and recommended to Ferroni that we leave, but Titus held up a hand in protest and asked if he could show us one of his own paintings in the next room.

Ferroni ogled him from head to toe. 'Oh? Another painter in the Van Rijn house?'

'Very well,' the Prince said. 'Show us.'

The four men stepped into the hallway with Titus leading the way, but I trailed behind them as they ducked under the dusty chandelier then filed into the next room. Pausing in the doorway, I watched as they approached Titus's painting, which from a distance I immediately knew as a classical work depicting Meleager and Atalanta, the beautiful daughter of King Schoeneus of Boeotia, who runs faster than anyone, and with her skill, is the first to wind the monstrous boar of Calydon. One day, Meleager, after dispatching the beast, kneels at Atalanta's feet, giving her the head and hide as a trophy, and in turn wins her heart. Titus's painting of this story, though beautiful and reminiscent of his father's style, was somewhat of a disappointment due to its crowded composition, but I did not want to make a hasty judgement from so far away; after all, the parts could easily 'mingle and become confused'. Besides, the Prince and Ferroni, their eyes fixed on the canvas, seemed interested enough to begin negotiation, so I decided to join them in case they needed to avail themselves of my expertise.

Yet, as I started to make my way inside, something stopped me. This 'something' was the most acrid smell of paints and oils breezing down the hallway, which I knew had to be coming from Rembrandt's workshop. I peeked down the long, dingy corridor, and after seeing it was empty, reversed out of the room without any further thought about where it might lead me or what the consequences might be. I followed the potent haze, my heels barely touching the floor, embued with a spurt of energy so foreign to me it seemed that all those sedentary hours at my desk had stored themselves up for that moment. When I reached a dead end, there was a door, slightly open. Leaning down, I peered through the crack and caught a glimpse of colour, red on canvas. This entirely absorbing patch of deep scarlet convinced me: *I must go in.* After checking for any signs of suspicion from the others that I had left their midst, and without hearing the slightest noise except for the mumbling of Titus's voice from the salon, I touched open the door.

I was expecting something unusual, but not *this*: the workshop of the master was not a glorious or spacious temple, but a dim

cavern, hoary and humble. The fug was so intense I had to cup
my hands over my nose to keep from falling over. Sunlight from
the tiny windows trembled downwards, revealing a cosmos of dust
particles in the air as I followed the glow of a single oil lamp
down a path that had been cleared through the objects stacked on
the floor. These many things choked into a small space unnerved
me, not because they were misplaced and disordered, but because
of their stiff imprisonment and incalculable age. The rickety
furniture, dingy bottles of pigment, cracked jars of oil, charred
creatures and crusty cloths, swelling with grotesque proportion,
seemed to have endured centuries of decay. They were the possessions of an artist who was prepared for death or who already
considered himself dead, I thought, as I pulled the flask from my
pocket and held it above my mouth, only no drop emerged. *There
is no antidote against the Opium of time, which temporarily includeth all
things.*

A pale mirror on one wall of the room summoned me. Standing
before it, I placed my two feet on the rutty floorboards and
observed myself the way an artist might do, not by registering the
features, but by seeking out the emotions in tone and shadow. The
grey glass echoed back a man aged well beyond his twenty-four
years. He had a miserly brow, lugubrious grey eyes and cowardly
lips that retreated into an avid mouth. The face, its pale skin and
odd definitions, appeared to be created by clumsy gestures, with
discarded remnants. He seemed lodged in a state of *continual becoming
and never being*. What was he, a dreamer or an impostor? Worse
still, a fanatic? I could not be sure, but he reminded me I had
entered into a private space, uninvited. Now I recalled the flash of
deep red colour that had called me into the room. An easel stood

in the corner, and upon it, Rembrandt's latest work in creation. The paint – still wet – was layered loosely and roughly applied. Here is what I saw.

A man and a woman standing in a garden. With their heads bent together, their faces were tenderly pink. The man wore a golden costume and black brimmed hat with a cap underneath. A lock of hair fell across his forehead as if he were perspiring. He gazed down at his companion – who peered beyond him, into the distance – his arms embracing her. The man's left hand rested on her shoulder, the other on her breast. She had lain her hand over his, so that her fingers touched him, apart from her pinkie, encircled by a ring of pearls. Her other hand rested on her belly, clutching a scarf against her crimson costume. A watery red washed over the woman's skirt; flakes of gold and green skittered across the man's billowing sleeve.

The picture defied all my previous conceptions of beauty, neglecting elegance and charm, and yet I wished for hours or days to spend before it, because the more I looked the closer I felt to forbidden things, the unnamed and the unnameable, all those things I had denied myself for too long. My eyes feasted on the pale hands of the two lovers – the husband's bulging veins; the wife's soft fingertips – merging in body and spirit: *and the two shall become one flesh*. The movements of the paint captured the very depths of that touch, all the feeling behind it, while no words could convey that feeling. But in this place, there was no need for words – only gestures; and so, despite my resistance, I entered the painting and the couple's most secret moment. I became the man with a firm hand on my beloved's breast, pledging my devotion, guarding her safety. Her gesture, her love for me was both gentle and enduring, and when I pulled myself away, it was difficult to renounce so immense a desire. At that feverish instant, for the first time, Rembrandt's genius as a painter struck me, for I experienced the coincidence of someone else having created something that felt my own in both mind and heart. I had buried myself in the picture, then it had buried itself in me, and I knew it would remain long after I left this place, trailing me and watching me.

Suddenly, I heard footsteps muttering across the corridor. This is the end, I thought; someone has realized my absence and is about to catch me out. Stricken with guilt, I wanted to show my face and confess my sins, but that feeling quickly subsided as the footfalls neared, because my embarrassment overpowered it. I glanced around for somewhere to hide, and spotted a cranny into which I could squeeze myself, underneath a battered desk piled with books and sketches. Fortunately, I had closed the door behind me: its rattle would warn me should someone come in. There was just enough time for one last glimpse.

That is when I saw it, an irresistible arm's-length away, crying out for my attention. On the desk, amongst Rembrandt's other belongings, was a faded black leather tablet, rounded in form from intensive use. Some of its pages were torn or uneven, and several cream-coloured corners poked out at the top and bottom edges. I laid my hand on the cover then picked it up and ran my fingers along the two golden clasps engraved with leaves and the metal needle. I suspected it was a sketchbook or journal or both; in any case, it appeared valuable, and I thought that if only I could possess a small token of my experience, like Atalanta with her head and hide from the slain beast, a small token . . . If I could simply borrow it for a time and then return it – perhaps it would contain a scrap of this mysterious man I had just discovered, or perhaps even a marvellous reality. My hand trembled on its cover, feeling the bulge of its contents, and *the great ocean of truth lay all undiscovered before me*. Then again, I thought, how often the prospect of happiness is sacrificed to one's own impatience for instant gratification.

The choice was made for me when the footfalls stopped, just outside the door, and an incredulous silence followed. I peered over my shoulder, but the door had not been opened. A furry moth pinged against the oil lamp. The handle rattled. I threw the book down, its pages fluttering, and dropped to the floor. On my knees, rear in the air, I wriggled my way under the desk.

Abruptly, the door burst open.

With my long, awkward body rolled into a ball, I trembled in dirt and filth.

Two boots, daubed with paint, made their way towards the desk, a few inches away: Rembrandt's feet.

My heart thundered in my chest.

A grunt, a sniffle and the shuffle of paintbrushes in a jar.

I stayed motionless where I was, hugging my crumpled stockings.

The edge of his smock brushed his shins as he tinkered with his jars.

Head lowered, I closed my eyes and tried to steady my breathing.

Rap, rap, rap. One foot tapped against the wooden floorboards.

My muscles ached. How long will I have to endure this? Could I slip out while his back was turned?

Suddenly, he bellowed, 'A whip is for the horse, a bridle is for the ass, and a rod is for the idiot.'

I sucked in my breath. Was he speaking to me? Was I the idiot?

He spoke again. 'Are you planning to come out from there?'

Whatever I was planning, it was too late; there was no other choice than to reveal myself. In shame, I crawled out slowly and rose up before him. Rembrandt stood still, a bulky mass against the feeble light, his lips quivering, his fists shut tight.

'I am very s-s-orry, Master,' I bumbled.

He spat at me through the mouldy air. 'If the Prince was not here, I would hit you!' He raised his arm to slap me across the cheek, but his hand stopped — stained, stony and callused — in front of my nose. The fingernails were cracked and black.

I shrank. 'Please don't . . .'

'No one enters my workshop uninvited!' His burly figure was so close to me I could smell his breath, stinking of tobacco and alcohol, and see his face — the skin damp with perspiration, as if made of wax; the cheeks drooping over the corners of his mouth; the eyes murky and sad. He lowered his hand and clutched his hip.

'Your door was open and I just happened to see the red—'

'Enough!' he said. 'What were you looking for, aye?'

My eyes darted about the room and settled on his book. Did he notice it had moved slightly?

He wheezed, 'Sit down.'

'What?'

'Sit down.'

I backed my rear end on to the stool behind me.

Surprised, and unsure of how to respond, I squinted at him. So this was what people meant about his uncertain temper . . .

'You are a publisher, aren't you?'

'Yes, I work for my father, Joan Blaeu.'

'*The* Joan Blaeu, the famous mapmaker?'

'Yes, that's the one.'

His voice was deep and hoarse. 'I expected . . .' He paused. 'Ask him about Elsje Christiaens.'

He expected what? He was obviously going to say something and changed his mind. Elsje Christiaens: what did he mean? I suddenly remembered that my father had been involved in her trial several years before, but she was one among many criminals and nobody special. If Rembrandt were holding her conviction against my father, it would be difficult to comprehend why.

'I don't understand,' I said, which was partly true.

He gave me a hint. 'She was an outsider, like me.' After a moment in which he seemed to be putting his thoughts in order, he changed the subject. 'So, do you plan to carry on the family venture?'

I hesitated, musing on how to proceed: though my distaste for mapmaking was obvious, I had never admitted as much to anyone. Since I was a boy, Father had insisted that I carry on the business in all its facets – globes, maps, books and slaves too – whether I wished to or not, and with his same, unwavering dedication. My grandfather had set the cornerstone for all Blaeu men by making his elaborate atlases, and in my father's hands, the business became a success. Doesn't every man want money, power, fame? Well, here they were, blazing before my eyes, but the pyre was about to consume me. I could no longer keep to myself what had been weighing me down, and somehow this hoary creature seemed the only one with whom to share my confession.

'Well, I enjoy my work as an editor, but I'm not remotely interested in cartography.'

'What are you interested in?'

I almost choked; no one had ever asked me that question before, other than myself, at least not out of sincerity. 'Well, I want to write my own books.'

When his face softened, his thin moustache stuck to his upper lip. After musing a moment, he said, 'Tell me a story then.'

'What?'

'Do you know Ovid's Pyramus and Thisbe?'

'Of course, Master van Rijn.'

He pulled a pipe from the ragged pocket of his smock, and began filling it with tobacco. 'Tell it to me then.'

'Oh . . .' I wondered whether he was serious or not. What were his intentions? Did this have anything to do with Elsje Christiaens? I could not guess, but the little dignity I had left told me to honour him with the tale. It had been a while since I visited *Metamorphoses*, so I started with little confidence and creeping words, hoping he would stop me after a few sentences.

'The setting of the tale is Babylon, and Pyramus and Thisbe were the most beautiful people living there. They were neighbours, who fell in love, but their parents forbade them to marry . . .'

My mouth was dry, and demons tussled inside my stomach. Looking to Rembrandt for assurance, I received a vacuous stare above the glow of his pipe. That is when I noticed his right eye was slightly lazy. I thought my own eyes were playing tricks on me, but looking again, I confirmed that one pupil wandered away from my face while the other watched me directly. How could I have failed to notice before? It seemed strange considering his profession. Waving a hand in the air, he encouraged me to continue.

'In order to speak, they had to exchange words through a crevice in the wall between their houses, and when they said goodnight, they kissed a different side of the wall. Then, one day, the lovers made a plan to meet under the moon on a certain night, at a tomb, I think it was . . .'

'The tomb of Ninus,' he interjected.

'Yes, and near a spring, under a mulberry tree with snow-white fruits. When that night came, Thisbe reached the desired place, but instead of finding her lover she encountered a lioness, fresh from the kill and drinking from the spring. Thisbe, who was very afraid, fled into a cave and dropped her cloak on the way. The lioness ripped it to pieces.'

He nodded, then blew a puff of smoke at me.

My nostrils flared: if I were a woman that would be sexual invitation! Still, I ignored him and went on. 'When Pyramus arrived and saw the animal's footprints and the bloody coat, he cursed himself. He felt great shame for making Thisbe come to that dangerous place. So, taking the sword, he plunged it into his side. When the blood poured out of his wound, it ran all over the mulberry tree and dyed its berries dark red.'

He began pacing the room as I continued. 'A short while later, Thisbe came out from her hiding place to find her lover. At first, she did not recognize the tree because its colour had changed. Then she saw Pyramus lying on the ground, and his eyes met hers one last time before he expired. Immediately she cast herself upon his sword, which was still warm from his blood and . . .'

'And?' he prompted.

I finished, with emphasis, 'From that day, the mulberry fruit, when ripe, was always dark red.'

After clearing my throat, I stayed quiet for a time, musing over the absurdity of the situation, the significance of the story and his mysterious reasons for requesting it. Did he think I was interested in unrequited love? *Na, na.* Was he telling me that he wished to paint this scene? *Possibly.* But I came up with a better idea. 'Is that where you get your red?' I asked, provoking him to give up his secret.

'No,' he said, curtly. An awkward silence fell between us, and it seemed to stretch out for an eternity, until he approached his painting and pointed at the woman's dress. His voice was hollow, without passion. 'Look here, this colour is carmine, made from the kermes insect. The bug is as tiny as a child's fingernail, but when boiled and dried in the sun becomes a deep scarlet.'

'Why carmine?' I asked.

'From the Sanskrit, *krim-dja.* Some wrongly believe it is a berry.'

'Ah!'

'Don't forget your bag,' he muttered, and with a swift swoop, grabbed the bundle from underneath the desk. Amidst the confusion, I had forgotten. When he handed it to me by the strap, his calloused finger scraped against mine.

'Sorry for disturbing you, Master.' When I held out my hand, it hovered between us like a pesky fly because he did not shake it. There was time for one more question. 'Your painting, what is it called?'

'Two Years!'

Thinking *how perfect*, I smiled at him then left the room with my bag flattened to my chest and pressing against my ribs.

A few minutes later – how had I gathered the strength to leave the house? – I was standing in the cobbled, dingy street, and Ferroni was asking me where I had gone. 'Trapped in the privy,' I said. 'Rembrandt had to prise the door open.' He rolled his eyes and Cosimo laughed, but both seemed satisfied with my explanation, and anyway, they were absorbed in themselves, discussing the success of our visit (for it *was* successful). Although exhausted by the morning, and despite it being a bitterly cold day, I decided not to accompany them but to walk home, saying I fancied a stroll. Ferroni promised to keep me in mind as a guide for future tours, and the Prince suggested we meet again if ever I visited Florence. Before they ascended into their carriage, I made them a low bow with my knee deep in the snow, feeling insignificant and small. Though disappointed in myself for blundering the end of the tour, I was also overly conscious of the contents of my bag, which, due to my cowardice, was lacking one special item.

As I walked across town, time seemed to flow downstream, and somewhere in that web of narrow streets the significance of my morning became visible. Instinct told me that, if given the opportunity, Rembrandt and I would become closely acquainted and perhaps even great friends, for despite the uneven ground between us we were kindred spirits. No one had interested me or, indeed, found me interesting in a long while. Besides, I was privy to something no one else knew: he had been keeping a journal. I could not prove it, but what else could it have been? A sense of failure descended upon me, making me feel silly for letting that treasure slip away. I was a habitual passer-by of opportunity; I had lived without having lived! Of course, if I had stolen the tablet, I would also have been guilty of a crime – no better than the common criminals my father had sent to the gallows. The worst sort of crime, if it were a diary as I suspected, because I would have cut short his life and broken a natural human course – a cruel sentence against someone I was just beginning to know and respect. The world belonged to people who could ignore other people's feelings, hopes and futures, I thought, but I had always been different – fearful of hindering pathways or muddling constellations.

Now, imagine it.

The sky is a pale-green curtain. A raven flies overhead. Snow fleeces the rooftops and edges the thin branches of barren trees which line the frozen canal. People skate and gather on the ice: a young man pulling an old woman on a handmade sled; a girl offering a hand to her companion who toddles behind; a skinny dog with a curly tail shivering near a hole; three children in a circle playing a game of dice; a stall selling food and drink; a pair of lovers skipping along in clumsy harmony; one woman in a red coat, having lost her balance, sits on the ice, and no one is helping her up . . .

The fallen woman floundered near the edge – close to where I stood – crouching upon one leg and frowning. Her red skirt billowed up, revealing her stretched-out leg – a thin, stocking-covered ankle and a small boot attached to a skate shoe. A white scarf concealed her head apart from a few strands of strawberry-blonde hair, brushing against her wan face and long neck. The simplicity of her form touched me, and with her chin tucked into her chest, she reminded me of a swan. She lifted her eyes to me with a seriousness that made me feel she was sad. Or could she read my thoughts? I wanted to offer her a hand, but my body was immobile and all I could do was return her gaze. When she did not lower her eyes, I blinked once then turned away. Heading down the Bloemgracht, I suddenly thought of Elsje Christiaens and remembered that a few years previous she had been depicted by the artist Anthonie van Borssom hanging on the gallows, alongside four other corpses, wearing a crimson-red dress. In fact, she looked very similar to the woman I had just seen and left behind. When I looked back over my shoulder, she was still stretched out on the ice but waving her scarf to attract my attention. Did I know her? Despite my curiosity, I carried on, for there was another image invading my mind, and it would remain long after I left this place, trailing me and watching me.

Neeltgen's Story

When Neeltgen's husband, Harmen the Miller, went blind, he was sitting in the chair near the fire. He cried out to her from the front room, my wife, my wife, please come. Neeltgen, the baker's daughter, stopped plucking her duck and went to him immediately. She moved swiftly for a buxom woman of sixty years, so the keys on her silver belt jangled and her bouncing pomander released its aromatic scent into the hallway.

What is it? she asked. Harmen gripped her arm and said the universe was growing distant. He could not feel the earth under his feet. Even worse, he could no longer see her, his wife of forty years. Oh, Jehovah! she gasped, how can this be true? Do you see this? She waved a hand in front of his face. No, he replied. What about my red slippers? Look here! She lifted the edge of her linen dress to give him a better view. No, he said again. Can you see anything at all? Yes, he answered, blurred lines and a stubborn fog. But do not fret, my love, I recognize your voice and it is the sweetest melody to me.

Neeltgen took his soft face in her hands and held it against her apron. Lord have mercy, what shall we do? She looked to the heavens, then sought her answer in the darkened room, which resembled a slightly skewed box. The wide-open shutters coaxed the light and air from the courtyard. The table was covered in a blue carpet speckled with white paint, because her son, a painter, had used it for a drapery. Four porcelain jars and a pair of roemers sat atop the oak chest. The four chairs sank on their turned legs. The white walls attracted flies. She blinked away her tears: all appeared the same.

Shhh, Harmen murmured, your prayers are no use. I will get the doctor, Neeltgen said, or should I fetch the boys? No need, he said, no need to alarm them. She released her husband and sat in the chair opposite him. His hands, scarred from an accident with a musket, shook in his lap. His eyes, which were open, were still the green colour of olives, but they did not sparkle or shine or follow her movements. They were like two dead circles, and the thin lids around them were red. She felt their emptiness. There is no way out for me, her husband said, I need you to be my eyes. Positively I will, she declared, but I cannot abandon the hope that your sight will return. Perhaps, if you hang on to my voice ... My beautiful bird, he interrupted, do not speak of such things, for I am resigned to living in darkness. I beg you, please, to stay by my side and be my eyes.

For years, Neeltgen stayed by her husband's side, being his eyes. Although she ceased reciting her prayers aloud, to avoid upsetting him, she kept hope while clothing and feeding him and making him warm. On cold nights, after combing the tangles from his long white beard, she read to him from the Holy Book as he would have done himself if he had had his sight. The stories of faith might especially touch him, she thought, as she resurrected Job, Noah and other righteous souls. Once, Harmen's cheeks rose and his ears twitched when she related the story of Tobit, so she told it again the following evening, and again ...

Tobit is a devout Jewish man who suffers calamity one night because of giving burial to executed Jews. As he sleeps beside a grave, a shower of sparrow guano falls into his eyes and blinds him. Without sight, he must depend on his son Tobias for guidance. Still, he needs him to recover the money he has deposited in the land of the Medes, so he sends his son away on a journey. During this time, Tobit starts to believe his boy will not return, and prays to God for death to deliver him from this burden. On his journey, Tobias is joined by a stranger, who saves him from being killed by a monstrous fish leaping out of the Tigris. After killing the creature, the stranger tells Tobias that he must keep the heart, liver and gall because of their magical healing powers. When Tobias returns home, accompanied by the stranger, he realizes that he has nearly lost his father, so he spreads the gall on his eyes. Tobit recovers his sight and sees the stranger transformed into the angel Raphael, who leaves in a blast of radiance. It is a miracle of God.

Whenever Neeltgen finished the tale and closed the book, she wept silently. Even when she recited with the greatest emotion, Harmen did not respond. She wiped his rheumy eyes and asked questions, but he behaved as if he could not hear her. He spoke of the past as if it were his present, and she thought, *with no vision, a man becomes unrestrained.* She wept silently because her husband was slipping away from her. Her youngest son Rembrandt felt the same way, which is why, after Harmen went blind, he sketched his father sitting in his chair, eyes wrinkled and sealed like two pie crusts. As he worked, Neeltgen brought him frothy beer and herrings, and sometimes she watched without making her presence known. She tried to understand how this talented creature had come from her blood, her body. She did not know what time might be. It seemed a short while ago that she had swaddled him to help his bones form; sung him to sleep in his wicker cradle; rubbed juniper oil on his gums as his teeth grew; and taught him to walk with a helmet on his head to protect him when falling down. She would have been proud had Rembrandt become a miller, like his father and her son Adriaen, or a baker, like her father and her son Willem. But she was delighted that he had become a great painter; it had proved his Fate. Harmen was pleased too: with his monies they could live comfortably.

Early one morning, Neeltgen remembered that it had been three long years since her husband went blind. It was her body, not her mind, which informed her that she had spent days on end fetching this and that for Harmen, in addition to her regular routine: scrubbing and scouring the reception rooms, dusting and polishing the bedrooms, washing cloths and cooking meals. Now her bones were telling her with a great aching that work had dried her out. Setting her broom to one side, she thought, I am not a young woman any more. My role is to sustain everyone and now I am exhausted. Harmen was not to blame – he had always told her to give more duties to Miken, and she had ignored him because, if she could give birth to ten children and hold back six of them from death, she must be created from the strongest fibre that the Lord could bestow on a woman. Besides, she had given up going to market on Tuesdays, and allocated the most difficult tasks to Miken, like removing cobwebs and insect droppings, clearing termite nests and suffocating the cockroaches.

Early one morning, while sweeping the front porch, Neeltgen knew she needed to rest, so she folded inwardly with slackening muscles. She drifted into a deep, pleasant sleep for what seemed like two minutes and was really two hours, until the sound of trampling feet and rattling floorboards roused her. Her son shouted, Moeder! Please wake. Smacking her lips, she opened her tiny lids like a newborn bird. Rembrandt leaned over her. She straightened up with a jolt. What has happened? Where is Father? Tucked in his bed, her son breathed, do not worry, but I have terrible news. What do you mean? There's been a fire in the city, he said; the madhouse is burning. I do not believe it! she shouted. Come and see for yourself, he said and took her arm, guiding her from the silence of the parlour into the street. There they encountered a deafening noise: the clamouring of townspeople and the miaowing of frightened cats. Even the stray dogs, which could not be stirred by barbarous brawls or pitiless weather, were huddled in packs, shaking and howling. Neeltgen and her son stayed on the edges, near the house. A foul, peppery odour filled the alleyway. She coughed into her hand.

Flames leapt towards the clouds, crackling and sputtering near the city gate. The sky glowed with crimson light as timbers cracked in the distance. Neeltgen put a hand on her son's arm; how did this happen? Earlier this morning, he explained, Lievens and I were working when we suddenly heard shouting in the street, and seeing the fire, I immediately rushed home to warn you. What if it spreads to the brew quay or even here? she wondered aloud. I would not worry, the sanatorium is near the water, and I saw many men on their way to help . . . Do you think I should go too? Stay here with me, she said. Rembrandt put his arm around her and held his gaze upwards. The changing colours of the flames flickered in his dark eyes. Brimming with questions and capable of causing the greatest unease, they reminded Neeltgen of the reasons she fell in love with his father. The rest of him resembled her own father – the puffy cheeks of a cherub, the heavy muscles of an ox, the vigorous chin of a goat. She did not know where he got his nose, which was large, waxy and round, but she was often tempted to kiss it.

There was a loud shrieking, and two men hurried down the street toward them. One was barefoot, eyes full of fear, wearing a torn and ragged housecoat. He galloped by them, spitting from his mouth, Fire! Fire! Haaalp! The other followed closely behind, running with his underpants around his ankles, his testicles swinging between his thighs. When he snarled at Neeltgen, showing his rotten teeth, she cowered against the wall. Rembrandt grabbed the man's arm and tried to console him. Don't be frightened, he said. The doctors are on their way. But the man only grew more excited and tried to break free of Rembrandt's grasp. After they had struggled for a minute, two soldiers charged through the crowd, seized the man and carried him away. Neeltgen shuddered, looking at her son, his face beaded with sweat.

Soon the flames began to settle, and clouds of smoke billowed upwards, advancing towards them. A dozen or a score of figures scurried away: some headed for home, while the more curious folks, wishing to assess the damage, moved towards the Vrouwenkerksteeg. Neeltgen tugged on her son's dingy doublet; why has this terrible thing happened? It must have been an accident, he replied. No, she said, it is a portent, something bad will come, I can feel it in my bones. You worry too much, he said. Let me take you inside, so we can tell Father. Leading her by the hand, he brought her indoors and they told Harmen the news. The fire is over now,

Rembrandt said, touching his father's shoulder. He described his morning and the incident with the madman, then speculated on the number injured and the amount of damage. Flames shot up and streaked the sky with fiery shades, he said. I have never known a more brilliant yellow or bright orange, Papa, and that deep red was the purest colour I've ever seen, as if it were God's shadow.

Later that evening, when Neeltgen had returned to her high-backed chair and while her husband was asleep, Rembrandt sat nearby. He said that he had spoken to some men at the tavern. Little remained of the madhouse but not many were injured, and everyone had been moved to the hospital. A night watchman, still on duty, had smelt the burning and warned the patients, but when he stayed behind to help everyone, he was trapped inside. That poor man, she said, folding her hands across her lap. It could have been Father, Rembrandt said, if he hadn't stopped his duties. You shouldn't say that, she told him, lest he overhear you. He cannot hear me, her son shouted, he cannot hear or see us any more, that is the truth and we must accept it.

A short while later, in April 1630, as if in response to the prophetic fire, Neeltgen's husband, Harmen the Miller, slipped into his last darkness. The following day, her sons carried his body in procession to the burial place at the front of the pulpit in the Pieterskerk. Neeltgen, being a woman, did not attend, though she heard the chiming of the bells at midday. After the funeral, she served a lively feast to her six children and her friends, at which she drank spiced wine in excess. That night, when the watchmen blew their horns, she said her goodbyes and imagined Harmen's body ascending like a dove into Heaven. She thanked the Lord for having given her forty-three years with the humblest man in Jerusalem.

The days were getting warmer, so Rembrandt bought a patch of garden on the right-hand side of the Witte Singel, where the wind bounced off the water and the tulips swayed in full bloom. Neeltgen enjoyed the quiet of solitude while her son made sketches from nature. There he told her of his plan to move to Amsterdam and seek patronage for doing portraits. It is my only chance to survive as a painter, he said, if I do not go to The Hague. And there is not enough work in Leyden, please understand. Her throat contracted. I do understand, she said. Don't be sad, he said, Adriaen will look after you. I am not sad, because I have always known that you were meant for larger things. In truth, she added, when you went the last time to study with Lastman, I wished you would not come back. He draped his arm round her bony shoulders. Well, I did, and I have been happy here with you and Father, but it has been five years and everything has changed. Perhaps you will find yourself a wife there, she said, if you do not get fat. He scowled, his face turning a dusky red. Lievens is leaving too, for England, he told her, to become a painter at the court of King Charles. She sighed, what has happened between you? Nothing, he said huskily, looking at the grass. It's time we stood each on our own. When will you leave? she asked. Perhaps in a year, he said, so I have time to paint you as the prophetess Anna.

When Neeltgen was ready to play her role, Rembrandt rummaged for the proper costume in his sloping room in the eaves. Over her own plain scarf she slipped on an earthen-coloured silk headdress, and over her linen skirt, a red velvet mantle. She donned a grey-green fur collar with matching sleeves. The canvas and pigments were already prepared, and Rembrandt's easel positioned accordingly in the upstairs room. He sat in front of the small panel, his face tense, his eyes clear. Gripping the palette in his right hand, he looked like a crafty spider eager to weave his web. If she wanted to see him, she only had to look from the corner of her eye, but once he started, she waited, not stirring.

He told her to relax as he worked. She had heard this before, yet it was always difficult. Neeltgen liked to imagine that two large stones were tied to her wrists, pulling her shoulders downward, or that she was a sparrow flying above the treetops. She liked to pretend that she was anyone other than herself. In this case, she placed herself in the role of the prophetess. He had already shown her how to perch on the wooden chair in the corner, in front of the tawny plaster wall. With her buttocks tucked into the shell-shaped seat, which sat low to the ground, the open book — her own copy, bulky and yellowed — rested on her propped-up knees. She leant forward slightly and placed her right hand on the left page, where the light glowed on Luke's Gospel.

There was a prophetess called Anna, Phanuel's daughter of Asher's tribe, a woman who, well along in years, had lived with a husband for seven years from her virginity, and became a widow eighty-four years old. Anna had put her hope in God, and was never missing from the temple, rendering sacred service night and day, persisting with fastings and supplications; she returned thanks to God and spoke about the Christ to all those waiting for Jerusalem's deliverance.

She devoured the words line by line, without taking her eyes off the page. Her eyes lost focus and all human noise grew very far away. She heard only the sound inside, the humming in her mind.

Thoughts floated perpetually in her head, thoughts of the passage of time and the reversal of life.

She remembered sending Rembrandt to Latin school, where he made his first drawings of cats and dogs, and in particular, the first day she walked him there. When she kissed his forehead goodbye, he cried and wrapped his arms tightly around her legs. He pleaded to stay with her, but she prised each of his fingers loose and told him he had to behave like a grown boy. Although he shouted as she turned away, and his anguish pelted her like hailstones, she did not look back but told herself she had done the right thing to enrol him there, in order to ripen him into a serious, learned man. Since then, Neeltgen had witnessed the hardening of his soft edges and the opening of his intellect. Never again had he been prone to weakness nor shed a single tear in her presence, not even when his father died. Soon, she thought, he would go away. Her pain heightened with the recognition that she might not see him ever again.

Her son behaved as if he could not hear her thoughts, or as if she was not there. In truth, she no longer knew where she was, after sitting and musing for long hours. Her limbs went numb and her eyes drooped with tiredness. When she closed them, he immediately scolded her; his enthusiasm seemed to have no practi-cal limit. But the following day he allowed her to rest, and the process continued for several weeks, until he told her he would apply the last touches in the workshop alone. Finally, he revealed the painting in its completion, and she smiled at him with tenderness. He had captured everything: the creases at her nose, the crinkles around her mouth and eyes, her scraggy neck, the wrinkles on her hands. She thought the number of lines equalled the sum of her years and hardship. Her portrait was more than a good likeness, it was a gathering of the difficulties she had overcome. Neeltgen, the dead miller's wife, praised the Lord, for she had become Anna, a prophetess, a widow, who would forsake herself for all others. She would spend the final years of her life, long after her son went away, sitting in her chair by the hearth, reading the Holy Book.

Leyden, 1629

Fashioning Oneself for the Cream of Society

My tiny bed is moist and cold. I lie still, my hands tucked into my armpits for warmth. The pigeons coo on the roof. Miken has already visited my room to stoke the fire and leave a pot of fresh rainwater. After saying a little prayer, I scramble out of the bedclothes and creep over to the mirror. My fingers fumble to light a candle.

The man staring back at me has dark puffy eyes and a scraggly beard. I wriggle my nose, then my dungy breath fogs the glass. The occasion clearly calls for some primping. First, I scrub myself all over with a hard-bristled brush. Next, I shave my beard with a knife, and by a miracle, cut myself in only three places. My hair looks like a bird's nest when I start out, but my orris-scented comb works miracles. In the end, a soft lock trails over one shoulder and a springy curl rests on my forehead. After slipping into my underclothes, I don my best: a white shirt and cuffs and an embroidered gown. Should I wear my felt hat with the upturned brim? My jewelled hatband with the ostrich plume? Oh, I had better wear my gorget collar-piece and black velvet beret. As Lastman used to say, 'Neglect nothing that can make you great.' Alas, here he is: Rembrandt, the burgher.

Moeder is still asleep — I can hear her snoring — or is that the dog? Though I want to kiss her goodbye, I must be on my way. After dusting my boots, I secure my Judas painting under my arm. The Hague is twelve miles away, a long and silent landscape. Hear my heart rejoice!

The Boy on Crutches

The ragged road meanders south through marshes, then winds west through low, grassy meadows filled with cows. My steps lead me across rickety bridges, alongside clumps of willows and windmills, past thatched cottages, farmhouses and barns. If only I had time to make a country scene ... Why is it that these things stir me so much? At this early hour, the atmosphere in the south, near the horizon, has a dim haze of rose-flushed clouds, redder towards the west. In the east, the damp vapour shows brighter while the houses are scarcely visible. The entire field is bathed in a diffused light and dancing with shadows.

Halfway to my destination, I consider stopping at an inn to refresh myself, but then I see a peaceful river and a hollow there. Leaving the road, I make my way towards the water through tangled grasses and weeds resonant with flies. There I find a large elm tree with a great split in the centre, and take shelter in its embrace. A small group of peasant fishermen crouch on the riverbank, casting their lines. Another onlooker is standing close to the water: a young boy dressed in rags, holding himself up with crutches. One of his legs is distorted. He has a lovely elfin face, purely cut, and brown hair falling on his temples. Hands folded at his breast, he is seemingly preoccupied with his thoughts. As the men drop their hooks, he gazes tranquilly at the water. For a long while I, too, do the same.

Note: The oaks look much lighter on the side from where the wind is blowing because the wind turns up the leaves, always whiter on the underside. The surface of the water has two movements, one following the current, the other following the motion of the return flow. The greatest depth of river water is always below the strongest current. In drawing, hold to nature and no other rules!

The boy turns his head to look at me as if he were a hunter, and I a deer. Lord knows why, but my skin prickles. Lowering my head, I notice that my clothing, previously starched and clean, is now wrinkled and dirty from travelling. The breeze has probably wilted my curly hair. I scramble to my feet and stretch my arms in the air. Avoiding the boy's gaze, I turn in the direction of the road. But after a few steps, when I glance over my shoulder, the boy has not stirred. His eyes remain fixed in my direction as if I were not there, peering into some unknown space. Their solemnity and reserve frighten me.

I press on along the broad path, absorbed in the scents from meadows and carried away in a sort of dream. Currents of air stir the dust on the path and the tops of trees, so that everything seems to be swirling around me — things, places, years. It seems as if I am headed for the Promised Land. For a moment I see the future and myself, the aged artist wreathed in glory, drenched in recognition and applause. Oh Lord, I want these things and I want them quickly ... Please rid me of these frustrations and fears! Soon enough, the sky and fields cause my future to slip away. Out here in the open, who can say what the years will bring? No matter how untrod my way shall be, I must persist in following my own road.

How an Artist Establishes His Reputation

The Hague seems a world away from Leyden. Hours later but still early in the day, I enter the city from the north, beckoned by the church towers rising among the trees. Rather than the expected military barracks, I find an *endless spread of stables, fencing academies and stately buildings. The precincts of the court overlook the flowing Vijver. Inside those tall, brick walls are the medieval palace and living quarters of the Stadhouder, the Prince of Orange, which stretches over a considerable distance. A space to conquer!*

Knocking on the heavy door, I wait thinking of Rubens, who, when he had been made Knight of the Garter, was bestowed with a diamond ring, a hatband and a sword by King Charles. I do not expect as much from the Prince, needless to say, but when prompted I proclaim my name with the confidence of a regent — Rembrandt van Rijn — to gain admittance by the guard.

Huygens, draped in a black silk broadcloth, sweeps along the corridor to the reception room. He greets me warmly by extending his hand. I accept it without reservation and with an earnest grasp, not because I am a friendly sort or at ease with the situation, but because I feel the very opposite. This extended hand, so familiar to me, offers safety. Here in the court it is the only available comfort. Why? Because I know these hands. I've seen them a thousand times since the winter. Their white, slender fingers with shorn nails, folded together, are reproduced in paint on an oak panel in my workshop. These hands are the only part of Huygens painted by Lievens on his initial stay, the only part I was able to anticipate. Now, releasing one of them and looking up, I complete the gentleman's portrait: his angular body swimming in the folds of his costume; his narrow face with brown eyes cast in reflection; his high-arching brows and pointed nose; his fastidiously trimmed moustache and beard; his cropped hair tucked under a stiff black hat; his neck concealed by a white ruff.

This is Huygens: lawyer, scholar, artist, musician, athlete (he climbed the spire of Strasbourg Cathedral), diplomat, Protestant, poet (in Latin, Dutch and French) and translator of John Donne, knighted by the last King of England. Next to him I feel like a bothersome vagrant who sits on doorsteps, along with his children, moaning all night until let inside. He lets me inside.

[*Enter Rembrandt.*]

The office is an opulent, grand salon with tall windows letting in a blinding amount of light and velvet chairs lining each wall. In the centre of the room is a walnut desk, at the short end there is a marble hearth, and on the other, a cabinet inlaid with tropical woods and encasing ivory and mother-of-pearl curios. Numerous paintings — landscapes, seascapes and still-lifes — grace the walls alongside embroideries and tapestries.

SCH: Pleased to meet you at last, Rembrandt. How was your journey?

RVR: Not too bad, Sir Constantijn. I fancy a stroll now and again.

SCH: You walked? I am charmed. I have never seen such dedication and persistence in other artists — in other men! — as I have seen in you and Lievens. You must be tired, won't you sit? *Gestures to one of the armchairs then takes the other.* Your friend, as you may know, was so eager to paint my portrait he arrived long before the appointed date, and his desire to impress me has made him very restless these last few weeks.

RVR: Is that so? He is still painting then?

SCH: Well, he tells me the portrait is finished.

A young maidservant arrives, crossing the room to where the men are seated, and sets a tray on the table between them. The painter notices, beneath her bonnet, her eyes like slits and her pallid lips.

SCH: I am the one with reservations. *Leans forward, seemingly bothered by the girl, who clumsily pours two cups of tea.*

RVR: Are you displeased with the result?

The patron's hands are steady as he lifts a silver pitcher and pours, in one swift but graceful movement, the milk into his tea.

SCH: Lievens wreaks miracles in painting the human countenance, but this one does little justice to my vivacity.

RVR: *Tilts his head, waiting for an explanation.* (*Aside*) Hmm, Lievens's colours do run down his pictures like dung!

SCH: Well, it is my fault. Please have a drink, Rembrandt.

The painter takes a cup of tea. Unsure of where to settle his eyes, he watches the servant as she leaves the room in haste, her white frock grazing the back of her legs.

SCH: Lately I have been involved in a serious family affair, you see, my wife passed away. And so, no matter how much I tried to conceal this when I was sitting, it is clearly reflected in the expression on my face.

RVR: *Fidgets in his chair, his leg never still.* I'm sorry, my lord. Have you discussed it with Lievens?

SCH: I have, but you know how resistant he is to criticism. *Pause.* Please don't misunderstand me, I'm convinced his strength is in portraiture, but he is unlikely to match your spirit of invention.

RVR: *Springs to his feet.* Would you like to see my Judas?

SCH: *Sips his tea then smooths his moustache.* Well, you're not one for idle talk.

The patron rises from his chair, walks over to his desk and removes a pair of eyeglasses that are resting there amongst a scramble of things: a large globe, a compass, a stack of books. Meanwhile, the painter takes the panel and walks ten paces to the other side of the salon to hold it up with both hands.

SCH: *Seated once more, pinches on his spectacles and stares at the painting. After a stretching silence:* Have you reworked any of the passages?

RVR: No, sir. (*Aside*) That is a lie. I have added a new figure and changed the background.

SCH: Do you realize what you have done? *Slides his palms up and down the velvety arms of his chair then gets up.* This has none of the refinements of classical history painting!

RVR: *Raises his voice.* Have you changed your mind? Is that what you are saying? Or would you still like it for the Prince's collection?

SCH: Extraordinary! *Clips his lips together.* Changed my mind? I am simply trying to say that you have made a daring leap.

RVR: Oh?

SCH: *Bending down before the picture.* Such command and honesty! Your figures are full of emotion, for instance, here – *points at the panel* – the figure of Judas on his knees, wringing his hands in self-hatred and pleading for forgiveness ... Who would have thought that someone your age, a miller at that, could put so much into a figure!

RVR: (*Aside*) Is that a compliment? (*To SCH*) Thank you, sir. It would show best in the Gallery of His Excellency, because of the strong light there.

SCH: I like your Judas, and I will give you one hundred guilders for him.

RVR: *Cheeks flush with heat.* It's worth at least two hundred guilders, because it has taken me a long time to execute, the main reason being that I was trying to express the most innate emotion . . .

SCH: Innate emotion?

RVR: I tried to achieve an immediacy with the figures that makes the Scripture breathe and come alive.

SCH: Well, this you have done, but I have made my offer, one hundred guilders, Rembrandt, and let me tell you why . . .

RVR: *Crosses his arms over his chest.* Why?

SCH: The architectural setting has atmosphere but no spatial precision. You see the canopied area? There is no relation to the pillar and the back wall. The incoherency is only emphasized by the cracked surface of the background behind the priests. I am also wary of the foreground figure, whose presence seems too calculated, as if you are trying to fill up the space . . . Yes, he simply does not belong.

RVR: Surely you can offer more, considering all of the positive things you have said about it! (*Aside*) That bastard! How am I supposed to feed myself?

SCH: Would you prefer I pay you out of pity? I have made my offer.

RVR: I don't want your pity, I want one hundred and fifty guilders, no less. *Recovers the painting with a cloth and places it under his arm.* Well, I'll just be on my way then . . .

SCH: Fine, Rembrandt. One hundred and fifty it is.

RVR: Thank you, Sir Constantijn.

The men shake hands as if old friends.

SCH: But there is something else I would like you to consider, a matter which I have also discussed with your friend Lievens. Please, sit down.

RVR: *Sits down.*

SCH: Until now, you and Lievens have been content to hide yourselves in your own little world, and though you have both grown in your skill, you have not yet achieved what you are fully capable of. There is one thing, and one thing only, which could perfect your artistic powers.

RVR: *Mouth twitches.* What?

SCH: Italy, of course. The pictures of the great Italian masters! You must go immediately.

Startled, the painter sits upright.

SCH: Well? What is the matter?

RVR: This is very unexpected.

SCH: Consider Titian, Michelangelo, Raphael — *with one hand leaning on his desk, he waves the other in the air* — you can learn from them, and how quickly you could surpass them all!

RVR: We are far too busy for that, and some of the finest Italian works can be seen here in the Provinces, in my very own collection of prints! I have learnt from them already. (*Aside*) My painting is a window to a foreign land where my feet will never walk, and a proclaimer of my name, which has no face. The better life resides in the imagination.

SCH: *Shaking his head.* I do not understand your resistance. Lievens is equally obstinate. How foolish of two artists otherwise so brilliant! Even your teacher Lastman made a pilgrimage to Rome, even your idol, the great Rubens. It was good enough for the two of them. Please go now!

RVR: Now? I can't go now! Let me think more about this and send word to you at a later time. (*Aside*) What about my old mother and my blind, crippled father? Now I truly am exhausted. I'd better find a seat on a passenger coach.

The Field of Blood

On the way home, at a midway halt, the coachman and other travellers stop to change the horses and take refreshment at an inn. I stay inside the carriage to savour some bread, cheese and herrings brought from home. What a stomach-rumbling day! I am slightly disappointed, having left the palace without my hoped-for two hundred guilders. At least I have a new patron, and Huygens promised to visit our workshop in the near future. If only he hadn't pressured me about going to Italy . . .

While I am gobbling down my food, the new horses get restless and begin kicking up their heels. Then, without warning, they bolt down the road. The carriage rumbles, tossing me from one side to the other. When I look out of the back window, I see our driver dashing from the inn. He runs after us, hitching up his breeches and shouting. While I give him a wave, the horses stop for nothing. They gallop at full speed, kicking up great clouds of dust in their wake. My rear bounces on the seat, up and down, up and down, as trees rush past my window and shadows hurl themselves across the road. Thank the Lord they're headed in the right direction! While the carriage dashes along, swerving wildly, I finish the story of Judas in my head. For, after he withdrew from the temple, he went off and hanged himself. The chief priests, left with the thirty pieces of silver, chose not to donate them to the sacred treasury. They bought a potter's field in which to bury foreigners, later called the Field of Blood.

Light & Darkness

Dürer regarded shadows as a darkening of the light, the absence of colour. While darkness increases the light effect, the contrast between the two must not be too sharp. I must continue to study how dark places in a large area of light are absorbed, how the edges are diffused and softened. Also, my lights must be dispersed, rather than limited to a single object. Otherwise, they will appear hard in the picture and their colour is destroyed. Shadows and light must stand not only in contrast of light and dark but also in coldness and warmth. Warm shadows imply cold light and vice versa. Only by an unremitting study of God's creation can I achieve my results.

PURCHASES

Item, a capon ... 10 g.

Item, Anchovies ...?

Item, Indian ink ... 25 g. 3 st.

Item, Charcoal ... 30 g.

On Judging Your Painting

Nulla dies sine linea! *Not a day without a brushstroke. You see, Huygens was somewhat correct in his criticism of my Judas painting, difficult though it is to admit. My background did not support the figures, and the picture was spoilt by an insufficient amount of paint. I have already used his advice in my latest paintings, which have proven to be of high excellence: David and Saul, Samson and Delilah, Peter and Paul. From the outset, everything must be rendered in harmony with the principal subject. If the original idea is not carried out to the end, it is best to start all over again.*

My painting of the artist in his workshop has been leaning against the wall for months now. I haven't been able to look at it, much less touch it. The time has come to take a long, serious look in the mirror. This is the best way to check for any mistakes in the proportions and relationships. The candlelight is sure to reveal any defects in the harmony of my picture, which, even in the darkest corners, must retain its inner light.

After I determine the problems, I return for retouches using my intuition and imagination. These essential forces are behind all of my paintings, driving me towards a strength of expression and something else: honesty. The artist in my painting has become none other than myself. The face, and the uninhibited light there, is deadly serious. The eyes fix the beholder and record every movement of my body. The figure remains the slightest insinuation of who I am — yes, the timid feet. With or without such a veil, no one will ever see me. I believe in mystery, perhaps at any price. (Oh, this may be an exaggeration! By the end of this journal, you may have unravelled me.)

Beggars and Rogues

Waiting for the paints to dry, I read Justinius, Ovid, Pliny, Homer and look at pictures, usually those of Rubens, whom I measure myself against with great admiration. I study the master's poses, compositions and subjects. I even emulate his characters and costumes. Today, I am drawn to a series of prints called Capricci di varie figure *by the Lorraine artist Jacques Callot, etchings which he has dedicated to Lorenzo de' Medici. One of these* capricci *shows a beggar man crouched under a tree, making water and defecating at the same time. Another figure is wearing a long, tattered cape. Balancing himself on crutches, he holds out his deformed and overgrown fingernails. I cannot refrain from thinking about the boy, shameless and strange, whom I saw on my journey to The Hague. I wonder if he was one of the victims of our town clerk, Jan van Hout, who expels the poor from our city, loaded upon carts. I suppose it is better than being whipped into submitting to a decent Christian life.*

I have the idea to do a similar series of figures with more realism, because Callot's rogues, while recognizably human, are shown as freakish objects of curiosity. Mine will not be pitiful or weak but crooked and dangerous, earthy and bold. To present them as faithfully as possible, I must hold fast to their humanity. On the street, I will capture them in their unconscious moments. In my workshop — a place no less appropriate for the tragedy and comedy of life — they will become my favourite biblical characters. These types are perfect for creating history scenes that are raw, startling and true (in keeping with the traditional masters, like Pieter Bruegel). I never undervalue my emotions, and paint only what is important to me. These are my heroes, my kindred spirits. Perhaps I will even put myself in their company, spitting into the eyes of magistrates, open-mouthed, sinful and foul.

Beauty Is Not the Only Aim of Art

On a day like this, when the air is filled with blue light and freshened by linden blossom, I put down my brushes and take a walk. Usually I bring several copper plates with me to do an etching from nature, after life. This may lead me to the Carpenters' Yard, where I watch the men erect buildings from timber, or further down the river, towards the meadows of poplars and sycamores, even to Katwijk. Today I will visit an old pharmacist, Christiaan Poret, to view his extensive collection of naturalia and artificialia. When I am successful I will be a great collector myself. It has already begun with these bare bones: prints, nautilus shells, Mughal miniatures and plaster casts. In the meantime, I am compelled to visit the pharmacy — my weekly brush with everything that is absurd and dazzling. From my house to the Maarsmansteeg, it is a ten-minute journey through crowded alleyways and past the cloth halls.

When I arrive, a young servant girl offers me a seat in the front room, where Christiaan stands behind the counter. He reminds me of Aristotle, an old bearded man with a crinkled nose, his back arched over a vial. I watch as he tinkers with bottles of toad and newt secretions, crushes the roots of liquorice and sassafras, grinds antler and coral then drops them into his concoction. Wiping the sweat from his wrinkled forehead, his rheumy eyes look up at me. He smiles kindly. Now, he is ready.

The apothecary's cabinet, at the rear of the house, heaves with rarities and curios from many corners of the world: healing stones, Chinese herbals, stuffed porcupines and pelicans, stag antlers, unicorn horns, optical lenses, an ivory globe and the green egg of an emu. The apothecary shows the painter a bezoar, an antidote to poison, set in gold and shaped like a cannonball, which comes from the stomach of a Persian goat.

RVR: *Gazing down at the object in his palm.* Is this real gold?

CP: Yes, but if you wish to imitate it, you can put a few dozen threads of saffron in a dish, cover it with beaten egg white and allow it to settle in to a crimson orange, which you can then apply to paper or anything else. Even eat it, if you like. Pliny says 'the hair of the crocus' is the perfect remedy after a night of merriment, though others say it revives the spirit.

The apothecary sets on the table two of his recent acquisitions, suspended in glass jars and immersed in formaldehyde, a neck of a savage and a strange leg of marvellous form. The two men lean over the table.

RVR: *Admiring the jars from all sides.* My Lord, Christiaan, they're pink and withered and grotesque. Not human at all, but severe distortions of nature. What delicious torture!

CP: Oh, you are mistaken. They are the truest form of nature.

RVR: (*Aside*) I feel a great sadness for them. Above all, I am sad for the man, this savage whose body has been flayed for all to see. What crime did he commit, to deserve this ghoulish end?

CP: Have you heard about Dr Tulp? He was recently appointed

praelector to the Surgeons' Guild in Amsterdam. He'll conduct the annual anatomies now.

RVR: Really? Not like the great Vesalius!

CP: *Begins circling the room.* Tulp's philosophy, and this could be called revolutionary, is cut and cut deep, and you will find the source of the problem.

RVR: Who is he again?

CP: I say, Dr Nicolaes Tulp.

RVR: Haven't heard of him!

CP: He's the son of a linen merchant, would you believe. Ten or fifteen years ago, he was a medical student here, studied under Dr Pauw, but then he was called Claes Pieterszoon. Do you know it? Pieterszoon. Recently he changed it to Tulp.

RVR: *With a shrug.* Because he likes the flower?

The apothecary remains silent.

RVR: Too early for a bit of pleasantry, old man?

CP: *Not smiling.* I will leave you in peace now, Rembrandt. I must return to ... I must ... *His voice drops off.* Oh, before I go, you might like to borrow this.

The apothecary holds out a large volume with the title De Fabrica. *Taking the book, the painter runs his fingers across the leather cover, then lifts it open.*

RVR: Where did you find it?

CP: When? Last week. It's the first anatomy book since Vesalius, written by Adriaen van der Spieghel.

RVR: No, where?

As the painter flips over the thick pages, he finds many elaborate illustrations and detailed diagrams of body parts he has never even heard of before.

CP: I have many sources, young man. *On hearing a bell — a customer has arrived — he advances towards the door.* Look it over, but be sure to return it.

RVR: (*Soliloquy*) Now that I am alone with the curiosities, who is this dead man? A thief? A murderer? A heretic? Do not despair, one of the thieves was saved; do not presume, one of the thieves was damned! The further away I go, the closer I will come to clarity. The secret is patience. I must bide my time and lie in wait. Sure enough, after a few minutes, this happens: the jars gradually vanish. Then the appendages stir and twitch in a frightful way. Oh Lord, what is happening? They are floating in the air! Eventually, they settle and seem to be lying on the table. Their pulpy tissue hardens, and the flayed edges lose their outlines. My mind begins to conjure up the missing parts — head, chest, abdomen, feet. Finally, I can see the man's entire body. His true form. This is the corpse before its dismemberment. He stretches along the table in milky serenity. The green light shines on his risen chest. I can see his face, drained of blood, his eyes, closed and sunken in their cavities, his stretched nostrils, his wrinkled mouth and the shadow there. His hands look as if they are struggling to grasp something. In fact, he seems to be alive. Even now, hours later, I see his eyes by the dim light of my lamp. But they are wide open, staring into emptiness.

My First Set of Eyes

I am seven years old, and it is a typical day at my Latin school on the Lokhorststraat, a brick prison which bears the limestone inscription Pietati, Linguis et Artibus Liberales. *The other children sit round me on the rigid wooden benches as we read Virgil. I am prompted to give an answer on particular citation. Who said this and where does it come from? I am unable to remember. My schoolmaster, Jacobus Lettingius, who never spares the rod, raps me over the knuckles with a large stick several times. With hands still stinging, I set off for another classroom for my drawing and calligraphy lesson. My favourite part of the day. There I feel at home, and take pleasure in learning how to make my first set of eyes.*

All Glory to Me, the Next Rubens

A letter from Huygens has arrived. I break the seal and begin to read:

> Most honoured Rembrandt van Rijn,
> I would like to commission two additional pieces for His Excellency, the Stadholder Frederik Hendrick, who intends to make a gift of them to Lord Ancrum, courtier to King Charles, on his visit to The Hague, where he will attend the obsequies for the son of the Winter King and Queen of Bohemia on 14 September.

*The Stuart King will be most pleased with this gift of 3 paintings —
one already in his possession, the second a self-portrait and the third of your
own choosing. I kindly request that to this task you apply all your skill, in
order that the King, as in my opinion, will recognize the work of someone
who can match the invention and genius of Master Rubens. I have full
confidence that, as with your Repentant Judas, you will devote your
concentration to achieving on a small scale a result that cannot be found in
the largest works of others. Leaving aside the many fascinating figures in
this one painting, the gesture of the despairing Judas I place against every
elegance that has been produced throughout the ages. All honour to thee, my
Rembrandt! It is a great achievement to have brought the laurels of Greece
and Italy to Holland, especially for a youth who has seldom ventured
outside the walls of his native city.I feel it incumbent upon myself to state
again how, if only I could drive it in your head to journey to Italy, you
could raise art to its consummate heights.*

*Further, whilst I admire your extreme dedication, Rembrandt — truly,
you are 'redeeming the time' — in your youth you seem an old man burdened
with age, to the extent that I fear these furies could lead you to darkness
and grief, as others of your nature, if you do not consider your constitution,
which a sedentary occupation has already rendered less vigorous and robust.
I should be pleased if you will send word to the palace whenever you find it
possible, so that I may serve the wishes of His Excellency, the Prince.
I commend you to God in health.*
Yours, &c., Sir Constantijn Huygens

There is no higher honour than being compared to the glorious *Pietro Paolo.*
Here I am, ready for fame and the glory days ahead! Oh, but a long silence
ensues. My pipe glows like a firefly and my heart sinks into my boots. The
pleasure of this news is not as great as it ought to be. Why should I release

my soul into the wicked world? What if I fail? Then again, I must take pride in something. Something other than my cock. If Huygens was impressed with such a trite piece, my greater works are bound to be approved. 'Be not concerned for the gallery, act to the stalls and boxes!' Oh, this is not the time to think about it. My musings will only carry me away from my picture. What does he mean by 'less vigorous and robust'?

INTERLUDE

A cock crows three times

RHL

With a few more touches, my painting will be finished. I do not mean there exists such a state of completion — there is always more to do, more to add. Yet the time comes when I must allow the subject breathing space. Even the most essential passages should not be heavily rendered. Remember, Pliny praised Apelles for knowing when to take his hand away from the picture.

Keeping this in mind, I return to my chair and attempt the last strokes on the panel. So as not to disrupt the previously rendered pigments, I use a maulstick to steady my hand. With slow, heady dabs of a miniature brush, I enhance the textures and tweak the reflections, applying beads of brightness. I enlarge the fissures in the wall and darken the bolts on the door. My palette knife makes additional scratches to the floor and chinks in the door. The artist himself, standing there, requires the gentlest touches to his dress. I also lay in certain details on his face, like the highlight at the end of his nose. This feature requires little paint but by its shape defines three different planes. How tiny he appears, yet so admired.

The processs takes several hours. When Lievens knocks on the door and cries, 'Come on, old boy!', my time has run out. Without further delay, I must leave my artist alone with his thoughts. He will live on as a memory while I, the artist, will set off from my obscurity. To revel in my youth! Perhaps we'll go to the gaming house or the brothel, just to celebrate our success. But not before I extract a fine paintbrush from one of my jars and dip it into the monochrome colour. Thinking of Aristotle — Art loves chance and chance loves art — with an extremely fine line, I apply three letters:

R H L *(Rembrandus Hermanni Leydensis)*

'Grooten atlas oft wereldbeschrijving'

The intolerable lucidity of insomnia needled me. I had stayed awake for a long stretch, through the night hours of despair and loneliness, during which I had only paused to piss in my pot or pour myself a tot of gin. Now it was late morning and I sat by the window, looking down into the cobbled street, where a cold sleet was falling. Inside, light suffused the room and all was the same, though my possessions seemed to be travelling towards their own dissolution: the narrow four-poster bed, the mahogany desk and shelves overweighed with books, a wing chair and an ebony mirror.

My temples clanged with the bells of the Oude Kerk, ten times. When I resurfaced, there was a banging on my door.

'Pieter, are you in?'

My father.

'Yes,' I coughed.

'May I enter?'

I stood up and tugged my cloak over my nightgown before opening the door. He stepped in and instantly filled my bedroom with his magnanimous presence as if he were claiming new territory. Draped in an elaborate costume of black satin with an excess of fabric on the sleeves, his arms ballooned outwards, obscuring the rest of his body. His slender hands hovered uncomfortably in mid-air. I glanced about, feeling that I should find them a resting place.

'Don't offer me a seat. It smells foul in here.' An authoritarian scowl spread across his waxy face. His rounded, seemingly endless forehead protruded into a black hat that matted his hair into a nest of curls. The thin moustache, recently trimmed, rose to a peak underneath his nose, and below his lip, one stubbled line tapered down to his chin.

His tone was caustic and censuring. 'We missed you at break-fast. Do you intend to report to your desk this morning?'

'Are you saying I'm needed?'

'No . . .'

Just as I expected.

'. . . But don't answer a question with a question.'

With an unusual boldness, I said, 'Then I won't be in today.'

'Are you ill?'

'I'm going out.'

His nose and his chin folded together into a sweet bun. 'I'll expect you tomorrow because we have to finish work on the Graswinckel. You also haven't told me about your tour yesterday. I had to hear it through Ferroni.'

'I'm sure he didn't miss a detail, but . . .'

'He said you blundered the whole way through and that, if it wasn't for him, the sale would not have happened.'

I cringed, the nerve of that bastard behemoth Ferroni! Without my help, we would never even have entered the Van Rijn house. 'Well, the Prince thought it was a success.'

'Consider being more prepared next time.'

I ignored this comment.

'Where are you going?' he asked.

I must escape, I thought, at any cost.

His eyes inspected me, clearly horrified. 'Well, wherever it is, have a wash first. And put on something respectable. You look pitiful.' With that, after giving me another disdainful glance, he turned around and left the room. I listened to his heels clicking down the stairs, and when they had reached a sufficient distance, slammed the door.

Taking a green-glass bottle from the side-table, I poured myself a drink. The hum of the presses through the walls made my head spin: my room's emptiness seemed endless, and its familiar things appeared foreign to me. There was my father's globe, with a walnut base and brass meridian, made by Jodocus Hondius the Elder in the South Pacific, and the first two volumes of the Blaeu World Atlas published by my late grandfather, Willem Janszoon, which I inherited as an infant. From a tender age I had carefully studied its pages, trying to find my journey through life, because I stupidly believed what my father had told me, that it was the geographical guide to my future. To others it appeared a fragment of the history of the world, for me it embodied the story of my existence – how I, Pieter Blaeu, came into being, and how – more importantly – I became entangled in this difficult maze. I wish I could tell the tale with passion and pride, and linger on personal details to make it more exciting, but as I do not own any of those feelings, you will have to settle for a straightforward historical account.

Born in Alkmaar in 1571, my grandfather Willem was educated as a clerk in the herring trade because his father was a fishmonger. I never met him because he died before I was born, but legend has it that, at twenty-three years old, he left home to become an assistant to the astronomer Tycho Brahe in his misty empire on the island of Hven. Tycho showed Willem how to fix the positions of planets and stars, and how to make maps, timepieces and scientific instruments. When my grandfather returned to Amsterdam two years later, with the ambition of publishing his own cartographic materials, he succeeded – first a globe, then a planetarium and a tellurium. He printed pilot books and sea charts while working closely with explorers who could supply him with information, along with curiosity items from all corners of the globe, if they were lucky enough to survive the tempestuous seas.

In the meantime, he married my grandmother, Maertgen Cor-nelisdochter, and they had six children. The first was my father Joan, born in 1596, who quickly developed an obsession with mountains, volcanoes and the inky deep sea. Without hesitation, after he graduated from the University of Leyden, where he studied Law, Joan worked alongside his father. Together father and son worked on a complete description of the earth, seas and skies, the largest in the world, but by the time my grandfather died in 1638, only two volumes had been published. In that year, my father began to navigate the business on his own, and succeeded Willem as hydrographer to the Vereenigde Oost-Indische Compagnie (VOC), which sent hundreds of ships to Asia, Indonesia and China for assorted plunder. As one of the 'Seventeen Gentlemen', he drafted manuscript charts amidst the aroma of cloves and nutmeg. Shortly thereafter he married my mother, Geertruid Ver-meulen Pieterdochter, the daughter of a pearl trader. They seemed deeply attached but had few things in common. My mother was a fragile flower who loved music and dreams while my father was a stringent gentleman, an influential scholar with no imagination. They, too, had six children. The first was me, born in 1645, who was sent, along with the other children of wealthy merchants, to the Van den Enden School where, under the direction of a former Catholic, polyglot and liberal scholar, I studied Latin, philosophy, medicine, physics, history and politics.

Meanwhile, the operation became the largest and most famed of its kind in Europe, officially serving the King of Sweden. The atlas expanded to a twelve-volume *Grooten atlas oft wereldbeschrijving* containing 600 hand-coloured maps, 3,000 pages of text in a large format with luxury binding and fine engraving, all housed in a custom-designed, carved, wooden display cabinet. Because my father was getting richer by the day, he needed assistance to meet the demand: as the eldest son, I worked at the original foundry, editing novels, plays, poetry, devotional literature and Catholic missals. My life was a sedentary one, confined to a desk, which my father strategically placed near his own so he could oversee my work and ensure that I undertook the path cut by my grandfather through remote islands, rocky coastlines and mysterious landforms. To him, my future looked bright, but he could not see that a shadow had passed across my sun. I was a simulacrum, appearing only in glimpses. Everything, especially my future, seemed insignificant.

Then, two years ago, my mother suffered a horrible, ridiculous death under a full moon, and a great sadness swept over me because she had been my closest friend. Now that she was gone, my life acquired a large empty space, which I moved through slowly and miserably. However, I learnt a simple but important lesson: our existence is but a small crack of light between two eternities of darkness, all things can change in the blink of an eye, *memory slips away, age, time, events pass mostly into oblivion* – no matter how steadfast they seem to be – so we should pursue happiness at all costs. Besides, my mother had always protected me from my father, and now that she was gone, I was forced to face him and an ugly reality: the atlas was not the irrefutable proof or universal truth of my existence. This Blaeu *Bijbel*, as I liked to call it, had been hindering me and holding me back from something more significant or noble; if I did not redirect its purpose it would mask me entirely . . . *regressus in infinitum.*

This revelation occurred slowly over time and had many contributing elements, but one thing in particular brought these thoughts to the forefront of my mind – a missing link. It was nothing less than my chance encounter with Rembrandt, my moment in his workshop and the glimpse of his book. There was no other way to describe it: Fate was telling me that the tablet should be mine. When I mused on what it might actually contain, distant worlds flooded my mind, worlds more exotic than any my father had to offer. I imagined that it was a compendium of artistry with stories, drawings, recipes and a secret coverted between its pages. A personal commission was hidden in its lines – it must be – if only I could obtain it. The question remained, how? As I sat by the window with the snow falling outside, the prospect alone made my head clamour and I badly needed some air. My father would rather be stricken with boils than see his son in society looking and smelling like a vagabond; nevertheless, I would! He held the reins so tightly he would never allow himself to be grimy, hairy, smelly, dungy, warty, even if he had no plans to leave the house. Yet I was not my father: for my own dignity I washed my face and tidied my hair then, in a private act of defiance, neglected my armpits, groin and buttocks. Feeling deliciously perverse, I meandered through streets and alleyways to find a quiet tavern. A dull hubbub floated over me as I kept pace with the city.

It was difficult to find an alehouse that was not full of rowdy creatures, even in the morning, so I gave up trying when I reached one of my favourites on the Rapenburg, 'De Druif', where a boy in ratty clothing sat on the porch, drumming his *rommelpot*. After giving him a stuiver, I went inside. Immediately my knees buckled from the fumes of smoke clogging the damp room. Hardened puffers sucked their clay pipes and scruffy topers clutched their roemers as if they had already reached their nightcap. I headed for the bar, trying to avoid tankards, cats and puddles of melting snow on the floor. The tables were crowded with patrons soaked in beer and brandywine, tottering on their benches. A gnome-faced woman in a black hood greeted me from her stool with a tar-blackened smile.

I ordered a dram of genever and looked among the revellers for my old friends from school. When I did not recognize anyone, I sought the most respectable place to sit at a table near the fire. There a young woman, wearing a lemon-yellow overskirt and white headdress, talked to her neighbour in a coquettish manner. I could not fault her: the man was handsome, with shoulder-length brown hair, a sparse whisker and a tall hat. As soon as I perched on the bench, he raised his pul of ale in a salute, toasting me to good health. I peered at the opaque liquid in my glass and downed it, savouring the taste of the juniper berries; then he gave a hearty laugh and staggered to the bar for two more. Opposite me sat a well-clad man with drooping lids, who, when opening an ornate nutwood tobacco box, revealed its inscription: *Des menschen leeven vervliegt als roock*. Man's life passes even as smoke.

Soon the clinking of glasses and chatter in the room was accompanied by the gentle sound of music. As the stranger wove his way back from the bar with our third round, I swiped aside the flagons of wine and half-eaten bread on the table to clear a place for our glasses. Abruptly, a gruff-bearded lout with a large belly passed by and bumped my arm, causing me to knock over the full glass of a woman sitting near me. A lake of beer spread all over her skirt. The woman, obviously from the local brothel, twisted around and slapped my face with her hand and a miasma of fetid breath. I recoiled, and had I not been astounded and weary I would have hit her back, but my patience was rewarded when she became ill in the corner and had to be trundled from the tavern in a wheelbarrow.

The stranger and I continued our contemplative swilling for many hours, and only stopped when we were seized with the desire to kiss, in alternate turns, the tiny woman with the yellow apron. Meanwhile I thought more about Rembrandt van Rijn. My publishing work was interesting enough to keep me occupied, I supposed, but I had never encountered something that seized me by the neck and shook me around, not in this way – and it belonged to me alone, not to my father or anyone else. What were these distasteful paintings I found so hard to forget? Who really was the man daring enough to paint them? What secrets was he withholding? It seemed imperative that I should seek the answers to these questions before they scattered away with the wind and time. Rembrandt was a man soon to pass out of this world and I wanted him to endure, if only inside my mind. I would make his discovery my primary quest, for I trusted that while everything occurring to a man from his birth to his death is predetermined, we could turn our opportunities into our own fortunes or misfortunes, *and through those fortunes a coward can prove himself.*

As I savoured the harsh bouquet of the genever, I let my gaze wander over the tavern, which by now had turned riotous, and meditated on a way to approach my task. Although an initial failure was inevitable, I would begin my investigation by going to the man himself. Surely, if he had spoken to me once and trusted me with some of his trade secrets, he would do so again. Everything else I sought was near at hand (as most things are): the stories of those who knew him, friends, neighbours, models, sitters, patrons, the characters in his paintings . . . even the dead. By hearing their sides of the story and allowing them to speak, I would draw close to my subject. This was my personal commission, and once I reached it, time would stop. Nothing else would matter. I had earned the right.

If only inside my mind.

Time would stop.

I had earned the right.

I repeated these three phrases in my head until I was no longer merely pickled with gin but half-seas over. The face of the stranger faded, the racket of the tavern drifted away and the light trickled down into darkness. The words divided and multiplied in my brain then carried me from the tavern until I was deaf, blind and boggled, and had fallen fast asleep with my heavy, wet cloak settling around me.

For what seemed like days or months, I dreamt of the book . . .

Then someone nudged me with their foot. Slowly I returned to my senses. The hairs on my body stood up with cold. My clothing had formed icicles, and my back stiffened against the snow. Where was I? Almost underground. The tops of the grey trees were asleep and a hazy star, flickering in the sky, dizzied me. Each tiny sound stood out nervously: the canal water slapping against the bridge, the whining of cats, the drum-roll of the sheriff in a steady banging, the treading boots of the nightwatch.

I heard a woman's voice: 'You've missed the curfew.'

I gazed up at her in astonishment, my breath balled in my throat. The darkness trembled round her except where the blond light of the moon shone on a hole in her stocking, disclosing a tiny bit of her leg and a fresh scratch the same colour as her red skirt billowing in the wind. Spriglets of strawberry-coloured hair poked from the edges of her white scarf, which hugged her plump, cherubic cheeks. She was like a little gnome, pale and frail but utterly clear and calm. My head was reeling; had Elsje Christiaens returned from the dead? Then I recalled the image of this same woman sitting on the ice with her legs outspread, a dumbfounded expression on her face. The person standing above me was the fallen woman. Could it really be? I wished I could see her neck again, to be sure, and because it had reminded me of a swan's.

My lips cracked as they parted. 'Are you the fallen woman?'

She looked at me with her green eyes, and their lids drooped as if on the verge of closing. 'Come, we must go,' she whispered.

Holding out her hand, she pulled me to my feet. Her hot palm invaded my whole body as I scrambled up to meet her. 'You could have helped me the other day,' she said. 'An ordinary man would have . . .'

'What? How?' Everything was topsy-turvy, so I focused on my breeches, soaked through and caked with mud.

'But you're stubborn, I guessed that.' The tone of her voice suggested she might have been smiling.

Still clutching my hand, she pulled me away from the tavern and the piled-up crates along the curve of the wide canal. We moved slowly through alternating patches of light and shadow into the intimacy of the impending morning. The city was asleep apart from the beggars, whose tussle over a blanket or a bed of hay echoed from a distant alleyway. The hazy houses – their colours hardly distinguishable – spread out before my wistful eyes, and the whirling winds howled against them, rattling the shutters. Our boots crackled against the blue moonlit snow, and we walked in harmony, though our movements had no knowledge of one another, and neither did we, nor did we ask.

She ushered me down a side street and into diverse clusters of darkness. A trapdoor had been shut over the sky, leaving no above or below. My eyes saw spots as if I were caught in a mist or swimming in the deep sea. A sense of panic welled up inside me when something scrambled over my foot, squealing all the way. A rat? A rat! I stumbled and nearly fell over, but the woman yanked me towards her, and I felt the touch of her hand though I could not see her.

'Are you afraid?' she asked.

'Of course not.'

'Then why are you trembling?'

Before I could answer, she stopped in her tracks. I pricked up my ears: a sharp echo of footsteps travelled towards us from the far end of the passage. Vague voices rushed in our direction, and though I could not hear what they were saying, it sounded like two men – one whispering, one growling. My blood froze. Were they drunken sailors or sentrymen? I focused my eyes on the woman, blurred and shapeless. Without a word, she clapped her hand over my mouth and yanked me into the nearest entranceway. We fell against the door and clung to each other like barnacles. As the two men marched in our direction the sound of clanging metal grew louder and louder. Helmets and knives, I thought, my heart sinking into my boots.

'Stop breathing so loud,' the woman whispered, clutching my arm and the layer of thick wool between us.

'The noises came from down here, I'm sure of it!' one man grumbled.

'I don't see anyone,' the other man squeaked.

The bakery behind us was shut for the night and completely quiet, but I expected it to light up suddenly and burst into action, exposing us to the watchmen, as my companion muttered, 'Be still.'

Two ominous shapes loomed out of the mist and stopped directly opposite us, their swords gleaming in the dark. As they craned their necks and sniffed around, I prayed they would not smell my liquor miasma, which filled my own nose with disgust. Burying my chin against the woman's soft hair, I drew a long shuddering breath and silently counted the seconds. When I reached thirty, one of the men stepped closer, only a yard away. His face whirled into view, horribly disfigured by disease, and his eyes burned with gloom in the lifeless air. For several minutes, there was no sound save his breathing and the faint ticking of metal at his hip. Then he began to laugh, showing off his rotten teeth. We could not fool him, he was saying, and though I was unable to move a muscle I sweated from every pore.

'See? Nothing,' the other man said.

The first man shrugged, stepped back, and started off in the direction from which they had come. Then he stopped again and spat over his shoulder into the entranceway, right on to my boot. I watched the phlegm seep over my toe, but I dared not move as they carried on, their footfalls sinking into the fog.

My companion giggled and leapt into the alleyway; did she think this was fun? To me it seemed closer to torture, all this suspense, but perhaps I had never loosened my reins enough to learn what fun was, which is why I remained behind with a mounting nausea in my stomach until she extended a gloved hand to coax me out of my hiding place. Soon we began cutting a zig-zag path through the labyrinth of streets, and with my vision no longer mine, I relied on her like a child and in a way that I had not done since I lay in the arms of my mother, silently and without fuss. In fact, this unknown woman reminded me so much of her, and in the wake of our bizarre, frightful episode, I felt an impulse to break the silence between us.

'My mother died two years ago,' I told her. 'But I can recall so little of her now, except that she looked like an angel and smelt like roses.'

'Really? Most women do.'

It seemed a cold reply, considering my heartfelt revelation. 'You mean, die, look like angels or smell like roses?'

'All of them. But I presumed you'd be thinking about paintings.'

How did she know? After searching my stagnant brain, it dawned on me. 'You've heard about the Prince?'

She stopped walking and brushed a stray hair from her face. 'Everyone has. You're as famous as your father now.'

I blushed, not quite believing her, and anyway, the last thing I wanted was to become my father. Still, I could not fault her for being generous, and her words lifted me from my wretched state. I stepped towards her, wobbling on my long heron's legs, and saw that we were standing in front of my house (so she knew where I lived, too?)

'After you've had time to get over the shock, you must tell me what happened. What he said and did, everything. Because I would very much like to help you with your work.'

What work did she mean? Even if she had heard about my visit to Rembrandt, she could not possibly know of my intentions to find out more about him or to commit my thoughts to paper. 'How do you imagine that happening?'

There was a moment's silence in which she lowered her eyes then she pivoted on her heels and scurried away into the night. I did not even get her name; yet later that night, in the green solitude of my room, I found myself creating one for her, a heroine's name that ended in *a*, like Leda, for she reminded me of a swan.

Portrait of Father and Son

June 1653

My Dear Son,

I write to you with a terrible aching for our old affection and a keen desire to speak with you even if there is little to say, because your journey shall always be my journey — and what was the possibility of shipwreck on your passage to London? I suppose I could tell you about my own recent visit to Delft, which met with few immediate results though not without its possibilities, for I brought my *camera obscura*, and was accompanied by Drebbel, that marvellous inventor of microscopes and clavichords amongst other things, truly one of the great thinkers of our time, unequal in rank but not in talent to Sir Francis Bacon. Perhaps I once spoke of our first meeting in England, when he constructed a submarine and submerged it under the Thames to the delight and wonder of the English court, but unfortunately proved futile when tried as a weapon against the French at the siege of La Rochelle. What a curious figure he is!

There were others amongst us, the young scientist Van Leeuwenhoek, conducting all of his observations with single lenses, and the painter Samuel Van Hoogstraten, who, formerly apprenticed to Rembrandt van Rijn, has developed a fascination with perspective illusion. These illustrious men wanted us to introduce the device to a promising young painter who expressed an interest in experiencing this optical phenomenon, previously unknown to him, a Catholic called Johannes Vermeer. His workshop in Mechelen, the inn formerly owned by his family, has a wider frontage than the common Delft house, and therefore let in a sufficient amount of light, though not from the north, for our experiment. So that you may imagine it: Leeuwenhoek sat regally before a table on which was set by Drebbel a golden brown drapery, a sprig of oak with apples and a terrestrial globe by the late Willem Blaeu.

When young Vermeer peered through the lens, his eyes registered nothing initially, but in a matter of some minutes the image came into view, slightly blurred, as if covered with a faint bloom, a kind of smokiness that reminded him of lard. Diffused circles of light, not seen normally by the human eye, settled around it, he said, but figure, contour and movement harmonized in the most natural way. Nothing could have prepared him for the overall effect, that is: it gave him the sensation of being afloat. He asked me how it could be merely a 'topsy-turvy' reflection, a trick of the eye which cannot be trusted, because this was a place where his senses were most alert. I replied that yes, all painting was dead in comparison, for here was life itself or something nobler, if only there were words for it. Afterwards, we noticed that this young man's mouth was atremble from the revelation of an indefinable truth and offered him a cup of wine, but he could hardly partake of one sip without spilling a sizeable portion. Then Van Hoogstraten remarked that the sight of these reflections in the darkness can be very illuminating to the painter's vision, for besides acquiring knowledge of nature one also sees the overall aspect which a truly natural painting should have. I felt it incumbent upon myself to offer that the instrument could be used as a more fundamental aid to painting, if in their discernment they dared to take it to heights which transcend all others.

As you can imagine, I departed from Delft with the curiosity as to whether and in what manner they would further develop the uses of this magical chamber of secrets; yet, I must exercise utmost patience, for all will be revealed in time according to the intent of our Great Lord. So, dear son, this is where my words dissolve: a poem is calling to me forthwith, as is a telegram, which will hopefully carry news of your whereabouts and good Fortune.
I am –
Your loving father,
Sir Constantijn

October 1654

Dear Father,
Thank you kindly for the etching by Rembrandt van Rijn, who, to this day, remains the greatest painter of the Soul. This elderly man, with a tuft of hair on his bald pate, has a head of the most unusual oval shape. Do you think his torso is too large in relation to it? The man's eyes, nearly closed, make me wonder if he is falling asleep or blind. He seems to be waiting patiently for something, or he could simply be weary, but the cross-hatchings on his chin appear to quiver, and the wavy lines on his brow speak of the futility of Life, a Vanity and striving after the Wind! I cannot stop staring at it, perhaps because I see myself in him. Is this what I will be like in old age? A man should not be able to observe his own face: there is nothing more ominous.
Yours very truly,
Christiaan

November 1654

Dear Son,

O Time is the great devourer, and slowly gnaws with its teeth, but remember that he who sows virtue reaps honour. That is why one part of the painter's art most pleases me, that piece which lays its hand to slow the wheel of time, and places the grandfather of my father's sire now in my sight, as if he lived today or yesterday, and allows my children and grandchildren to inherit the countenance that goes with me to death and to decay. Is the painter's skill not more the master than indeed is time? It preserves in its oil all these perishable things, so that as a perfect memory everything long past seems related to the present. There was no greater worker of the aforementioned wonders than Rembrandt, I agree, who chose in his youth not the court and its splendour, neither Italy in its glory, but the vanity of the city, seduced by a flame which eventually consumed him to the disappointment of us all.

I remain, your loving father,
Sir Constantijn

Postscript: Please pardon my haste; these days I do not feel equal to long stretches of writing on account of my sore hands, though they have improved greatly upon application of Bacon's mysterious tincture.

Feb 1656

Dear Father,
I discovered a strange wonder that I should like to make known to you as a trusted companion who is bound up with my gazing,

keeping it a secret from the promiscuous public, however, until the time when my work is published. As you are already aware, I have been studying Saturn's puzzling protrusions, which Galileo called Lobes but, in my opinion, resemble Handles coming out from either side. When I initially observed this mysterious Planet, my eye did not notice its odd shape – or in fact that these Handles seemed to have shrunk into little discs – as much as a bright Star which lined up with it, and imagine my delight after some weeks of observation in realizing that this very Star was moving around Saturn. Yet, my studies suffered from the use of inadequate lenses, so in order to learn more, I constructed a telescope with greater magnitude and resolution to resolve that the Star was actually an orbiting Moon. Further, I discovered that the plane of the Ring tilts 20° to the plane of Saturn's orbit, and the Ring maintains a constant orientation as the planet orbits the Sun. The varying appearance of Saturn to us on the Earth can be explained by the angle changes of the ring during its orbital period, which I have determined as 15 days, 23 hours and 13 minutes.

I intend to publish a book which will discuss my theorems and axioms, but since I am diligent at work on the pendulum clock, which I will soon tell you about at length, I have penned a very brief treatise that formally announces my discovery, and so as not to give away my idea I have disguised it in the form of an anagram: a a a a a a a c c c c c d e e e e e h i i i i i i i l l l l m m n n n n n n n n n o o o o o p p q r r s t t t t t u u u u u. If someone should introduce a similar notion, I will reveal my anagram as, *Annulo cingitur, tenui, plano, nusquam cohaerente, ad ecliapticam inclinato* OR It is surrounded by a thin flat ring, nowhere touching, and inclined to the ecliptic.

Even so, very much hard work remains to be done and one needs not only great perspicacity but also a great degree of Faith, for we shall be less apt to admire what this World calls great when we know that there are a multitude of Planets inhabited and adorn'd as well as our own, with their Dress and Furniture, nay and their inhabitants too. I wish that Mother, whom you tenderly called your Star, were alive on this Earth to partake in the discovery with us, dear Father, for however frequently I imagine her enchanting spirit in the glowing fires of the skies, my yearning for her is a disease which weakens both my Heart and Soul. It seems inopportune to feel this way and indeed to make it known to you at a time when my advancement and success are most imminent, but equally, perhaps these pangs of loss are the natural reaction of a man foreboding one's own glory and fame.

Your devoted son,

Christiaan

March 1656

Dear Son,

Is it not the heart-kernal of Life, these dark sorrows which draw us to eternity? If only you knew that I, too, weep for the loss of the lap where I laid my head, the hand I was given to hold, the arms that once coddled and embraced me. Behind this stern exterior there still courses through my blood a sublime love for your Mother, which remains as active as it was in the beginning, if not stronger after her death. Yet, the grief is no longer master over my life and my intellect as it once was, when I could hardly tear it out of myself in order to achieve what I had set out to do; and there was plenty to be done! Indeed, I was a man of no hope, who believed he was learning how to live whilst he was learning how to die – so that even my sleep was tortured and more closely related to oblivion than anything else. Then alas, after endless stumbling, the ground grew steady under my feet, and I found in my possession a language which could span time and reach for that Eternal Paradise where my Stella resides and to which I am going. You, too, possess that living language, dear Christiaan, which breathes in your theorems and hypotheses, your axioms and equations. Never doubt that you can find your sweet mother in indescribable majesty amongst your treasure-house of nature that honours the infinite wisdom and power of God.

And now that I have confessed all this in a rare moment of weakness, I am driven to share with you a poem I wrote long ago, when you were but a child of eight years, because I would like to prevent your thinking with contempt on me during those years of silence and severity to which I can never return but will always regret for your sake, my young son.

Your loving father,

Sir Constantijn

Enclosure: *To Stella, My Dearest Wife, Now Dead*

With elements disordered, fostering nature

   Orders their sorrow to my suffering.

White day breaks, black night dies, you die with them;

   My Star, my days all perish in your death.

March 1666, Paris

Dear Father,

What a glorious city! King Louis XIV has provided accommodation for me in the spacious quarters of the Royal

Library, and I have been invited to organize the *Academie Royale des Sciences*, an assembly of the 'choicest wits in Christendom' along with G.D. Cassini. There is a meeting every Tuesday at Montmor's house, which I never fail to attend, and where gather twenty or thirty learned men, including two French mathematicians, Monsieur Fermat and Monsieur Pascal, who often call at my quarters to speak of the force of Water rarefied in cannons and of methods of flying, and to examine my telescopes, and how frequently I share with them your thoughts on midges, ants and mice . . .

Amsterdam, 1631

My New Home

This narrow room is my new home with a desk, a box bed for sleep and a row of windows so I can look out from among skulls and manikins. I have already seen a hundred subjects for paintings and have started some in my head. Opposite the canal, a row of narrow houses with assorted gables and tilting facades. Rising behind them, the tall brick Zuiderkerk tower and its wooden spire and golden clock face. On my left, beyond the river Amstel, sails, flags, towers and windmills parting a host of feathery clouds. On my right, the yellow light blazing down to the watery mouth of the sea, filled with small ships rising and falling with the waves. In the distance a forest of masts along the curving bay, where East Indies and Baltic fleets, lying at anchor, send in their wares on barges. Below me, the street seethes with activity. Children throw stones at strangers. A group of skullcap-wearing Jews converse in whispers. A woman with a giant pan flips hotcakes. I imagine my new neighbours, the printers and painters inside their shops, quietly working.

I have moved into a large house by the Sint-Anthoniesluis at the edge of the Jewish district, owned by Hendrick van Uylenburgh, a Polish Mennonite and art dealer. He is a kind and solemn man who, appropriately, resembles a large sausage. I met him three years ago when I came to study with Pieter Lastman, and when I wrote to him of my intentions to move to Amsterdam, he invited me to work with him. He runs a successful business from home, importing cargoes of paintings from Italy and Germany. Inside, there is a showing gallery, a storage place, a press and a large workshop. I have invested 1,000 guilders to work as a teacher and run his workshop. In turn, he will allow me the space, money and time in which to create my paintings – then sell them for me. What a relief! I will not have to deal directly with patrons, who expect me to flatter or court them.

Hendrick assures me that within two years I will be allowed to join the Guild of St Luke. An artists' guild! When I am a member, they will help me to carry on my craft and stop outsiders from taking away my business. They will also look after my family, once I have one. The group includes painters, bookbinders, glaziers, playing-card and compass makers. In Leyden such a guild is unheard of – painting is still considered a lowly trade. That is the reason I came here – for numerous opportunities. A court painter for the Prince of Orange, where would that have led me? I only hope that Hendrick is as trustworthy as he seems. His Mennonite patience, charity and morality are exemplary. Throughout the workday, during his free minutes, he engages in silent prayer. It is strange to think that this arrangement, too, would not have happened in Leyden. The one between him and me, I mean. In my hometown the Reformant preachers stand on their pulpits and rage against the men of his faith. In Amsterdam – though not without its feuds – Gomarists, Arminians, Catholics, Jews and Mennonites seem to live and work together happily. Although I could not call myself any of these, I find goodness in all of them.

An Encounter in a Dingy Alleyway

I do not know her real name, but she calls herself Pussy Willow. I meet her on the Niewendijk, lined with filthy hovels and slop joints, on my way to the market square. She is worn and dirty, with a heavily crayoned face and tousled black hair, though less blemished and shrivelled than the others. I am tempted to follow her into the brothel because she looks delicious. More than six months have passed since my last whore. Then again, I do not want to soil my godly mind. I have not even begun to arrange my new home, much less put a brush to canvas.

PW: *Stopping him in the tiny street, tugs on his coat.* Come, lovey, won't you feel me? There's no one in the city better than me. *Thrusts her bulging bosom against his cheek.*

RVR: *Brushing her away.* No, I must . . .

PW: Are you new here?

RVR: Only arrived yesterday, from Leyden.

PW: *Wriggling her fleshy hips.* You'll need to make friends.

The painter nods at her heaving breasts.

PW: What's your name?

RVR: Oh, well, Jan Lievens.

PW: My name's Pussy Willow. They don't call me that for nothing. *Flutters her eyelashes.* Now, let me see how equipped you are.

RVR: *Throwing back his shoulders, sucking in his stomach.* You won't be disappointed.

PW: *Plunging her hand into his breeches, she feels around and squeals.* That's a big boy! Come inside!

RVR: *Adjusts himself.* Perhaps later . . . (*Aside*) What torture!

PW: Join us tonight at the musico!

The painter gives her arse a tight squeeze then waddles down the street like a duck. As he passes, the other whores, lingering in doorways, snigger at him.

A World of Colours, Smells, Sounds

The white tower of the Oude Kerk, stretching into the marine sky, leads me to the Dam Square, a world of colours, smells and sounds. The salty steaming of the summer air mixes with the stench of fish and pungent aromas of ginger and cumin. The crowd moves slow and fast in all directions. My limbs feel weak as people dance around me, brush past me, bump into me: men and women carrying carrots and artichokes; bargemen counting their money; craftsmen blowing smoke through their noses; old hags looking for handouts. Everyone is shrieking or shouting, trying to make a sale or negotiate a good bargain.

A butcher with beefy arms strings up plump pigeon and woodcock. He handles his purple slabs of beef and ox, then wipes his hands on his apron, streaking it red, and offers me one. I decline. A woman scampers by, pushing a wooden cart. Her red dress, wet with perspiration, clings to her round rump. My eyes follow the movements of her jiggling backside until she is lost among the crowd, when I see another, more beautiful woman in a blue chemise, carrying a wicker basket overflowing with fruit — jostling peaches, cherries, watermelons. Then another woman comes, clutching a pair of oozing white cabbages, and another with a barrel of pickles ... They seem to be everywhere: sinewy, nimble, statuesque, buxom. I see all of them without their dresses or corsets or girdles, with their stockings rolled down below their knees, their feet waving in the air. I think of Pussy Willow with her hand in my breeches. Why didn't I go to her bed? Desire is getting the best of me and I cannot concentrate. Already, for these sinful thoughts, I will have to ask the Lord for forgiveness. May God help me. I should find my way back to her or eat something. Yes, I must eat something ...

I stop at a fish stall, before a mountain of fleshy-coloured seafood. Shiny flounders, dabs, cod and turbot slime over the table. The cured red herrings look as irresistible as cow's tongue. My mouth drools as I reach into my pocket for my purse. My purse. My purse? That accursed woman has stolen my purse. What a stinking Jezebel! There must have been at least 15 stuivers inside, enough for the herrings, a loaf of rye and a glass of Rhenish. I knew I should not trust her. And I did not want her anyway! Pussy Willow must be dealt with immediately, given a good walloping, or I may never get my money back.

My First Experience in the City

The painter rushes at the whore, who dallies in front of the brothel.

RVR: *Shaking his fist.* You wretched creature, where is my purse?

PW: What purse?

RVR: Don't play dumb with me . . . I know you took it!

PW: *Slaps him across the face, her nails scratching.* How dare you!

RVR: *Groaning.* Minx! Give it to me now.

PW: You want it now?

RVR: Yes, you thief.

The painter grabs the whore by the arm and sticks his hand down the front of her dress. His fingers fumble with her corsetry and graze her wrinkled skin. When he does not find the purse, he clutches her skirt and begins to pull it up.

PW: What're you doing? Leave me alone! *Bites his ear.*

RVR: Ouch! Where is it?

PW: I already said, I don't have it.

The painter takes hold of her hair and drags her to the stoop.

PW: *Kicking his shins.* I hate you, I hate you!

RVR: Enough, woman! I'm going to search your room.

PW: Let me go, Madame will be very upset . . .

RVR: What's her name?

PW: *Narrows her eyes.* Tryn the Cupping Woman.

RVR: *Shouting.* Well, she stinks too! And how will you feel when I have you locked up, aye?

The painter opens the door and pushes her inside. They pass from light to darkness, from distinct shapes and certain brightness to a world that is cloudy, boggy and muddy. The brothel is a snake-pit, a poisoned sea infested with hissing women and slithering sailors. They wind and stretch around one another, their long tails and scaly bellies sweeping the ground. The men, weak with hunger, have eyes glaring like candles and sharp, pointed teeth. They emit an infectious smell, fouling everything. The women, flapping their red tongues, call their lovers with a whistling sound, then they swoop down with opened mouths and devour what they see.

AN UNSEEN MAN: *Shouting,* Come on, Wafflewife, lemme stick my arse on your head!

AN UNSEEN WOMAN: Shut up and slip me that old mackerel!

RVR: (*Aside*) Perhaps I was not drawn here simply because of my missing purse.

The room is small and dark. There is a simple wall-bed, a straight-backed chair and a single cupboard covered with flies. The shutters are closed and the air is heavy with piss, penis porridge and other thick body odours. The painter releases the whore then tells her to sit down. When she does, her skirt settles around her like curls of butter. He begins scouring every inch of the area, foraging through her belongings.

PW: *Yelling repeatedly.* I shit on you! I shit on you!

The painter finds in her bed two silver spoons, obviously stolen, and in her cupboard, along with a few items of clothing, four linen napkins, also obviously stolen. He holds them in front of her nose.

RVR: Aha!

PW: Those are mine! And I don't have your lousy money.

RVR: (*Aside*) She is right. My pouch is nowhere to be seen. But I am sure she has it hidden somewhere I have overlooked, like in her knickers. Her knickers? There is only one way to find out . . . This scrubber has stolen what belongs to me, and I will not leave here in the wrong. Her dishonesty must be exposed!

The painter corners the whore and clumsily works his fingers on her buttons, laces and clasps, then dismantles her bonnet, chemise, skirt and petticoat, corset, girdle belt with attached pincushion, knickers, stockings and mules. Five minutes later, his hair is dripping with sweat. A hill of damp cloth lies on the floor — but no pouch.

PW: *In the nude, scowling.* Pay me twenty-five stuivers.

RVR: But you already have fifteen! (*Aside*) She, like the others, is a deceptive serpent, and knows I am within the sticky reach of her tongue. Experience has taught her how to read a man's face for yearning, how to detect a weakness in his flickering pupils. She is tall, broad-hipped and older than I originally thought — at least fifteen years older than me. Her stomach is distended and her flabby breasts have round, dark nipples. Purple flog-marks cover her legs and backside, which sags to the back of her knees. She is repulsive and beastly but strangely arousing. I have an overwhelming desire to possess her, but only for a brief while. Afterwards, I will recite my prayers and feel no remorse.

PW: Don't give me trouble, Jan. *Breaks into a guffaw, snorting through her nose.*

RVR: *Laughs, reminded that he lied about his name.* You're the dangerous one.

The painter steps towards her, a hazy figure in the grey light. The whore pounces on him like a wild cat. They tumble backwards on to the bed. She removes his breeches in earnest then scrambles on top of him. He enters her with a gurgle. She plants her dirty feet on the soft bedding and hops up and down, up and down, making the walls of the wooden coffin creak. The copper warming-pan rattles to the floor with a clang.

RVR: (*Aside*) My first experience in the city!

INTERLUDE

God is watching me in the half-light. He watches my eyes meditate on the wall, my hand trace the contours of my face. How vile I am! The cratered skin, the wispy moustache, the gobs of spit at the corners of my mouth. I no longer fear the glass or what it will tell me. I do not distort my visage or escape from myself. My purpose has changed. I want to discover the truth of who I am, to find my reflection faithful and still. I am so happy I feel drunk, in a city with many mirrors of water.

When a Painter Treats His Pigments as Living

My pupil, Isaak Jouderville, the innkeeper's orphan, has followed me here to continue his lessons. Like me, to make his name in the world. But I suspect he will not stay very long. He is a slow learner. The contours of his figures are flat and out of proportion, and he does not drape their clothing convincingly. He applies his highlights too randomly, which creates the effect of concentrated brightness all over his pictures. He must do as I do — build up the paint so it reflects natural light and casts shadows as would real objects. Unity in this effect should be the guiding principle of any painter's work. Pigments can be full of life and expression if handled properly. That is why he must value the paint's capacity to be worked and moulded. He must continually learn about his substances and experiment with them, an early lesson Lievens taught me. (Oh, I miss our tiny studio and the way we worked together, playing off each other's strengths, avoiding each other's weaknesses!)

The work of the hand must be evident in what is seen. I think of this often — that a hand is an instrument as good as a talon, a claw or a horn, or any other weapon or tool, because it contains them all. Aristotle says that man is the most intelligent animal, and his hand is the counterpart of his reason. When a painter treats his pigments as living, they can become anything. Titian is the master at this: he begins with a translucent brown base then builds up his textures slowly, using almost-dry, thin washes of glaze. He scrubs and smooths and blurs his pigments to add harmony. His lights move into his shadows, as if caressed and stroked. I must remember to tell Isaak.

PURCHASES

Item, pair of French stockings ... 14 g.

Item, cuirass ... 41 g.

Item, halberd ... 35 g. 4 st.

Item, velvet ... 9 g. 2 st.

Item, prints by Adam Elsheimer ... 50 g or more.

The Drawing Lesson

This morning I give my pupils a lesson in drawing from life. The studio is large but stifling in the heat of midsummer. When I enter, the ten boys immediately take their places, squatting in the middle of the room. Our model, a tall middle-aged man like a sculpture of a Greek god (one of Hendrick's), stands in the corner on a low plinth. I set up mirrors to expand the space so they have various ways of looking at the subject, and tell them we will make three sketches — from life, from reflection and from memory. The boys seem nervous, even afraid of me, and I don't know why. Before they begin, I offer them a few basic tips to prepare them for the task.

— Protagoras says that 'man is the measure of all things'. To draw a man, you must know his anatomy. Do not neglect the wonderful workmanship and divine symmetry you will find there. I have several scientific volumes that you are welcome to use, but I encourage you to look at Vesalius, de Ketham, van der Spieghel and Paré.

— Study the body and all its proportions, scrutinize the shapes, layout, powers and functions of each of its parts. Understand the workings of the muscles on the arms, the rotation of the hips, the bones at the knee, the grip of the hands. Know these concepts by memory. When you begin drawing, examine your figure and see its points of action. Feel the energy of the body and capture its sensitivity. The exterior of a person should manifest his inner character.

— Work for order and balance. Your model always changes, so do not lose focus or drift. Your picture must not follow him, it should stay in one chosen moment. Choose the most important element of your subject and eliminate the rest.

— Show the activity of the mind in the face. The eyelids and the lips

should correspond the same feelings, whether anger, surprise or disgust. An eye is an expression; a nose is a direction. A neck expresses character and imagination.

— And, most importantly, do not sketch the person, but your own feelings when observing him. The deeper you go below the surface, the better you will see. Know thyself!

With squinting eyes, backs bent over their tablets, they start to work. The younger boys sketch directly in their tablets, using silverpoint on vellum, because it leaves a fine, controlled line and is easier for learning. The more experienced ones, along with myself, use a grainy white paper already tinged with a brown hue and a pen or chalk. I perch on a stool and work alongside them, for my own practice and for their benefit. I will refer to my drawings later when they get in a muddle.

The naked man stands in a traditional contrapasto pose: one leg poised in front of the other, his head facing towards me but tucked into his chest. I make quick strokes with a black chalk, forming his outline, paying heed to the proportions of his shoulders, his torso and the muscles in his right arm, flexed and tucked behind him. The muscles are relaxed in his left arm, which hangs at his side, forming a line to his outstretched foot. I draw the thick chords in his thighs, the left one flexed and holding all his weight, the other loose and extended.

Once I have the form of a hero, I search his face for what will express his mind. I think about Heracles, the supreme rescuer and harrower of Hell, of his mighty strength, which carried him through the Nemean lion, the Hydra of Lerna, the boar of Erymanthus, the Cretan bull, the girdle of Hippolyte, not to mention the triple-bodied monster Geryon. His downward gaze warns me to keep away. In his eyes is a look of madness, belonging to a man who has wrestled with Death ... I concentrate on one eye, and make all lines lead there, following my sense of it. I touch quickly and lightly to form the other eye, then his nose and lips. My chalk presses firmly against the paper when making the wrinkles across his forehead. These strong lines express his anguished thoughts. I run a ripple around his chin, pinched in turmoil. Then, in white, I add his tangle of hair and neglected beard.

Turning away, I observe his reflection in the mirror. From this angle, I repeat the same process in reverse on another piece of paper. When that is complete, I approach the whole thing from my head. In the end, my three sketches are similar but not entirely the same, because the one done by memory expresses more emotion in the lines.

By that time, our model blinks with fatigue, and a drop of sweat runs down his cheeks. It is time to examine what my students have done, so I circle the room, peering over the boys' shoulders. They have a lot to learn. Most of them have added too many details, and some do not comprehend proportions. I point out their mistakes, one by one.

— You lack continuity. A line should hook all the vital parts together. If you examine your work through half-closed eyes, you will be able to detect the distractions.

— Remember the face has three sections: the hair and forehead, the nose, the chin and mouth. The distance between the outer edges of the eyes to the ears, and the midpoint of the nose to below the chin, are both equal to half the face. The space from the mouth to below the chin is a quarter part. The slit of the mouth to the base of the nose is one-seventh. Don't just stare at me, write this down!

— Your shadows are misplaced. They should be darker close to the object and gradually fade into the light as if they have no end. Focus on the light and you will see the shadows.

— Yours isn't a strongman, it's a fat cow! The muscles should be pressed together so that no air can come between them.

— Develop your visual memory by learning to close your eyes.

— The penis arises at the middle of the man, and from there the distance to the knee is a quarter part of the man ... By the way, his penis is far too small. This is Heracles!

— Your man appears wooden. His legs look like gherkins! If you cannot draw a man standing, how will you be able to draw him walking, running, playing, dancing, sowing, hammering, fighting, fishing, climbing a slope, throwing a spear or firing an arrow?

And to Isaak (who, I have to admit, was the best of them):

— An outline should define the places where the body is soft and where it is hard. You should not emphasize all of the body's muscles; one part of its muscles must relax while the opposite ones tighten. Seldom does a man, unless he is very old, rest his weight on one leg. Keep the rhythm in your forms.

I end the lesson by telling them never to throw their sketches away.

— Take them outside and study their faults in another light. Judge yourselves!

Then I set them to grinding the colours in the mill and mauling them on the stone. Tomorrow the pigments will be ready, mixed with oil and stored in pig bladders, and we will begin painting.

Spiders and Flies

Now that Pussy Willow has come to recognize me, our encounters bring chaos to everything else. In my workshop I see definite shapes and feel confident about how to conquer them. I am like my black spider that connects his tiny strands to weave a picture in the corner. In her room, the shapes are disguised and retreat from my gaze. I become like her flies, making mad sketches on the walls. It is an uncommon feeling as if I am diseased. Though

I can put off the desire, our afternoons continue to pervade my mind: the drizzle of rain on the window, her stockings balled up on the floor, our silk and wool rubbing together, my grip on her neck, her chubby hand on my thigh, a string of saliva dangling from her lips. Perhaps I am her chosen one. The proof is in the spicy odour of my clothing, the stale taste of sex in my mouth. These reminders unravel me from my morning work — the time she ate an entire apple while we were making love! — but I must push them away, lest they lead me from the narrow road — it helps to write them down.

Diana and Her Nymph

Lately my pictures are heavy with mythological subjects because I have been re-reading Livy, Euripides and Sophocles. (I first encountered them in Latin school, where I spent too much time daydreaming.) These stories have a long history in art, and I feel impelled to respond to them. My collection will one day sit alongside the great masters, whose works I own and use for study purposes. I have been accumulating prints from shops and auctions, storing them in wrappers and albums. Some of these I will eventually trade; others I will keep for my ever-growing survey. My very favourite etchings, those by Dürer, Lucas van Leyden, Sebald-Beham and Tempesta, hang on the wall above my desk. I am consulting Carracci's Susanna because I want to imitate his poses for my next pair of etchings — Diana and her nymph Callisto.

This is Ovid's story, in brief: Jupiter seduces Callisto, who is expected to be as chaste as the goddess Diana herself. When Diana discovers that Callisto is pregnant, she angrily turns her into a bear and sets the dogs on her. Jupiter intervenes and rescues her. Later in the legend, Diana transforms the hunter Actaeon into a stag when he accidentally encounters her and her nymphs while they are bathing. His own hounds tear him to pieces, so he is prevented from telling his friends that the goddess has shown herself to him naked.

Eventually I would like to merge these two separate events into one piece, but for now I will focus on the moment when Diana is discovered near the stream. I am going to ask that damned hussy if she will play my Diana. Is that a good idea? No. But I won't be going back to the brothel, she will come to my studio. Besides, the models that Hendrick has supplied are not raw enough. What I mean is: I prefer a washerwoman or a peat-treader or a whore to play one of my goddesses, rather than any fine lady who resembles a Greek Venus. I hope we can begin soon, for gloom envelops me when I am not making art. Nothing else holds me or makes me feel enduring.

Sweet Lady of My Desires

The city glares white and glitters in the heat. The warmth of the air is sweet and painful, filled with the sound of bells. Strong shadows fall from houses and trees as the painter walks east towards the docklands. He passes a heap of mangy cats fighting over scraps of rubbish. At the brothel, he is greeted by a shrivelled hag of nearly fifty, a German woman with matted blonde hair, who tells him he can find Pussy Willow in her room.

GERMAN WOMAN: Sure you don't want me?

RVR: *Eyes wander over her.* Yes, I'm sure.

The painter ducks inside the brothel. As he walks along the dark corridor the walls shake with activity — men grunting and groaning, women cackling and screaming. A dishevelled whore pokes her head out of a door, waving a fan at her neck, and calls him a bishop-beater. After scrambling up the stairs, clutching his case, he stops outside the door to catch his breath.

RVR: *Raising a fist, bang, bang, bang.* Dearie!

PW: *Half-asleep or half-devoured.* Who is it?

RVR: An old friend. Open the door.

PW: I'm busy. Come back later.

RVR: Are you alone?

There is a clatter of wooden clogs on the floor. When the door opens, a line of flies escapes the crack and swarms by the painter's head. The odour of sex assaults him before he sees the whore, peering round with an angry fat face and a flap of pap.

PW: What do you want?

RVR: *Straining to see inside.* Is someone there?

PW: Mind your fat nose.

RVR: I thought I heard voices.

PW: *Pulls back the door and reveals herself, naked apart from her mules.* I talk in my sleep.

RVR: May I come in? (*Aside*) Her navel is even hairier than usual, not to mention her . . .

PW: *Snorting.* I'm tired.

RVR: Ah, you have been busy then!

PW: You're jealous!

RVR: Don't be ridiculous.

PW: *Heaves a hand on his collar and yanks him close.* I work late at night.

RVR: I want you to pose for me, for a picture.

PW: Me? Don't you know any beautiful ladies?

RVR: I want you. Be a sweetheart and sit for a while.

PW: *Frowns.* Not today.

RVR: I'll pay you.

PW: Really? How much?

RVR: Ten stuivers.

The painter pushes past the whore and slams the door behind them. She draws his thumb to her mouth and sucks it for a minute until he pulls away.

PW: Don't you want me?

RVR: *Perspiring.* I'd like you to do this first.

PW: I know you want me . . .

RVR: *Takes her straggling hair in his hands, and begins to bundle the locks into a ball.* Do you have pins? I want you to wear it on top.

PW: I haven't said yes. *Sighs.* They're in my box.

With his hands still tangled in her hair and his calf muscles straining, the painter walks her towards the table. Her sagging breasts smother him as she reaches for the pins in her box. She hands him the pins one by one, and he presses them into her hair until it forms a bun at the back.

RVR: There! (*Aside*) Ah, look at her: the curve of her cheek, the angular bones under her eyes, the blush of her nose, the tiny double-chin! With her hair off her shoulders, I can see her delicate collarbone and the down on her neck.

The painter opens the grimy shutters, letting in a view of the blue sky and the smell of seawater. Heavy sounds fill the room: honking ships, ringing bells, barking dogs, hurdy-gurdy tunes. From his case he extracts an embroidered robe and drapes it over the back of the chair so it resembles a mound, then he shows the whore how to pose. She props herself sideways on the seat with the sheet pulled over her thigh to conceal her groin. He positions her left arm on the robe, and brings her right arm towards it, so her arms form a circle.

RVR: Relax.

PW: How can I? It's too uncomfortable.

RVR: You may move a little, but be natural.

The painter crouches on the floor with the tablet propped on his knee. As his black chalk hovers over the paper, trickles of sweat run down the sides of his face.

RVR: (*Aside*) The lady of my thoughts, no, the lady of my desires. I search for the beauty in her, what I want to capture in a rare moment when I forget the kind of girl she is, when she could almost be a housewife. My own wife.

PW: *Fidgets with the drapery.* Make me look beautiful.

According to Pliny

Pliny tells the story of a young woman from Corinth who says goodbye to her lover before he sets out on a long journey. While embracing him that evening she notices his shadow on the wall, cast by the light of a candle. Without further ado, she reaches out for a piece of charcoal from the fire and fills in his form on the wall. Pliny suggests that this maid is one of the first known artists. If so, then my craft has its origin in love and passion.

My Etching Process

1 *To prepare the varnish, take Virgins' wax, Mastick and Spaltum and beat them into a mortar then melt them together. Add water to form the mixture into a cocoa-coloured ball. A soft resin allows you to draw freely.*
2 *Take an ordinary piece of copper and hammer it flat until very thin. Only when the plates are fresh can they hold all the ink needed for a strong, balanced print. Clean and polish the metal.*
3 *With the varnish wrapped in fine linen, heat it over a chafing dish where there is a moderate fire, so it will dissolve when passing through the cloth and fall easily on to the plate. The copper must be covered in a thin and*

even wash; smooth it on using a feather. Next, apply a second layer of ground, a mixture of lead white and egg whites.

4 *After turning the buttoned side of your sleeves round, set to cutting the grooves with needles of broad and sharp edges. The various sizes create diverse sorts of lines — wide, thin, straight, crooked. For figures use a duller point; for shadows use cross-hatchings. Details in the foreground, do not work up. By merely implying a body, it will protrude from the background, which should be drawn in a much livelier manner, using abstract scrawls or violent gestures.*

5 *Prepared a day ahead, the acid is a weak mixture of vinegar, saltpetre, sea salt and verdigris, which will act slowly when it contacts the metal. Pour the liquid in a steady stream while turning the plate sufficiently eight or more times, removing the varnish between the tiny hatchings. When some of it is trapped, use a soft-grained wood to rub it away. This is the tricky part, because sometimes dust collects in the grooves.*

6 *Examine what has been done, and fix the spots that require the burin or that need to be etched further by the acid. This may require several rounds before it is ready to print.*

7 *Apply a thin film of ink on the copper's surface before laying over the sheet, dipped in water to take up the tone. The texture of the paper should be of quality: sheets from the Orient are smoother and catch less ink. Warm the copper and apply the ink with a dauber, gradually working down into the grooves and pits. A final surface cleaning with a cloth must be done gently, so the ink stays in the lines.*

8 *Push the plate through the press by cranking the wheel. Once you peel the paper off the metal, hang it to dry. The initial impression you should keep for yourself and for posterity, so others will be able to imagine your process. There are times when you will change your mind while working: leave even these discarded thoughts in plain view.*

Nicolaes Ruts, the Polecat

Early days here and many new commissions. Hendrick has referred me to a man he knew long ago from the Mennonite community, who approached him about having his painting done. He is Nicolaes Ruts, a Flemish exile and fur trader, who needs me to promote his image. When I am through with Ruts, he will have the magnificence of an aristocrat and the humility of a carpenter! And I will charge him one hundred guilders.

The moment he enters my studio he fills it up with shoulders and head-to-toe sable fur. Its odour is that of a cat's, only more pungent, like a pickled seal. Probably because it has endured a six-week journey through the rough waters of the Arctic. Some poor Russian traded that for whale fins and horsecloths? He is an old man from Cologne who reminds me of a polecat, with a soft grey beard and pristine moustache, dark beady eyes, pale skin. When he thrusts out his hand to give mine a hearty shake, I realize what most interests me about him. Somehow I must use this firm feature in the portrait. After a disdainful glance over my room, he steps up to the mirror and begins preening himself — though he already looks impeccable — adjusting his hat, combing his whiskers. I watch him out of the corner of my eye as I finish mixing my pigments.

NR: You're using the panel I've chosen?

RVR: Of course. (*Aside*) For the support, he wanted me to use an elegant mahogany, which I ordered from the joiner and has milled edges because it used to be a box containing sugarloaves from Middle America. I prefer tropical woods anyway — when the glue reacts with the common oak it turns yellow in colour.

NR: *Pulls in a sudden breath.* Where would you like me to sit?

The polecat thrusts out his tail and lowers himself on to the leather chair. He lifts the edges of his enormous coat, heaving them over the sides as if a giant skirt.

RVR: Stand behind it, with your right hand rested on the back.

NR: *Coughs and gets up.* Show me exactly what you mean.

RVR: Like this, see?

The painter approaches the chair to demonstrate the pose. When the polecat takes the same position, he stands like a rigid soldier.

RVR: Hmm . . . Turn yourself slightly towards the door, yes, that's it . . . and cock your head to one side . . . no, *against* the direction of your body . . . Hold it. Perfect.

The polecat's beard nuzzles his white collar and his gaze falls beyond the painter. With his right side to the windows, the high afternoon sun catches his face.

RVR: (*Aside*) What should he do with his other hand, awkwardly bent at his side?

The painter scrambles to his desk for a tiny piece of white paper, his shopping list from yesterday, and pushes it under the polecat's left thumb.

NR: *Nose twitching.* So, how long have you been painting?

RVR: *Sketching the composition on the panel with his brush.* Ten years or so. (*Aside*) Would someone ask a butcher how long he has been flaying meat, or a tailor how long he has been sewing buttons?

NR: I'm a partner in one of the guilds. We've been exporting from

Arkhangel'sk for nearly thirty years. It's not only sable, you know, our agents try to buy up all the Russians' winter stock. Marten, ermine, wildcat, mink, wolf, Arctic fox, squirrel . . .

RVR: What about polecat?

NR: Oh yes, polecat too. *Shoulders slump slightly.* I've known Hendrick for a long time, since my family moved from Cologne. I was raised as a Mennonite, you see, before I turned to the Reformed Church.

RVR: (*Aside*) Why won't he shut up?

NR: He tells me you're the best young portrait painter in Amsterdam.

RVR: *Continues to lay the paint on the panel.* I make the most of my trade.

NR: Why haven't I heard of you before?

RVR: Perhaps you haven't travelled in the right circles.

NR: *Tiny pupils darting.* That's not it. You certainly haven't painted anyone *I* know.

RVR: I've only recently arrived here. You can see my portraits of Maurits Huygens, Jacques de Gheyn III and Amalia van Solms in The Hague.

NR: Ah, you've been commissioned by the difficult Princess of Orange!

RVR: She had particular tastes, but at least she was a quiet sitter.

NR: I've come to you because Hendrick assured me you could produce something, well, bolder.

RVR: (*Soliloquy*) What an insult! He probably means something in the Hals or Van Dyck style, with a broader range of expression. Of course I could do that – better than all of them. Yet is this really what he wants? For he, like the others, wants the portrait to conform to his own idea of himself, which is dignified and noble, without the pockmarks, warts, moles, bulges under the eyes, unusual longness or shortness of neck, big ears or yellow teeth ... And what if I refuse to do so? What if I catch him at his game, when he is not accepting himself? That is the subject in truth, which is why, when I begin painting, I feel as if I am attacking him in his own house. I am so much better at painting myself or, dare I say it, attacking myself. If I am to paint the intention of his soul, I must confront him, and in doing so, find the truth of who he is, which is someone other than his idealized self. For he could easily be a proud aristocrat whose ostentatious hat hides his shifty eyes and doubting brow. Someone who swindles in the morning, boozes at midday, visits hussies in the evening and goes home to his family with a fake smile. Perhaps he confronts his hypocrisy only briefly, while he genu‑ flects in church on Sundays, the one night a week he loses sleep from a guilty conscience. And this is the image we both fear, because if I am to fulfil my duties he must look as admirable as a hero. There is no way to return from it: my portrait of him will participate in eternity.

The painter continues smoothing the ochre down the length of his fur coat, and then, using the sharpened end of his brush, gouges the wet paint to make the individual hairs stand up. The fur trader's thumb trembles, and beneath it, the ink on the paper begins to run.

RVR: Would you care for some ale? (*Aside*) The light is changing anyway.

'Amoris Causa, Lucri Causa, Gloriae Causa'

Later that morning, I awoke with a start and a horrible headache. The memory of the previous night filled me with uncertainty, for a woman of implacable clear-sightedness had reached into my inner skin where even I was afraid to go. So why did I release her again? Perhaps the beauty of possibility was too impossible, or perhaps I had conjured up the whole espisode. Yes, surely, I thought, running downstairs and padding across the cold marble floor in my bare feet. When I opened the front door, a freezing wind hit my face and ruffled my nightgown. The ground was quilted with snow, though it had ceased falling, and dark purple clouds floated over the red-tile roofs. Although my fallen woman was no longer there, her tiny footprints remained on the pathway: two in perfect form, two others dragging off, which reminded me that she had not said goodbye, as if to deny a separation. I thought about following them, but it was her duty to catch me again – my secret sylph, my spirit of the air – and there was no sense in worrying about the future if I could neither foresee it nor determine what it would bring. She would only distract me from my journey, and I was anxious to commence my investigation of Rembrandt van Rijn, no later than today. My father had left the house early (who could ignore the click of his heels even in sleep?), and would not return to the foundry until the afternoon, which provided me with plenty of time to do my business without him ever suspecting my absence.

After boiling a pan of water, I washed and shaved then put on a fresh pair of clothes and combed my hair with excruciating care. Where to begin? I thought about returning to speak with Rembrandt or Titus, so I could ask them all the questions I had framed in my head these past few weeks — a tactic which would definitely bring me closer to my subject. On the other hand, such a bold move might close the door on any sort of intellectual or emotional discovery, for if I revealed too much interest in Rembrandt he would probably retreat into his shell, and my project would be foiled prematurely. Instead, I decided to head off to the home of Samuel Van Hoogstraten, the town gossip and Rembrandt's former student, who not only had a plethora of information about his master but a notoriously loose tongue. His stories had been floating around the district for years, stories to regard with suspicion because he was known to drink, and secondly, because he had betrayed Rembrandt by abandoning his manner and embracing the smooth, idealistic style so abhorred by him, not to mention the unforgivable sin: he had criticized Rembrandt for his excessive naturalism. But for six or seven years they were as close as two swallows in a nest; wasn't that a reason for letting him speak? I left the house and headed for the Lauriergracht, where Van Hoogstraten had taken up residence since leaving Vienna and his post as court painter specializing in optical deceits. He currently made peepshow boxes constructed of wood, with one missing side that allowed light to enter as if through a shuttered window and two small holes for viewing the painted panels of scenes inside. I had never seen one of these peepshows personally, and hoped he would have at least one to show me.

The city was peculiarly noisy and bright, so different from the previous night when it was veiled in a dark silence, and the warm timbre of the woman's voice haunted me. Why did she say I was different from ordinary men? She was not very ordinary herself, sneaking around the city's underworld of thieves, approaching a stranger after the curfew. What an embarrassing contradiction! Yet it gave me tremendous consolation that here was a woman accepting me, even welcoming me, in my normal pathetic state; at last I did not have to put on any airs. Without further thought, my soul had rushed to her in such a completely ridiculous way, despite the foreknowledge that if I allowed a woman – any woman – into my life she would destroy my peace of mind, which I had carefully preserved for a long time. Now that she was gone, I wished her to return immediately. Yes, were those not her eyes still gazing into mine as I walked under the arches of the town hall, following me through the market, where the butchers weighed their wares with bloodstained hands? As I turned on to the draughty little street, my heart beat anxiously with the thought of seeing her again. I paused, standing hopelessly in front of the grey house with its ornamental gable, staring at the wintry garden where a few blades of grass peeped sad and green through the snow. I walked up the drab stairs and read the engraved nameplate: Samuel Van Hoogstraten. Taking a deep breath, I knocked.

After the maidservant let me in, I waited in the entrance hall and listened to the echo of approaching footsteps with the sensation of all my obstacles dissolving. I vowed to get what I came for, even if I had to fight tooth and claw; but when Van Hoogstraten entered the room and leant in closely as if he were sniffing me, my whole body sank under his weight. He was a well-built man with a Herculean torso, padded limbs and a rugged face framed by long, greasy blond hair that was tucked behind his ears to reveal his giant drooping lobes. From the look of him he should have been unloading cargo on the wharf or sailing sheep dung to the tobacco growers (not that he was ugly, mind you, he had probably been handsome in his younger days, but the years had weathered him). His outstretched hand was coarse and muscular like the rest of his features, and nearly crushed my bones when I shook it and introduced myself in a bumbling manner. When I told him the reason for my visit, disguising my true intentions, of course, he seemed flattered by my interest in his peepshows and the origins of his work.

When Van Hoogstraten spoke, his accent was flat but his swollen lips made the most extravagant movements. 'I would be delighted to show my art to anyone in the Blaeu family. I've met your father a couple of times, a splendid man. Come into the parlour, I know it is still early, but do you care for a drink?'

I suppressed a chuckle as he motioned me into a room that was furnished in a simple and elegant period style, filled with a stupefying oil and glue cocktail creeping in from the back of the house. The floorboards were shining so brightly they mirrored every object nearby: six upholstered chairs decorated with cultivated flowers, an ebony pillow chest with four doors, glass bookshelves composed of numerous small panes framed in lead, a large writing table near the window. When Van Hoogstraten asked the maid to bring us a pitcher of ale, I noticed, hanging on the wall, a framed pen and ink drawing of Christ in the House of Martha and Mary. Approaching it, I thought it might be a Rembrandt print, because the style was in a brown wash: a contemplative Mary listens to

Christ in a softly lit interior room as her sister Martha labours after him.

He peered over my shoulder. 'This is an early picture I made shortly after leaving Rembrandt's workshop. It was hard to break away from him, I can tell you.'

I turned round; that was easy enough. I did not even have to raise the topic myself. 'So when were you his student?' I asked, feigning ignorance.

'Between '40 and '47, something like that, but we'll save it for a rainy day.'

'Well, it's a snowy day. Please go on, I'm interested in hearing more.'

His nostrils dilated as I waited for him to call my bluff. 'Here, take a seat.'

I sat down on the upholstered chair though he remained standing, pacing the room in his pointy black shoes. He seemed troubled, perhaps by something that had passed between himself and his master: I would have to proceed carefully.

He stopped, fingering his collar. 'Why are you so interested in him?'

'That's a good question.' I paused, formulating my thoughts. 'I met him recently, and I suppose he stirred me in a way. He seemed sad.'

Tugging on his earlobes, Van Hoogstraten sputtered, 'Then you misread him. Don't mistake his anger for sadness, though he always did have the habit of talking about death when he was talking about life, we used to laugh about it.'

I was taken aback by his comment, and was glad when the servant came back with a pitcher of ale and two puls. Van

Hoogstraten plopped himself in the nearest chair, leaning one elbow against the table so his hand was free to accept the first glass. His potbelly strained the clasps on his white shirt, and his legs were spread in the laziest position, showing off the crotch of his tight breeches and his bulging member. The ginger hairs on his strong calves poked through the netting of his pink hose. In fact, everything about him suggested shamelessness or excessive virility. When he curled his hand around the pul and took a long swig, I silently cheered (the rumours of his drunkenness were probably true, and it worked in my favour to loosen his already loose lips).

'Rembrandt taught us a certain style, *his* style of course, then expected us to cleave to it as if the entire globe should be made up of little Van Rijns. Heaven forbid one of his students should use his own imagination or intuition! You wouldn't believe what a demanding teacher he was — I'll show you some of my latest works after we have a drink — and maybe he's softened in his old age, but he's still a disgrace to our profession.'

I was baffled; this man did not possess even a lingering sense of loyalty to his master, and yet he owed his success to him. 'Don't you see him any more?'

'No,' he said hesitantly, then lowered his voice. 'I suppose it doesn't hurt to tell you this, most people know anyway, we parted on bad terms. But that was his fault. He drove me to tears and fevers with his insults, I even went without food and drink for days, trying to correct the errors he marked in my work, to please him.'

'Really?'

'Stubborn as an ox, that man, and not a kind word out of his mouth. One time, another apprentice, a friend of mine, kept asking him questions, but instead of giving him the answers, Rembrandt said' – Van Hoogstraten's voice slipped down to a nasty rasp – '"If you use properly the knowledge that you've already got, you'll find out more rapidly what you don't know." What gall! He also made extensive notes and erasures on our drawings or reworked them . . . Here, let me show you.'

Van Hoogstraten hefted himself from his chair and went to his desk, then scrambled around in a drawer as I silently rejoiced over my foaming beer.

'This is it,' he said eventually, holding up a piece of paper. He staggered back, the tassels on his shirt swinging wildly against his chin, and handed me the drawing. It showed the Holy Family at the foot of a large tree in a landscape, with a tower on a hill in the distance. Mary held the child on her lap and fed him with a spoon while Joseph, seated before a pot on a small fire, proffered a bowl of the food he had prepared. Beside him were a hat, a basket, a saw and a grazing ass.

'Turn it over,' Van Hoogstraten told me.

I did, and encountered Rembrandt's bubbly handwriting on the reverse:

It would be better if the ass was placed further back for a change and that a greater accent came on the heads; also that there was more vegetation by the tree. Joseph is straining too hard and too impetuously. Mary must hold the child more loosely, for a tender babe cannot endure to be clasped so firmly.

I re-examined the picture, which showed promise, but was poorly drawn. The foliage was very sketchy, and because he did not use enough shadow or outline, the Holy Family dissolved into the background. Sure enough, the mother appeared to be suffocating her child.

'Not bad advice,' I said hesitantly. 'Is it?' I did not want to offend him or appear overly confident.

Van Hoogstraten belched. 'Perhaps that wasn't the best example.'

'Where did you work, at the house he lives in now? It's terribly small . . .'

'No, he had an enormous house near the Van Uylenburghs then, but it wasn't large enough for all his apprentices and students, not with all the paintings he was turning out. Eventually we got shuffled over to the Bloemgracht.'

'That's where I live! What number?'

'You know the warehouse set back from the road?'

'It's in my neighbourhood.' My head began buzzing with ideas. Would I be able to see it? Who owned it now? Was it available for purchase? Probably not, or my greedy father would have bought it already.

'There was one large room where Rembrandt set up a space for each of us, separated by a canvas, so we could paint from life without bothering each other or him, of course. Aye, that reminds me of something. One time there was a pupil closeted in one of the private cubicles, working with a female nude model, and because it was summertime, and very hot, my friend decided to remove his clothes too. "Here we are," he said to his model, "naked like Adam and Eve in the garden." We all heard him and laughed, but so did Rembrandt, who then spied on them through a chink in the wall. He got very flustered and angry, and banged on the door with a stick, shouting, "But because you are aware that you are naked, you must come out of the Garden of Eden!" He then drove the two of them from the workshop, chasing them with his cane while they were hastily trying to get dressed, and would you believe it, kicked them right out into the street!'

Van Hoogstraten laughed from the depths of his belly and took another swig of beer. I laughed too, not realizing that Rembrandt had such a sense of humour, and it made me jealous, because I had not been part of the joke. Why had he been so reserved and serious with me?

'Tell me about his teaching,' I said. 'What did you learn there?'

'It was very interesting at times, I have to admit. We used the attic as a theatre and performed plays. What is good for the poet is good for the artist, he would often say, and encouraged us to act as a way of perfecting the proper movements and gestures of the figure.'

I could not resist imagining myself in one of Rembrandt's plays. What role would he have assigned me, that of Samson or another biblical hero, like Paul or David? 'What sort of plays?'

'Oh, meditations on particular stories, usually biblical or historical. We would do one performance viewed from alternate positions or different performances altogether, and Rembrandt would sit there drawing after us. Sometimes we had an audience, but that wasn't necessary because the purpose of this exercise was to educate *us*. It was a theatre designed for the actor, not the spectator.'

I was perched on the edge of a precipice. 'I don't understand. The artist is meant to learn from a model of his own body, which he himself can never see?'

Van Hoogstraten gulped his beer. 'We were learning how to

play scenes *in the mind.* If you want to win honour in history painting, he told us, you must transform yourself entirely into an actor.'

I tried to be coldly professional. 'What did you do with your sketches?'

'Our drawings were preliminary and usually became narrative paintings, but Rembrandt kept his own sketches completely separate from his other works.'

'Do you know why?'

'He believes that different media require a different approach and strives for perfection in each one. Sometimes he would spend two days putting on a turban according to his liking, or two months perfecting the light on a pearl! I cannot fault him there . . . Have you seen his painting of the Company of Banning Cocq? Even if he went too far in the detail, it is so powerful in conception that it will, in my opinion, survive all of its rivals. And yet now he is simply careless, like a ruffian flinging that paint on the canvas, smearing it with a trowel! Anyway, how did we manage to talk so much about him?'

Seemingly irritated or angry with himself, Van Hoogstraten jumped up from his chair and marched quickly out of the door, pul in hand, spilling his ale along the way. I followed him, hoping for another opportunity to bring the conversation back to Rembrandt, for if I left immediately he would call my bluff. When I met him in the hallway, he led me into the adjacent room, a surprisingly tidy space that seemed less for work than for display.

In the centre, on the table, was a box the size of a small cabin-trunk or Flemish *kist* with six sides. The outside was dark in colour and painted with emblematic figures – an artist with a gold chain and laurel wreath – to represent the motives of a painter: *Amoris Causa; Lucri Causa; Gloriae Causa.* At the two short ends, the rectangular box had a peephole on the horizon line, revealing what was within. I began with the left end of the box, where I discovered the inside of a house with various rooms and figures, not all at once but one by one. I saw a hallway, and beyond that, a living room where a woman sat with her sewing. In the far room, another woman sat by the front door, while through the nearby window the shadowy shape of a man appeared outside, standing on the porch, maybe just about to enter. This particular lady, tiny like a doll, wore a red skirt. Her bonnet, pulled back, revealed a few fine strawberry-blonde locks near her ears. In fact, she had the distinct look of my very own fallen woman, complete with those sibylline eyes. There she was, waiting for the man, and he was standing only a few steps away, bathed in the pale but glowing light of daybreak. Was he about to come in? Why was he watching her from outside? For one awful heartbeat I imagined that, despite his great desire to see her, he did not approach the door but disappeared into the morning fog. I cursed him for his lack of courage and for those tears streaming down the woman's cheeks.

Van Hoogstraten shook me out of my reverie, urging me to go to the other side. I walked round and peered in at the perspective changing like scenes in a play. In the bedroom was a woman lying in bed, plumped upon three pillows. In the hallway, near a chair, a springer spaniel sat patiently. The experience was delightful but made my head spin. No matter how much I tried, I could not conceive of how Van Hoogstraten had made it – and could only guess that the appearance of the objects were altered by a thickness of air present between them and my eye, or perhaps the image was just an idea in my mind. How could I know if it really existed, simply because I beheld it? Sometimes when we think we rightly perceive something we simultaneously persuade ourselves that it is true, but in matters perceived by the senses alone, truth does not exist.

Finally, he told me to look through the glass side, where the view was the same, in essence, that of a house with a series of adjoining rooms and passages, but the elements converged in a dissimilar pattern. Although I could see the whole picture from this angle, the image appeared distorted. For example, the chair in the hallway was displaced, its lines mismatched, and the dog was broken up so that his top half was painted on the wall, his bottom half on the floor. It reminded me of the catoptric theatres I had seen, where the figure inside is multiplied by the variation of the angles between mirrors. Only recently I had been editing the works of Athanasius Kircher, in which he described his own polyhedric box: sixty little mirrors line the inside of a large chamber, transforming a bough into a forest, a lead soldier into an army, a booklet into a library. If you put a coin in, you could watch people grab for illusory riches; if you put a cat in, you could watch it chase the many reflections of itself until it went insane.

'It's wonderful. How did you do it?' I asked.

His chest expanded to the size of Africa. 'A work of art requires as much knavery and deceit as the perpetration of a crime. If one wants to fool the sense of sight, one must have every understanding of the nature of the eyes and what they are capable of. Tricking the viewer is part of the artist's role, my role, and I can't reveal my secrets.'

'It reminds me of something I've been working on lately. Do you know the Jesuit Athanasius Kircher?'

'I know of his strange fancies and unique inventions. Didn't he lower himself into Mount Etna, and invent a magnetic Jesus that walks on water?'

'Precisely! Well, in his *Oedipus Aegypticus*, he has a picture of Harpocrates, the god of silence, holding a finger to his mouth, and above him is the phrase, "Only by this do I reveal secrets."'

He petted his side-whisker. 'Are you publishing his works then?'

'Yes, everything he's written, a total of sixty volumes.'

'I wish you luck, Mr Blaeu,' he said curtly. 'But now that you've seen what you came for, I'd better return to my work. Thank you for calling.'

My chin quivered. Was that it? I wanted to cry out, *Wait, we're not finished yet! What about Rembrandt?* However, I took his brusqueness as a warning to be on guard: if I pushed him into revealing more, most likely he would turn on me, and I would forfeit my chance of hearing the rest of the story.

I shook his hand. 'Thank you, Mr Van Hoogstraten. It was my pleasure.'

Abruptly I left the room, telling myself it was better this way, for once again I had exercised mournful patience. But, walking home, I began to fear that I would spend the rest of my life waiting for something extraordinary to happen, and it never would, not for lack of opportunity but because I could not pluck up the courage to follow it through, like the man in the box wavering on the threshold.

Kircher with His Magic Lantern

1. Make a wooden box, ABCD, and attach a chimney to it so that the lamp may let out its smoke. The lamp itself should be placed in the middle of the box, either suspended by a metal wire or placed on a stand, M, opposite the hole, H. Place a tube, with the width of a hand's-breadth, no less, into the hole, mount a lens of good quality in the front end of that vessel, I, and a well-polished, flat glass in its rear end, H. (Note: the tube may point either inwards or outwards, but both approaches are equally good, and this is more a question of judgement.)

2. On this glass, you can paint any picture you like with transparent watercolours (they may be joyful, solemn, horrible, frightening, immoral, and for those who are ignorant of the cause of their appearance, even prodigious). Place the painted glass in an inverted position on a white-painted wall, VTSX. This will cause the light from the lamp, as it passes through the lens, to exhibit the picture enlarged and in proper position with the natural rendering.

3. In order to intensify the light of the lamp, use a concave mirror, S, behind the flame, though darker is the more preferred.

All these steps should be carefully considered at least to some extent, and in the end, you can do anything you like in a dark room. I have my own preferences, but I think the process has been explained thoroughly enough, and one will understand it better if one attempts it oneself, rather than if I try explain it, by means of my expertise, in a multitude of words.

Amsterdam, 1632

My Shell Collection

Here are my shells, orderly to the eye, mysterious to the mind. Some are rough and grainy, others are soft and pearly. Mine are all empty, but out in the sea there are empty ones too — as many as there are full. When the creatures emerge, they leave part of themselves behind. That is why I think of these spirals as living though they are asleep in their forms.

Many of the items in my collection once belonged to my dear old friend, Christiaan Poret. That visit I made to his pharmacy three years ago — when he lent me his Fabrica *and I marvelled at his outlandish specimens — was the last time I saw him. He passed away shortly thereafter. What a blessed man! He left me his shells and his emu egg, knowing how much I loved them. But I regret that I did not have the money to purchase the remainder — like the unicorn horns or the stuffed crocodile. Now his curiosities are in the hands of those who did not know him, collectors who bought them at the auction. When these objects are removed from their original surroundings, they take on a new life.*

My most recent addition is an orange starfish, curling its arms to welcome an embrace. I bought it while snooping around the harbour, from a sailor who found it in the East Indies. I also have an assemblage of eight shells made by a mollusc that grows on the wood of ships. The entrance at the top closes out the world by means of little doors joined together. Inside, it seems like any old house with joints and seams and roofing, but these molluscs do not create their manors like we do — they exude them from within. And while we build our houses for living, they live for building their houses. I have heard of an enormous mussel shell constructed by the tiniest, limpest, flabbiest being into which many people can fit. In China, the rich mandarins use them for bathtubs! Until I can obtain one I will be content with the shell of a snail, which in winter plunges deep into the ground, shuts itself inside a coffin until spring comes, then lets down its walls and reveals itself, full of life. Ah, to appear and reappear, to live alone ... If I could crawl inside that sleepy interior, I would find a different sort of beauty.

The Van Uylenburgh Party, a Reunion

Dear Lord, forgive me for eating so much. I ask you in advance because I have only passed through the kitchen, where the servants are preparing food for the evening feast. There are heaps of artichokes and cabbages on the floor and piles of fish on the cutting block, awaiting their Fate. The scullery boy turns geese and capon on the spit. The servant girl draws a turkey pie from the oven. The cook makes marzipan and a fruitbread stuffed with currants. I can almost taste the Brazilian sugar! Please Lord, pardon my weakness for anything sweet. And do not let my teeth fall out.

This is what I pray while sitting over a hole in the outside privy, with the gulls mewing on the roof. Tonight the Van Uylenburghs are having guests, and the house bustles with life. Servants scamper along the corridors with their brooms, cooks dash in and out of the house, and the children take their turns in the bath. There is no particular reason for the dinner, only that Hendrick wants me to meet his relations. I will force myself to attend though I would rather be at work on my painting of Ruts, or daydreaming, or visiting my *Pussy Willow*. The mere thought of having to converse with other people jostles my nerves. As soon as I even make an attempt to speak, I become muddled and utter something out of turn. My capability for witty or clever remarks exists only in my mind. Besides, when most people gather together their conversations turn sordid and trivial, and I find it extremely boring.

Nevertheless, I find myself framed in the doorway, wearing my Sunday best: black breeches and matching doublet with gold buttons, a white shirt with a pleated collar and sleeves, a tall hat. I seize my chance to examine the oblong room, which, usually dark and agitated, is lit up with tapered candles and decked out in finery. On the table, covered in a red damask cloth, there are pitchers of wine, baskets of bread and an arrangement of cheeses and fresh oysters. One wall has a row of windows facing the courtyard. I will sit there, I decide, where it is cool, and because I do not like having my back to open space. Amongst the crowd of elegantly clad women and gentlemen, I spot Hendrick standing near the banquet, with a red face and a felt kolpak hat upon his head, his mouth swollen with food. As he chews, little crumbs fall on to the front of his lumpy coat. When he sees me, he waves his hand to beckon me inside.

HVU: *Spitting.* I'm glad you decided to join us!

RVR: May I have a glass of wine?

HVU: Of course. *Plods over with a glass of wine.* I'll introduce you to the Frisian-Calvinist branch of my family. Not all of them are Polish Mennonites like me.

RVR: *Eyes wandering back and forth over the oysters.* (*Aside*) Should I tuck in immediately or wait until they are offered?

The art dealer takes the painter's arm and pulls him towards an old woman wearing a white bonnet over her grey hair, tight against her forehead with its arched wrinkles. Her fierce mouth stands out against her soft cheeks. The art dealer introduces her as his cousin Aeltje Van Uylenburgh. She clutches the arm of her elderly husband, Johannes Cornelisz Sylvius, Predikant of the Oude Kerk, who resembles a goat with his long white beard. His face seems to begin halfway down his egg-shaped head.

AVU: *Offering him her wrinkled hand.* Hendrick has said wonderful things about you.

RVR: Thank you, and now I have the opportunity to tell you how kind he's been to me.

JCS: *A muscle throbbing above his right eye.* You must come to visit us at the church on Sunday.

RVR: Oh? (*Aside*) Already, I've lost. If I say yes, I am rejecting the Mennonite family into which I have been accepted so graciously. If I say no, I am rejecting one of the most respected ministers of my community. The family division is a bore. How can I be honest and not offend them? (*To JCS*) I would be very interested in hearing your views on the Scriptures. I support all of God's friends.

JCS: *Nods his head in thought.* You will, perhaps, be surprised to hear, I myself have sometimes wished I was a member of no religion. But I have learnt that the way of Jesus of Nazareth can be better taught by living the right life than by the thunder of the voice.

By the light of a flickering candle, the Predikant's shadow is thrown in a black outline upon the wall behind him. An odd glow like a halo trembles above his skullcap.

JCS: We may expect you, then?

RVR: I would like to speak more about this, perhaps after the meal?

JCS: Yes, but remember, he that sows sparingly will also reap sparingly, and he that sows bountifully will also reap bountifully.

RVR: But let each one do just as he has resolved in his heart, not grudgingly or under compulsion.

HVU: *Nudging him.* Shall we greet the others?

As the two men nudge through the swarm, the art dealer points out his young niece, Hiskia, short and stout, laughing up her sleeve. Her husband, Gerrit van Loo, is secretary-clerk of the township of Het Bildt, a group of farming villages northwest of Leeuwarden. He has an unsentimental face, as if he would rather be fishing or fowling, and his dark eyebrows travel round the side of his head. The men stop to chat with the art dealer's wife, Maria, whose blonde hair, softly curling, is cinched in a band and decorated with a single violet flower. She wears an old-fashioned costume of borato and holds a handkerchief with tassels. Suddenly, a hand reaches through the tangle of arms and tugs the painter away from his hosts.

RVR: (*Aside*) Such delicate fingers with bulging veins! They belong to my first teacher in Amsterdam, the history painter Pieter Lastman. It must be eight years since I saw him last. Those eight years have been unkind to him. His lips part in that same dry smile, but a million wrinkles crease his purple cheeks. Without these familiar gestures, he could be anyone – just any old weak and debile man. Yet this man painted in Rome alongside the great Pietro Paulo, and created the most fiery of histories in Coriolanus and the Roman women! His passion and excitement, which once flooded from his every crevice, have subsided into lethargy and boredom. Is this what I will become in later years?

The teacher, a warped figure, stoops in the slightly illuminated room. He is wearing his usual thick coat over a brown vest with tiny buttons, though the edges are frayed, and the pelt on his collar stinks like a tannery.

PL: *Wheezing.* My good boy, you do not seem happy to see me.

RVR: Master, I am overjoyed!

PL: But I hear you have given up history painting. *Thrusts a pipe into his mouth from which he begins to puff white clouds of smoke.*

RVR: Do you mean, because I have been doing portraits?

PL: Yes, I was sad to hear that, my boy, considering my hopes for you.

RVR: You mustn't jump to conclusions. Portraiture is simply the way to money. I'm busy at work on narrative paintings, too.

PL: *Chokes.* Money! You have always been rather ambitious, haven't you? Lofty dreams of becoming a burgher and so forth.

RVR: Money, of course, but freedom too. Freedom to do whatever I want! Besides, my portraits are more than just portraits, they are histories. I assign my patrons their parts and they must play them.

PL: You do not serve your patrons, then, they serve you?

RVR: Precisely.

PL: *Laughs, showing his yellow teeth.* Is it freedom, working in such conditions? You can't fool me. I've heard all about the cramped spaces and tiresome hours, the young students with no sense of history or technique . . .

The maidservant steps between the men with a pitcher in hand. As she refills the painter's goblet, the folds of her skirt brush his leg.

RVR: True, it's not *your* workshop but I've made many friends in high places. My biggest ambition is to be a history painter, you know that, and I will never compromise, not even after I receive the gold chain!

PL: You will paint yourself wearing the gold chain. What difference would it make to have a real one?

RVR: Are you mocking me?

PL: Certainly not, I admire you. Most people are satisfied with too little.

RVR: You, my teacher, admire me? You're too kind.

PL: It's not in your nature to have an attack of modesty, Rembrandt. *Rests a hand upon his hip.* Please tell me about your latest project.

RVR: I will paint history scenes of fathers and sons, or friendships between men, Abraham and Isaac, Tobit and Tobias, Jacob and Joseph, Saul and David . . . (*Aside*) Ha, there's a woman I have not seen before! She is sitting at the table, well out of our way. A country girl, I am sure, because she is fresh and innocently beautiful like a well-bred cow. She wears a fur-trimmed blue jacket and a yellow silk skirt with brocade. Her plump shoulders droop and her chin leans forward over her bosom. Her ginger hair, swept up, reveals her wide neck and the damp strands of hair trapped there. Her eyes are two almonds with puffy lids. Is she tired? She knows she is being watched and meets my eyes with her own, smiling over her shoulder in a bold gesture. Who is she? My eyes want to follow her everywhere.

PL: *Following the painter's gaze.* Hendrick's niece, Saskia. Have you met her?

RVR: Not yet, but I'd like to.

The art dealer rejoins them, chomping another mouthful of food.

PL: (*To HVU*) We were just discussing your niece.

The painter pulls a short-stemmed clay out of his pocket, puts some tobacco in the bowl and pokes it with his little finger. The maidservant is quick to offer him a light from her candle.

HVU: Oh, I knew you'd like the look of her. *Claps the painter on the back.* Your new friend Sylvius is her guardian. Her mother passed away when she was six and her father died about nine years ago.

RVR: So she's an orphan? Who was her father?

HVU: My father's brother, Rombertus. He was a lawyer and the

Burgomaster of Leeuwarden. Left Saskia a sizeable inheritance, I tell you. Do you think she's pretty?

RVR: (*Aside*) From the corner of my eye, I catch a glimpse of her soft, downy cheek. She is talking animatedly to her sister, but I am too far away to hear the sound of her voice, which I imagine to be light and airy, the tone of a fife. She is far more than pretty. I will confess nothing.

HVU: *Chuckles.* Perhaps she's the one to get you out of the brothels, eh?

RVR: Oh, sure. (*Aside*) But I've been keeping my visits to the docks a secret.

PL: *Interrupting.* That Sylvius, he certainly has an interesting face. Don't you agree, Rembrandt?

RVR: I was thinking the same thing earlier. Would he sit for me, Hendrick?

HVU: That man has preached all over the Friesland. He'd be a very intriguing subject, indeed. Why don't you ask him?

A hush descends on the room, and the guests disperse to the table.

PL: *Whispers to his former student.* I will have to leave early.

RVR: *Whispers back.* Wait until the fruitbread arrives! (*Aside*) Maybe I will have a chance to speak with Hendrick's niece, if the wine will allow me such boldness.

The painter heads straight for the empty chair across from the strange Friesland girl, and near the window, but nearly knocks over the scullery boy, who bears a tray of freshly carved goose.

PREFERENCES IN THE MARKET
Catholics: History paintings from the New Testament
Calvinists: Landscapes & Still-life Paintings
Orthodox Calvinists: Paintings, figures from the Old Testament
Jews: Etchings of figures from Old Testament, Portraits
Mennonites: Portraits, Vanitas still lifes

The Idle Hour

This is the idle hour. Stretched on the floor, I fold my arms above my head and cross my feet. It is the position I like best when my humour is in a stir. All the bad energy pours out of my fingertips. Breathing is easier too. As the presses creak in the next room, the planks quiver against my back. There is a strange glow on the ceiling. When I close my eyes, it lasts for a moment, then great blue spheres explode one after another — a shooting comet. The early morning hardens around me minute by minute. The apprentices will arrive soon and the workshop will become a chaos. The longer I wait, the fewer minutes I have to paint in solitude. And what will my students think if they find me here? I suppose it does not matter, when they already suspect I am a madman.

The thought of Hendrick's niece, Saskia, comes into my mind. Will I see her again? It seems impossible that her guardian — the pious Sylvius! — would ever let me near her. Wait until I am wealthy, and a famous painter at that! I could find another excuse to travel to Friesland. Fishing, perhaps?

Oh, the echo of her high voice and strange dialect sings in my ears. I am almost lulled to sleep.

I imagine my father watching me from Heaven above. Up there, his vision is perfect and takes in everything. Is he happy with what he sees? Is he proud of me? I imagine we are two points composing a line, here to there, and drift close together to form a pattern, near and far. My grief for him is mute, but he never leaves me. A diffused yellow light enters through the window and catches me out of time and place. 'Life is short and art is long.'

Fathers, Brothers and Sons

The beauty of sons is their fathers, but sometimes jealousy and greed find a way into their hearts. Remember Cain and Abel. Think of Saul, greedy for power and jealous of his son Jonathan because of his affection for David. Why else would he take up a life-long campaign to slay his son's friend? Or Esau, who vows to kill his brother Jacob, greedy for his birthright and jealous of his father Isaac's love for him. Then Jacob, who loves Joseph more than all his other sons, because he was the son of his old age, and had a long, striped garment made for him.

Joseph's brothers know that their father loves him more than them, and so they begin to hate Joseph. When Jacob sends Joseph to check on his brothers as they are tending their flocks, and they catch sight of him from a distance, they plot to put him to death. As soon as Joseph comes upon them, they strip off his garment and pitch him into an empty waterpit. Then they sit down to eat bread and decide to sell him to the Ishmaelites for twenty silver pieces. After Joseph is taken away, the brothers slaughter a male goat, dip Joseph's garment into the blood and carry it to their father, who then exclaims, 'A vicious wild beast must have devoured him! Joseph is surely torn to pieces!' Jacob rips his mantles apart, puts sackcloth on his hips and mourns his son for many days. As his sons and daughters try to comfort him, he cries out, weeping, 'I shall go down into Sheol mourning for my son!'

Only the Master Decides

The face of Joris de Caullery, a young marine soldier, looms out of the surrounding darkness. The light falls on his right cheek, warm and rosy-coloured, and the gorget collarpiece resting alongside it. His eyelids are puffy and white with barely discernible lashes, and lights rim the greasy skin underneath. A few dabs of red rest in his eyes' inner corners, which are closely set.

JDC: *Raising his voice.* Why has the portrait taken you so long to complete? I've been sitting still for two months!

RVR: It hasn't been nearly so long.

JDC: Perhaps it has been three . . .

RVR: *Shouting.* What do you expect, that when you blink it will suddenly appear?

JDC: No need to lose your temper.

RVR: No need to be greedy. You and your friends can wait for perfection! *Leaps from his chair and throws his big, unhappy feet around the room. (Aside)* What gall! While I've been working my hands raw, this man has sat day after day with lazy limbs. Now he is thinking only of impressing some pompous fools, and of the glory he may or may not receive.

JDC: It looks fine to me.

RVR: It will look even better if you just stay quiet and do as you're told. Actually, why don't you go? I can finish without you.

The painter stomps back to his easel and stares down at the palette with its bevy of ochres, umbers and lakes. He squeezes a drop of bone black from a pig's bladder and drops it next to the cassel earth.

RVR: (*Aside*) Did I forget to order more schulpwit?

JDC: Don't be angry. You understand my predicament.

RVR: Only *I* decide when my paintings are finished, do you hear? Only the master decides.

JDC: *Nods, jiggling his jowls.* The master, hmpf.

RVR: *Dips a tiny brush into a mixture of carmine red and yellow ochre then touches it against the panel.* Let me finish.

JDC: Let you finish? With pleasure! *Relaxes his arms, one of which holds a small musket, the other a golden trumpet.*

RVR: What do you think you're doing? Hold still.

JDC: You told me to leave. Besides, I have an important matter to discuss with my associates.

RVR: *Hands curled into fists.* What occurs in this room stays in this room.

JDC: The matter does not concern *you*, sir, it concerns my trade.

RVR: And your trade is more important than mine?

JDC: *Steps backward.* Send word when it is ready.

RVR: Don't be a fool. Sit down. (*Aside*) He is not listening. Look at him hustling to the door, pumping his strong arms! When he turns round, his mouth hangs open, his cheeks grow pink and his wisp of beard quivers. An ensemble of plum-coloured veins dances on his forehead. Watching him in great distress, his senses in full flare, I rejoice. This is what I have been seeking through all these months, and I want more . . . Emotion! Passion!

JDC: You have two days.

RVR: *Shouting.* I have as long as it takes!

When the marine soldier leaves the room, he slams the door behind him.

RVR: (*Soliloquy*) Why can't my clients be patient and understand that only *I* decide when my painting is finished, because only *I* know when my intentions have been satisfied? Further, how can I explain that my painting might seem finished to him but seems suspended to me? When I seek to perceive it, I am more conscious of the activity of creation than the product itself, and in my mind I re-create it, step by step. Everything breaks down into fragments which, in turn, are fragmented. That is why I do not feel good about releasing his portrait – or any other painting – because there is always the opportunity to change that tone, that mark, that shadow. My compulsion is to return to the passages over and over again with a kind of fever.

INTERLUDE

A woman is warbling in French. Her soprano notes skip over the canal and waft into my ears like the cry of a baby bird.

Man's Inexorable End

Hendrick wants me to be kinder to my clients. He says my stubborn attitude could adversely affect the business. But I am not stubborn. Also, my De Caullery portrait proved a success. Further commissions are coming to me in pushcarts. This month I am going to paint Marten Looten, cloth merchant and Flemish émigré. The best of the news is: I have been commissioned to do a group portrait of Nicolaes Tulp, praelector of anatomy, with seven other doctors of the Surgeons' Guild. I will charge him 150 guilders and an extra 100 guilders per head! I have yet to meet the doctor, but I have been told a lot about him. His carriage, painted on the side with a golden bloom resembling a pointed turban, often rolls through town while he makes his house calls. Apparently, he heard about me through Barlaeus, an orator and poet friend from my Leyden days. Barlaeus recently moved here to become one of the new professors at the Athenaeum Illustre. He is not only a friend but also a patient of Tulp's, because he has trouble sitting down (he believes his backside is made of glass).

What do I say about Tulp? Formerly known as Claes Pieterszoon, he studied medicine at the University of Leyden before starting a large practice in Amsterdam. He teaches special courses to midwives, rejects the ever-

popular medieval apothecary and believes in unity between body and soul. Barlaeus tells me that Tulp resembles a Roman Senator and is a lover of the arts. They are both members of a circle that gathers at Muiden Casle, the home of P. C. Hooft, along with the great poet Vondel and Maria Tesselschade Visscher. She's the wild daughter of the poet Roemer Visscher, and I sometimes see her swimming in the canals.

I have begun my research by scouring anatomy books and old prints of dissections. For ideas on background, lighting and grouping, I have studied other group portraits. In Rubens's The Tribute Money, all the figures, clustered to one side, gaze at the Lord with the utmost concentration. Each wears a different expression. If I am to achieve such diversity in my composition, I will have to conduct preliminary sketches of the individual doctors. Finally, I will take my place at the Waaggebouw for the grisly dissection ceremony in January (the corpse keeps longer in winter). Everyone will be stooping over my shoulder — senators and rectors from the university, burgomasters, aldermen, students and citizens. My primary subject, besides Tulp of course, who will he be? A common criminal, disgusted with the world and everything in it. At this moment, he is a free man. He has yet to commit the crime that will put him on the slab, at the behest of Tulp's tweezers.

These are the prints of dissections I found: Anatomy of Dr Sebastiaen Egbertszoon de Vrij *by Aert Pieterszoon, 1603, a rigid, over-extended piece of twenty-eight surgeons;* The Osteology Lesson of Dr Sebastiaen Egbertszoon *by Thomas de Keyser, 1619, a more centred composition in which the same doctor conducts a bone demonstration; and* Anatomy of Dr Joan Fonteijn *by Eliaszoon, 1625, a pyramidal structure with the head surgeon pointing his index finger at the corpse. After examining these pictures, I came up with several requirements:*

1 *The praelector should be the primary focus.*

2 *Each doctor must have a recognizable likeness without detracting from the unity of the group.*

3 *The members should be differentiated by rank and function.*

4 *At least some figures must address the beholder directly, to show their roles in society.*

5 *A unity must exist between the subjects themselves, and between the subjects and the spectator.*

Most importantly, I must include a memento mori: 'We are but dust and shadow'; 'Man is a soap bubble.' The bodies of the dead silently teach justice and medicine to the living!

The anatomist is the true eye of medicine, and an autopsia is an act of direct witness. But these early anatomy paintings do not reflect a true eye at all. Where is the revelation? The artists have portrayed their dead man in a stilted manner. They have hardly cared to show his full form, and his face is the same colour as those of breathing men. Of course, I will have to overrule reality in some respects. Tulp will commence with the most gruesome aspect, by opening the stomach like a pomegranate and removing the intestines. I would rather focus on the extremities — arms, legs, feet, and especially, hands — which are left to the end. You wouldn't believe the stink! The cadaver cannot be thought of as a sophisticated arrangement of organs, I mean. He is alive with the spirit of something greater. Though he has closed his eyes on time, he is timeless. But how do I uphold the vitality of a man whose vital organs are hanging out? I must reveal rather than conceal him. It is impossible to brush aside the idea that life rises out of what is not life and vice versa.

On my shelf is the 1543 edition of De Humani Corporis Fabrica

Libri Septem *by Vesalius. Before he was famous, he dug up corpses in Paris cemeteries to perform experiments on them. His atlas demonstrates the ingenuity of the members in the most detailed charts. Some even have paper flaps to disclose overlying or underlying parts. The woodcut frontispiece shows him opening the abdomen of a woman in front of a large group of Paduan spectators. He outlines his procedures, narrating what he removes or displays at each stage. I have learnt all the Latin names for body parts, but I am only beginning to understand the essential harmony of man. I wonder, of what use is it to determine the components of a lifeless member, when the living one is not examined? Between life and death, many changes occur in the body, so it is hardly the same entity.*

MY PORTRAIT PRICES, INCREASED

Head-only ... 50 g.
Half-length ... 100 g.
Life-size ... 500 g.

Contrast & Harmony

Colour of an object must always depend on its surroundings. For example, the colour of a red house appears different under a clear blue sky than under an overcast grey one. To achieve this harmony of colours in a painting, one must vary strong colour tones with contrasting ones. But contrast alone creates too harsh an effect. That is why I alternate warm and cold shades in variations, each complementing the other. In choosing these complements, I always follow the dominant tone that carries the mood of the picture. In nature, a dominant tone is everywhere:

whether in grey weather or the golden light of evening or the bright blue of midday.

A Visit to Willem Blaeu, Cartographer

One of my painter friends has referred me to a man who lives near the Nieuwe Kerk. He has a collection of bird skulls, fish jaws, dragon bones, elephant teeth and possibly other things I would like to use for my paintings — costumes and suits of armour. His name is Willem Blaeu, a cartographer who works from his home on the Bloemgracht. Last week I wrote to him about my voracious hunger for curiosities and about my recent project. Hopefully he has something from which I can make my anatomy drawings. Wish me luck, for anyone pocketing the vital organs at the lesson, when passed around for inspection, will be fined six guilders!

This afternoon, a ruthless rain attacks the city. The canals are overflowing and the dogs run dizzily over their bridges. I blink my lashes free of water to see hazy figures whirling around me: a baker sways under a large breadbasket; a milkman jangles his jars; a warehouse worker gathers up sacks from his doorstep; a man in a black frock-coat wanders like a shepherd among the blind. The cats, eyes like moons, hide in corners and spit from their wrinkled lips. I patter down alleyways, following a pack of rats until it ducks into a hole under a tavern. Deus est anima brutorum. God is the soul of the beasts.

Eventually I reach the red-bricked dwelling, cloistered in itself, with varnished wooden shutters and a plaque on the facade engraved, 'Geography is the Eye & the Light of History'. A small side-addition to the main house clatters with activity: the Blaeu printing works. My heart pounds with a sense of adventure as I give the door a forceful bang.

The painter is greeted by a tall, stooping figure whose face, with its tuft of silver hair, is a befuddled yellow under his spectacles. The cartographer is perhaps sixty years old, and has a nose like an eagle's beak.

RVR: Pleased to meet you, Mr Blaeu. (*Aside*) I like him immediately — for his dusty, ink-stained housecoat rolled up to the elbow.

WB: *In an exotic baritone.* Come in, the hour is at hand.

The cartographer ushers him down a long hallway and into his chamber of artifice, a square room filled with the vapour of Eastern scents. The red curtains are parted to reveal two large windows, overlooking an abandoned street where the rain keeps sadly falling, but they afford very little light. A lone candelabra, burning high, brings into view the glittering objects in the room. Uncertain shadows creep on the white walls, reflecting the stuffed animals dangling from the ceiling: an ostrich, a crocodile, a pelican.

RVR: *Absorbed in contemplation.* Well.

WB: *Jounces his overgrown eyebrows.* Rembrandt, did you say?

RVR: Yes, sir, I run Van Uylenburgh's workshop.

WB: Don't be bashful. Have a look around. But I think I have what you need for your project.

RVR: Thank you, sir.

The painter approaches the glass-fronted wooden cases extending along the left wall, which hold all conceivable kinds of shell, starfish, mineral and horn.

RVR: (*Aside*) I feel curiously weightless. These objects seem to be floating in the sea or enveloped by a snow-white mist. *Hopping from foot to foot.* The longer I perform this exercise, the more I realize how silly it is. How could I try to remove the veil which nature has created for these creatures?

At the next cabinet, the painter sees that each object is systematically labelled but their arrangement obeys no rules at all. Two items resemble shrunken, deformed prunes, whose labels read, the hand of a mermaid and the hand of a mummy.

RVR: Is it true that some bitumen is made from ancient Egyptians?

WB: That's the common belief. The Egyptians used to pull the brain through the nostrils with an iron hook, wash the corpse with incense then cover it with linen and the bitumen we know as mommia, which smells like garlic and is rather pasty. Excellent for shading, I hear?

RVR: Yes, though I prefer asphaltum, which is more lustrous and translucent.

WB: *In a slow, affected style.* If you want to make Egyptian brown yourself, you can take a carcass of a young man with red hair, not having died from disease but killed, let it lie for a day in clear water, cut the flesh into pieces, add myrrh and aloe, then allow it to absorb turpentine and wine. It's also a good way to expel wind out of the bowels.

RVR: I may try that.

The painter admires in the next case at least a hundred round parrot eggs — oval, pristine and pearly. There are also Javanese shadow puppets, African calabashes and an enormous boar's head.

RVR: (*Aside*) That overgrown pig gazes at me over his sausage nose with an incredibly solemn expression. His mouth is open wide and drooping at the corners. Then something else hovers above me like an apparition. On closer inspection, it proves to be the body of the most dazzling creature: a medium-sized bird, like a crow, with short velvety feathers – black on the breast, reddish-brown on the back and orange on the sides. The head is golden and the throat is emerald-green. It possesses neither a tail nor legs. (*To WB*) What glorious colours!

WB: *Standing behind the painter, his voice booms in his ear.* Paradisea apoda. The Spanish named them Birds of Paradise because of their great beauty. This one comes from New Guinea.

RVR: Where are its legs?

WB: No one knows. I have heard they don't possess legs at all, and keep flying until they die.

RVR: That doesn't make sense. Mustn't they rest?

WB: Their friends, the Colibris, drill their beaks into trees and stay fixed there, so the birds can rest upon them.

RVR: Ah, I would love to draw it . . .

WB: *Rubbing his broad forehead.* You are a painter, aren't you? Then you understand that nature is not at variance with art, because nature is the art of God. They are both servants of His Divine Providence.

RVR: While art is the perfection of nature. *Pause.* Would you sell it?

WB: I couldn't bear to part with it, not now, though I assume you will visit again?

RVR: *Shakes his head up and down.* (*Aside*) An Aristotelian place and a man after my own heart!

The men stop in front of a large map of Africa displayed on the wall above the mantelpiece.

WB: You're one of the first to see that. I've only recently finished it.

RVR: It's as if I am viewing another world from another world! With the landscape opened up and flattened, I see everything and yet, somehow I feel separate from it, like an eagle flying overhead.

WB: *Smiles gently.* Then I've achieved my purpose. A good map should enable us to contemplate the things that are farthest away right before our eyes.

RVR: Is this what you specialize in?

WB: If you mean mapmaking, yes. Now that I work for the VOC, we're sending men to chart routes to the Indies and Brazil. I also make navigational tools and optical instruments. Those ones over there are mine. *Gestures towards two side-tables scattered with globes, compasses, sextants and sundials — one of which holds a statue of Atlas, the carrier of the world, and the other, Minerva, the goddess of wisdom.* Now let us find what you came for. I don't allow many people this privilege, not even my son.

RVR: Well, thank you. Your son, he's a cartographer too?

WB: Yes, Joan, but he's incorrigible.

The cartographer guides the painter to a mahogany cupboard crowned by oriental porcelain and opens the double doors to the inner sanctum, a series of shelves lined with jars containing human and animal parts preserved in liquid.

RVR: *Pointing to a bottle.* What on earth is that?

WB: A dog's stomach. Oh, you haven't seen the best of it. *Holds out another jar, green and mouldy with age. With two hands, he carries it over to the table.* You won't believe this, but it's the very fore‑arm that Vesalius dissected in *De Fabrica.* Do you know the frontispiece?

RVR: *Walking on the cartographer's heels.* I was just looking at it the other day. You're right, I do not believe you.

The cartographer holds the jar under the candlelight and rotates it slowly.

RVR: How compelling. (*Aside*) With the bulging muscles and tendons revealed, the arm seems grotesquely out of proportion. I cannot be sure which side of the man's body it originally belonged to. The right, the left? The longer I examine it the more displaced it seems. What must the owner of this arm have been like? What had he used this hand for – to create, carry, murder or plunder? Suddenly a jolt of energy runs through my own arm, from elbow to wrist, pumping through my veins and massaging my muscles.

Then my limb seems to swell and stretch. When the aching travels down my fingers, they start to tingle and twitch. I close my eyes to end this absurd reaction, but nothing happens. When I concentrate all my powers on filling in the man's form, he resembles not a common criminal but me – bulbous nose, glowing monstrously. I can only imagine myself suspended on the gallows, twisted round and laughing in a horrible way. Below, a stranger stretches out his hand to me, and in the teeth of fear, I venture ever closer to him. At last, I can touch him.

WB: *Snaps his fingers for the painter's attention.* We study the order of things, but we can never grasp their innermost essence.

RVR: *Dizzily.* That is precisely what I was thinking . . . and if it is true, how can anything ever present itself to me, if it inevitably breaks down and falls into mere illusion?

WB: Every perception is a communication or a communion, because an object is always inseparable from the person perceiving it. Your experience naturally breaks forth and transcends into whatever you see. *Puts a finger to his lips.* Do exactly what you have just done.

RVR: What do you mean?

WB: Identify with the dead man . . .

RVR: Who is lifeless and dull?

WB: We never remain suspended in nothingness. All things desire to endure in their being. Even after death the face is doomed to express something. Truly, I have seen corpses with faces bearing expressions of surprise, peace or discretion, as if they were conversing with me.

RVR: (*Aside*) His face, in the circle of the light, is definitely that of a living, breathing man, but there is something immortal about it.

WB: You have the chance to prolong his life.

RVR: Well, I like to say, eternity is a gift only God and the painter can bestow.

WB: *Sinister laugh.*

RVR: Does it belong to a pair, or is this the only one?

WB: The other exists, but I am only interested in selling this one. That is, if you are willing to pay a good sum for it.

The cartographer sets the jar on the table and watches the painter over the top of his spectacles, his eyes grey and shrewd.

RVR: *Digging in his purse for coins.* (*Aside*) Please Lord, bless me. I must have this specimen!

A violent gust of wind thrusts open the windows and flaps the red curtains. An angry, sleety rain begins to pour in, splashing upon the cartographer's coin collection and stirring up a harp-like melody. The painter jumps back, retreating behind the table as the angry wind rushes into the room, shaking the ostrich, the crocodile and the pelican on their ropes. The jar containing the ninety-year-old, sinewy forearm flies off the table and shatters on to the floor. Wringing his hands, the painter watches tiny pieces of glass scoot across the marble. A quaggy liquid seeps over his stockinged feet, and a putrid scent rushes into his nostrils. The candle flames grow frantic, rising and falling, then die abruptly. The room goes dark.

Philosophers Sitting by Candlelight

On 31 January 1632, Dr Nicolaes Tulp conducted an anatomy lesson before hundreds of onlookers at the Waaggebouw, on the corpse of a petty thief, Aris Kindt, who had been hanged for his misdemeanours. Afterwards, two men who had attended the event – until then strangers to one another – met in the back room of the residence of him who, though being a Frenchman, made his temporary home in the slaughterhouse district of Amsterdam, where he lived 'as in deserts most remote' due to the discreet manners of its inhabitants.

The Frenchman, René Descartes, was a *philosophe* who began studying scholastic doctrines at La Flèche from the age of ten before receiving a law degree at Poitiers, and at thirty-six years old, was in the midst of writing a treatise on universal science. He was small in appearance with a large head, a prominent nose, a projecting brow and dark hair hanging in his eyes. Dressed in a long woollen coat, he reclined on a chaise longue as he often did in the evenings: one boot crossed over the other and beside the fireplace, in a yellow gleam, close enough to nudge the turf if the flames died down. The bookshelves lined the walls behind him, so that if he wished to pull down one of the scientific volumes he had only to extend his right arm (or so he liked to believe, for this action would merely allow him to reach the bottom two shelves). Although he appeared feeble

BROWNE: With pupils that are dancing ghosts! *Lowering his voice.* Be wary, Plato died in a dream. *Approaches the bookshelf.* Yet persons of radical integrity are not easily perverted in dreams. Think of Luther or Alexander! I confess that, with or without the assistance of narcotics, I am able to manipulate the sequence of events at will, compose a whole comedy, behold the action, apprehend the jests and laugh myself awake. Yet, afterward, how can I describe it? I am left with insufficient judgement. I forget the story and can only capture a confused and broken tale of what has happened.

DESCARTES: Often at night I find myself in this particular place – right here! – dressed and seated near the fire, while in reality I am lying undressed in bed. I am in the habit of representing to myself the same thing or even less probable things in my dreams than those who are insane whilst awake! Oh, but I am a captive who enjoys an imaginary liberty. When I begin to suspect that my liberty is a dream, I try not to awaken and conspire with the illusions to prolong the deception.

BROWNE: Yes, the night supplies us with fictions and falsehoods; yet, however fallacious our dreams may be concerning outward events, we are more able to sensibly understand ourselves through them. It is like men who, when they are dying, speak and reason above themselves because the soul is beginning to be freed from the body, as if inhabited by some mysterious fire . . .

DESCARTES: Thank you for the reminder. *Without getting up, he snatches the poker and stokes the fire.* Now, what were we saying? Ah, yes, when we realize how greatly the body and soul differ, we understand much better the reasons why our soul is entirely independent of the body, and is not liable to die with it. Then, when we observe no other causes capable of destroying it, as we did in the theatre today, we are naturally inclined to judge that it is immortal. For all we know, my mother could be floating around in this room with us.

BROWNE: Your mother? I do not detect her, unless that whistling sound is not really the wind, or that cat in the corner is simply an inhabited carcass.

DESCARTES: Where? *Sitting up, he looks frantically about the room.* What cat?

BROWNE: You are frightened? Enough of these chestnuts! I only meant to emphasize that there is nothing strictly immortal. Things that have no beginning can be confident of no end, all other things are within reach of destruction. As Paracelsus says, man has an invisible sun, a life-giving force that allows us to live . . .

DESCARTES: You follow the Hermeticians!

BROWNE: In philosophy, where truth seems double-faced, there is no man more paradoxical than myself. *Snorts and collects his thoughts.* I was introduced to the writings of Paracelsus while studying in Padua, in fact. Returning to your earlier point, my good sir, about these particular spirits trapped in the body, have you thought there might be a universal spirit common to the whole world trapped in nature? This was the belief of the Hermetical philosophers: if there is a common nature that unites and ties individuals into one species, there must be one that unties them all.

DESCARTES: If you mean, do I believe that art, nature and the universe are the proof of the wisdom of God, then yes.

BROWNE: *Sits down in his chair.* All physicians and scholars should seek truth in the light of nature, for it is the second book of God and shows evidence of His power and wisdom.

DESCARTES: *Wiping his nose again.* One has to be cautious of blind curiosity, however. That is, some men seek out things that are rare solely to wonder at them and not for the purpose of knowing them.

BROWNE: I agree, though I myself am a collector of rarities.

DESCARTES: Of what kind?

BROWNE: Of several kinds, scarce or never seen by any man now living.

DESCARTES: *Raises his eyebrows.* Excluding you, I suppose, unless I am dreaming again.

BROWNE: I could not begin to tell you the contents of my cabinet, there are too many to name. The important thing is, I do not acquire these objects simply for the purpose of wondering at them like a common fool. Every essence, created or uncreated, has a final cause or some possible end of its operation, which is precisely what I seek in the works of nature, on which hangs the providence of God.

DESCARTES: Please, tell me about your cabinet of curiosities.

BROWNE: Well, I am only beginning to form my collection, which I call my *Musæum Clausum*, although I have, for example, a magnified amulet made of deerskin and containing tortoise legs that were cut off alive; a concoction of spirits and salt of Sargasso covered with vegetables, excellent against the scurvy; a crucifix made from the cross-bone of a frog's head; a poem by Ovidius Naso, written in the Getick during his exile at Tomi and found wrapped up in wax on the borders of Hungary; an extract of liberans, that famous and highly magnified composition used in the East Indies to repress the fuliginous vapour of dusky melancholy . . .

DESCARTES: *Yawns.*

BROWNE: A petrified hedgehog; a cock with four legs . . .

'Nosce Te Ipsum'

How vulnerable I was in the emptiness of my room as the light rose from the high window, for during the night, I had been awakened by a vision of the girl-mouse with pink ears. Standing at the end of my bed, she gazed at me with her green eyes, her lashes dragging down her lids as if she had been waiting a long time for me to notice her. The blood rushed to my head, and my legs scrambled under the linens: my happiness at seeing her again equalled nothing else. A mere slip of a girl, her aura eddied around me and held complete domain over my heart. I rose out of bed and crept towards her, but immediately regretted my haste when she backed away, gliding further and further into the distance. Then, like a phantasm, she vanished into the chink of my door. I groped the darkness, feeling the wooden boards with my palms, and peeked through crevices, because I wanted to follow her every-where, but she had not left behind the slightest trace. *Oh love, just a fancy on the inside of my eyelid!*

Waking again to the Oude Kerk's seven bells, I wished to snuggle in my bed a little while longer with the drool running off my chin, but the servants were making a racket – scurrying up and down the back staircase, beetling from room to room (their keys jangling), stirring up fires or scrubbing floors, banging pots in the kitchen. When I pulled back the covers and planted my bare feet on the cold floor, my nightgown froze up around my bones. Instead of warming myself near the hearth, I opened the window, for there was nothing more refreshing than pressing my face to the piercing wind. From an overcast sky, the snow swirled down in scattered flakes to blanket the red tiles of the sloping roofs, and the icicles, hanging in different lengths from the eaves, looked like waterfalls of crystal. Pigeons perched on the lower sill, shitting on the frosty bricks of the courtyard below. Our chickens ran about, having escaped from their coop, wobbling their wattles and flapping their wings. I wished I were one of them: at least they were making the most of the morning, the little time they had remaining. Like them, I felt unrestrained and yet confined, free but not at all free.

It was almost too late for one of them; the maid stepped out of the back door, bent her knees and lunged at the group of fowl with outstretched arms. Then she began her chase for the midday meal. The squawking grew louder as the chickens dispersed. Run, I tried to scream – run, run! – but all that came from my mouth was a rasp, and by then she had cornered one strutting blusterer near the gate. She grabbed it with both hands, and holding it out like a screaming baby, made her way towards the kitchen. The plump bird struggled beneath her grasp, throwing up a cloud of loose feathers. The girl's face contorted in concentration until she noticed me grimacing from the second-storey window. Stopping for a moment, she smiled, blinking against the flakes, and forcefully tucked the chicken under one arm. Her tawny mantle and poke-bonnet were beautifully piled with snow. I smiled back.

With a curtsey, she called up to me, 'Good morning, sir.' When the chicken pecked at her sleeve, I waved and told her to get inside; it was painful to watch, and besides, she was shivering. 'A message arrived for you this morning, sir,' she said. 'I'll bring it to you.'

I quickly dressed before she rapped on my door a few minutes later, and when I opened it a crack, she stood there sniffling. My springer spaniel, sitting beside her, perked up when she saw me. After dashing under my legs, she stretched herself flat on the floor near the fireplace, yelping loudly (I called her Echo, for her voice was alive and could be heard by everyone). Without a word, the girl handed me the message, then scampered downstairs to return to her duties. The letter was damp in my hands, and the seal on the outside was frozen, so I used my fingernails to prise it open. I carried it over to the window and held it towards the light. There were delicate indentations in the paper where it had been folded, and the ink was dark in some places, light in others, but I did not recognize the script. The characters came very close together as if they were afraid to let go of one another.

> *Dear Pieter Blaeu,*
>
> *When dawn appeared, I could not help feeling rather gloomy. I should have liked to stay a little longer. There is something in my possession which would be of great interest to you. Please swallow your pride and meet me in the Cock and Bull at Four o'clock this afternoon.*
>
> *Yours Sincerely,*
>
> *The Fallen Woman*

The paper shook in my hand, and I became very unsteady on my feet. She had written, she had written! My heart wanted to erupt from my chest and fly out of the window. Who was she, and what was I to do with her? The very answers to these questions were lying in my palm, but Echo's outbursts were making it impossible to concentrate. After dismissing the bitch with the kindly toe of my boot, I re-read the message then, like the earnest editor, read and re-read it again, picking apart each sentence and phrase with the aim of piecing everything back together.

When dawn appeared; did she mean this morning or yesterday morning? *Feeling rather gloomy*; was this slightly gloomy or very gloomy, and why gloomy at all? *I should have liked to stay*; again, was she referring to last night or the previous night? Had she really stolen into my bedroom? The *should have liked* part especially confused me; did she mean there somewhere else to be, or was it a polite excuse for leaving abruptly? What could this object in her possession be, and how did she know it would interest me? *Swallow my pride*, what pride? I was no one other than her humble slave, and she would have been convinced if she were spying on me in receipt of her letter — so happy and delighted that I pressed the paper to my face and held it there for a while, feeling it with my lips. As I breathed in the scent of the parchment, which seemed a mixture of vanilla and cinnamon, I wanted to believe it had lingered from her skin. Certainly, it had, though I could not be sure because I also smelled parsnips and hay, with the understanding that the letter had been passed through the hands of a messenger and then my maidservant. Which of these scents belonged to my girl-mouse? Ah, she had signed it *The Fallen Woman* — a careful, clever choice. She must have heard me refer to her as such; so had she made the connection? Was she trying to form a kinship with me or was she simply trying to conceal her true identity?

These questions, among many more, followed me to my desk in

the factory and tormented me throughout the morning as I gloated over Athanasius Kircher's tattered books amidst the drone of the presses. It seemed that Kircher and I were undergoing a similar struggle: while he attempted to decode the mysterious language of the Voynich manuscript (a 200-page volume filled with strange symbols and figures), I was trying to uncover the secrets of the Fallen Woman's message. How on earth should I answer her letter? When I picked up my plume and dipped it in black ink, my clothes were bathed in sweat.

Dear Fallen Woman,
The perfume rises to my head, a symphony of...

Dear Fallen Woman,
I sit beside a lantern in the coloured dusk of my room. Confused shadows flicker on the...

Dear Leda (for she reminded me of a swan),
I woke alone as the snow scurried in the coiling wind. I do not know what time is, or how we measure emotion, but the day is no longer frozen and cold.

Dear Leda, Fallen Woman, Lady of My Thoughts, Anon.
What should I call you and who are you? Why did you follow me? I do not understand why you wish to see me again, for I will only make your life miserable and you mine. You say I am proud but you have misunderstood me: I simply feel accustomed to being alone in my superior fortress with its strangling vines, where the darkness forbids even a dream of happiness. I am snarled in bitterness. My arms are so long they get in the way when I walk, and my hair is thinning...

Two hours later, I sent for the same messenger to carry back this reply:

> Dear Mevrouw,
>
> *Please do not be gloomy because the night will never end. My mind is disordered, but I am eager to see what you have for me. I will meet you at the proposed time in the proposed place. The path is slippery, so be careful not to fall on the ice.*
>
> *Yours Truly,*
>
> Pieter Blaeu

I left early, at three o'clock, after an unusual amount of primp-ing – wearing a wide-brimmed hat to conceal my bald patch, of course. The tavern was only a ten-minute walk from home, but I wanted to arrive first and sit quietly, gathering my thoughts and drinking a calming beer. I turned my collar as high as it would go and set off down the street into the stiff easterly wind, the ground crunching beneath my feet. The clouds were thick with a storm, and the birds swooping over the bare trees predicted another flurry. The gusts flung the snow about, drifting against the shop doorways like heaps of salt. No wonder the city was quieter than usual, and the chimneys were choking the air with smoke: this was the coldest day of the year yet. A wan wisp of light from the sun gave some shadowy hint of life on the frozen canal; a delivery barge was surrounded by bergs nearly two inches thick. The ice was groaning as the bargee attempted to crack it with an axe. There will be a shortage of water and fish, I thought, then people will use melted ice from the Amstel for drinking, and catch the disease.

Luckily, the Cock & Bull was not very crowded, and its few

customers were hazy-eyed, warming themselves near the open fire, sedately puffing on their pipes or consoling themselves with gin. I spotted an empty seat in the corner, affording me a view of the door so I could watch for new arrivals. After ordering a pul of ale, I slipped onto a bench and tried to assume an air of having been there long enough to appear comfortable, not long enough to appear desperate; yet soon the colour rose to my cheeks, a restless vein broke out on my brow and my heart beat wildly in my chest. I decided to distract myself by reading the day's newspaper:

A house partially collapsed on the Haarlemmerplein during a funeral dinner. Drunken orators and guests crashed through the floor, rolling helter-skelter like a pot of pears. The table, glasses and bottles were all broken.

A Lady of thirty-two years was taken to her grave at the Oude Kerk in a six-horse coach after a bizarre illness that left her without stool for 50 days.

A Spanish sailor emasculated himself with a razor out of despair, after an unsuccessful visit to the local brothel.

A woman was found frozen to death in a room on the Hoogstraat. She was lying in a box-bed on some straw with her three children, and another child was sitting on its potty, dead. There was nothing else in the room apart from the potty and straw bedding on which the dead woman had lain with her children.

This exercise was clearly not working; it only made my nerves twang. While reading I kept an inward count of the time and frequently glanced up from the paper at various stragglers coming in from the cold, like frozen ghosts, but the tension of waiting for her made my undergarments feel tight in the groin. The hour was nearly four. Where was she? Perhaps she had fallen on the ice in spite of my warning.

I could have been right, I could have been wrong: in any case, she appeared late and stood in the doorway, a lily in the sepia gloom of the tavern, draped in snow. I identified her immediately, for there was something entirely unique in the way she removed the shawl from around her shoulders and shook off its flakes, smiling as if she were the only person in the room. After stamping her boots, she walked straight towards me, a little elfin creature. My fingers gripped the edge of the table, and my mouth dropped open slightly.

'Good afternoon,' she said, with a nod, and glided next to me on the bench, only a hand's-breadth away.

I quickly swallowed my last drop of ale. Imagine me with my shyness, my cowardice, trying to think of what to say first – the experience of being alone with a woman was utterly foreign to me – as I turned my head and our faces were close enough to have been kissing. Her full lower lip glistened in a pout, and melting snow dripped from her cap and trickled down her round cheeks as if she were crying, but her green eyes were clear and watchful. Her clinging yellow mantle marked every soft line of her bosom, and her patrician hands, nestled in her lap, were red and chafed from the cold. They seemed to be trembling – another frightful, infinitely alluring dream.

I resorted to the second thing that leapt into my head (the first thing too intimate to mention). 'You forgot to tell me your real name when we met the other night.'

She narrowed her eyes into slits. 'I didn't forget, but you can call me Clara.'

I blushed at her deliberate attempt to be mysterious. 'Yes, Clara, it ends with an *a*. How perfect. My name is Pieter, but of course you already know that.'

'I know that and more,' she said.

What did she know, and was she intentionally toying with me? I told myself not to become overexcited about it; these snippets of knowledge would be revealed in due course – and she would not have tried to see me if what she heard were disagreeable. Perhaps she even found me intriguing. Her slender nose, dotted with freckles, made me lose my breath – it touched me so deeply – so I avoided her face and stared at her right knee, the one closest to me, like a walnut underneath her blue skirt. After considering it a moment, during which she was silent, I followed the curving line of her thigh. She must have noticed my stare, because she lowered her hands down her lap to cover her legs.

'What do you have for me?' I asked, peering stiffly ahead.

'A sketch,' she said, stopping then starting again. 'I thought you might . . .'

'Oh, forgive me,' I said, jumping out of my seat. 'May I buy you a drink?' I cursed myself for forgetting and because, in a matter of seconds, I had managed to behave like an idiot.

She arched her thin brows. 'Wine, thank you.'

I dashed to the bar, afraid to leave her for too long, and quickly ordered her a wine and a second beer for myself. After the bartender fulfilled my order, I returned with the two glasses, but not before mopping my forehead with a handkerchief. A lantern was now resting on the table in front of a large-sized sheet of paper;

she must have placed them there when my back was turned. The flickering candle gave a lunar tinge to the smoky air.

'What is this?' I asked, taking my seat.

'Have a look.' She splayed her fingers and pressed down on the corners of the picture with the balls of her palms.

The bench creaked as I leant in and caught a whiff of cinnamon. We hunched over the paper together, my ear vibrating close to hers. The drawing was on grainy vellum, a sheet from a portable sketching tablet, and done in fine silver lines. It showed a girlish woman wearing a straw hat, very popular in the country, over a simple coif. She sat behind a table of sorts and bent over it so that her bosom fell against her reclining right arm. Her left elbow was propped on the table, and her hand cradled her face — the little finger pressing against her cheekbone, the underside of the thumb supporting her neck. In her other hand she held a drooping flower, perhaps a poppy. Under her wide-brimmed hat, which was encircled by more flowers, her face was round with almond-shaped eyes, a button nose and a pretty mouth, grinning. A curl of hair lay against her right cheek, suggesting there was a slight breeze. A linen shawl was tied over her shoulders and the gathering folds of her chemise; a pearl necklace rested round her throat. Her head and torso drowsed in a dewy summer light.

'Perhaps they had stopped somewhere on a country stroll in June,' Clara said.

'What? Who?'

'Read the inscription,' she said, pointing.

On the lower half of the paper were the words, *This is the likeness of my wife Saskia made the third day after our betrothal, 8 June*

1633. How could I be so silly? It was my Rembrandt, of course! I already knew that his late wife was called Saskia.

'I was thinking,' she began, with a faraway expression, 'they had walked down muddy paths beside streams brushed with willows, and then went out into the fields full of rape, linseed and magpies. There must have been magpies, where they picked those flowers . . .'

'I suppose.' I did not want to give her too much credit, feeling slightly exasperated that she was already several steps ahead of me on my quest. This was supposed to be my own particular interest, and now she seemed to have taken it as hers with equal enthusiasm. I was both terribly envious and in awe of her.

'Where is your imagination?'

I ignored her. 'Where did you find this?'

She pulled away and fingered the stem of her glass. 'You ask a lot of questions.'

'Well, you have so many secrets. For instance, who are you?'

She put two fingers to her lips. 'I am Clara de Geest, daughter of the painter Wybrand de Geest and Hendrickje Van Uylenburgh, both deceased. My mother gave me this picture before she passed away.'

I stared at her in disbelief, goggle-eyed. Could this really be true? And was it Fate who dealt me these lucky cards or was it a blessing from the gracious hand of Jehovah? 'The world is bound with secret knots,' I said, remembering Kircher.

'Pardon me?'

I cleared my throat. 'Your father's work is wonderful. You are a relative of Saskia, then, from Friesland.'

She nodded. 'She was my cousin, from Leeuwarden too, but later she lived in the nearby village of Sint-Annaparochie. Rembrandt used to visit her there when they were courting.'

The ale and the pleasure were making bubbles in my stomach. 'Have you ever met him?'

Her pupils danced. As she crossed her legs, the soft folds of her skirt brushed against my calf. 'Yes, when I was a little girl hiding under a table. He saw that I was crying because a dog was trying to bite my pancake. So he fended off the dog and danced for me, to make me laugh. I remember his boots, splattered with paint, such tiny feet! He was always kind to children; in fact, he seemed to prefer them. Anyway, I see him and Titus now and again.'

I grinned. 'I'm sure he doesn't dance for many girls. But tell me more about *her*.'

'I'll turn my pockets inside out and show you everything, but first you must promise me something.'

As I waited for her to continue, she took a slow sip of wine as if testing my patience. 'Promise me that you'll let me help you with your work.'

'You said this before, but I'm not sure which work you mean.'

She brushed a wisp of strawberry-blonde hair out of her eye. 'Pieter, don't be coy, I know you have been snooping round about Rembrandt. Aren't you going to write about him?'

'I don't *intend* anything. I simply must know . . .'

'Knowledge is nothing if not put to use,' she said.

I agreed with her to some extent, and was also convinced that she would not divulge any more information unless I consented to her request. 'Very well, I promise.'

She clapped her thighs in triumph.

'You were talking about Saskia,' I prompted.

'Yes, well, let me tell you without too much exposition. Please don't interrupt me. We can discuss the details later.'

I nodded.

She licked her lips and began in a very serious tone. 'Saskia Van Uylenburgh was the youngest of four girls, one of eight children. Her mother, Sjoukje Ozinga, died when she was just seven years old. Her father Rombertus was a burgomaster, and founded Franeker University. He died when she was twelve years old, leaving her most of his estate. Afterwards, she was shuffled between her sisters' homes in Sint-Annaparochie and Franeker. Hiskia was married to Gerrit van Loo, secretary-clerk of the township of Het Bildt. Aeltje was married to Johannes Cornelisz. Sylvius, minister and Predikant of the Oude Kerk.'

I spoke, thinking aloud. 'Rembrandt did a portrait of him, an etching. He's the funny-looking, goat-like man with the long beard.'

Clara narrowed her eyes at me. 'But he provided a godly, sober house for Saskia. Rembrandt courted her there in his parlour. My mother said they liked to talk and play backgammon.'

'Then they got lost in wedded bliss,' I said sarcastically, hoping she would tell me about the wedding.

Ignoring my tone, she scarcely faltered. 'A year later he and Saskia went to register their marriage at the Oude Kerk sacristy, and Sylvius was their witness. They married in Friesland on 22 June, 1634, during the time of haymaking in the meadows. She was twenty-one and he was twenty-eight. When they walked through the door of the church in Het Bildt she was wearing a silk black dress, a white lace collar and cuffs, a crown of flowers and fruit and a string of pearls. My mother said she looked beautiful but frightened. Rembrandt wore a sober black suit with a wide-brimmed hat, and new shoes he had bought especially for the occasion. He had a fluff of hair on his head and a big smile on his face. During the ceremony, he gave her a gold ring to wear on her first finger.'

'Because he was marrying above him,' I added. 'Who were the guests?'

'Hendrick Van Uylenburgh, with whom he lived at the time, his wife Maria, Saskia's three sisters and their husbands – Titia and François even travelled up from Zeeland – and my father and mother.' She paused, shaking her head. 'Would you believe it? None of Rembrandt's family attended.'

'What a shame. Why?'

'I'm not sure,' she replied. 'His father was dead, but apparently his mother Neeltgen was still in good health, and had gone before the notary in Leyden to give consent to the marriage. I suppose he was never very close to his brothers, and felt it unnecessary, because he had become part of another family?'

'Or felt embarrassed by his own, because they were poor.' Then I reasoned to myself aloud. 'No, I don't think so. It was probably too difficult to see his family and then have to say goodbye again, realizing he'd never be able to return. And his new life was so different . . . So, what about the wedding feast then?'

When Clara, who had been sipping her wine, pulled the roemer away from her mouth to speak, a few drops trickled down her chin and dripped on to her skirt. She did not seem in the least embarrassed, and brushed the mess away carelessly as if such things had no importance in her world. This disdain for vanity or what was proper might have bothered me in another woman, but in her it was overwhelmingly agreeable, and I wanted to lie like a dog at her feet.

'I heard it was similar to most Friesland feasts,' she said, 'and took place at Hiskia and Gerrit van Loo's house in Sint-Annaparochie. There were copious amounts of food – piles of sweetmeats, spiced breads, marzipan, pitchers of ale and wine steeped in cloves and ginger. Marigolds everywhere! They stayed at the Van Loos' for at least a week afterwards, because Saskia had to sell her share of local farm property, then they moved into Hendrick's house on the Breestraat.'

'But they didn't stay there for long.'

'Right,' she said excitedly. 'Well, imagine him trying to create paintings amidst all the hubbub – apprentices, painters and etchers working, buyers coming and going – and no offence, but Hendrick's enormous personality, his dutiful wife and six children must have driven them mad. Poor Saskia. No wonder they moved out within a couple of years.'

'Is that when he bought his own house?'

'Not immediately. First they stayed in the Nieuwe Doelenstraat, near the Amstel, then on the island of Vlooienburgh in a sugar refinery, with a view of the river and quays and the countryside.'

'And surrounded by three synagogues. So they moved back to the Breestraat in 1639?'

'Yes, perhaps we can visit there together, if you'd like.'

'I would love to.' Everything around was very quiet, faintly dimpled by the intensity of my attention to her. My eyes wandered over her pale face and her frail frame. 'But you're tired.'

'Yes, I am rather tired and cold.'

I had not noticed before: her shoulders were slightly hunched and quivering. We exchanged a long look, during which I wanted to touch her but did not dare, and prayed that I would not faint. The conversation had slowed and grown thin, not out of a lack of words but because we were comfortable with our thoughts, and any attempt to communicate would be too obvious an attempt at concealment. Besides, the silence said everything. I should have rejoiced in the watchfulness a while longer; instead I became ruffled, timid and hysterical. 'I did not expect to meet you again, and hoped that . . . what I mean is, I'm glad that . . .'

I must have alarmed her, for she snatched the picture away and tucked it into her side-pocket. Lowering her voice and shifting in her seat, she said quickly, 'There is more to discuss, about a scandal between Rembrandt and the members of my family, but we are out of time. I must go now.'

'Wait!' I cried, thinking that she was about to disappear as she had done in the past. Standing up, I banged myself on the table-top. The candle flame flickered, and a thunderbolt of pain ran through my knee. When I looked down, my face flushed with embarrassment: she had not gone but was waiting patiently, her arms crossed and her eyebrows raised. *Every gesture, every action ripples and reflects*, I thought, *and violates an inner secret*. I had never felt more vulnerable.

'There are numerous things we might talk about,' I added, by way of explanation.

'I just said that,' she smirked.

'Oh, but you left too abruptly last time! Tell me where to reach you.' Laying my hand on her shoulder, I imagined the heavy material falling away, exposing a fleshy curve and a jutting bone.

'We'll find each other somehow. Will you fetch my shawl?'

She swatted a fly buzzing around her brown bonnet and got up. I gulped down the rest of my beer and followed her to the door with crushing regret; the back of her head made me homesick for a home I did not know. While I removed her damp shawl from the hook, she spoke: 'Why did you say the night will never end?'

I considered her question, seeking the perfect answer, and once I found it, counted *one, two, three* before turning round to her. She stood with her toes pointing outward, so I took a deep breath and spoke to her closed eyelids: 'Because I had been dreaming of it too vividly for too long.'

When still she did not open her eyes, I moved behind her to drape the shawl over her shoulders. As I bent down my nose hovered near her neck, and there, on that downy slope, I found the vanilla.

Amsterdam, 1635

The Tobacco Wards Off Pestilence

The plague is cleansing us of our sins. In the evening, the coughs and screams are louder than the cooing pigeons and church bells. During the night, all is calm except for the wind blowing. Then I know they have found relief. When I awake, and the first rays of sun peer through the window, I hear the cart's rattle. A man trudges behind it, crying out for the dead. When my neighbours toss their cadavers from the windows, we are plunged into darkness once more. All is vanity and vexation of spirit. This is why I pray incessantly for deliverance and safety. To God we are as scummy dross, the seventy thousand men in Israel. Our bones have become dry and our hope has perished.

The dogs have demons in their fur, so the militiamen are shooting them. Could they be the same creatures in my drawings, curled up and free from harm? Like them, we have no escape. Torches burn on the canals to rid the air of disease, but sometimes that means fire. The poor who reside on the inner alleyways are even more unfortunate, suffocating in the foul vapours. I have stopped eating meat because it is infected, and when I am not rinsing my mouth with vinegar, a pipe is between my lips. A friend of mine, a doctor, says the tobacco wards off pestilence. He smokes three pipes after breakfast alone! Though I am not afraid for myself, I will do anything to protect my dear wife and our unborn child. It must be a son on the way, for

Saskia's belly is swelling as if she had swallowed Jonah. I will love them both with all my soul and leave my disposal to God.

A Shot of Hootch

From the window of my attic workshop, I watch the flowing grey bog of the river Amstel. We live on its west side, the narrow strip that curves north where the boats moor. Lately, cats and pigs rise to the surface. With the help of our Van Uylenburgh cousins, Hendrick and Maria, we have moved our belongings into a house built by Willem Boreel, Pensionary, on the Nieuwe Doelenstraat, number 20. The house is new and large with three floors, split down the middle. Our landlady Maria lives in the other half. Boreel, our neighbour, is an important man to have as an ally. He has ties to pastors, burgomasters, shipping magnates and traders — many who wish to commission paintings from me.

Hendrick and I still collaborate on various projects, but we have drifted apart over conflicting interests. He stifled my ambitions, and most of my time was taken up with his complex operation instead of my own projects. Besides, his house didn't have enough space for two lusty newlyweds. Saskia and I spent the first year of our marriage grinding our teeth about the lack of privacy there. If we had had it our way, we would have spent most hours bouncing on the box-bed! Whenever Hendrick and his wife stepped out, I pulled their niece into dark corners. Isn't that the beauty of first love or love at all, for that matter? When you are most assured not a single being can change you, you surrender and pass into another existence at once. The effect is similar to swallowing a shot of hootch.

Eventually we grew tired of stifling our sighs and screams, so our intimate moments became few and far between. Now I fear we frequently disturb Maria, probably even the wealthy lawyer. How the walls rumble! That doesn't mean I am neglecting my work, which is prospering more than ever before. I have finally become an official member of the Guild of St Luke, and am in the midst of an ongoing project for Prince Frederik Hendrick, a Passion series. As an independent master, nothing can hinder me. Not even the plague. While I am painting, time falls away.

AT AUCTION

Piece by Adrian Brouwer, a pastry cook flipping her hotcakes over an open fire ... 140 g.

Eight sets, Dürer woodcuts on the life of the Virgin ... 224 g.

Liefde Baart Kunst

Love gives birth to art. In her most unguarded moments, when she is dressing, sleeping or sewing, I make intimate studies of Saskia with my pen and dry-point. I dress her in all sorts of beautiful costumes, re-create her as heroines and goddesses. Even Flora herself!

Last summer the burgomaster's daughter became my wife, but in my latest painting she is my whore. I, her husband, have chosen the role of the prodigal son, a dandy in a red doublet. I wear a plumed hat over my long brown curls, a golden sword under my belt. With a tall flute of sparkling wine in one hand, the other holds Saskia's back as her rump rests on my knee. I am cackling with a toothy smile. She glances over her right shoulder, hardly smiling, though her mouth is slightly open. Her coppery hair is styled in the same way as when I first met her — and it still makes me wild — pinned up in curls, revealing the graceful ivory nape of her neck. A peacock pie and a knife rest on the table behind us. In the brothel, we will eat and drink then succumb to our passions and fall asleep. This is me, before marriage and children, the Prodigal Son before his repentance and return.

When Saskia enters my room, she tells me she has been burying onions in the floor to suck up the evil worms. Her eyes are still puffy from sleep, and she looks paler than usual, almost like a child herself. She clutches a rag in her reddened hands. Her gaze roams around the workshop — to me a beautiful array of jars, brushes, pigments, mannequins, costumes, helmets, daggers and drapery; to her a horrible mess. I have been careless of late, restless in art. She has been sick in the mornings and growing plump. It would be better to tuck her into bed then stroke her hair until she falls asleep. But I cannot wait any longer. I must show her the painting.

She looks at it for a minute then sits down, pursing her lips. Sometimes silence is the best applause, but I know she does not understand. A marriage portrait, with her as a strumpet and me as a sinner? She seems afraid to speak. Sometimes I lose my temper with her. There is a hidden demon in all of us; mine is just less capable of hiding. He rushes out at the world quicker than a bee whose nest has been disturbed. When Saskia catches me in a rage, smashing things, she cries for her dead mother. The yearning to please her settles like a weight in my stomach. I want to tell her she is everyone to me, past and future. If we are not these very two lovers then they exist somewhere, like Adam and Eve, Isaac and Rebecca, Boaz and Ruth. Yet I cannot find the words. I hope she will find the truth in my face, which is always a mirror.

I place my hand on her ripened belly and kiss her forehead. She snuggles up to me, nibbling my earlobe. The soft downy hairs on her face brush my cheek. Her hot breath ripples through my whole body. No talking, no illusions, just the warmth of each other's skin. If she keeps this up, I will dive out of myself and into her … I must return to my work … Her hand

*wanders under my shirt and tugs on the hair at the hollow of my back. I
fall over her, burying my beard in her bare neck. My big nose lingers on her
scent — perfume, sweat and vegetables. She is ticklish, and giggles. On her
way out, shaking her arse, she yells over her shoulder, 'I am not your
whore!'*

Belshazzar's Feast, Part I

*Without my vermilion and gold, I could not tell the next story. Every
colour has a distinct quality and a unique essence. While red is a life and
blood pigment, gold is harmonious and perpetual. Red invades the eye and
brings the muscles outward, away from the body. Gold has a fluttering
effect, like a sound which vibrates in a flute. These two colours are essential
to my painting of the biblical drama, Belshazzar's Feast: a lesson in
overindulgence, false worship and God's justice. No narrative is more suited
to my exploding expression because of its visionary possibilities. This is the
cautionary tale.*

*Belshazzar the king of Babylon held a big feast for a thousand of his
grandees, wives and concubines, during which he sat with them eating and
drinking wine until he became intoxicated. Then he ordered his servants to
bring in the vessels of gold and silver that his father Nebuchadnezzar had
taken away from the temple in Jerusalem. After the vessels were carried in,
the people drank while praising the gods of gold, silver, copper, iron, wood
and stone.*

*At that moment, the fingers of a man's hand came forth and began to
write upon the wall of the palace. As the king watched, his complexion
changed and his thoughts began to frighten him. His hip joints loosened and*

his very knees knocked each other. He called out for the conjurors, Chaldeans and astrologers, and when they arrived, he said to these wise men of Babylon: 'Any man that will read this writing and show me its interpretation will be clothed in purple, with a necklace of gold around his neck, and will rule as the third one in the kingdom.'

When the magic-practising priests attempted to interpret the inscription, they could offer no solution. So the king became very frightened. The queen suggested he call in Daniel, whom Nebuchadnezzar had brought out of Judah, and who was able to interpret dreams and untie knots. When Daniel came before the king, he said to him: 'The Most High God gave to Nebuchadnezzar, your father, the kingdom and the greatness and the dignity and the majesty. Yet he killed, struck and humiliated whomever he wanted. His heart became haughty, and so he was brought down from the throne and made to live like a beast, dwelling with the wild asses, eating vegetation like the bulls until he learned that the Most High God is ruler. As for you, his son Belshazzar, you have not humbled your heart, though you knew all this, but against the Lord of the Heavens you have exalted yourself. Your servants brought before you the vessels of your father's house, and you have praised mere gold, silver, copper, iron, wood and stone, which are beholding, hearing and knowing nothing.'

Daniel continued, 'This is interpretation of the words, Mene, Mene, Tekel, Upharsin. Mene: God has numbered the days of your kingdom and has finished it. Tekel: you have been weighed in the balance and found deficient. Upharsin: your kingdom has been divided and given to the Medes and Persians.' At that time, as Belshazzar commanded, Daniel was clothed in purple, with a necklace of gold around his neck, and became the third ruler in the kingdom. However, that very night, Belshazzar the Chaldean king was slain.

INTERLUDE

Someone in the neighbourhood is playing a viol for his own pleasure, and without tuning it. He needs a better teacher!

This Is Mokum

My friend Menasseh Ben Israel is a rabbi who speaks ten languages, fills his life with preaching and writing, and runs a printing press. He opens his mind very sincerely to me, and I gain everything by listening, especially to his insights on the Book of Daniel. A year ago, I peeked through his window to look at his movable type press but saw his face instead. Like a fish behind the bevelled glass! He immediately stopped his work, came outside and snatched me by the ear. But it was just to tease, because then he laughed and invited me in. We have been friends ever since.

Today I am going to his house on the Breestraat, to talk over tea and Turkish figs. This is Mokum, the New Jerusalem, separated from the rest of the city by the Amstel and three canals. My stomach is already growling for the figs, almonds and raisins from Turkey and Cyprus. Alongside the sluggish river, brawny men are unloading timbers and pilings from their barges, stacking them on the wharf. When I give them a wave, they reply with uneasy looks as if they have just seen a ghost. Entering the narrow and deep labyrinth, I see no further than a long, dismal corridor. High up is a crude grey strip of sky. Below is the world of age-old tales and divine myths. All around is the stench of fish, piss and straw. Death stalks me like a shadow, and its silence is terrifying. I hold a handkerchief over my mouth and hurry past the cadaver of a dead horse, lying on its side, covered by a thick cloak of flies ... The wooden houses, stripped and faded, are the homes of the poorer Jews, the Ashkenazim. Who have already escaped the worst, I think. As long as they can worship their God freely, they demand little else from life.

On the corner, a fiddler in a skullcap plays a soulful tune. I drop a few coins into his bowl, plenty to spare. Several groups of men converse in the street. They wear ragged cloaks to the ground, beards to their chests and tall, misshapen hats. I strain my ears to hear, but I cannot understand their ancient language in voices so nasal and uncultured. The men, conversing and waving their hands about, seem oblivious to the whole world struggling around them. They do not even notice me, the intruder. I curse myself for not bringing my sketching tablet, though I am afraid to stop. Then one man's dark eyes drift loose from his friends to catch me sneaking by. My face is strange and unknown to him. He glowers, telling me I do not belong here. A sense of shame overwhelms me, so I avert my eyes. Will he warn the others? My back tightens as I continue walking, waiting for the first stone to be cast. Did he look at me long enough to sense something beyond my pity? Because there is envy too. I fear he only saw the pity. Now all eyes are upon me. Rounding the next corner, I leave their stares and nudges in my wake.

This next street is uneven and littered with hay, crackling beneath my feet. Menasseh brought me here before, to visit the printers, wigmakers and tailors making prayer shawls. This time I move quickly to keep in step with the chickens and goats, as restless as me, expecting a storm. I duck into a tobacco shop, and when I come out with a new pouch, two ragged children snicker at me. They follow me on to the busy Lange Houtsraat, close on my heels, looking for handouts. When I enter the Four Sugarbreads, the two boys loiter on the doorstep as I purchase a cake spiked with cloves and candied ginger for Saskia (oh, to make her smile), and a sweetbread for myself. On my way out, I give each of them a handful of almonds.

Once I reach the synagogue, the Neve Shalom, the houses are larger and fancier, brick with stone trim. The Sephardic Jews are a proud group of people, and resemble aristocrats with their shortly clipped beards, costumes of black velvet, white linen and lace. Menasseh is one of many who, having escaped religious persecution in the Iberian Peninsula, set up in the city as merchants and traders. 'The Lord shall scatter thee among all people, from the one end of the earth even unto the other.' Menasseh's father was tortured on three occasions by the Inquisition before escaping from Lisbon to Madeira, where Menasseh was born. In Amsterdam, son vindicated father. Menasseh became a member of the Hevrah in the Talmud Torah congregation at twelve, a Hebrew scholar at seventeen and a rabbi at twenty. Now he is widely praised for his knowledge of Scripture, famed for his powerful sermons. He leads a comfortable life on the Nieuwe Houtmarkt, and his house smells of rosewater. A mere two years older than me, he is an old sage whom I could not admire more. We are two wheels on the same axle.

The Writing on the Wall

Inside the house, everything shines or flutters with green and blue. The two men sit near the fire in a respectable room not lacking in finery. On the table is a teaset and a notebook. The murmurs of prayers from unseen members of the family filter through the walls. The rabbi perches on his chair, his black leather shoes barely touching the floor. His olive-coloured face appears fatigued, from work or worry. He has a squat nose and woolly beard hanging down to his white starched collar. His fidalgo garb is complete with a black vest and breeches and a floppy brimmed hat.

RVR: *Leaning forward in his chair to take a cup of tea.* Have you been busy lately?

MBI: *Nasal voice rises and dips in a sing-song.* I feel strangled by my work, no exaggeration. Let me tell you how I allocate my time each day. I devote two hours in the temple, six to the school, one and a half to the Pereira's academy, of which I am president, two for proofreading texts, because everything published must pass through my hands and the others are too incompetent, then I also lecture on the Talmud, regularly assist my neighbours in their affairs ... oh, and answer four to six letters per week. Besides, everyone wants to learn Hebrew these days. It is even fashionable for Christians!

RVR: Yes, I was going to request that you tutor me, too ... (*Aside*) Should I offer him some of the spicecake I bought for Saskia? Probably not. Lately she gets very hungry in the afternoons. And she will be happier about me having gone out in the plague-ridden streets if I have something to show for it. Besides, there is still a good chance his servant will bring in the figs.

MBI: How is the Passion series coming along?

RVR: *Face sinks.* As you already know, this project will bring me further commissions and the recognition I deserve, but I am finding it impossible even at the outset.

MBI: There is a proper time for everything. Work on something else until you are ready.

The prayers grow louder in the back room.

RVR: (*Aside*) It must be some kind of performance. If only there were a crack in the wall so I could watch them huddled in their shawls, folding their hands before an array of candles.

MBI: You mentioned you need help in untying a Gordian knot?

RVR: Yes, well, in most paintings of Belshazzar, either the inscription on the wall is in Latin or omitted altogether, which avoids one important question. That is, if the words on the palace wall were clear, why could no one but Daniel decipher it?

MBI: Do you know what you are asking me? I have been thinking about this question and I may have found a possible solution in – *lowers his voice to a whisper* – the Kabbalah.

RVR: *Lowers his voice too.* What is the Kabbalah?

MBI: It's a secret Jewish lore of letters and numbers which explains hidden meanings in the Bible.

RVR: *Claps his thigh excitedly.* Really?

MBI: Shhh. *Glances round the room as if they can be overheard.* Yes, and I think the reason they could not decipher the words was because the letters were written in vertical columns rather than horizontally, from right to left. A trick of the eye, see?

The rabbi opens his notebook and takes up his plume. His hand trembles over the paper, then he pulls back.

RVR: Is something wrong?

The rabbi shakes his head, then lowers his hand to write the esoteric lettering:

```
S  U  T  M M
      e  e    e
I  PH K  N  N
   a     e  e   e
N  R  L
```

RVR: But of course! What would they look like in Hebrew?

He rewrites the characters in his language in a box form.

RVR: Do you mind if I use this for my painting?

MBI: *Nostrils flare.* Not at all. But be forewarned, if someone copies down the words of the Kabbalah, it is said to come true.

RVR: *Twiddling his fingers on his lap.* Well, I'm not frightened.

MBI: *Gazing intensely through bulging, wide-set eyes.* Let me tell you this story. Not long ago, using the lost formulas of the Kabbalah, the Rabbi ben Bezabel made an artificial man to assist him in all the menial tasks of the synagogue. By the power of a magic tablet that the rabbi placed under his tongue, the creature's existence lasted only during the daytime. But one night the rabbi forgot to take the tablet out of the being's mouth, which would render him lifeless, so he escaped and ran into the dark alleys, frightening people, knocking them over. When the rabbi caught up with him, he removed the tablet, and the artificial man fell down. It was then decided that, whenever making such a creature, one should write the word *Emet* on its forehead, meaning Truth. When one wishes to destroy it, he only has to remove the *E*, changing it to *met*, or death.

RVR: I'll keep that in mind. What is the significance of the hand, I wonder?

MBI: *Tugs on his black beard.* In the Scriptures God's Spirit is referred to as his finger.

RVR: Ah, and I always thought it was a nebulous shadow floating overhead.

MBI: Well, the Spirit is that too. At the beginning of time, when it moved upon the face of the waters, I imagine it was like a puff of smoke drifting and eddying in the air.

RVR: Then I must have both, don't you agree? The hand could emerge from a steamy fog or ride in on a dark cloud, and the text will be sinister and glowing . . .

MBI: *Head bobs enthusiastically.* You must show God's almighty power in action. Remember, this is the Holy of Holies who rescued Shadrach, Meshach and Abednego from the fiery furnace! He is formidable, like a lion when he executes judgement.

RVR: *Frowns.* And his anger is blazing against us now.

MBI: Because we have been warned, and yet we keep taking God's precious things and desecrating them. *Pause.* But the plague is not a dream, it resides everywhere, in our tea, our sugary cakes, our books, even in your paintings, Rembrandt. Do not neglect your prayers. God is a refuge for those loving him.

RVR: Sometimes I think this could be the end of the world.

MBI: Soon — *slurps his tea* — not yet. According to Nebuchadnezzar's dream, the Messiah is coming to end the long travail of my people. But before he does, we will be thoroughly dispersed from one end of the earth to the other.

RVR: How do you know they are not?

MBI: News has reached us that a traveller, Aaron Levi de Montezinos, found the ten lost tribes of Israel in Ecuador, but that's only one end of the earth. The other end is England, from which we were expelled in 1290, and we must first re-establish a community there.

RVR: England? *Laughs in disbelief.* My old friend Jan Lievens is in England. Ha, so he's at one end of the earth . . .

MBI: By the way, who will play the role of Belshazzar?

RVR: *A smile creeps across his cheeks.* Your friend, Isaac.

MBI: *Looks up, as if seeking Isaac's face in the air.* He was wonderful as the turbaned Turk in your painting of St John. Oh, and the formidable Persian King Cyrus, I nearly forgot! That was his best role.

RVR: I would use him in every painting if I could. Even I grow humble before him, and I'm the proudest man in Jerusalem!

MBI: *Chuckles.* Especially in red and gold, those are his colours.

RVR: Did you know that toads, living deep underground, grow lumps of gold inside their heads?

MBI: No, but I can tell you how to make edible gold, which cures all diseases of the lungs and heart.

RVR: Really? How?

MBI: When blue vitriol is mixed with tin powder it becomes the most beautiful yellow water in the world. Then you leave it overnight, and in the morning, pour it over gold leaves along with a very fine brandy. If heated long enough it will become an oil that can be taken internally, and will prolong your life.

RVR: Will it ward off the plague?

MBI: Drink melted mercury, but remember, some poison themselves in fear of the infection.

RVR: Is it a symptom of melancholy to be afraid of death yet sometimes desire it?

MBI: No, Rembrandt, it is a symptom of being a man.

Belshazzar's Feast, Part II

The gold shines on Belshazzar's ornate cloak, speckled crown, bejewelled necklace and crescent-moon earring. It even shines on the vessels and the banqueting plate. The room is full of other precious metals which behold, hear and know nothing. My vermilion brightens the onyx and rubies on the king's chains and brooches; it radiates on the plumed women all around. On Belshazzar's head, the turban glows like a pearl in the light.

The king cranes to look over his left shoulder. Having just watched the hand emerge from a sleeve of billowing grey clouds, his fatty throat compresses in shock. His eyes bulge from their sockets as they fix on the glowing text. The yellow letters I painted just as Menasseh showed me, in vertical lines from right to left. Though I have remembered his words of warning: the hand's third finger pauses in mid-air before writing the final letter, sealing the fate of the king. No wonder Belshazzar's hip joints have loosened, his very knees knock each other!

As the king stretches out his left arm to shield himself, his body jolts backwards and he knocks over a vessel of wine with his other arm. The woman behind him does not notice the stream pouring over her lap. She expresses horror in her widened eyes, her hands clasped in fear. The grey-bearded man beside her has thrust forward his chin, opening his mouth wide to expose his bottom teeth, rotted from overindulgence. Only the courtesan at the far left is aloof, sitting still in the bright light with her plumed hat and pearl necklace. The fourth woman shrinks back from the king's massive arm, and her golden pitcher of wine spills in a cascade, the same colour as her deep red gown. She leans so far back from the vision that the shadows creep across her shoulders and neck.

There is another person here, whom I nearly forgot: the woman in the far background, holding a recorder to her pursed lips and gazing at the viewer. She is saying to the people of Amsterdam, 'Watch out, the Lord's judgement is upon you'. Everyone else leans outward, so they might topple off the canvas, but they have no means of escape. Just as we, the people of Amsterdam, are suffocating in the foul vapours. God shall cover me and in Him I shall trust. May His wrath be merciful.

The Utmost Forethought

My pigments retain their body as if they were painted yesterday! I alternate the application of the most opaque tones wih the finest glazes applied with my fingers, the ball of my hand, or with a rag. And not merely once: the great Titian testified to using thirty or forty glazes ('Svelature, trenta o quaranta!'). Into these glazes, I set strong accents of light and shadow to avoid flatness in the final character of the painting. These touches must be spontaneous and quick. I set the colours into, not over each other, wet in wet, so the undertone always exercises its effect throughout the whole picture. My pictures are not produced hastily. They are always done with the utmost forethought on every possibility.

My Workshop a Theatre, the Floorboards a Stage

Several of my students cannot attend class today. Contagion has struck their families, or they live in restricted areas. I am teaching the others how to act. A good drama will keep their minds occupied. Each Thursday we have a full session. In the morning I give a lesson on drawing or painting, in the afternoon a brief lecture. 'Brief' means that it lasts either the duration of one sentence or as long as my wits wander, up to two hours, depending on my mood. Preparation is not my forte, but that makes for excitement. And I spare no expense, especially when it involves performance.

... Here I go, scrambling through my kunstcaemer, pulling out costumes, wigs, beards, headdresses, jewellery, face powder...

We are staging a narrative, something I like to do if my students are finding it difficult to draw with reality and emotion. I have chosen the account in Genesis, when three visitors inform Abraham and Sarah they are going to have a son. We will experiment with the scene by enacting it in various ways, making alterations as we go along. The painter is freer than the writer because he can start wherever he pleases, at the beginning, middle or end of the story. The writer is doomed to work in a straight line, from the ground up.

My students come from many different towns and countries because my manner is so praised. Now that Lastman has passed away, I am the best art teacher in the land. That is why I charge my pupils 100 guilders per year excluding room and board, while other painters charge twenty to twenty-five. Now that Govert Flinck is gone — a formidable talent but a disagreeable man — I have two promising apprentices: Ferdinand Bol and Jan Victors. Bol is nineteen years old, a doctor's son from Dordrecht, who shows great skill in portraiture though he is a chameleon painter, changing his colours for whoever strikes his fancy. Victors is sixteen years old, a poor tailor's son from Amsterdam, who shows talent in painting rural scenes but is rather conservative for his young age. As an orthodox Calvinist he follows the instruction in the Ten Commandments never to depict God the Father. He does not represent Christ or the angels, either. What else remains? His career is doomed! Still, just for him, my angels have put on wings — because if we adhered to the true biblical record, Victors would have to render God as a man, and he refuses to do so. These are the sorts of petty things my students demand from me.

The three angels gather round a table, covered with a blue and orange carpet and a white tablecloth, set in front of a door (the entrance of Abraham's tent). At the head of the table sits the dashing copper-curled Bol, draped in a white silk costume enhanced by gold embroidery. The Almighty himself! Victors stands to his left, a slight, dark-haired man with pointy features and a serene face, which matches his white costume. He does not have a big speaking part and possesses a clear voice, so I appoint him as narrator. A fair-haired little boy angel, played by one of my younger apprentices, Otto, wears a pair of downy blue feathers on his back. Near the open door, but partially concealed in the darkness, is one of my female models named Marijke, representing Sarah. Abraham, played by faithful old Frans — recruited from the street long ago — waits to one side, ready to take *his place at the table. In a fur-lined robe with gold clasps, he looks a hundred years old with his shrivelled face and scraggly grey beard.*

Some windows are shut, others open, to let in the proper amount of light. I pay particular attention to the deportment and gestures of the figures and to the direction from which they are seen. I might ask my players to move a little to the left or come forward or stand still. Who should be in shadow and who in light? Who should command the eye's attention? My adjustments to the props include positioning three mirrors around the room. Now the students can watch themselves as they read from the text and act out their roles. Meanwhile, I will circle round my apprentices, my players, listening and correcting.

RVR: *Shouting.* Now, begin!

NARRATOR (*Victors*): God appeared to Abraham among the big trees of Mamre, while he was sitting at the entrance of the tent in the heat of the day . . .

RVR: Fan your face, Frans!

NARRATOR (*Victors*): When he raised his eyes, he saw three men standing some distance from him. He ran to meet them and bowed to the earth. Then he said:

ABRAHAM (*Frans*): *Stops fanning his face, walks swiftly across the workshop and bows to the men.* If I have found favour in your eyes, please do not pass by your servant. Let a little water be taken, please, and have your feet washed. Recline under the tree and let me get a piece of bread to refresh your hearts. Then you can pass on.

ANGELS (*Bol, Victors, Otto*): *In unison.* You may do just as you have spoken.

RVR: You seem stiff, angels. Work on your harmony.

NARRATOR (*Victors*): Abraham went hurrying to the tent to find Sarah, and said to her:

ABRAHAM (*Frans*): *Scurries back to the door, where Sarah lingers:* Hurry! Get some fine flour, knead the dough and make round cakes!

SARAH (*Marijke*): *Eyes widen.* Yes, master.

RVR: Excellent, Frans. You sound very eager, breathless.

ABRAHAM (*Frans*): I am breathless.

RVR: Stay in character!

NARRATOR (*Victors*): Next, Abraham ran to the herd and got a tender young bull for his attendant, who rushed off to prepare it . . .

ABRAHAM (*Frans*): *Glances about desperately.* Where is the herd?

RVR: That line is not in the text, Frans.

A peal of laughter runs through the group. God (Bol) doubles over, clutching his stomach. He can barely contain himself, and causes the others to laugh louder. The teacher claps his hands to maintain order.

ABRAHAM (*Frans*): Seriously, though, where is the herd?

RVR: Pretend it's there. Let's move on.

NARRATOR (*Victors*): *Suppresses a giggle.* Then Abraham took the butter and milk and set it before the men.

ABRAHAM (*Frans*): *Takes a silver platter with meat and bread from Sarah's hands, and places it on the table, then sits down.* Please, eat.

Two Angels (Otto and Victors) take their seats, one (Bol) remains standing.

ANGELS: *In unison.* Where is Sarah your wife?

ABRAHAM (*Frans*): *Points towards the rear wall.* Here, in the tent.

RVR: When you say this, Frans, peer over your shoulder and look frantic.

NARRATOR (*Victors*): Sarah was listening at the tent entrance, which was behind the man, when the angel said:

GOD: (*Bol*): *In a monotone.* I am surely going to return next year at this time, and look, Sarah your wife will have a son.

RVR: (*Aside*) What? Bol thinks this an acceptable delivery, for such a crucial moment? *Walks over to the angel and thrusts a nose in his face.* (*To Bol*) Is that supposed to be the voice of God, speaking that? Where is the power and emotion? Pretend I am the other person and repeat it to me.

GOD: (*Bol*): *Throwing his arms in the air.* I am SURELY going to return next year at this time. And look! Sarah, your beautiful wife, will have a SON!

RVR: Better.

NARRATOR (*Victors*): Abraham and Sarah were old, being advanced in years, and Sarah had stopped having a flow of blood.

ABRAHAM (*Frans*): *Tenderly places a hand on his wife's shoulder.*

RVR: Wonderful improvisation, Frans.

NARRATOR (*Victors*): Hence, she began to laugh inside herself, saying . . .

SARAH (*Marijke*): *Not laughing.* After I am worn out, shall I really have pleasure, my lord, being old besides?

RVR: Touch your face and the wrinkles there.

GOD: (*Bol*): Why was it that Sarah laughed? Is anything too extraordinary for Jehovah? At the appointed time I shall return to you, next year, and Sarah will have a son.

SARAH (*Marijke*): I did not laugh!

GOD: (*Bol*): Nay, but thou didst laugh.

RVR: Nay, but thou DIDST laugh!

GOD: (*Bol*): She did not laugh. I didn't hear her, anyway. If she doesn't do her part, I cannot do mine.

RVR: *Shouts.* Not aloud, Bol, that's the point, you ass! Now read the last line, Victors.

NARRATOR (*Victors*): And so, just as God said, at the appointed time the following year, the child was born and appropriately named Isaac, meaning Laughter.

RVR: Very good. Now I want you to do it again, this time

without interruption or prompting. But I am going to move you around first.

The students sigh and groan, but after a little prodding they start to shuffle around the room, resituating themselves to their teacher's direction.

BOL: *Dashes back and forth across the workshop, flapping his wings.* Where's the herd, Frans? Where's the herd?

Eventually we get it right, or nearly. In the end, Victors's drawing is best; he demonstrates his great ability by giving the angels' wings the quality of a still life. Yet I am trying to discourage him from sticking to a fixed repertoire of figures that turn up repeatedly in his paintings. He confuses inner tension with affected, statuesque poses, so his characters are not convincing. With a little more acting practice, his scenes will seem less like judicial hearings. Bol is once again unimaginative; he copies exactly what he sees. While his figures are beautifully rendered, they do not have a sense of mystery. I lean over his shoulder, seize his chalk, and make a few lines to demonstrate the difference between a good drawing and an excellent one. What I tell him, is:

— I sense no spirituality here, apart from the presence of the wings. Imagine how you would feel if, today, you were visited by the Lord. Could you know him in a crowd, if you were face to face? What sort of faith would you have? Would you trust his word? Use your powers of creativity! See the roll on the table? What if it were not an entire loaf, but partially eaten? Explore all the possibilities!

Then we disassemble our theatre and the students assume their places for my lecture — perched on chairs, propped against the wall or sitting on the floor. As in every school around the world, the intelligent ones take notes; the mediocre pay attention but foolishly think they will remember what is said; the ignorant fill their heads with lusty dreams. Half-seated on my worktable, I do not speak from a prepared script. I like to expound and use my hands for emphasis or demonstration. The following is an excerpt of a speech that emerges from my mouth even better than I imagined it upon waking:

— I, in opposition to many painters, challenge the correctness of the tradition that light passages advance and dark ones recede. I say, this is a blindness that is still profound to this day! Do light passages ALWAYS advance and dark ones ALWAYS recede? Consider the sun, which is very bright though it is not seen as being near at hand. Think of the fish swimming in a clear stream. The ones that are closer to the surface of the water appear darker than those at the bottom. Also, it has long been known that a landscape takes on an increasingly lighter hue as it recedes into the distance, and that more distant shadows are lighter in tone than those nearby.

— If one renders a blue sky with clouds on a piece of blue paper, one never loses the impression that the paper is very close to the eye, while the sky itself is infinitely distant. Your piece of paper, however smooth it may appear, has a certain perceptible roughness into which the eye can stare, wherever you choose, which is not possible in the blue of the heavens. The coarse surface of a paper gives the eye something to fasten on, where it can focus, making it appear substantial, perceptible and close at hand. I maintain that it is not lightness or darkness, but perceptibility alone which makes objects seem near or far. Coarseness makes them advance while smoothness makes them withdraw.

— So, in practice, you should paint that which is receded more neatly and purely, and that which is in the foreground, roughly and briskly. This is where daubing comes in ... Remember what I taught you last time, that you should richly differentiate your use of paint to create spatial effects. I

repeat, not one colour will make your work seem to advance or recede, but the perceptibility or imperceptibility of the parts alone.

When I finish speaking, the boys look at me for the signal to leave. This is their signal, my final bow. I bend at the waist like an actor on the stage, one foot sliding backward, my hand rolling through the air. The young ones scoot by me, heads lowered, afraid to meet my eyes. The older ones move slowly, waiting to catch my attention, and nod appreciatively. Bol claps me on the back and smiles. He is always the most splenetic while I am teaching, but in the end, shows me the utmost admiration and respect. After the last inferior trickles out, the sound of Saskia's humming wafts through the corridor.

Sleeping Saskia

In the darkness of our chamber, Saskia is lying in bed, hair spread over the pillow. I hold a lantern in my hand and my breath in my throat, listening to the sounds of her body. Her breathing drops and falls, gurgling through her nostrils. I wonder what place she visits in her dreams and wish I could go there with her. Oh Lord, I cannot sleep lately. These nights I am a phantom, lurking in the coloured dusk of my rooms. The house preserves the same solemn silence as in my paintings while the echoed cries of the dying grow louder and deeper.

My girl looks so peaceful I almost do not recognize her, free of her daytime worries. Careful not to rouse her, I approach the bed and begin tracing her face with my fingers. I lightly sketch her heavy eyelids, her snub nose and her Cupid's-bow lips. My thumb gently presses the dimple on her chin. I sink a finger between her breasts and follow the trail of longing. Shhhh, sleep on my darling. If I could crawl inside her open mouth and inhabit her breath, I would truly make her mine. As if sensing my desire, *her legs shift under the sheets. She blurts out a word, an underwater babbling. Is she talking to me? I murmur her name, 'Saskia', half-hoping she will awake so we can make love like cats. After she emits a sigh, her head drops against her shoulder. She gives a little snore.*

Through the long-suffering night I watch over her, while sitting in the bedside chair where she usually does her darning. In spite of all the sleep weighing me down, and the profound need to piss, I do neither. Shafts of cold air seep through the floor and into the holes of my stockings. My pipe glows in the darkness. Sunk in the cushion, Saskia resembles a polar bear with her growing belly, where my child is keeping her warm. It must be a boy! As the forces of nature prepare him to come out, I am beginning to feel like a father. I have already arrived at who I am; what will he be like? Will he have this broad, bulbous nose? These wild black eyes? This dishevelled mane, proud mouth and wispy beard? I pray that he inherits his mother's beauty and her divine kindness.

How I Learned to Use My Eyes

I wish I could remember who I was as a child. My past is still there like the hum of the sea inside my shells, distant and strange. I do not know whether it is relief or misfortune, only that I have not returned home since leaving four years ago. Though I faithfully write letters to my mother in Leyden, I can hardly imagine revisiting my former surroundings. That one-day walk would seem like a trip to the other side of the world. I feel like a beggar waiting outside a closed door, but I prefer it that way. Here, I can forget my old self and take on various guises, repaint my past on a whim. Besides, I do not need to see the sunset in Leyden to conjure it. My imagination is more vivid than my senses themselves. Here it is . . . a muted orange glow fading into yellow beyond father's windmill. The rosy tint of the sky gleams on the long green fields running down the Rijn.

One memory stands out unlike the rest — the days when I learnt to use my eyes. Because my right eye was slightly weak, I tried to make it stronger by pushing it to the limit. My gaze could be quick or slow, depending on what was in front of me. In my room, I tried to understand the spaces between objects. When I closed one eye then the other, the vase, pitcher or bed-warmer would start out over here and end up over there! When I looked at a table or a chair, I plunged myself into it and lived there for a while. I examined all lines and shapes, trying to discern which ones harmonized or disagreed. In time, my pupils were as keen as a falcon's. After spinning myself round, or turning somersaults, I would stop abruptly so the earth rocked beneath me. My arms swooped in the air. The ceiling became the wall and the wall became the floor. Our spaniel Hagar took flight around the room, barking madly! Though Mother warned me against it, I would stare at the sun until my eyes boiled. Then I'd turn away and watch the light spiralling in front of me. I especially liked the shadows crawling across the walls in a candlelit room. Sometimes I watched them, at other times I chased them. My hands, held up to the lantern, created creatures of all shapes and sizes — a swallow, a goat, a woodcock.

My gaze was long and languid when I spied people through dimpled windowpanes, observing their distorted movements. At first they were simply tall or short, fat or thin, young or old, but then I began to see them as weak or cowardly, pompous or humble, faithful or deceptive. There was a feeling behind every face, secret and mysterious. Each told a story worth as much as the other. I fell in love with their differences.

In the dark with my eyes closed, or wrapped in a scarf, I tried to acquaint myself with that strange affliction called blindness, which I read about but never witnessed first-hand. How did it feel to be Polyphemus,

Tiresias, Timoleon, Tobit or Samson? What did they see or not see? Was it any different from Oedipus, who blinded himself with his own nails? If only I knew my father would be stricken blind in his old age, never to recover his sight. For him, it was death. For me, it was a game.

All of the world was blackness as the air closed around me. I had no idea of space though I was in my own living room. Where did it end or begin? Sounds became crisper: the swish, swish of Mother's broom on the floorboards; the rustle of a cockroach in the corner; the chilling slice of Miken's knife in the kitchen. Smells became more pungent: sweet tulips in a vase, crackled wheat on the underside of father's shoes, burning peat in the hearth. There was no warning for voices, touches, movement. Things came out of nowhere, then disappeared again. So I learnt to trust my hands, which followed the grainy surfaces of our tables and chairs, skipped over the cracks on the walls, fingered the thick woven draperies. I lived inside my mind, recalling the wan yellow light that peeped through the panes in the afternoon and settled on mother's tattered red shawl. There was a violet halo round her white hair, brightening the blue Delft tiles of the hearth beside her. This is how I paint now, by shutting out the world and remembering. I am all eye. Still, the terror of blindness lingers. I never forget my father. Do you hear me, Father? I never forget you.

The hours I spent staring at my reflection! When my face wasn't rippling in the canals, it was creeping across Mother's silver dishes and beakers. Even the wan moon echoed my image. What did it see? Who existed before me? Though I seemed handsome from certain angles, my cheeks were too round and my nose never seemed to stop growing. When Father bought me a mirror, another mystery presented itself. The glass followed, watched and mimicked my every movement like a shadow. Yet my reaction to what I was seeing changed what I was seeing. It was impossible to catch my living glance.

Later I began presenting myself for the glass as if playing a role —
moving, miming and speaking. In my Latin school, I was learning pronun-
ciation, impersonation, including dramatic monologues, and visible eloquence.
I was so fascinated with performance that my dream was to be a director of
a theatre group. I followed the players from England and France every time
they visited our city, watching them perform: *The Trajedy of Samson*, *The
Life of Joseph*, *Esther*. But the best of all was *Aran and Titus*. One of the
characters collapsed on stage with blood pouring from a bladder concealed
under his jacket! Meanwhile, my room was my theatre. I could become
anyone I liked by changing my appearance and style of dress.

And so I came to love my own beauty, like Narcissus, who ignored all
other hearts around him. 'He thinks it to be a body, what is only a shadow'.
Perhaps, in death, I too will become a yellow flower with white petals, a
fugitive essence. When a copper pheasant cries for its mate, it is consoled if
one puts a mirror before it. What a beautiful thought. Porphyrus said that
God himself, who cannot be seen by either body or soul, allows Himself to
be seen in a mirror. Why? This has always puzzled me. The Almighty
has no need to situate Himself while a man does.

'Bene vixit, bene qui latuit'

It was really a matter of Fate that I found Clara again, an uneventful week after we had met in the tavern that afternoon, days of intense agony during which I tried to immerse myself in work while remembering vividly all the things that had passed between us. I happened to be strolling through the market on my way back from the dye factory, where my father had sent me to negotiate a new deal, and disgusted with myself for having mangled the transaction, sought comfort in the red cabbages from Muiden, the orange carrots from Hoorn, the green sprouts from Naarden. The sun was shining, and what remained of the snow sparkled against the blue sky as I passed tables and crates laden with butter, cheese, milk, eggs, chickens, ducks and fish. When I reached the meat section, I succumbed to purchasing a sausage – encased with flesh, offal and blood – then stopped to admire a gigantic wheel of cheese being chased over the bricks by a grubby boy, and him, by a swarm of flies.

That was when I glimpsed her, or the woman I thought to be her, a few yards away amidst the red-rind discs and cumin-studded spheres, speaking with a bushy man in a grimy apron. I did not peer more closely, assuming that this vision was another disorderly fallacy of my imagination, and I told myself: *The understanding of a wise man will not be deceived by these fancies.* Then a dog began barking in her vicinity, which meant I was forced to look in that direction – anyone would – and when I did, there was Clara de Geest habited in a dress the shade of poppy-juice. The effect was unspeakable: my knees became wobbly and my palms sweaty; the sausage slipped out of my hand and skidded across the slushy snow. She did not notice me, for she was tasting a piece of green cheese, the kind coloured with sheep's dung, head bent forward to reveal her supple nape. Rebellious strawberry-blonde curls sprung from her bonnet while the seagulls swooped above her, flapping their wings in a fit of greed.

As I bent down to recapture my sausage, the stray cats were already poised to attack it. I shooed them away then remained squatting, deciding how to approach her. Nothing graceful came to mind; instead, I imagined facing her and spurting out a string of incomprehensible sentences, or even worse, being struck with dumbness. When Clara turned away from the cheese counter and began walking in my direction, I ducked behind a cart of stinking fodder, but she looked straight ahead without slowing down. With her nose in the air, she reminded me of a cockerel. As easy as that, my next opportunity presented itself: here was Fate allowing me to to see her in truth, stripped of any airs. So I sneaked into the crowd and began to trail her, keeping close to the stalls for cover. My great height allowed me to peer over the sea of heads, but I dared not stop as she kept up a good pace, slithering and darting like a charmed snake. I nudged myself through elbows and shoulders to catch up with her, and after a long succession of nudges, broke through the congestion, leaving the market's hissing vapours behind. Where was Clara? A few paces ahead of me, and no one was between us.

She was ogling a magpie hopping next to her along the stones, poking at the slivers of straw stuck in the crevices. I swung round and scratched my head in a pathetic attempt to appear lost. After counting to ten, I craned my neck to peep at her. Thank the Lord, she was already carrying on, because I could not afford to make that mistake again. With her mules pointed slightly outwards, she scooted over the cobblestones as if she might take flight, and the breeze picked up, ballooning her skirt. I glimpsed a bit of her stockinged calf when she turned on to a narrow lane. Where was she headed? The Westerkerk's spire taunted us from above the red rooftops, making my skin itch. Could she be going to church? My father had forced me to attend every week when I was a boy – we had a reserved pew – but horses could not drag me back, not even a beautiful woman. She was two blocks ahead, a tiny mouse scooting round another corner. I broke into a run, but rounding the bend, I crashed right into her for she had slowed to a stroll.

After straightening herself up, she swivelled round, gripping her skirt with both hands. Her face was bright red and her lips hung in disgust. She lunged forward as if she were going to strangle me, but her tiny stature made it impossible, so she waved her arms in the air instead.

'Why are you following me?' she spat.

I shook my head, spinning from the crash. 'I'm sorry.'

'I want an answer.'

I sputtered, 'To see you. I like you.'

She gave a hoarse little cry, showing off her large teeth. 'What a ridiculous way to show it!'

'Fine, I'll go.'

As I stepped back, she grabbed my arm. Her dark green eyes

sparkled in the sunshine, and the arched brows above them were very fine, sketched with a crayon. She was even more beautiful and fiery than I had remembered. 'You're not going anywhere, Pieter Blaeu.' Her voice softened. 'Actually, I'm glad you found me. Tonight is a dinner celebration for Titus van Rijn and his soon-to-be bride, Magdalena van Loo. Rembrandt will probably be there. If you're lucky, you may accompany me.'

My chin dropped to the ground and wonderful visions arose before my eyes. 'I may? Do you mean it?' When she batted her eyelashes at me, I hated myself for every action I had taken until then and for the weak pucker on my chin. Why wasn't I blessed with a sanguine humour? 'I'd be honoured,' I added.

'Then go home and change into a proper suit. Meet me at the Gilded Scales at six o'clock. Be punctual.'

'Should I not escort you?'

'It's better this way. I'll explain later.'

Thus she spoke: and at once from his sight, like a wisp of smoke thinned into air, was gone. Wildly he grasped at shadows, wanting to say much more . . .

Alone in the street, I looked down at my crumpled suit: it was time to have my yearly bath – a gruelling chore and my last desire, which just proved how much I wanted to please her.

I knew about the Van Loos only from peripheral observation. Magdalena was the niece of Saskia's older sister, Hiskia, and Gerrit van Loo, making her Titus's distant relative; they had known each other since childhood. Her father, Jan van Loo, had been a successful silversmith, and her mother, Anna Huijbrechts, was descended from an old goldsmiths' family in Bruges. Jan died when Magdalena was young, leaving her mother to care for nine children in their substantial house on the Singel, opposite the Apple Market and famously known as the Gilded Scales for the ornament of a herring boat on its facade.

That evening, I arrived as the bells of the Nieuwe Kerk rang six times, feeling especially agreeable in my new skin. My jacket and breeches, usually clinging to my body, settled around me softly; I actually thought Clara would find me attractive. Torches blazed outside the house, leaving a silvery glow on its fish scales as I stood at the bottom of the stairs and gazed up at the entranceway. There was no sign of her, but it was still early, and if our last meeting was any indication she was likely to arrive late. When the maidservant appeared on the stoop, I shouted up to her, 'Has Clara de Geest arrived?'

'No, I don't think so, sir.'

'Then I would like to wait for her.'

She winked at me, and hands folded across her waist, stepped back inside. As a bitter wind whistled through the trees, I leant against the red bricks and swigged the gin in my flask. With the fires dancing above my head, the red flames rising and falling, I could hardly see down the long, gloomy corridor. The shadows embraced the neighbouring houses and the canal lay sluggishly still, as if hiding something in the slow twilight. Then, in the distance, I saw a little lantern coasting above the ground. The dot of light flitted along the deserted street like a firefly, growing larger as it advanced, but I could not be sure that anyone other than a ghost was accompanying it. When I strained my ears I heard the echo of footsteps, slow and scraping. Shielding my eyes, I peered into the endless and uninviting fog. The lantern, obviously extinguished, left a haze of desolate emptiness.

'Who's there?'

No one answered.

'Who's there?' I asked again.

This time, a low gurgle broke the silence and a nebulous figure dragged itself before me. The torchlights from the house cast his face in wan, livid hues, deepening the pits of his cheeks, the crags on his nose, but I knew him immediately: Rembrandt.

I jumped back. 'You scared me!'

'To live well, you must live unseen,' he said.

We stood close like two frightened boys, and his eyes sank almost out of sight but examined me with a vacant air of listening. I was not sure if I should re-introduce myself because he seemed to know me. Then again, I could never be sure.

'It's Pieter Blaeu,' I said, nodding.

'I know who you are.' He swaggered backwards and forwards in a maelstrom of alcohol or tiredness, I could not be sure, until I gulped a puff of his dingy breath and decided on the former.

'Are you sure you want to go in, Master van Rijn?'

He flung one arm before his face, his voice rough and crude. 'Of course! Don't be ridiculous!'

His protest suggested he was afraid, but of what? Perhaps of the Fate that awaited him inside: old friends, some loyal, some disloyal, all with judgements, not to mention his son's future. I wanted to reassure him, but on seeing his stubborn scowl I was confident he would not welcome an encouraging word, especially from a near-stranger. Perhaps there was another way to show him I cared? This was the great hope I was clinging to when I took his arm and uttered with a big smile: 'Then let's have a drink and celebrate.'

We announced ourselves to the servant though there was no

need, and when she offered to take our coats, I handed mine over, but Rembrandt carried on down the hallway in his own woollen cloak — its collar and sleeves frayed — as if he had not heard her. After I met him in the doorway of the dining room, we stood side by side, taking in the lively scene and listening to the hubbub of laughter and the rustling of silks. The table was lit up with flickering tapers and glistening silver dishes, festooned with red tulips and spread with a banquet of exquisite foods. The dozen or more guests engaged in lively banter — the men in black satin, the women in bright fabrics and gemstones — and around them the noble works of art stood out against the yellow‑papered walls, making strong contrasts with the embroidered blue carpets laid about the floor. On the back wall, a fire blazed in the hearth, whose large chimneypiece had solid marbled columns, and above it, a gilded mirror revealed in its reflection a woman standing before a virginal, tapping out her high notes. The jolly music and fumes of wine put me in a *gaieté de cœur* — only occasionally was I seized by affability, and it was usually the result of such sensual surroundings. When Rembrandt began fidgeting inside his pockets, I motioned to the sideboard which held a sumptuous display of cheeses, figs and almonds, but as we made our way to the corner all gleaming eyes followed us: he could not avoid the attention even now, twenty years past his prime.

Many of the guests I did not know, and assumed they were either the Van Uylenburghs or the Van Loos, but the few I recognized made me feel as if I had stepped into a gallery of portraits. Standing near the hearth, the stout Jeremias de Decker sucked on a clay pipe, filling the room with fumes. He was a famous poet and an old friend of Rembrandt's; he had often flattered him in his poems, admiring his ability to 'bring the dead so well to life'. Speaking with him was a silvery fox called Abraham Francen, the apothecary, who lived in the same district as Rembrandt and acted as his attorney through the financial troubles. He held out a long-stemmed glass, an orange peel hanging over its rim, as the servant boy poured him some wine from a pitcher in a long stream. Meanwhile, Harmen Becker, a dealer in jewels and textiles whose swarthy skin matched his nature, was charming a very young girl who clearly found him repulsive, cowering into her rollmop.

Titus was seated at the head of the table with an air of self-assurance, his long coppery hair cascading over the shoulders of his red velvet coat, which was accented by a white cravat. On his right was a dark-haired woman in a satiny indigo dress, whom I presumed to be Magdalena because she was smiling like a child who has just been given a new toy. Seated next to her was an old woman who must have been her mother, Anna, possessing the same severe chin and flaunting a scintillating brooch. Most importantly, there was my lovely Clara, whose beauty was enhanced by the light-green dress that accentuated her eyes, the yellow ribbons that adorned her curly hair. Had she come alone? What was she doing here already? Had she intentionally told me the wrong time, so that I would meet Rembrandt outside? When I looked to my companion for reassurance, he gave me a sidelong leer, then excused himself to say hello to Abraham Francen. I had failed already, for I had not even poured him the drink I had promised.

Not knowing what to do with myself, I decided to approach Clara, following Rembrandt's trail through a group of children who were leaping over candles placed on the floor, then another group playing a game with empty oyster shells. Upon seeing me, she waved me to her side. My hand sought hers – a tiny, pale, ungloved hand – and when she clasped it, I could not believe how natural it felt, palm on palm, our fingers equally bony. At that moment, everyone else in the room faded away and all that remained was the image of her, gazing at me ardently like a wood nymph.

She released my hand. 'You're here.'

'I would never miss such a blessed occasion,' I said teasingly, and entranced by the freckles on the bridge of her nose, instantly forgave her for leaving me outside.

'Really? I hate weddings and engagements.'

'You do? Why?'

'It is better to go to the house of mourning than to the house of feasting,' she said soberly.

'Is it?' I asked, but she turned her head to gaze at Rembrandt who, having arrived at the table and taken a seat on Titus's left side, was reaching for a glass of wine. Titus was running his fingers caressingly over the lapel of his jacket, and when he noticed that we were looking, fiddled with his little moustache. Because I did not glance away, he stood up and offered his hand.

'How nice of you to join us, Pieter. You know my cousin Clara?'

'Yes, but not very well,' I replied, inching away from her out of embarrassment. 'Congratulations on your engagement.'

'That's very kind of you. Well, won't you take a seat?' He gestured to the vacant chair between Rembrandt and Clara, then spoke in my ear: 'I hope you don't mind watching over my father. I think he is slightly . . . tipsy.'

If I had been nervous before this, I certainly was as I sat down, feeling the warmth of my two favourite people on each side of me and the weight of heavy responsibility on my shoulders. Rembrandt was gloating over his roemer, one elbow propped on the table, his cheek nestled against an open hand. I had the feeling that he was musing *de vanitate mundi et fuga saeculi*: on the vanity of the world and the swift, frightful passing of time. The bowl of potatoes in front of him steamed with a thick vapour.

'Titus is about to propose a toast,' Clara told me before resuming a discussion with her neighbour.

I had no choice but to renew my conversation with Rembrandt, for his son did not appear ready to give his speech, planting kisses on Magdalena. I nudged him. 'What did you mean earlier when you said, you must live unseen?'

'Why do you ask such things?'

'Well, it's an odd expression for someone who paints so many self-portraits.'

'Ah, you make a grave mistake,' he said, raising a finger. 'Why should you think that my pictures are me? They may resemble me in different airs and attitudes, but not one or all of them can ever reveal how I would think, speak or act on any occasion of life.'

With that, Titus lifted his glass and cleared his throat – 'Ahem!' The virginalist stopped playing and a hush fell over the room. Titus looked down at the pigeon serenely spread before him on a platter as if his thoughts were contained there. His lips quivered with uncertainty, showing off his large gums, a pale red above his broad teeth.

'Thank you for coming tonight,' he said, adjusting his beret.

'We feel very honoured to celebrate our engagement with you.' Pause. 'First I want to thank my future mother-in-law, Anna Huijsbrechts, for accepting me as part of her family and blessing me with her daughter, whom I promise to look after and to love and cherish as my own self. I would also like to salute my father for passing on to me his intelligence, talent and charm, not to mention his beauty' – we all laughed, but Rembrandt did not budge – 'which is why I managed to win the hand of the loveliest woman in Amsterdam. It saddens me to leave you, Pa' – his voice trembled as he eyed his father – 'but we will visit you often, and soon enough you will hear the pitter-patter of tiny feet through your house . . . That is, if my wishes are granted.' He turned towards Magdalena, who gazed at him adoringly. 'May God bless everyone!'

'To Titus and Magdalena!' someone yelled.

'To Titus and Magdalena!' echoed the rest of us.

Around the room, glancing tears shone among the smiles. When Rembrandt and I clinked roemers, his distorted features met me through the glass: a grimace pulled his lips to one side, his dark-rimmed eyes wrinkled up like apricots and his bulbous nose glowed monstrously. As he took three deep gulps, his prominent Adam's apple bobbed in and out. *For now we see through a glass, darkly: but then face to face: now I know in part; but then shall I know even as also I am known.*

When Clara and I clicked glasses, the edges of her mouth curled into dimples.

'You look lovely.'

'I thought you liked me best from far away.'

'Nonsense!' I took her hand, which lay on her lap underneath the table, and gave it a squeeze. 'Would you like to go for a stroll tomorrow? Together this time?'

'Perhaps,' she said. 'But I can't help thinking that you're after my . . .'

Just then, I heard a loud crash and felt a warm, oozing sensation on my neck. When I looked over my shoulder, Rembrandt was leaping out of his chair, trying to avoid a steaming pile of potatoes and a trail of broken glass on the floor. He straightened up and violently cursed himself while swatting at the sticky mess on the front of his breeches.

'It's all right, Pa,' Titus said, but Rembrandt stood disoriented and speechless, his face swollen, his cheeks and nose bent out of shape. He shook his fists at Heaven in all directions, then kicked the leg of the chair. The guests halted and stared at him, some with food on the way to their mouths, waiting for an explanation.

When I stood up to offer Rembrandt my napkin, he dismissed me with a wave, then headed towards the door in a whirlwind: his coat tails flapping, the tapers flickering, glass crunching under his boots. On the way he brushed Clara's shoulder very tenderly with his hand. Was that an intentional gesture, and did he realize what he was doing? I watched Clara as her back tightened and her face blushed pink.

From the doorway he shouted, 'I didn't mean to ruin your party, Titus, my good boy!' He frowned, raised one shoulder in a gesture of rejection, and was gone. After the front door banged shut, the men laughed and began to joke, and the women kept silent, but no one seemed terribly shocked either. Within a few seconds, the sound of clattering utensils broke the awkward mood.

Clara's face had hardened into stone, making me wonder if she was withholding something, but I did not have the courage to ask. She said quietly, 'You should go after him.'

I wanted to go, but how could I? He despised me! Besides, I wanted to resume my conversation with her. What was she about to say just a minute ago, before Rembrandt's awful outburst?

Titus turned to us. 'I'm terribly sorry, I'd better follow him. He might fall into the canal.'

I placed my hand on his arm. 'Allow me. You should stay with your guests and enjoy the party.'

'Are you sure?'

I wiped my neck again, this time with Rembrandt's napkin, which, although unused, gave me a tremor of excitement because it had been meant for his own lips: I would journey even a thousand miles to reach him. 'I am happy to do it.'

Titus smiled nervously. 'Be patient with him, Pieter.'

Although I nodded, the importance of his advice did not sink in immediately, because I felt torn between two different kinds of bliss: the one that lay ahead and the one I was leaving behind. After kissing Clara on the cheek, I said, 'I'll call tomorrow,' but a day seemed too long to wait because she had only begun to open herself to me. When I examined her face to determine whether she wanted me to stay, she looked pleased – smiling eyes and lips. Was that because she did not like me or because she wanted me to be with Rembrandt? I could not be sure. At least she had consented to see me again.

I dashed out of the room, down the hallway, through the reception room and into the street. Seeing no sign of life, I grabbed a torch from the wall and began heading in the direction from which he had arrived – the long, gloomy corridor. As he did not live a great distance away, I was fairly confident about catching up with him. It was colder now, so I pulled my scratchy collar up to my cheeks, and stirred by anticipation, walked more gracefully on my lanky limbs than ever before. With the greatest speed possible, considering the unevenness of the road, but with the aid of my own light and the moon's reflection on the water, I followed the line of the canal. My eyes darted back and forth along the path, searching for man, beast and mongrel. Not even a twig moved. The blood throbbed in my head: if only Clara could see me now! She is probably laughing with Titus or cutting into a juicy beefsteak or being pawed by that lecherous Becker, I thought, unless she is bored to the bone without me ... I regretted not having brought her along. When I crossed the bridge, through the stench of fish, I began worrying that Rembrandt had fallen into the canal, and gazed down at the bilgy water, waiting for it to give up its secrets. The surface yawned, profound and silent, but there was nothing to see apart from a floating log of shit. Carrying on, I entered the poor edge of town with its warehouses, brothels and ramshackle houses, then began to doubt myself. Had I behaved too impulsively? Should I turn back?

A few streets further, I saw what appeared to be a carcass or a pile of rubbish on the ground, but upon stopping, I heard it groaning and mumbling. When I bent down to examine the specimen in the torch light, I was startled at the sight: an old man was slumped against the wall, tangled up in a shabby cloak, and his hat had fallen off to reveal a pile of dirty white hair so scant I could see his scalp. A familiar face whirled into view, but his features had collapsed inwardly, and sweat sprang from his every

pore, trickling down his wrinkled forehead though he was shivering with cold. Rembrandt's black eyes, his unmistakable eyes, gave
me a stare like those of a cornered animal as they peeked above the
collar of his coat.

'Are you alive?' I asked.

Nothing could prepare me for his answer, which emerged as if
from a gushing wound: 'I am a dead man who has to go on living
though my candle has burnt out and my art has abandoned me,
and all that is left is this broken voice, this dry hand, this big belly,
and her face in mere shadow, her beautiful face . . .' He tremulously
raised his voice. 'My God, look at the gathering clouds! There is
going to be another storm.'

My heart rushed to him as I reached for his arm, but he shrank
back into the stinking mud.

'You will freeze if you stay here. Let me take you home.' Using
all my strength, I managed to get him to his feet and, taking his
arm, draped it over my shoulder. 'Steady. Try to hang on,' I said,
leading him – almost dragging him – down the path while trying
to carry the torch. He merely cleared his throat, then hocked up
a generous wad of phlegm which he spat in the street. I had
imagined this moment for so long – being alone with him, that is
– but the reality of it was far different. He was supposed to be the
father, and I, the son. How could I admire and respect this pathetic
old man? Yet somehow I carried the burden with pleasure.

So, once we had attained a good rhythm, I asked, 'What were
you saying before?'

He did not answer, and for the following minutes we advanced
in silence as I tried to get my bearings and remember where he
lived. When we reached the Prinsengracht – quiet, muddy and

slushy – I spotted the Nieuwe Doolhof, the garden at the southern end with its labyrinth of hedgerows and elaborate fountains. We were drawing close now, lurking past the little houses and the filthy alleyways between them where the pigs wandered. Then there it was, number 184; this time without a Prince on the doorstep or a curious crowd loitering behind.

When I released him, he staggered slightly but seemed able to stand on his own. I propped the torch against the house, then opened the door and led him over the threshold into an impenetrable darkness.

'No need to come any further,' he said.

'Are you well enough?'

He nodded, and in fact he did look better already. The thought of being at home seemed to comfort and settle him, though his right eye wobbled a little from tiredness.

Not wishing to leave, I made another attempt at conversation. 'Were you talking about Saskia, earlier?' I asked.

He flinched and started to close the door in my face. 'Don't ever mention her name, you hear me? Never! Bugger off, you stockfish!'

My heart hammered wildly. Was this all a test? He had not shut the door completely, allowing me an extra second to respond. 'I'm sorry, Master. Please forget I asked.'

He spoke through the crack. 'Pieter, I've known you since you were a child, don't you remember? You have always had trouble understanding your place.'

'What? How? I thought you hated my father!' My mind drifted back to our first meeting. So he had known my face all along; why didn't he admit it then?

'Your father means nothing to me. I was a friend of your grandfather's. He was a wonderful man. A fine figure! I thought that something of his brilliance had passed on to you.'

I felt the need to defend myself. 'Oh, I assure you, it did.'

'Prove it to me,' he said, and slammed the door.

In the Valley

Between dawn and nightfall, his position determines the tide or the hour. He is your travelling companion, for everyone walks in vanity and disquiets oneself in vain. Cannot you see him, growing out of your feet or lying under the comforting trees? Look there, in the dusty corner. Remember, his shapes tend to be elusive and strange and full of tricks. He hides his face, for he is mysteriously reserved. Do not mistake him for friend or foe, neither father nor son, nor mother or daughter.

He is a simulacrum, that is all.

Be curious but do not break him, for he partakes of the nature of universal matter, a matter more powerful in its beginning and weaker towards its end. Wait and he will seek you out, flee and he will catch you in ambush. As soon as you grow near, he will contract and fade, but if you observe with respectful distance, he will voluntarily stretch himself across the land and the house. Watch him creep up your wall like a climbing vine or a restless branch then burst into life like a young animal at play: rabbit, dog, rooster, spider.

Each day he has a different story; sometimes it is of trust or concord, sometimes of enmity or treachery. On his journey he may meet success or failure, life or death. He may be brave or cowardly, friendly or shy, righteous or unjust, which is why, depending on the hour, you find him suspicious and frightening or comforting and pleasant. Yet, whatever his nuance, you cannot escape him. As you move he moves, pursuing his mate, *chasing, chasing*, enduring cold. Then, without warning, he abandons you and walks away.

Where on earth could he have gone?

Amsterdam, 1636

The Executioner

I am an executioner, clutching the cross, breathing on Christ's nailed feet. His blood runs on to my collar. Understanding my imperfect ways, he bears my sorrows. My sins may be as scarlet, but he will make them white like snow.

> *It is I, O Lord, it is I who have done this to*
> *Thee*
> *I am the heavy tree that was too much for*
> *you to bear,*
> *I am the stout rope with which you went*
> *tightly bound,*
> *The nail, and the spear, the scourge that*
> *flayed Thee*
> *The blood-spattered crown worn upon your*
> *head:*
> *For my sins, alas, brought all this to pass.*

This is one of the two scenes I have already completed in my Passion series for the Oude Hof Palace: The Elevation of the Cross, which accompanies The Descent from the Cross, based on prints by Albrecht Altdorfer. Now Huygens has written to inquire about the other three pieces: The Ascension,

The Entombment and The Resurrection. Can't they wait? I must haggle some additional time ... I could suggest to him that it would be more beneficial to finish all of them before they are delivered, rather than sending each piece individually. Yes, and if I muster up enough courage I will request twice the usual amount — 1,200 guilders — enough money for an initial payment on a house. Besides, my kunstcaemer has been neglected of late. Imagine the number of costumes and curiosities I could obtain, if these commissions keep coming my way.

The truth is, I can hardly bear to extend my arm and paint them. For compositional ideas I have leafed through my prints album, looking at engravings by Schelte á Bolswert after Rubens and a Descent engraving by Pontius. But how do I shrink these sensational episodes into a small format and make them contemplative? They must emphasize belief and grace, a nearly impossible task for someone like me, who cannot call himself a Mennonite, Catholic, Jew, Remonstrant or even a Counter-Remonstrant. Do not think for a minute that I am fickle. I simply want to worship God in my own fashion.

AUCTION PURCHASES
From the Jan Basse collection:
Lucas van Leyden prints ... 607 g.
Proofs of engraved landscapes, corrected in Rubens' own hand ... 424 g.
Prints by Dürer ... 127 g.
Miscellany:
Helmet of a Turk ... 71 g. 3 st.
Tinkling Cymbals ... 28 g.
A Large Ostridge's Egg ... 13 g. 2 st.

The Slumber of the Body, the Waking of the Soul

The early-morning light leaks through the cracks in the shutters. Dawn breaks above the street coming to life. My wife stirs, kicking her legs, and I open my good eye. The blanket, having slid down her body, has accidentally exposed the soft flesh of her thigh. Was it accidental? I put my hand there, gently caressing her. For a moment, not a muscle moves on her face.

She surfaces from her dreams. Her lashes flutter as she looks at me, a newborn bird smacking her lips. She says nothing. Her eyes are teary with sadness as if something has been stolen from her. What was she dreaming about, that reality should be so disappointing? Had she found Paradise? Her head shifts on the pillow. She gazes up at the ceiling, breathing heavily. A tear travels down her cheek and drops from her chin, painful and afflicted.

RVR: Why are you crying?

SVU: *Whimpering.* I'm not crying.

RVR: You are. Tell me what's wrong.

SVU: *Sniffles.* I'm waking up, is all.

RVR: (*Aside*) Her mornings are racked with nausea, but not often sadness. Is she hurt over something, or angry? She is difficult to understand, and I like things as clear as possible. I should be patient. But look at her silky nightdress! I can't help but pull it over her huge, round belly, where the skin is stretched to transparency, exposing the green veins underneath. She seems like another woman with this body. I am afraid to curse the blessed womb, but desire might get the best of me.

SVU: Let me rest a minute.

RVR: (*Aside*) She must still be upset over last night. Somehow, during a pheasant feast, our daily dialogue meandered into a heated discussion about money. She is afraid that I have been spending too much at auctions, buying things for myself. What was the word she used? Oh, yes, *greedy*. That is utterly untrue! I'm tired of having to justify my spending to her. After all, it is my money. I earn it. We have not even begun to tap into her inheritance. Is this why she is upset? I thought we settled it. Maybe she is just irritable from the morning sickness.

SVU: Tell me why you got up during the night.

RVR: I couldn't sleep.

SVU: Again. Why not?

RVR: This commission from Huygens is turning me into a madman. Or perhaps it is the plague that's troubling me, I don't know. Yesterday, I saw a death-cart piled with naked bodies, maybe fifteen or twenty of them. They had just been dumped there, as if they will not be counted. (*Aside*) Is she trying to make me feel guilty, and if so, for what? I could be Atlas, with the amount I carry on my shoulders!

SVU: I'm sorry you are worried about the commission, and I'm frightened of the disease too, but I haven't been sleeping well either, you should know, because I can hear you creeping about or working, or sense you in the corner of the room, smoking, reading and writing in your book, not to mention the candles . . .

RVR: You're forgetting one thing, sometimes I watch over you and the baby. (*Aside*) I am trying to soften her. There is nothing worse than the day getting off to a bad start. It sets off an entire series of miscalculations.

The husband bites his wife's milky shoulder, where her skin has not yet aged or wrinkled. His hand finds the nape of her neck, underneath the copper curls, a white valley. Her eyes are tense, wide open. He sucks on her bottom lip, dry from sleep.

SVU: *Pulls away suddenly.* You're the best painter in the city. Everyone admires you!

The husband falls back into the cushions and lifts his hands in the air to stare at the hands: the flaccid skin with a blue network of veins, the thick callused fingers and their dirty curved nails.

RVR: I want to buy a house for us.

SVU: If you counted your costs . . .

RVR: *Voice booms.* Stop, Saskia! *I* am the head of the household and *I* earn the money. Be grateful for what I provide.

SVU: Wait and see, Rembrandt van Rijn, if you're not careful, one day you'll have nothing and then you'll wish . . .

RVR: *Shouting.* That's enough! (*Aside*) Doesn't she see that my entire life is her, her, her? My throat burns as the demon struggles to emerge. My heart beats rapidly with adoration for this woman who carries my child.

SVU: I was trying to help.

RVR: I don't have to justify my spending to you or anyone else, but if you really want to know, I've been commissioned to do four portraits this month, two dull marriage portraits, which will make me more than what I just spent at the auction.

The painter's wife snuggles up to him, purring into the pit of his arm, but his body grows cold and all his desire sinks into his boots.

The Sacrifice of Isaac

Our baby should be arriving any day now! That is why I am painting the sacrifice of Isaac for my Jewish patron. No story better illustrates the strong bond between fathers and sons. Though I have read the account many times, only recently has the intensity of it reached my heart:

When Abraham was 125 years old, God put his faith to the test. He said, 'Abraham!' and Abraham said, 'Here I am!' Then God said, 'Take your son, your only son whom you so love, Isaac, and make a trip to the land of Moriah. Offer him up as a burnt offering on one of the mountains that I shall designate to you.'

At the prospect of carrying out this command, Abraham's hair immediately turned white. Yet he displayed his usual prompt obedience and did not question God. Rising early in the morning, before it was light, he saddled his ass, then asked for two attendants to accompany him, along with Isaac, who was twenty-five years old. Since Abraham was aged and weak, and the journey took three agonizing days — mostly an uphill trek — his son carried the wood without knowing its ultimate purpose. Meanwhile, Abraham wondered, why had God blessed them with a child in old age, only to request that he be killed?

When they reached the top of the mountain, between the Kidron and Hinnom valleys, near the ancient city of David, Abraham said to his attendants, 'You stay behind with the ass while we go over there and worship. Then we will return to you.' So Isaac took the wood, Abraham took the slaughtering knife and both went on together. Isaac said, 'My father!' and in turn, Abraham said, 'Here I am, my son!' Isaac asked, 'We have the fire and the wood, but where is the sheep for the burnt offering?' To this Abraham replied, 'God will provide the sheep for the offering, my son.' He was convinced that God, who loved him like a true father, would only make a necessary and proper request, and he trusted Him.

Abraham stacked one log upon another to build an altar. By now, Isaac must have understood what was going on, and if he wanted to, he could have easily resisted his elderly father. He could have kicked down the altar or run away. Instead, he submissively allowed Abraham to bind him, hand and foot, and put him atop the wood like a lamb. 'Listen, O sons, to the discipline of a father and pay attention, so as to know understanding.'

Abraham covered Isaac's face, thrust his head back and exposed the white of his throat. He extracted the knife from the sheath and raised it in the air. As he prepared to lower the shimmering blade, God's angel called out of the heavens, 'Do not put out your hand against the boy. Do not do anything at all to him, for now I know you are God-fearing because you have not withheld your son, your only one, from Me.' At that, Abraham raised his eyes and saw, deep in the foreground, a ram caught by its horns in a thicket. So he took the ram and offered it up in place of his son. This is why it is said, 'In the mountain of God it will be provided.'

Opening the Shutters

The street is quiet and then I hear screaming. They have detested me, they have kept themselves far from me; and from my face they did not hold back their spit. *When I look closer, I see a naked man covered in a rash and boils running towards the canal.* A brother to jackals I have become. *He jumps into the murky water and vanishes beneath the surface.* But no one jumps in after him, much less stops in the street. I cry to you for help, but you do not answer me. *He has probably just had his swellings burnt off or cut open. Now he has found relief, may the Lord bless him.*

A Letter to Huygens

I had better get my quill to paper and respond to Huygens, so he does not think I am a lazy goat. Besides, if I wait too long to reply, the mood will pass.

> My Lord, my gracious Lord Huygens,
> I hope that your lordship will please inform His Excellency that I am
> very diligently engaged in completing as quickly as possible the three
> Passion pictures, which His Excellency has commissioned me to do: an
> Entombment, a Resurrection and an Ascension of Christ.

Well done, if I may say so myself. A respectful address and concise opening.

> Of these aforementioned pictures, one has been completed, namely Christ's
> Ascension, and the other two are more than half done.

Not entirely a lie!

> Should it please His Excellency to receive this finished piece at once, or the three of them together, I pray that you will let me know concerning this matter, so that I may serve the wishes of the Prince to the best of my ability.

A bit of bumbling, but I think this will do the trick. Damn him if he does not grant me more time.

> And I also cannot refrain, as a token of my humble favour, from presenting my lord with something of my latest work, trusting that this will be accepted as favourably as possible. Besides my greetings to your lordship,

Generosity always works like a charm. Insert etching of an old man wearing a skullcap.

> I commend you all to God in health.
> Your humble and devoted servant,
> Rembrandt

Oh, just in case he has not saved my previous letter, I had better be sure he has my address.

> P.S. I am living next door to the Pensionary Boreel, Nieuwe Doelenstraat.

Ha, my proximity to Boreel is certain to impress him . . .

Two Sets of Hands

I have consulted Lastman's painting of The Sacrifice of Isaac for its emotion, an engraving of Rubens's Sacrifice for spatial ideas, which are well defined, and prints of Caravaggio's St Matthew cycle for the theatrical use of light and shadow. After numerous sketches, my painting will have two diagonals: the approaching angel and Isaac's prone body linked by Abraham's outstretched arms. The emphasis will fall on the hands — the most important aspect of the scene.

There are two sets of hands: the angel clutches Abraham's wrist while his other hand gesticulates in the air. At the same time, Abraham's right hand is releasing the knife while his left hand covers his son's face, suffocating him as he pushes his head back. Isaac's hands are tied behind his back, his knees bent, his toes curled and digging into the earth. There is a pot of fire burning in the background but no ram, because God has not yet intervened.

An Arrival in the Van Rijn Family

Loud voices shake the workshop floor. The painter's eyes squint like a bat's, straining to hear the conversation through the floor.

RVR: (*Aside*) Couldn't they possibly be quieter? I myself make a lot of noise, banging around, but I have little tolerance for other people's noises. What could be going on down there? Perhaps Saskia is yelling at our servant for stealing something or at the deliverymen, for bringing the wrong items. That would not be uncommon.

A WOMAN (*offstage*): Master Van Rijn!

The painter wipes his paint-stained hands on his apron, throws down his brushes and heads for the stairwell. Mariët, the maidservant, is on her way to meet him, gripping the edges of her skirt, hurrying up the stairs. When she sees her master, she says nothing, only stops and widens her eyes. She beckons him by waving her hands over her shoulders, Come quickly.

RVR: *Gripping the banister.* (*Aside*) This must be the moment we have been waiting for ... the baby is on its way! A week early? Heaven forbid there are no complications.

MARIËT: It's the mistress. Her water has come out.

RVR: Is the midwife here yet?

MARIËT: I've sent for her, Master, but she is delivering another child. She thought she wasn't needed until next week.

Together the husband and the maidservant cut round the corner and hurry into the bedroom, where the wife sits in the birthing chair with a blanket laid on her lap and over her legs. She clutches the sides of the chair as her body convulses with pain.

RVR: (*Aside*) Could this really be my wife? She has the pale face of death. It is I who have done this to her!

SVU: My love!

RVR: *Dashing to her side, he smooths back her hair.* Are you all right? Is it time?

The husband makes several laps around the birthing chair, then stops and glances about to get his bearings. His head spins, and the light of the fire dances across his view. The wet linens hanging near the hearth form a dripping curtain. The maidservant blots the wife with towels — she soaks through them in no time — and tosses the dirty ones into the basin.

RVR: *Running alongside the servant.* We can't do this without the midwife!

MARIËT: She'll be here soon.

The maidservant gathers up a pile of clean sheets from the laundry basket, which she then dumps into a pot of boiling water on the peat fire. The room, already warm and sticky, begins to fill with steam as she slowly stirs the linens with a giant wooden spoon.

RVR: *Shouting.* Soon? We need her now! (*Aside*) We paid a large sum for this midwife, and everyone else has fled to the countryside!

MARIËT: *Eyeing the door.* Any minute, Master. The servants from next door will help in the meantime.

Two elfin girls hasten into the room, carrying supplies: a fire basket with hot coals, a catheter and shears, which they set in order on the table near the birthing chair. They go over to the wife, who is sobbing for breath, and adjust her pillows and speak to her in whispers, their bonnets bent together. The wife clutches the sides of her large belly; it expands then contracts and rumbles like a volcano.

RVR: Try to relax, my love. (*Aside*) My hands! What should I do with my hands?

SVU: *Sputtering.* I can't. You must . . . take . . . the baby.

RVR: Yes, of course. (*Aside*) Me? No! Is she crazy? I haven't even seen a cow give birth. Or a pig even! Wait a minute. I was there when Moeder spit out my siblings. But what did the midwife do? All I remember are her strong, greasy hands.

The husband looks at the maidservant nodding her head in encouragement.

RVR: Mariët, fetch some oil.

MARIËT: What kind of oil, Master?

RVR: Olive oil?

MARIËT: We have none.

RVR: There's some walnut in my workshop, the jar next to my easel.

After the maidservant dashes out of the room, the husband pulls up a chair and sits between his wife's legs, ready for anything that might happen. She is panting through a horrible wave of contractions, closer together now.

RVR: (*Aside*) Could this really be the appropriate position? With the blanket draped over her, I will not be able to see what I'm doing!

SVU: Please! I have to push!

RVR: Don't worry. I'm here. *Steadies his hands between her legs, which are bent at the knees. He peers over his shoulder to sneer at the elfin girls loitering nearby.* (*Aside*) Look at those wenches, utterly useless! They may be childless themselves, but their master and mistress have had six babies. Didn't they learn anything?

When the maidservant returns with a bottle of oil, the husband pours a few drops into his hands and begins lathering them.

RVR: Where is that damned midwife?!

MARIËT: Please don't shout, Master. The mistress is almost ready now. You'll have to grab the baby.

RVR: I know that. Do you want to do it?

MARIËT: The three of us will hold her.

The servants gather around the wife, pinning down her arms and yanking her legs apart. The husband slips a well-oiled hand into her cavity.

RVR: (*Aside*) It feels like warm grease or porridge. Normally I would find that arousing. But who is this gushing woman? She does not seem like my wife at all.

THE THREE SERVANTS: Push, push, push!

The wife strains with all her might. The bulge of her belly heaves as she screams at the top of her lungs. Her face changes from red to purple.

RVR: (*Aside*) My hand is growing numb. I'm going to vomit up those herrings from breakfast. This is chaos: something terribly close to death itself. I look past Saskia, hoping to draw comfort from the arched niche, where a pot rests on the sill, and the long bench running along the far wall with an oval basket and washing bowl. The room feels unfamiliar now, with its lengthening shadows, as if it has gone completely still. Is this the same place where we sleep, where we conceived this very child? My eyes wander over to the window. Though the panes are fogged from the intense heat inside, I see beyond them to the knotted tree with its golden leaves.

THE THREE SERVANTS: Keep breathing, keep breathing.

RVR: Push, push, push! (*Aside*) So much stronger am I than the gods, and stronger than mortals!

SVU: *Spitting.* Oh shut up, you vile beast! Stop telling me what to do ... You're always trying ... and don't know anything, you pizzle! I curse the day I met you!

RVR: *Turning to Mariët.* What's come over her?

SVU: *Screaming.* Get out, you hear? Just get out!

MARIËT: *Whispers.* We should put something in her mouth.

RVR: I know. Use my paintbrush! *Gestures toward his pocket with his chin.*

SVU: Leave me alone, you coward!

The maidservant pulls out the brush then grabs hold of the wife's mouth and thrusts it between her teeth. She turns to her master.

MARIËT: Can you feel the baby now?

RVR: *Wriggles his fingers.* I think so. Mostly all I feel is blood and slime. Unless this is the head?

The husband holds his breath and slides out what he believes is the baby's head, slowly, but surprisingly without effort. The wife screams as her body lurches through long minutes. Then she grows quiet.

RVR: (*Aside*) I no longer hear her, because my spirit has fluttered away, drifting. I am thinking about the baby. Will it be healthy? Will it have a nose and a mouth? Will it inherit my lazy eye?

Surely, the most blessed beauty of all creation! Please Lord, let him share my love of art. I will begin teaching him the secrets of my trade, fresh out of the womb. By the time he is my age, he will be a great master.

The room is frozen in silence, apart from the heavy breathing of five people.

RVR: *Cries out, and holds a tiny, slithering body in his hands.* Could it really be? God Almighty be thanked! *He stands up and raises the messy creature in the air.* It's a boy! (*Aside*) Oh no, he has a slightly misshapen head. But two perfect brown eyes, a nose and a mouth, all of his fingers and toes!

THE THREE SERVANTS: *Clap their hands and cheer.* Praise the Lord!

The maidservant slaps the baby's bottom, and he begins to cry.

RVR: What was that for? Saskia, we have a boy!

The mother's eyes flutter, barely alert, then she smiles. The maidservant brandishes the shears to sever the cord.

RVR: You know what you're doing?

MARIËT: I've seen it done before. Hold still.

The maidservant grasps the cord between two fingers and cuts it, then ties the rest. She scrambles in front of her master, works her hands under the sheet, then pulls them out to show him a revolting organ of some sort.

MARIËT: How do you think it looks?

RVR: *Shrinking back.* I don't know.

MARIËT: The afterbirth, Master.

RVR: How's it supposed to look? Throw it in the fire!

MARIËT: Do I have your blessing?

RVR: Yes!

The maidservant tosses the afterbirth into the fire, then sets to cleaning the mother with the towels. The father hands his son to the other servant, who brings him to the fire basket, where he will be warm. She wipes him with a soft wet cloth, and swaddles him in linen from below his neck down to his knees. When she hands the infant back to his father, he carries the bundle to his wife, the mother.

RVR: Look, my love! (*Aside*) My wife and firstborn: this is the portrait that I want to keep for ever.

SVU: He's beautiful.

Father and mother dote on their newborn for several minutes, trying to fathom the idea that they are no longer two but three. After the maidservant takes the baby and settles him in his wicker cradle, the father lifts up the mother, a mass of limp limbs, to carry her over to the freshly made bed, where she can rest peacefully.

RVR: (*Aside*) She is so fragile. Withered and stripped of her spirit. Her whole body submits to my bosom, but where is my wife? What I have done to my wife?

The servants hang a paper and lace notice on the front door, telling the world about the Van Rijns' new child. A boy! Then they scurry off to prepare the evening meal. The father pours himself a glass of sweet wine spiked with cinnamon and a cup of mild broth for his wife. He sits next to her bed while downing the warm liquid. Moments later, there is a banging on the front door. Before answering the call, he dons his paternity bonnet with its green and yellow feathers. At the door, he finds a plump middle-aged woman.

THE GAP-TOOTHED MIDWIFE: *Breathless.* Am I too late?

The New Theatre

A stone building called the Schouwburg, designed by Jacob van Campen, will replace the former rickety hut run by Samuel Coster, teacher and playwright. Sadly, the Calvinist elders pushed him out. This new theatre will be financed by the regents of the orphanage. I watch them building it in town: an apron stage, two tiers of boxes with privacy curtains, an orchestra for trumpet, cello, violin and lute. Vondel is writing a play especially for the inauguration called Gijsbrecht van Amstel, which will celebrate our city's glorious beginnings!

Saskia's Milk

In the middle of the night, our baby is crying. Saskia does not sleep soundly any more, since he was born. I have never slept soundly, except now I have a good reason. She has learnt to distinguish his different types of fussing, whether he needs to be fed, changed, coddled or rubbed with rosewater and vinegar for fever. Regardless of the reason, and despite the frequency, she always responds. We called him Rombertus after Saskia's dead father, *because that is what she wanted. Our firstborn should've taken my father's name, Harmen.*

Her puffy eyes blink with tiredness. He is hungry. After slipping out of bed, she tiptoes to his bassinet. She carries him over to the nursing basket near the hearth, where she can sit with him on her lap, one knee raised under her crumpled skirt. This maternal compassion springs from her heart naturally. She never stops thinking about him or questions whether or not she should nurture him. He is only a few weeks old and already I slightly envy him for the affection he has snatched away from me. He never seems to stop wanting and needing her, my wife. So I am learning patience and generosity, those qualities I have never been forced to cultivate. At times, I completely forget about him and have to remind myself that I am a father. I cannot get used to the idea that he is alive, another human being who will always be there, to whom I must surrender my soul. When he cries for help, 'Abba, Father!' I must respond, 'Here I am!' without hesitation.

I prop up on my elbow as Saskia lifts her chemise and offers her swollen breast to his mouth, wincing as he latches on to her nipple. He gurgles then follows a rhythm, suck, suck, suck, swallow. After a minute he becomes relaxed, and the pattern changes, swallow, take a deep breath, swallow again. His eyes move, surveying the world. The soft texture of his cheek presses against Saskia's bare skin. There are creases of fat in his arms, one resting at his side, the other lifted into the air. He grabs her with his miniature hand, pale and dimpled. He is miraculously growing every day, but we always fear that some contamination will affect him, as it does many babies in the first months. There are stories about mothers infecting their children and vice versa. Some had been found dead together, the infant still latched on to its mother's teat.

Rombertus is fragile in spirit like Saskia, who has tuberculosis in her family. That is why she makes sure to drink stewed apples and to avoid bad cheeses and powerful spices. We never take the baby in the fresh air, either. Because of the plague, I keep my house like a garrison. Even if it means enduring his cry all hours of the day.

Only her pure milk can silence him.

Saskia's pure milk, a blessing from God to ensure our baby's survival, growth and prosperity. What on earth must it contain? I ask her if I can taste it. She blushes at the question and does not meet my eyes, but carries on as if I had said nothing. The silence stretches out until Rombertus has finished eating. As she wipes her nipple with a soft cloth, I ask her again. With quick fluttering lashes, she consents to 'just a taste'.

I get down on the floor, near to her and almost touching, heart whispering to heart. She shifts Rombertus to her opposite arm to offer me the other, less sore breast. With eyes wide open, I ogle the enlarged areola, the small bumps and hairs decorating it. Then I bring my mouth to her nipple and suck carefully, not wishing to hurt her. It takes a minute, but finally, a few warm drops fall into my mouth, creamy and sweet. The drink of the gods! It is nothing like cow's milk, closer to the juice of figs. Saskia's whole body stiffens, and she blinks uncontrollably. I grow hard inside my breeches. My lips slip off her nipple. My hand wanders between her legs. When she swats me away, I fall back on the floor with a dead thud. Crossing my hands under my head, I sulk. She hasn't wanted to make love since the baby was born. She constantly declares that she is ugly with this new body. No matter what I say, I cannot reassure her.

She lays Rombertus on my chest, so his head rests at my shoulder. As he burps in my ear, I breathe in his clean, powdery smell. My son, here I am! His hair is a lustre of red atop his head. He has a wide face and a pale *complexion, my nose and his mother's full, red lips. My large hand covers his entire back he is so tiny. I touch lightly, his entire life cradled in my palm.*

I ask Saskia to put some milk into a jar for me. She gazes down at me with her pale green eyes, a stare to expose my secrets. Smoothing her hands over her hips, she tiptoes to the basin and says she will bring it to the studio after her next feeding. After scrambling to my feet, I hand her the baby then kiss her snub nose.

Creation of the Sacrifice

I am taking advantage of the few hours before the apprentices arrive. My work proceeds far better in the solitude of these four walls. The paint spreads like a disease over every surface: curdles over the table, trickles down my easel, forms a sludge on the floor, oozes from the ceiling. The room's sharp odour tempts madness, making me blink, gag, itch, laugh and shout. No place for the timid!

The painting of Abraham's sacrifice is about to begin. Alas, I am a father and ready for the task (if only Rombertus would stop bleating). From the bolts of fabric leaning in the corner, I cut a sizeable piece of canvas, using a fabric with a fine weave so there is not much penetration between the threads. After I stretch the canvas over a wooden strainer, I lace it against the bars. To tighten and seal the surface of the canvas, I size it with animal glue. After it dries, I apply a primer in two coats of glue and chalk to smooth out the irregularities. Now, what Titian calls the 'making the bed of a picture': I brush on the ground in two layers, red ochre then warm grey (a mixture of lead white with chalk, ground in linseed oil, charcoal, raw umber and earth colours). Do not imagine that the ground is a heavy cake, nothing of the sort. I lay it down in a thin, transparent wash.

What happens next? After everything dries, a blank space awaits me. I face the easel, knowing that once I begin, the picture will take on its own personality. The best elements of a painting happen without my knowledge, so I have no way of repeating them, not even if I perform the exact motions. I must work out the idea in the making, like an alchemist gathering all the parts of the world into a new unity. Creation begins with chaos and ends in perfection.

I start slowly with a monochrome sketch, a transparent grey-brown applied over the ground to set down the composition. My emphasis is on casualness, avoiding sharpness in the contours. My brush marks the outlines of Abraham, Isaac and the angel — forming the two diagonals. I always work up the painting from back to front to produce a skilful arrangement. Other artists seem to sketch everything at first then build up the paint like pieces of patchwork. As a whole, people pay little attention to harmony though it constantly surrounds them, whether they are looking at a landscape or objects in a house. For me, every individual part should combine to please.

A New Formula

Saskia steps into the room, holding a glass jar and wearing a grin. My good girl. She is efficient and always listens to me. Who has a more beautiful and obedient wife? She sets the half-empty jar on my worktable and tells me to put it to good use. I hug her playfully, but she can easily detect my impatience. My pupils jump from corner to corner. Inspiration has seized *me by the neck! Saskia smacks her lips, then flounces out of the room. The practice of art demands a man's whole self.*

Let me tell you my idea.

My paint is usually no more than a mixture of pigment with viscous oil, but sometimes I add a drying agent (a small amount of umber, perhaps), an emulsifier (egg) or a foreign material (beeswax or resins from exotic plants). Depending on what I add and how I mix them, the textures of my paints can change: butter or mucus, silks or slugs. I constantly experiment with the substances, learning how they resist or submit to one another. The notion that hit me earlier was: what would happen if I added Saskia's breast-milk to my pigments? It is the same colour as flesh, the colour of life. But would it mimic the skin in texture — flaccid, slabby and supple? Would it cause the paint to wrinkle and crack?

I stare down at the flask, where the white liquid appears to be working a natural magic. As it gently swirls, I absorb with my senses the continuing events. The longer I stare, the more it changes. The milk thickens slowly, then separates into two parts: a creamy layer atop the watery deep. Then the glass seems quiet. It must be ready. I lift the residue off with a spoon and add a small portion to the pre-mixed pigments: lead white, light ochre, vermilion, terre verte and charcoal black. As I stir in the milk, the paint becomes shiny and resilient, fatty and almost rubbery like melted wax. It takes on a glorious opaque quality as pearly as a shell. I could not have judged it more perfectly. The result is ideal for Isaac's skin, if only I can attain the proper texture in application.

Imagine me now, a figure in the grey light outlined against the glow. I extend an arm, clutching my brush. A nervous energy seeps from my every pore. The great indescribable spirit! I add the colour layer upon layer — a dab, a sweep, a fleck, a stroke. On Isaac's throat the fatty mixture leaves a mark like raw tissue, on his risen chest a natural sheen. The milk spills over Isaac's curved belly and swirls over Abraham's claw-like hand. I think I have found the perfect formula for my tribute of father and son. It is all for you, Rombertus, whose entire life is cradled in my palm. Your mother may seem absent, off in the distance somewhere, but she is truly here.

ADDITIONAL PURCHASES AT AUCTION

Set of drawings by Hendrick Goltzius ... 106 g.
Bust of Roman emperor Tiberius, marble ... 204 g.
Prints by Raphael, rare ... 161 g.
Drawings by Pieter Bruegel ... 92 g.

Liberty & Audacity

I find myself imitating Rubens in certain effects, especially in the dynamic energy of his figures. Like him, I paint the spirit. Even if he often lacks refinement, Rubens always has the courage to be himself. He paints with liberty and audacity to bring vitality to his forms. Let me assert that there is nothing wrong with imitation. No one can make something out of nothing. Even the great Raphael imitated his master and his predecessors. It is a fine line to walk if one does not want to be compared to anyone. The Emperor Tiberius said he avoided anything that would give people cause to compare him to Augustus, whose memory was pleasing to all. For how do you outshine someone who is without fault?

Oh, Dear Rombertus!

An evil spirit has stolen our newborn baby. He is lying in his crib, eyes cast upwards, his chubby arms folded over his belly. I kiss his dimpled cheek. There is no breath from his pink lips, only silence. 'Out, out brief candle! Life's but a walking shadow.' Oh, dear Rombertus! Why not me, God? Why not me?

The Woman with the Big Bosom's Story

There once was a woman with a big bosom stretching from earth to sky. Although the rain and wind sometimes lunged at her, she did not tremble, and when the snow leant on top of her, she did not droop even slightly. What fortitude she possessed with her fitted framework of three floors, a garret and cellar, her lofty windows and stone doorway! On the outside she was built of strong brick, but inside she was downy and warm, and her arms were outstretched if only someone could accept her, for over the years she had grown tired of emptiness, a vast and deep silence that crept from room to room, an inertia that hummed in her hallways. During the day, the drone and buzz of the street might have vibrated her walls or made the glasses sing in the cupboard, but each night the chambers had sighed and groaned together. Although their harmony was beautiful at times, she yearned for the cacophony of ordinary life.

This loneliness continued until one day, in 1638, a man named Campen came in and widened her top floor, replacing two windows with four, and turned her step-gable into a classical-style triangle with an oval window. She knew this renovation could be for one reason alone: someone had noticed her and desired her as his own. Sure enough, she heard the solicitors talking in the front room, and the date was set for 1 May. That morning she kept vigilance through her windows, waiting for the new master to arrive. She wanted to make a good impression, so instead of hunching her shoulders as she wished to do, she girded her loins, held her head high and thrust out her chest. A perfect location if you asked anyone in the city, back from the row of trees that lined the lock, and second from the corner, near the diamond merchant's. Even if she were built on soft sand, running along a dyke, a nobler blood could not be found on the Sint-Anthoniesbreestraat, number 4, and worth a hefty 13,000 guilders! Most people would think it was beyond their means, but not this new man, who must consider himself wealthy enough to afford me, she thought, or is showing off to his friends. Her old life already seemed distant.

Oh, but he was just another beast who would adore her for a while, avail himself of all her comforts, steal inside her secret chambers, then pack his bags and desert her like the others. How long had it been since the last? Back in '36 . . . nearly three years, she calculated. Her plumbing must already be clogged and rusty. What mould or ordure would be found in her crevices? What bilgy stench in her recesses? She felt used and abused from the ground water ebbing and flowing, which dried out her piles and wet them again, as much as her lovers coming and going without explanation, having plundered her stability, safety, security – the things that most women desire. Those souls, who had shared their laughter, tears and nakedness, were lost to her now. There were no more passions or disappointments, triumphs or humiliations, kind-nesses or crimes, only an echo of retreating footsteps, the last traces of sulphur and sweat, the tattered books murmuring of the past, a shadowy image in the mirror that faintly resembled someone she used to know. What had happened to faithfulness? No one visited or wrote to her, either. She did not believe in ghosts — those horrible mythical creatures — but even in her darkest hours she wished she did, if only for some semblance of permanence.

A horse-drawn cart rumbled down the wide street, clattering over the stones and keeping to one side, avoiding the traffic, as its back end heaved with furniture and knick-knacks. That must be him, she thought, and as he drew closer she leant in for a better view. An interesting specimen! The first thing she noticed was his conk, large and curdled, the second was his muscular hands, stained and craggy as if he were a seaman or a builder, but when the wind ruffled his long wiry hair he clearly resembled a sooth-sayer. His brown eyes were dark and wild, encircled by soft pads of pessimism. He was in his thirties, perhaps — the same age as herself — and wore a young man's sparse beard (the moustache slightly curling), though his forehead, where the skin glistened, was marked with numerous horizontal lines. He seemed to be sur-rounded by a cloud of emotion, which might burst at any second and rain down his anxieties should the earth move even slightly under his feet. Accompanying him was an older, taller man with a shiny bald pate, reminiscent of a large sausage. Though they appeared comfortable with each other, as if relatives, they did not look anything alike.

When the cart's wheels came to a halt, the men jumped out to survey her, and she returned their smiles with red shutters wide open. Although her master was married (they all were), she was confident he would submit to her in no time, considering her numerous assets. The men followed the footpath leading up to her front door, painted green and set in the lower half of one of four equal-sized window embrasures. When her owner stepped into the entranceway, he marvelled at the shiny condition of the marble floors and the hewn oak ceiling beams way above. Their deep voices filled the entranceway to the brim when, clapping his friend on the back, the sausage man said, 'A bit dusty, but well done. Imagine the number of paintings you can fit on these walls!' Her master replied, 'All I need is a workshop.' She knew then that he was a painter, and rejoiced, for her neighbourhood cared for the city's best artists and dealers. It was only a matter of time until he found that perfect place to work; she already knew where it would be, and all her parts creaked and squeaked, eager for the attention they were about to receive. To get the larger items like furniture on to the upper floors, they would have to activate her pulley. Her pulley? No time to oil her gears beforehand, she brooded. It took hours for the men to bring everything in — one group roping up the furniture in the street, another on the second storey catching the heavy objects as they swung towards the glistening panes of glass set in lead.

Later that day, as she predicted, her new owner happened upon that special thing which would make it impossible for him to leave her. She wondered if it were love at first sight, as it seemed when he beat up and down her stairways, hauling crates of painting supplies — brushes, pens, chalks, paint bladders, stretchers, rolled-up canvases, reams of paper, earthenware pipkins — and took them directly into the large room on the third floor. There were many windows letting in the north light, each with bottom shutters that pushed back against the outside walls and top inside shutters that hoisted up against the ceiling. Two cast-iron stoves sat on either side of the room, allowing 'a sufficient amount of heat', her master remarked. He began filling the room next door with all kinds of

bizarre objects, most of which she did not have names for —
costumes and bright robes, seashells, gourds, coats of armour,
spears, busts, helmets, headdresses, coins and books — making it
his *kunstcaemer*. He must be one of the greatest collectors in the
world, she thought. Halfway down the spiral staircase was a small
room the families usually used for storage, but no — this man
would bring in a wooden printing press to make his etchings there.
An entire floor for creating, what artist wouldn't dream of such a
thing? Therefore, she knew for certain that he would not leave, at
least by choice, yes, only if he were forced out — which is eventually
what happened, but she could not foresee this at the moment, and
for the present, she wanted to believe he would stay for ever.

As for her other rooms, they were furnished by the end of the
week then gradually filled to perfection; and time flowed so swiftly,
so swiftly indeed that it seemed to her he had always been in her
life, that no one else had ever understood or adored her. The side
room, to the left of the entranceway, functioned as the receiving
room for his numerous visitors, with its fine walnut table and seven
Spanish chairs covered in green velvet. It only seemed appropriate
that such a sacred room in an artist's home, afforded with a generous
amount of light from the casement windows, should have a host of
paintings on the walls. He had converted it into a small art gallery
— an ingenious idea, for when people stopped by he could offer
them a glass of wine from the marble cooler and allow them to
look. How the woman loved those moments when she could fancy
herself up and make a good impression on her master's visitors! For
after looking, they would buy, and such a process would make him
wealthy and earn him his fortune. If they were generous enough to
be invited, guests stayed overnight in the spacious box-bed not far

from the wood fireplace with marbled effect. Although she hesitated to remember, or even say the words aloud, this is where some of her master's most violent rages occurred, to which he was susceptible from the very beginning: wrecking tea canisters, hurling decorative plates and brandishing antique statues like the weapons of a spoilt, arrogant child. The woman hated being shaken in this way, and sometimes it made her feel worthless, but the man was lovable in his own way.

His wife, Saskia — she had known there would be a wife — made herself comfortable back in the kitchen with its yellow-ochre wood and white tiles, near a large fire burning in the open hearth. There she prepared meals for their lavish dinner parties, or else sewed and darned. A small table, draped in a white cloth and in the centre of the room, was the ideal place for family meals, underneath a canopy of raw meats hanging from the ceiling. There were windows above the draining board, next to which a door led into the courtyard, brick-paved, with a few shrubs and a little vine growing over the roof of the privy and lean-to. In the chicken coop, the birds squawked to high heaven without let-up.

The staircase, twisting tightly with narrow and steep steps, secured a private room behind it — her master's office, in which he conducted his book-keeping or sold his most famous paintings over the years (sometimes he sold them and bought them back, to increase their worth), and at his desk he counted up his fast-growing fortune. When he and Saskia discussed financial matters, the woman left them alone, for she did not wish to intrude on their privacy, but when her master closed himself off and slumped over the papers to weep, for instance, on the occasion of his mother's death, then she softened her walls and held him in an embrace.

The most important place she could offer, apart from the workshop, had a cosy appeal despite its large size — the parlour, where her master and his wife sat near a fireplace with caryatids supporting the mantelpiece. There was a small cedar cupboard for their linens and an oak table at which they talked or played backgammon in the evenings. When Saskia was in a pleasant mood, she sat at the dressing table, making up her face and singing quietly to herself, and if they were going out to dine or to the theatre, he would help her put on a necklace, which she referred to as 'my wedding pearls'. In the bed enclosed by blue curtains, plumped up with a feather mattress and embroidered down pillows, the couple made love regularly, not only for the purpose of conceiving a baby, the woman thought, though this happened quite soon after they moved in. Their third child, born in 1640, would die in infancy like her previous two siblings, one of which was also called Cornelia. So, in order to endure the pain of loss, the couple immediately set about producing another baby, and were successful the following year when a second son, Titus, was born. However, the labour of his delivery proved distressing for poor Saskia.

The little boy Titus would lie in his bassinet as his mother tried to recover, too weak to sit up. Hands folded across her blanket, she slept. Though her master was in the midst of running the most influential workshop in the country, he often kept vigil over his beloved. With her pale face and sunken eyes, Saskia was fragile like a delicate piece of pottery. It seemed she stayed there for months, coughing and sputtering, and it must have been months, for during this time her master created one of his largest paintings. The woman wondered how Saskia could rest through that racket, for she herself had barely slept a wink while the officers of the militia marched up and down the stairs, performing just as they would out in the streets: banging their drums, raising their muskets and pikes, wielding their swords, barking like dogs and waving flags. Perched on a ladder before his large canvas, her master encouraged them by shouting, 'One, two, three, Load, Shoot, Blow!' He not only painted, he also behaved as if he were part of the troop that marched forward through the city and over its bridges, from darkness into light. In any case, she thought her master had gone mad, and the spectacle was enough to rattle her windows, rumble her floors and buckle her walls, especially when the painting had to be hoisted out the window and lowered on to a cart, which required an entire day. He had earned 1,600 guilders for the commission; she saw him counting each bill with a smile, locked in his office. Yet her master's work only served as a temporary distraction from the anguish in the room down the hallway. When Saskia's condition worsened, he was forced to hire a nurse to stay with her during all hours.

One morning, in June, just after Whitsun, a notary came for the purpose of sealing Saskia's will. In earshot of the discreet woman and in the presence of two witnesses, Saskia declared Titus as her heir and gave use of the estate to her husband to trade, consume or do anything else, provided that he bear the cost of the child and his board until he came of age or married. It was stipulated and agreed upon that if her husband should remarry, he or his flesh and blood would receive half of the remaining estate while the other half would go to her sister, Hiskia van Loo. Saskia then waived the requirement that her husband provide any kind of inventory of her property to anyone in the world, confident that he would acquit himself very well in all good conscience.

A week later, Saskia passed into death at the young age of thirty, when Titus was only nine months old, but within her walls the woman could never speak about such things with her master, his son, the maids or the nurse — even if she could, they would not hear her. So she observed them closely, and what she saw was disheartening in every respect. First, her master grieved in the normal ways — weeping at the most unexpected moments where she alone could see him, secreted in the privy or the workshop. Then he began filling his belly with meats, cheese, eggs and all varieties of sugary treats, or he would stop in the midst of a painting, rush from her protection and roam the streets. When he returned several hours later with dust on his jacket, his soiled boots making muddy streaks across her marble floors, she knew he had been to the countryside. He also went to public sales and bid so high at the outset that no one else came forward, acquiring clothes that struck him as bizarre or picturesque — at times, downright dirty — or beautiful curiosities that he took pleasure in hanging on her walls, such as arms, drawings, engravings and medals, anything which might replace the loss. At night, as her master lay in his bed, eyes blinking against the darkness, he would call out his dead wife's name, 'Saskia!' Sometimes he twisted up in the blankets, at other times his nightmares knocked him out of bed and he fell on the floor with a groan. Often he would take his dead wife's dress out of the cupboard and fall back asleep with it nestled against his cheek. Titus, the only family he had left, was a reminder of Saskia — so as much as he loved his son, he could hardly bear to hold his baby or gaze into his dotty little eyes. As Titus grew older and they grew closer, he still did not tell him much about his mother, even then he would not speak of her but chose to share his feelings in paint or in a tablet that he carried with him everywhere.

For that while, the woman had her owner all to herself except for the child and the maidservant, though they did not pose a threat to her, tiny in comparison. At least, that is what she originally thought, so she was horrified when in a matter of months, the nurse, Geertje Dircx, who had stayed on in order to care for Titus, began sleeping in her master's bed. He sketched Geertje from Waterland as naked as Eve and bestowed upon her his dead wife's precious jewels. But the woman could not hold a grudge against her master; how could she? It was not her position to judge, and he always managed to charm her out of any bad feelings. Besides, it was better this way, she thought; the gems and pearls would have been taken away from Saskia eventually had she lived, for in later years her master lost his entire wealth, not to mention his wife's inheritance, because of his inclination to spend and borrow freely.

The many difficulties and tragedies that befell her master thereafter could fill hundreds of pages if they were written down, but the woman with the big bosom would never reveal them, nor the secrets of his workshop and the mysteries of his *kunstcaemer*, for that would have constituted a betrayal of the most cherished man in her history, to whom she was devoted for all of her days, long after those twenty eventful years which he spent at her bosom. What fortitude she possessed!

'Boelering'

A woman with a wide face and broad forehead half rises from her bed, richly decorated with embroidered linens and pillows. Her chestnut hair is pulled back tightly into a gilded cap that resembles an upturned metal fruit basket. A patch of bare shoulder and one white breast peeps out from the plain shift wrapped round her as she extends an arm as if beckoning her lover, pulling back the fringed red curtain with a large dirty hand, belonging to the kind of woman who washes laundry and scrubs floors. The deep expanse of her bed is cast in a distinct shadow, *and on the eyes, black sleep of night.*

Who is she? I wondered, stepping back, and who is she waiting for?

'Geertje Dircx,' Clara said, honey-voiced at my arm and reading my mind again. I had the boldness to call on her that afternoon, still drunk with excitement from the events of the night before and with only an hour's sleep behind me. We looked up at the painting from 1647, hanging on the wall amidst countless pieces by local artists, most of which Clara had inherited from her father.

'Oh, *the* Geertje Dircx? Are you sure?' I knew it must have been one of Rembrandt's lovers, but the woman in the picture eluded me for she bore something of a resemblance to each of them. So this was Titus's dry nurse: the trumpeter's widow.

Clara nodded, and I swung my head round to peer at her. At one end of the room, two large doors connecting the parlour to a smaller gallery and library were wide open, allowing the sunshine to enter through the windowpanes and stretch across her like a meridian. It might have been the light or where she was standing, or some change she had made to her hair, but suddenly Clara looked different from the portrait I had made of her previously – the one I'd carried in my head for all this time; in fact, she bore little resemblance to this woman standing before me. I could not pinpoint what had changed about her, if she had changed at all, though I noticed small details – the soft down that spread across her cheeks and the crescent-shaped scar near her right eye. I wavered, thinking: if I suddenly do not see her as the same person, perhaps she does not recognize me either, in this light, or where I am standing, or with this coarse stubble on my face; perhaps we have both been mistaken in what we had understood about each other. *Stand to face me, beloved, and open out the grace of your eyes.*

Every second that passed seemed crucial to our fate, so crucial that the drumming of my heart drowned out the ticking of her upright clock . . . The world was merely marking time. Yet, while I was planning to confess my love to her, she was living only in the present, worrying about whether the tea would be hot enough or whether I thought it was too rainy for our proposed walk. Perhaps we should have drunk our tea earlier, but we had been enjoying the painting instead, and why should we care, as long as we were in each other's presence? It did not matter that it was raining, and still would not matter if it were snowing or blowing a gale, because every step we had taken in our lives until then had been directed towards each other. Why did she not declare it once and for all? Perhaps she was waiting for me to take the lead, I thought, so with all the courage I could muster, I hushed her concerns.

'I don't mind cold tea, and I am more than happy to stay inside.' I bent closer still. Then the rest came naturally: I cupped her face in my hands and planted a dry but insistent kiss on her mouth.

She pulled away and raised her fingers to her lips. 'What was that for?'

I shrugged and looked down at my boots, pointed and polished beyond reason. I hated myself for them; they were the kind my father would have chosen. Rembrandt was right to say that I had let him down, and that I had inherited nothing of my grandfather's intellect, charm or good taste; he would not have worn this type of boot for this occasion nor would he be gazing down at them at such an inopportune time. There must be something in my character that paid tribute to him, I thought, if only I could call it up. What would Willem have said to my grandmother when they first fell in love? And if she had resisted his advances? I supposed he would have stuck his neck out even if his sweetheart were poised to lop off his head.

I cleared my throat. 'Clara, I adore you, and I've adored you since I first saw you sitting on the ice. That's why I called you the Fallen Woman, didn't you know? Because you resembled a swan, but also because you were dripping like a wet myrtle. In any case, upon my honour, I cannot do without you, will you marry me?'

The words did not emerge as rehearsed (dripping like a wet myrtle?), especially not the last part – the proposal had not been in the original equation. How had I managed to blurt that out? One sentence had ruined the effect entirely, and it hung in the air between us as the clock chimed and then stopped, returning to its gentle ticking. Even her calico cat, which had curled itself around my leg, seemed to be waiting for a reply.

From her half-open mouth, the saliva glistened on her teeth. 'That's very sweet of you, Pieter, but you don't even know me. I am certainly not the woman you peeped at, ice-skating.'

'Well, no, I didn't see you skating, I saw you *after* your fall. But if I am wrong about you, rather than complain about it set me straight.'

There was no sign of a lip-quiver, an eye-dart or a chin-wobble. Her face was blank, her eyes like a bird's hypnotizing a snake. 'Then listen to me.'

With my hand supported against the wall, I endured the forthcoming confession, when Clara told me that she was 'an independent woman' with a classical education – grammar, logic, rhetoric, science, history – who had lived in Paris for a time to study French culture, who had had her portrait painted by Lairesse, and who had a seat in a literary and philosophical salon that included Espinoza. She was a poet, fluent in Latin, Italian and Hebrew, and furthermore, her patience wore thin with those who suggested that women's minds were not made for intellectual pursuits, or that they were in any way inferior. For that reason, she was determined to remain single. Why should she need a husband? She had inherited a sizeable wealth from her father, including the paintings he had obtained on his journeys, and besides, she was a Catholic.

She summarized most of her history in a cold and dismissive manner as if she were writing her biography, even talking about someone else. Obviously, I did not understand at first — lacking long hours to analyse her words — so rather than retreat as would be expected, I only desired her more. My calm outward appearance concealed an inner turmoil: perhaps my stomach was chewing up my heart, or my heart was trying to creep through my rectum. A rushing current carried my body away while I ridiculously, desperately tried to find some part of her to grasp. My arms reached out . . .

Then I became dizzy. The light jabbed at my eyes, and my face wrinkled up in defence. She probably thought I was smiling. My hand was clutching her breast? I blinked. No, my hand was on her arm. With my four fingers nestled in the fabric of her chemise, I tried to think of what to say, but I could not respond to everything — the fact that she was a Catholic, for instance — and my mind dwelt on one thing: the revelation that she had turned down many marriage proposals before mine, which made me want to retch.

I raised my voice. 'I do not care if you have refused other men, because you told me in the very beginning I was not like them. You said I was unique!'

She smirked and shook her curls. 'I would not have used that word, unique. I think I said "odd". But if you're not like other men, then why are you acting as they do? For heaven's sake, let go of my arm.'

I released her abruptly then walked ten paces to the other side of the parlour and stood in the doorway of the library with my back to her. Shelves lined with brown and green volumes reached from floor to ceiling, and paintings hung around them in any available space. This was her utopia, the place of dreams and invention and poetry: a small writing desk sat in front of the window stacked with more books (sure enough, there was Anna Maria van Schurman's Latin tract, *A Maid May Also Be a Scholar*), parchment paper, various plumes, ink pots and little trinkets that seemed to originate from distant lands, gifts from ancestors or other gentlemen, I did not know – in any case, her talismans. As she wrote, she might clutch them in her palm, drawing in their inspirational power, or she might stare at them, opening her mind to new worlds. Although I could not witness the creative process at first hand, the inertia of it hummed in the room, and a mist seemed to rise up from the desk and eddy around in the air – faces, places, sounds, smells. Irresistibly drawn inside, I began walking the length of one wall, trailing my fingertips over the smooth leathery spines.

I looked up to find her carrying in the tray of tea – despite her gracefulness and perfect posture, the cups and saucers made an awful racket, rattling against one another (she was not used to performing such menial tasks) – and she placed it on the table. Then she slipped into her seat and folded her pale hands over her lap.

'Dear Pieter,' she began, as if writing me a letter. 'Why can't we remain as we are? People like us, who cherish their freedoms, are not meant for marriages. Can you imagine me as a wife? There is no more loyalty in me than in a stewed prune! Most of the time I do live on a cloud with Zeus or some other hero, even you for instance, but I am wise enough to realize that no two mortals can ever attain that kind of bliss or intimacy because, by nature of their togetherness, they inevitably ruin one another. Every marriage, no matter who is involved, is based on a fallacy. The longer people stay together the more insincere they become. I never want to grow accustomed to that or grow accustomed to being accustomed. I would rather we be friends – lonely, honest friends who cherish each other's minds and words.'

The rejection was too much to bear; the word 'friends' shone at me like a beacon. I jumped up and began flailing my arms around the room. 'You're right. How silly of me to believe I was worthy of you. A ridiculous idea!'

She stomped her foot, shaking the table and the cups, spilling some of my tea on to the saucer. 'Don't be childish.'

I turned to her, hands on my hips, and glared. 'You're the one stomping your foot!'

'Because you make me angry, no one makes me so angry!'

'I'm sorry, but people who avoid love are just plain cowards,' I said. 'Because it brings happiness, too – not just occasionally but every day, in all the tiny things that add up, you know, the way someone looks at you with adoration or desire when you don't feel you deserve it, or brushes your arm in understanding while passing on their way to something else, or holds you in the middle of the night because you cannot sleep for fear of ghosts though they want to be sleeping themselves' – I noticed Clara stirring my tea for me – 'or thoughtfully stirs your tea even if you make her angry.' She blushed and dropped the spoon. 'We don't have to grow accustomed to anything, and we'll have servants – as many as you wish!'

She thought for a moment, her left hand kneading her opposite shoulder. 'You want to impose your idea of happiness on me, but have you ever considered whether I'm the right match for you? I suppose it has not entered your mind. How would you know, anyway? We've only met a few times.'

I walked over to her, then crouched near her chair and counted the lines encircling her neck, which reminded me of a tree stump with its succession of deep rings. 'I was just thinking the same thing, that every single individual is unknowable and full of contradictions. Does that mean we don't try to understand? You speak of time, well, one can live with a person for even fifteen years and never know them. What I see in you at this moment is what I will always see, and I like what I see!'

Leaning forward over her lap, she glowered at me. 'You contradicted yourself.'

She was right, I was a man who had shat in his own hat and set it back on his head. 'Then you understand what I mean.'

'Yes, you belong in an asylum.'

'Well then, before they cart me away . . .' I began, but our faces were so close I could see her nose hairs twitching and feel her breath clipping my mouth. She must have eaten pheasant or capon for her midday meal.

She looked at me squarely. 'You're incorrigible.'

'That's what my father always says.'

'Handsome, though. Sometimes.'

I raised my chin. 'You think so?'

'Yes, I like your high forehead, it rumbles when you're thinking, and I like your lips, the way they form tiny peaks, and I especially like your letters, even if they no longer fit into my box.'

Was she saying all this merely out of guilt or pity? I did not care, only that I had caused her to retreat with her shiny lance, or even to hide it, say, under her chair. I leant closer. 'You should reply more often, and at greater length.'

When she nodded, I pecked her on the nose.

With that out of the way, a silence that would normally have frightened or embarrassed me was a moment of pure joy, and I actually started to feel proud in my pointy boots. My knees creaked as I stood up and pressed down on the wrinkles in my breeches.

She sat upright in her chair, and a veil of reticence fell over her face. 'Why don't I tell you more about the painting, about Geertje.'

'I'm listening,' I said, sitting down next to her and plumping up the pillow behind me, then, when I was still unsatisfied, stuffing it under my arm. I looked at her out of the corner of my eye, hoping she might suggest I kiss her again, because I was not ready to listen: my mind was slipping backward to what had just happened between us, then time was passing and leading me to another, distant moment in which the two of us — she with silver sprigs, me with a receding hairline — huddled together in that very room, reading our books, silently sharing our disappointments. Once I was able to bring myself back to reality — it required a few proverbial slaps to my face — this is the story Clara began to tell me, more or less, based on the gossip around town from her intellectual circle and the Cock & Bull tavern.

'Let's see,' she said, smacking her lips. 'Geertje was born in Edam in 1605, and later worked as a waitress when she met a ship's trumpeter, Abraham Claesz, whom she married in 1634. Her husband died before they conceived any children, so she began keeping house for a lumber merchant. She also worked for her brother, Pieter, a carpenter employed by the VOC, and he knew Rembrandt somehow.'

'How?' I asked.

'The details are unclear, but apparently Rembrandt lent their family a great deal of money to ransom Pieter from the Barbary

Coast. In exchange, Geertje came to work for Rembrandt in 1642 as a housekeeper, and helped his wife through her illness. But when Saskia died a few months later, not yet thirty, Titus was only nine months old, so Geertje stayed on as a dry nurse. Within a year, she became Rembrandt's mistress and model. Would you believe he used her in a series of lewd prints?'

'I've heard of them. Have you . . .?'

'I know about one, a monk and his temptress!' Her face flushed. 'But only because I am writing a few poems in tribute to Rembrandt's etchings.'

'You are?'

'Don't get overly excited, they're for no eyes and ears but my own . . . Anyway, when Geertje became ill in 1648 she made Titus her heir, but by then the relationship had cooled. She and Rembrandt began to quarrel over the new servant girl, Hendrickje Stoffels, who was younger and more beautiful.'

I laughed.

She shrugged, annoyed. 'Geertje was eaten up by jealousy, so she took leave of the house. Then she had a legal document drawn up, accusing Rembrandt of breaching his promise to marry her. The Commissioners ordered him to pay her a sum of money to discharge her debts and an annual pension. Both were unsatisfied with the terms and their disagreement carried on for months – one day she would agree, the next day she would not agree – until they finally settled it. He was obliged to pay her 200 guilders up front and 200 guilders per year.'

'How ridiculous!'

'Still, it was not enough for Geertje. She sold Saskia's jewels and some of his paintings too. Apparently, she then began leading a disreputable life.'

'Is that how the painting came to you?'

'Well, she gave it to a female friend, who eventually sold it to my father.'

'Then what?' I asked.

'In 1650, Rembrandt returned the blows when he solicited the neighbours for negative comments about Geertje. He composed an affidavit saying she was mentally unsound and had her imprisoned in the House of Corrections in Gouda. As far as I know, she never got out.'

That was, essentially, the end of the story and our conversation, because Clara had to attend an underground meeting that afternoon, though she agreed to see me the following day. To keep my mind from sinking into lustful thoughts, I decided to journey to Gouda immediately with the intent of speaking to Geertje at the House of Corrections. Apart from Rembrandt's children, she was the only living person who would understand him.

I paid my dues for a seat on a wagon that was due to leave shortly and would carry me to my destination in a couple of hours, perhaps slightly longer because of the mud, which tended to slow the wheels. Settling myself in the dark compartment nearest the window, I avoided the eyes of the few strangers also heading south on the road in case it sparked a conversation, for I wanted to admire the landscape, which was always more enjoyable at a distance, from within the carriage walls, my boots nestled in the straw. Although I had spent most of my childhood out of doors – playing in the streets all day – I was never comfortable in the open air.

When the wagon pushed off, I grabbed the handle to steady myself, but leaving Amsterdam was as easy as moving from one room to another, the dividing line between city and country was so pronounced: soon after we had crossed the bridge outside the gate, the road gave me a view of small farmhouses, the mood of barren fields and the stench of manure. Although it was still early, the morning sun had already extinguished the last traces of snow. On the horizon, the rising windmills and church towers appeared insignificant against the large clouds soaring over the patchy flatlands. Sparrows flew out of the wind-ruffled birches, and even the sheep seemed to move with us.

I drifted into a reverie though my eyes remained open, thinking about Geertje, the peasant woman, small in figure but plump. How would she have changed through the years? Her heart-shaped face would be cut with wrinkles, I imagined, and her once chestnut-coloured hair would have turned a whitish-grey. It would be difficult to believe that she had once been beautiful, except perhaps when she smiled, though she would still be wearing a northern dress with fur around the collar, tightly fitted and strained into creases. I could just about hear her strange accent, belonging to the unknown north. She was whispering.

'It's all her fault,' she said.

'Who?' I looked up and glanced around me. The other travellers were already asleep; they had not muttered a single word and had not heard me, either. As my gaze drifted out the window, I strained my ears for that voice again.

This time it was louder, rough and guttural. 'Hendrickje Stoffels, that twenty-three-year-old tart. I was in full charge until she came along. I cared for Rembrandt and his little boy for seven years! But she turned my man against me, always causing trouble. One time she broke his sheep's skull, then turned round and told him I was the only one with a key to his cabinet, when I sure as hell lent her the key!'

From the window I glimpsed the roof of a cottage nestled in a dale, a shadowy cave with sprouting weeds and flowers. I imagined Rembrandt walking out here, wandering through the meadows and woods then hiding in a tree hollow to make his etchings: a windmill, a couple on a picnic, a man with milk buckets suspended from a shoulder yoke. Afterwards, he would follow the dyke roads, stopping along the way to chat with the fishermen or to draw the boats leaning in the breeze.

Geertje rocked in her chair, clasping her stubby hands. Her nails were torn off, showing the raw skin underneath. 'She acted as if Titus were *her* child, then she tried to seduce my man, flouncing her bosoms around, half-dressed. What man would be able to resist such advances? You wouldn't, would you?'

'Well, no . . .' I said hesitantly, then glanced at the strangers, but they had not budged.

'I couldn't bear to stay there any longer. So I threatened Rembrandt, "She goes or I go!" and he said, "Well, then – go!"'

I nearly jumped out of my seat. 'Did you go? Where did you go?'

Her brown eyes widened, creasing around the edges. 'A miserable little room in a shoemaker's house on the Rapenburg. What was I supposed to do? Just because I was barren! Wasn't one son enough for him? I thought he wanted to marry me. I sued him for breach of contract, that showed him.'

'Is that what he said, he would marry you?'

She opened her mouth to reveal a set of rotten, black teeth (so I had been wrong about the smile). 'He gave me a silver marriage medal and his wife's expensive jewels. Why would he do such a thing?'

The carriage passed a country house situated beside the road, nestling among its sheltering trees. A roofed-over hayrick, loaded to its limit, became visible behind the barn. A lone figure stood at the gate, half in sun, half in shade. Was he a herder? His cattle were roaming out in the green pasture.

'I don't know,' I said. 'Men behave strangely when they are in love.' I thought about my encounter with Clara as a perfect example. Why did I have to be so impetuous? At this moment, she must be regretting that she ever met me. 'What happened when you sued him?'

Geertje cackled, but it was a laugh of pain. 'He would not appear in court, so she did, and swore under oath about everything she had overheard in the house. She lied through her teeth, saying Rembrandt never promised to marry me. How would she know? Then she told them I willingly put Titus in my will. I was only being loyal to Rembrandt because he wanted his property to go to Titus.'

She paused, sucking her gums. 'I had to go to the notary and agree to the annual payment. If I didn't promise to keep the deal, I would have to return all the money. When it came to signing, I threw the plume at Rembrandt and yelled, I cannot sign it! What if I got sick? I might need a nurse. How could I live on this sum? After all my years of service, all my love and devotion, you beast! I demanded that he marry me or I would not sign it, I said.'

I did not know whose side to take because I felt sorry for both of them. Rembrandt was definitely headstrong, but Geertje was clearly unreliable and horrifying. 'What did he do?'

'He ran around the house, up and down the stairs, from top to bottom and back again, smashing things as if he had gone completely crazy. Stubborn as an ox, that man, and ugly as sin. Do you think I stayed with him for his fat nose and lazy eye? He gave me money and loved me like a charging bull. But Titus was crying, and I loved him, the poor boy, so finally I agreed.'

Near the roadside cottages of timber and thatch, a man with a brace of dogs at his heel walked towards us on the winding lane, carrying a knob-tipped pole over his shoulder: a hunter on his way to flush the rabbits out of their holes.

'Didn't you think Rembrandt was being generous enough, I mean, considering his financial troubles?'

'Well, I had no choice but to pawn the jewels – three gold rings, one with a diamond cluster. When my brother collected my first payment, because I was in debt to him, Rembrandt persuaded him to redeem the jewels and promised him part of the sale. And Pieter did, that traitor! Then they all went against me, saying I was mad, so they could lock me up in this wretched place!'

Beyond the wooden pier and wharf, a single oarsman with ginger hair rowed amongst paddling ducks. Near a clump of bushes, an angler crouched at the water's edge while his spotted spaniel trotted over the bridge. We were almost there.

Already I had been privy to Geertje's deepest secrets, apart from one. It seemed the proper time to ask her about the pictures; where they had gone? 'By the way, what about those pictures . . .?'

She bent forward and whispered, 'The naughty pictures? Ha! I knew you'd ask. You look like a gentleman, but you're just as filthy as the rest. I have one of them. Do you want to see?'

'Yes!'

She pulled a piece of paper out of her apron and handed it to me. The small etching was fingerprinted and worn from use. That was no surprise: the small scene was extraordinary. At the edge of a field of tall corn, a man and a woman copulate like animals. The man is on top of the woman, and he leans his weight upon the knuckles of his right hand. The woman's right hand clasps him to her, and her legs entwine with his. She is barefoot, but the monk has lost one of his sandals in the activity, his foot braced against the ground for support. The woman is a milkmaid; her jug lies to the left of them, tossed aside. In the background, the corn is being cut into swathes by a figure swinging a sickle in his left hand. I supposed some would find it offensive, but I found it hilarious. Rembrandt is playing the potent monk, I thought, laughing.

'Are there more?'

She looked at me, nostrils flared. 'We did it everywhere, in the fields, in the courtyard, in barns and on haystacks, everywhere. Then he'd go off and sketch our positions. Too bad for you, he kept them.'

She stood up, bent down and thrust her face at me, glaring with wild eyes. Her stinky breath blasted me as she screeched, 'You know what? Rembrandt *paid* to lock me in here. He's still paying for these sheriffs and wardresses to torture me. Look at my face! Look at my hands! Do you want to love me? Do you want to fuck me? I curse the hour I met him, and if I ever get out, I will kill him. You hear me, I'll kill him!'

I shrank back, clutching my face in my hands. What could I do? I thought about hitting her, but my courage had melted down like wax, bubbling and swirling. My voice squeaked. 'I'll get you out. Tell me what to do and I will, Geertje, I promise!'

'You're useless. No one can help me. I've been alone in here for twenty years, saying my prayers, listening to sermons. Would you believe it? No one to talk to.' She bent her head on her shoulder, blinked and strained a small smile.

Just then, the carriage hit a bump and jolted me back to my senses. I glanced around to see that only one traveller remained, sitting across from me. Had he overheard my conversation? When I tried to read his face for signs of fear or disgust, his eyes were kind and watery. He tipped his hat as the wagon came to a halt.

'This is where we part ways,' he said, nodding.

I gathered up my bag and said, 'Good day.'

When I climbed out, my knees buckled − though the time had gone so quickly, I had been cooped up for three hours. The driver directed me to the House of Corrections by pointing to a lonely road where all was quiet and there were no buildings in sight apart from the church spire in the centre of the town. I stretched my legs, hopping from one foot to the other, then dizzily followed the path through the budding trees and spreading foliage without knowing whether this was, indeed, the right way. The sky was full of billowing clouds, bright against the muted landscape, and the air smelt of earth and straw. The beauty of the countryside dazzled me, and I stepped slowly as if one irreverent move might cause it to crumble. The remoteness of the spot was deep and unbroken until I rounded a curve and the dingy grey walls of the house loomed at me. When I reached the main entrance, I met a sheriff who flashed me a strange look, as if surprised that anyone would be visiting here, then led me inside.

The room was a solemnly silent nook pervaded with an acrid smell that seemed to filter through every crack in the wall. From the adjacent rooms I heard a loud clacking and women's voices. When the guard left me, I walked up to the desk and smiled at the wardress, a stout woman with rosy cheeks and fuzzy hair.

'Name.'

'Geertje Dircx.'

She examined me, raising an eyebrow. 'Your name, sir?'

'Oh, Pieter Blaeu.'

She fingered through a few papers and glowered. 'Are you committing yourself?'

God forbid I be mistaken for a vagrant! 'I'm a visitor.'

'Have you notified us through a solicitor that you were coming?'

I towered over her. 'Actually, no, but I am here to see someone who has been here for a long time, probably without visitors, and I would appreciate your help.'

'The name was?'

'Geertje Dircx, she was admitted in 1650.'

'I'm afraid . . .'

'Please, it is a very urgent matter.'

'Unless there has been a death in the family . . .'

'Yes, there has been, you see.'

Her mouth twitched. She knew I was lying, but she must have liked me, or was too tired to argue, or was lonely. 'I will have to check my documents.' She began scrambling through stacks of papers in a tall wooden cabinet behind her. I was ready to offer some sort of advice, but it was intriguing to watch her, a squat, rotund figure trying to climb the shelves.

'What are they doing?' I asked, as the clacking noise grew louder, not sure whether to refer to them as patients or prisoners.

'Spinning, of course,' she said, over her shoulder. 'That's what they do all day long, until their fingers are worn to the bone.' She seemed agitated; perhaps she took an immoral delight in making this revelation, or perhaps she was a cruel woman who revelled in other women's distress. So that was what I had smelt: the lye.

Darkness lay over the room, obscuring its corners and cracks. The window was shrouded in a black cloth. The fire in the small hearth afforded little light, and the candle on her desk flickered pathetically due to the draught. No wonder she squinted, and I thought she would never find the records.

'Ah, there it is,' she said, bringing her parchment back to the desk. 'Well, according to this account, she's no longer here.'

'What do you mean, this account?'

'That's what it says. She was discharged in 1655.' She smirked. 'You're thirteen years late.'

'Are you sure?'

'Yes, in fact, she is out of her misery, so to speak.'

'What?' My fist pounded the desk.

'No need to get upset, but she's dead, sir.'

Two Men in Tall Hats

When the time for our meal had come,
    My loyal maid confessed,
After she scavenged round for some,
    'No mustard for the guest!'

'Hurry, hurry, buy some quickly,
    Follow the winding shore;
Can't you see the man is prickly?'
    (He's actually quite a chore.)

By the window he stood forlorn,
    Gazing across the field
At bramble and hollow and thorn,
    To see what it might yield.

An empty boat sat near my bridge,
    The lovers out of sight;
He said, 'Let's search the heaving hedge,
    And give them both a fright.'

Then turning to me, wild-eyed,
    He shook his money purse;
'I'll bet you every coin inside,
    That you can't write a verse

Before she has done her fetching,
    In half-an-hour due;
By the time I make an etching
    Of tree and spire too.'

Because I was low on mustard
    To spice our hearty meal,
His usual envy festered,
    And caused this whole ordeal.

With an idea in my head,
    I searched for book and plume,
But he was cutting lines like mad;
    My rage began to fume!

A copper plate upon his knee,
    A burin in his hand,
He surveyed what his eye could see:
    The beauty of my land.

The light spread over field and thatch,
    Whilst shadows led the way
Toward the Amstel's muddy path
    With budding trees asway.

They leant on the bridge's railing,
    Two men in their tall hats,
The leisure boats were sailing;
    Old fishermen perhaps?

Above, the great expanse of sky
    Was tinged with green and blue;

Van Rijn

And no words could describe the high
  I felt, after verse two.

When I looked over my shoulder,
  He'd almost reached the end.
I wished that my poem was bolder,
  And worthy of my friend.

The Oude Kerk tower was shewn
  From Amsterdam's north side;
The only thing he had not done
  Was check his work and sign.

Just then, my maid came down the road,
  The jar with her, God bless,
But I had failed to reach my goal,
  A poet nonetheless!

The sausage steamed and I felt wan,
  With nothing else to say;
I could not beat my paragon,
  Who proved his skill that day.

I handed him the money due
  And said, 'What's fair is fair.'
He passed it back, the picture too;
  'I really could not care!'

— Jan Six, 1645
trans. Pieter Blaeu

Amsterdam, 1654

Pinto's Piles

How can I work through all this noise? My head throbs. The workers keep coming and going, kicking up dust and dirt. They've torn down my wall, the one I share with my neighbour, Daniel Pinto. Now they have to rebuild it. The floodwater damaged both of our foundations, but Pinto's piles sank further, so he is raising the level of his floor. By three feet and two thumbs! He is using the opportunity to create additional space in his cellar for storing his goods — tobacco, sugar and spices from the Caribbean. When I agreed to the proposed alterations, more for his benefit, I had not foreseen that it would take so long. The carpenters refuse to work on Sundays and during the Sabbath.

I still owe half the price of this enormous house, almost the largest on the Breestraat. Some of my friends have lent me money, but my creditors want the full amount plus interest. No one is having financial success these days because of those damned Englishmen. I say, the war is going badly! To top it off, Pinto is taking me to court. He claims he was charged for my lumber. Even with the other problems, this construction mess is the heaviest burden of all — it means I have been painting very little of late. The pounding and banging never seems to stop. There's a stranger round every corner, conducting his business as if he owned the place.

A Prayer of Thanks

Dear Lord, I have much to be thankful for — especially dear Titus, who reminds me of his mother every day with his serene face and auburn curls. A son to carry on my name, and so well behaved! On the morning of St Nicolaes, he squealed to find his shoes full of sweets and gingerbread. On Twelfth Night, I made him a rommelpot from a jar, a pig's bladder stretched over it and a stick that moves up and down, so he could march in the procession with the other children. Not only that, he found a silver coin in his bread and became King for the day. I wish I could tell him how sorry I am, that life and death has separated them, mother and child. It has been twelve years since Saskia's death, but the loss is unbearable. All I can give him are these little gifts and my insufficient words to read when I am deep under the earth.

What would we do without Hendrickje, aye? This woman has the heart of a lion and loves us more than her very self. When I first met her, Eros shook me like a mountain wind falling on oak trees. Nearly five years on, I am still rattled to the core. Her body is beginning to swell: she is pregnant with our first child. At forty-eight, most men have to dip their members in eggs and oil to stimulate conception, or consume copious amounts of fowl and cow's milk to give their testicles energy. Ha, I must be as fertile as a crazed ox!

David, Uriah and Bathsheba

Bathsheba has always been a popular subject for painters, but my treatment must stand out amongst the rest if I am to rival the Italians. Return to the source, that's what Lastman taught me. Things always appear much different that way. I agree with Dante, who believes that every passage of the Bible has a fourfold meaning. Erigena says that those meanings are as infinite as the hues in a peacock's tail. This tragic tale comes from the second book of Samuel, and begins . . .

It came to pass that King David sent Joab, his servants and all of Israel to destroy the children of Ammon and besiege Rabbah while he stayed at home in Jerusalem. One evening he walked upon the rooftop of his palace and caught sight of a beautiful woman washing herself, so he inquired around his palace to find out her identity, and someone said, 'Is not this Bathsheba, the daughter of Eliam, the wife of Uriah the Hittite?' Immediately, David sent a letter to her by the hand of his messenger, proclaiming his love to Bathsheba with the aim of taking her as his own.

Note: *This is the most important moment in the story. What did Bathsheba feel when she discovered that the King had chosen her and sent her husband off to battle? After reading the letter, she had to decide between obedience to her King and fidelity to her husband.*

Although she was married, she had no choice but to comply with the King's request, and the timing was right, for she had just cleansed herself after her menstruation. Hence she went to the palace and lay down with the King. Some time later, she wrote a letter to David, declaring, 'I am with child.'

At this, David's messengers carried an order to Joab: 'Send me Uriah the Hittite.' So Joab released Uriah and sent him to David, who then questioned him about the people and how the war was prospering. After that he said, 'Go down to your house, and wash your feet.' David thought, if Uriah went home he would sleep with his wife, then everyone would assume it was her husband who had impregnated her. Yet, rather than returning home, Uriah slept at the door of the palace with all the servants. David tried to stir him, saying, 'It is from a long journey that you have come, is it not? Why did you not go down to your house?' With a noble heart, Uriah replied, 'The ark, Israel and Judah abide in tents, and my lord Joab has encamped in the open fields. Shall I then go into mine house, to eat and to drink, and to lie with my wife? As you are living, and as your soul is living, I will not do this thing!' David said, 'Dwell here today and tomorrow, then I will allow you to leave.' Uriah did just so, and David gave him plenty to eat and made him drunk.

In the morning, David wrote a letter to Joab and sent it by the hand of Uriah, sealing his Fate: 'Set Uriah in the forefront of the hottest battle, and retreat behind him, that he may be struck down and die.' When the men went out to fight, Joab assigned Uriah to a place where he knew there were valiant men. Afterwards, Joab wrote to David: 'Surely the men prevailed against us, and came out into the field, but the soldiers shot from the wall on your servants and killed them; your servant Uriah the Hittite is dead also.' David replied, 'Do not let this thing displease you, for the sword devours one as well as another. Make your battle more strong against the city, and overthrow it.'

When Bathsheba heard that Uriah, her husband, was dead, she fasted for seven days. When the mourning period had passed, David fetched her to his house, she became his wife and bore him a son. However, the thing that David had done displeased the Lord. True to the prophecy of Nathan, their child died on the seventh day.

. . . I am already imagining her through the King's eyes, the eyes that are watching her in secret. I will paint her paunch with devotion, love and pity. Inside her, a child will form. The unfortunate bastard!

How Am I to Pay My Debts?

Somehow I spent nearly all of Saskia's fortune, 20,000 guilders. Over the years I've purchased curiosities, props, costumes, busts, prints and paintings, but these are the things an artist requires. And deserves! Besides, my profits once exceeded every craftsman's in the city. My early paintings were — and still are — fetching up to 1,600 guilders apiece. How was I supposed to know it would cost so much to run this household, the market would shrink and my style would become unfashionable?

I make a tiny profit on my recent pieces, and almost every buyer backs out for some reason or another. Jan and Hendrick say it is because I am a slow painter. How could I compromise? Most of my clients are preposterous, anyway. A few months ago, I made a portrait of a young girl for the Jewish merchant Diego d'Andrade. He decided midway that he did not want it because, he claimed, it showed no resemblance at all to his young daughter. What did he expect? The girl broke from her sittings and refused to follow my rules. Then d'Andrade brought in a notary, demanding that I finish the work immediately or else return the 75 guilders he had advanced to me. In the end, I won, but we parted ways.

Isaac van Herstbeeck and Cornelis Witsen lent me 4,200 guilders against my house and my possessions. I can pay off the conveyance tax and receive the deed, but I will still be in debt to my creditors. So I may be forced to hold an auction and sell some of my collection. Abraham Francen says I could fetch a good price for my prints by Dürer and Van Leyden. He has helped me with dealing on many occasions, so I trust him implicitly. Oh, no one will want to buy my own drab paintings. This is why my face sinks inwardly, rotting before my eyes. The Apelles of Amsterdam, nonetheless.

Hendrickje Stoffels, My Bathsheba

The model sits on a bank covered by a plain white shift. She supports her upright pose with her left arm, a slender hand planted on the drapery. Her other hand rests on her crossed right leg, clutching a letter, one corner curled back to reveal part of the script. The paper casts a warm shadow on her left thigh. Her gaze extends upward as she ponders her Fate. The light enters through the upper windows and falls on her oval face and sloping forehead. Her brown eyes are wide-set and almond-shaped, seemingly flat against her face, framed with heavy brows. She has a dimpled chin and full, pouting lips. Her wavy brown hair is pulled into a bun surrounded by beads. A long braid tied with a red ribbon hangs over her left shoulder down to her breast.

HS: Sweetie, I have a knot in my neck. I don't know if I can stay still much longer.

RVR: There are four hours behind you, only two left.

HS: What are you going to pay me?

RVR: You'll get what you deserve. (*Aside*) How should I direct Bathsheba's gaze to show her emotion? Hendrickje has been looking up, her eyes peering beyond the room and the picture. But something does not seem right.

The model lowers her puckered chin and looks at the floor.

RVR: Are you falling asleep?

HS: No, I'm sorry, I was thinking she would not want to face the Lord.

RVR: (*Aside*) Can she read my mind? She is young and uneducated but sometimes she understands even before I do. Why hadn't I thought of that earlier? With this small gesture, she is forced to retreat entirely into herself. (*To HS*) Yes, that's perfect. But tilt your head away from me slightly.

As the model shifts her head, the red ribbon dangling from her hair slides further up her décolletage.

RVR: Good. Pull the opposite braid over your shoulder.

With this gesture, the model's right cheek caresses one of her braids.

RVR: Now, hold there.

Time passes. The painter and his model grow tired.

HS: I'm hungry. May I tempt you with some herrings?

RVR: (*Aside*) She is eating for two. And she knows how to pull my strings. I can never turn down a herring, even if my brush is in the midst of a perfect stroke. Besides, the hammering has grown louder next door. They are about to fell the Levant trader's house. I would not be disappointed.

A MAN (*Offstage*): *Shouting.* Timber-r-r-r!

The house shakes and the windows clatter. The painter throws his brush at the wall. His model seizes the moment to escape and steps out of pose to slip into her housedress. After she scrambles downstairs, the painter wipes his hands on his apron and sets to cleaning the brushes. A few minutes later, the model returns and sets a tray of beer, cheese and fish on the table. Immediately she begins pecking at the food.

HS: *Cheeks moving up and down.* Someone's here to see you. It's Trijn Jacobsdr.

RVR: That old bat? What's she doing here?

HS: She wants to speak with you about . . . Geertje.

RVR: *Finishes off a herring with a burp.* How dare she intrude! Who let her into this house? (*Aside*) Trijn is one of two Trijns, both widowed friends of my former lover, who refuse to get it into their heads that Geertje has gone mad.

HS: Rebecca did not understand. Don't worry. I will see her with you, if you like.

RVR: Let's be done with it then. I want to enjoy my fish.

The painter and his lover clamber downstairs and meet the housekeeper, Rebecca Willems, who is clutching a broom, trying to clean up the dust that covers all surfaces of the house. The three of them walk into the front hall where the sinister old dragon is waiting, her face like the shrivelled skin of a peach. The painter and his lover stand side by side as the housekeeper flits over the floorboards, scrubbing corners.

TJ: *Breathing fire.* You beast! How could you do this to Geertje? She didn't deserve to be locked up, and now you want to keep her there?

RVR: *Holds up two palms.* This is the best thing for her. She is not well enough to be out in society. I have done my best and continue doing my best. I pay her a monthly allowance.

TJ: *Spitting.* You think you can rule everyone. You used her, you ugly ape, and you should have married her. At the very least that would have been, your *best*. Have you ever thought about your son? She raised him as her own!

RVR: My boy is not your business, woman. You have no idea of what passed between Geertje and me. Maybe I would have considered marrying her if she hadn't lost her sense . . .

TJ: *Shakes a finger at the painter's lover.* No, it's her fault! That filthy Jezebel!

HS: Are you calling me a whore?

TJ: No, I'm calling you a harlot!

HS: How dare you!

The painter's lover, scowling, charges at the old dragon. As she reaches her, the old dragon catches hold of her braid and yanks her hair. The painter's lover struggles from the old dragon's grasp, then stomps to the window and perches on the sill, her heavy-lidded eyes fighting back tears.

RVR: Don't touch my woman, you old bag! You already know that the will of my deceased wife makes it impossible for me to marry . . .

TJ: You only care about the money, you heartless ox! Well, I'm going to get Geertje out of there whether you like it or not.

RVR: *Raises his voice but speaks clearly.* I've made my peace with the Lord. Geertje will not be released until Pieter returns. I warn you, do not get involved.

TJ: *Flashes her overgrown fingernails, looming daggers.* He's betrayed her. How can she trust him? Someone must do something … She's suffering in there.

RVR: *Wags a finger at her, shouting.* Trijn Jacobsdr., you will deeply regret it if you cross me. Now get out of my house!

The housekeeper is swift to open the door and shoo the old dragon out with her broom. The whiskers swipe her backside one, two, three times until she is snivelling on the stoop. A cloud of dust envelops her. The painter's lover slams the door.

Two Letters

A courier brought two letters this morning.

The first letter informs me that my two burglars have been charged and arrested. During the winter, Eleasar Swab, a Jew living in the lumberyard, and his accomplice Hartog Abrahams, dealer in old clothes, made a habit of sneaking into my cellar in the middle of the night. Those crooks carried off sixty rolls of tobacco under my very nose! They were not my own goods, fortunately. I'd been storing them for the Pereiras. I feel pillaged all the same. Another unwanted disruption to my work! The second message comes from Delft and my former student, Carel Fabritius, a highly talented artist. He trained in my workshop for nearly two years, along with his brother, Barent. How I long for those glory days.

> *Dear Master van Rijn,*
> *After offering you my kind regards, I hope this letter finds you in good health and happiness. I am diligently engaged in making a portrait of*

Simon Decker, the retired verger of the Oude Kerk, who lives on the south side of Jan Voersteeg, trying to utilize all the skills you taught me in the handling of paint and in ways of composition. I have recently completed a little deceit on a tiny panel of wood from a cabinet. It is a depiction of my pet bird, a putterje, chained to a curved rail on top of its box in front of a mottled white wall. The broad brushstrokes are visible at close range, but at a distance the picture looks extremely life-like. I owe its success to you, my master. One day, you may see it.

With hesitation, I come to trouble you for your gracious assistance. After four years, my reputation is finally growing in Delft; many of my pictures are in the hands of good dealers, such as Reynier Vermeer, whom you may know, and a patron, Dr Theodore Vallensis, dean of the Surgeons' Guild. However, all of my works remain unsold. There is no money for artists in Delft any more, due to a shortage of commissions, and we find ourselves in debt. I, admittedly, owe a great deal of money to a waiter at the Doel Inn for food and drink. Recently, I painted two coats of arms for the town council and received a lowly sum of twelve guilders, which was only enough to pay my annual fee for the Guild. (Reynier's son, Johannes, a new member, had only one and a half guilders!) It seems opportune that I establish myself as a painter in Amsterdam, and if you provide me with any guidance in this matter, I will repay my master with service and friendship.

Your humble and affectionate servant,

Carel Fabritius

While most of my students ask for help, I respond to few of them — only those such as Carel, who work diligently and with great passion at improving their skills. What a wonderful young man! I will reply to his *letter as soon as I have a quiet moment this evening. With peace in the workshop, I want to return to my Bathsheba.*

THINGS TO DO:
1 *Pick up repaired breeches from the tailor's*
2 *Find Titus a monkey for his birthday*
3 *Sketch the actor, Willem de Ruyter, preparing to play the bishop in Gijsbrecht*
4 *Deliver prints to Ephraim Bueno. Return scalpel*

Portrait of Jan Six, the Poet

He knows I am inspecting him and turns away slightly. His cleft chin nuzzles his white collar, the edges curled out. After licking his lips, he closes them, though not entirely. What is he thinking as he stands in the light? Under his tall, wide-brimmed hat, his dark eyes meet mine with an inward stare. His pencil-thin moustache and eyebrows, fastidiously trimmed, frame his strong nose, set a little askew. Despite the dark pouches under his eyes, his curdled-cheese skin and his frizzy red hair, he is, nevertheless, handsome. This is my good friend Jan Six, wearing his finest clothes: a long grey coat parading many gold fastenings, matching knee-length panta-loons, white silk stockings and black Italian leather shoes. His face is a warm pink, but is it a loyal one?

I met Jan about eight years ago, when he asked me to make an etching of him in his workshop amongst his books. In fact, I made three because he was not satisfied with the first two. He is somewhat tetchy but I cannot blame him. He still lives with his mother, an overexcited woman, in the Blue Eagle on the Kloveniersburgwal. His father, Jean, died before he was born, so his mother, Anna Wijmer, took charge of his education. She sent him to Leyden University, where he studied liberal arts, then on a tour through the Alps.

There is no need to give a list of Jan's credits. Everyone knows he has made a great success of his life as a poet and a playwright. If they don't know, he makes sure they do. Unlike me, he is a great rhetorician, which is why he travels comfortably in the higher circles of society. When he tells me I should make more friends, I say, 'Friends or distractions?' He might admire me as a painter but he disapproves of my lifestyle. No need to say a word, his gestures tell me my women are immoral, my borrowing shameful, my dealings shady and my spending capricious. If you could see how he enters my house with a grand air then prances by Hendrickje without lowering his eyes — as if she does not exist!

Every so often, I visit his country estate at Ijmond to sketch the riverbank as the sailboats pass by. We chat for hours about our rival collections or consult each other on art purchases. I was sitting next to him when he bought the ninth-century Carolingian minuscule manuscript of Caesar's Gallic War! A few years ago, when his play of Medea proved a major success, he commissioned me to etch the frontispiece for the book. I also contributed two drawings for his Pandora, one of which showed a blind Homer reciting his verses, open-mouthed before an audience. Then last year, Christoffel Thijs began to pressure me about my debt on the house, so Jan lent me 1,000 guilders. Though the loan was interest free, he demanded a separate guarantee from Lodewijk van Ludick, the antiquary. This is something I cannot understand about Jan; he will make a kind gesture then almost retract it. No matter how much I try to despise him, he manages to seduce me by his mere presence into admiration. He enlarges my mind and makes me feel important, even glamorous. Now is my chance to repay him with a great portrait.

The canvas, three-quarter-length on an almost square support, rests on the easel in front of the painter. The poet stands against the wall, looming from the darkness. He fiddles with his vast white cuffs.

JS: *Glances around.* I'm sorry, this incessant banging is giving me a headache. How can you work through all the noise?

RVR: I manage. You'll be fine for a few more minutes.

Without warning, the poet drops his expression and walks to the door. Taking his scarlet cloak from the hook, he settles it on his shoulder in a determined gesture so it drapes over his shoulder, half-on, half-off. The gold of the lapel shimmers against the red fabric. He begins to put on his chamois gloves, which resemble his leathery face.

RVR: *Leaps from his chair.* Where are you going?

JS: I told you that I couldn't stay all afternoon.

RVR: No? (*Aside*) He's skipped five sessions already! He says he cannot pose for long hours because of his back and still expects perfection.

JS: I have some business to attend to.

RVR: What sort of business?

JS: I have an important meeting with . . .

As the poet rambles on, the muscles in his face relax, his jowls lower, his lips almost smile, and his pupils enlarge to at least twice their former size.

RVR: (*Aside*) How different he looks now, more vulnerable. Confident in uniform, unready in mind. So many pretences! Did he think he could fool me all this time? His face intrigues me, but I hate it. He must be willing to play his part and allow me to stick to my own perception. If I can paint him like this, his secrets are bound to open on the canvas. There must be a way to convince him to stay.

JS: . . . and it's likely to earn me a good sum.

RVR: Jan, step back into the light, but remain just as you are. (*Aside*) This moment will last only a minute. Two, if I'm lucky.

The poet removes one glove then begins tugging on the other.

RVR: Jan, please stay as you are.

JS: I will just return my cloak . . .

RVR: I SAID, STAY AS YOU ARE!

JS: *Crinkles his brow.* You old fusspot.

The poet scoots along the floorboards, careful not to disturb his appearance.

RVR: Pose as you were before. This time, hold your hands where I can see them, and get ready to pull on your second glove.

As the poet stands with an impatient flicker in his eyes, the painter tries to express what is around them, using airy strokes on the canvas.

RVR: (*Aside*) What vanity! If only it forced him to stay, rather than run away.

JS: *Moustache twitches.* This coat is getting heavy . . . But I'm getting an idea for a long prose poem.

RVR: Recite it to me when you finish.

JS: Do you wish to hear my idea?

RVR: *Peeks out from behind his easel.* No matter how talented he may be, the poet cannot attain with the pen what the painter attains with the brush.

JS: What are you saying? Poetry and painting have always had equal right in hazarding anything. They are both forms of imitation, the only difference are the means and manner in which they are represented.

RVR: *Scratching vigorously at the canvas with his knife.* Yes, but poetry imitates by language alone, which is not universal. Painting embraces within itself all forms of nature and is, therefore, universal.

JS: Well, the poet serves understanding by way of the ear and the painter cannot. *Smacks his lips.* Painting is dumb poetry.

RVR: Poetry is blind painting! What is the more grievous defect? The eye is the nobler sense.

JS: Yet above all is the mind itself. How can you represent that by action alone? There is no better route to the workings of the mind than through poetry, which is by its very nature philosophic and therefore of greater import.

RVR: *Stops and glares.* Paintings can reflect the workings of the mind in the movements and expressions of the figures. You have the effects of demonstrations alone, while I have the demonstrations of effects.

JS: *Speaking through his teeth.* The painter knows appearances only, and even they are only deceptions of Beauty, a kind of dream created for those who are awake.

RVR: A poet leaves only a convincing impossibility or an unconvincing possibility.

JS: Very funny. *Removes the cloak from his shoulder, tossing it over his arm.* Would you like to come to a dinner tonight at Gerbrand Ornia's? You might meet some important people.

RVR: No, I should work. That is, if you want me to do you justice. (*Aside*) Ornia is a pompous fool. His important people would rip me to pieces! Besides, I'd rather spend my evening with Hendrickje, and I cannot take her in public with her big belly.

JS: I have my eye on Nicolaes Tulp's daughter, Margaretha.

RVR: *Raises a brow.* Apparently, she is quite a beauty. Have you proposed to her?

JS: Once I find the perfect set of jewels.

RVR: Yes, of course.

JS: *Affectedly.* May I be dismissed, kind master?

RVR: I may send for you again.

The poet shrugs into his cloak and walks towards the door.

JS: *Over his shoulder.* Not in the next few weeks.

RVR: Fine, it is only your reputation at stake.

JS: And yours.

The poet descends the stairway, his long scarlet cloak dragging over the dusty steps.

INTERLUDE

Two men play knuckle-bones in the tavern. Dice which face inward are lucky, those that face outward are unlucky. A variety of faces brings fortune.

Here I Am, Titus, My Son

You sit at your desk, writing your lessons. With a quill in one hand, you hold your chin in the other. Are you thinking of an answer? Your eyes have that faraway look. They fall beyond the paper, towards the open window. A warm breeze ruffles your auburn curls and floods the room with a spicy aroma. Our neighbours are preparing their Iberian foods for the Sabbath. The red beret I gave you rests on the crown of your head. It matches your sleeves, bunched up and dirty round the edges. You must have been dipping your bread deep into the buttermilk. I wish you hadn't inherited my slouch. It makes you look lazy and weak. You bite your lower lip, not paying attention to your work at all. Do you wish you were outside, bouncing a ball with your friends? I would not blame you. Summer is on its way. Even I, your father, who exercises the utmost self-discipline, must resist the urge to abandon my paintings.

Amsterdam, 1654

In my workshop, I dream of the lone Amstel and its glittering fish under a clear, blue sky. Soon I will take you to a cherished spot of mine called the Omval, a spit of land dividing the river and a canal. We will bring our copper plates so I can show you how to use a dry-point. Last time, Hendrickje and I sat in a tree hollow amongst flowers and ferns, eating a meal as the boats sailed past. Then she picked daisies, and I etched a windmill squatting near the water's edge. Whenever I see these wooden fortresses I think of my own father, the grain-maker, and my poor youth. The sound of their creaking arms was my cradlesong.

On our travels we saw many peasant children, drunk in the meadows. Not the sort of life I wish for you, my son. That is why I am strict with you about your studies. Rain or shine, we must never neglect our drawing lessons. I do not tell you often enough: you are making good progress. No one can sketch dogs as wonderfully as you do! Soon you will be running my workshop. Promise me, long after I am dead, you will keep painting. Even if the house is pervaded by the smell of blossoms, tempting you outside. Even if, because of your art, you squander your fortune and your friends abandon you. That is why I keep you here, shifting in your seat. Lord knows what Hendrickje allows you to do while I work upstairs. A fly buzzes and settles on your paper. Your thumb pressed to your cheek, you do not notice it, or me. Crouched in the corner, I am sketching you.

The father scrambles to his feet and tucks away his sketch. The sound of rustling pages startles his son, who looks up, sighing slightly.

RVR: *From the shadows.* What are you working on, my boy?

TVR: *Wipes his lips with the back of his hand.* Calligraphy. It's awful. Look! *Holds up his paper and pouts.*

RVR: Seems fine from here. It's only important to memorize and pronounce the letters. Most artists are not good at writing anyway. Bring it closer.

The son searches his father's face to gauge his interest. He drops his quill and leaps out of the chair, then rushes toward his father with the paper. It is full of upper-case Greek letters, from Alpha to Omega — the beginning and the end.

RVR: This is quite good, Titus. Better than mine, less bubbly and more elegant. Your Deltas need a bit of practice.

TVR: But I know the alphabet by heart and can say all the letters too.

RVR: That's what matters. Are you finished with everything else?

TVR: *Picks at his collar.* Almost.

RVR: Almost is not good enough, but you can stop now. Why don't you go and find your friends? (*Aside*) I take pity on him. After all, it is Friday.

TVR: Really? *Tugs on his father's arm.* Thank you, Pa! There's a hoop-bowling game at Willem's. I'll be home at suppertime. *Bends down to tighten the laces on his boots, then bolts towards the door.*

RVR: Wait, you forgot to clean up!

A Secret Ingredient, A Grand Scope

I have created a unique concoction by my own hand. There is nothing more sympathetic to the movement of the brush. It's like painting into butter!

Every brushstroke is soft and glossy but preserves its shape. Sometimes the paint breaks off and sticks to the underlying layer, at other times it remains in rounded hills. When dragged at great speed, it leaves thick tracks that reflect light.

SECRET RECIPE FOR EGG AND OIL EMULSION:

1 *The freshness of the egg is important for the quality of the emulsion. Snatch them right from under the chickens!*
2 *Separate the yolks from the albumen then put them in a jar, one by one.*
3 *Mix yolks with a lesser amount of stand oil (if the mixture is too oily it later darkens the paint, and if there is too much yolk, it later cracks the paint) and a jot of turpentine. Then beat all the ingredients with a soft, long-haired brush for a good while.*
4 *For added shine or body, mix in powdered glass or chalk.*
5 *The result is a clear, turbid film, not very sticky, which, when added to the pigment, allows it to behave in many different ways.*

While most painters try to disguise their movements with the patience of saints, I am leaning towards a rough manner in my old age. While my brush moves very freely, the paint reveals my every gesture. The blurred strokes and defined bumps determine the overall impression of the painting. How can I explain? The combination of sharp and blurred elements stimulates the eye, allowing a sense of spatial illusion. This is a manner I did not attempt in my younger days because it requires maturity. If only I had as much confidence as Titian! His last paintings are composed of blotches, but when seen at a distance, they represent reality more convincing than any finely brushed work. As Horace says, 'A poem is like a picture: one strikes your fancy more, the nearer you stand; another, the farther away.' My paintings may appear unfinished to others, but they are as intricate as a map of the Cosmos. They owe their perfection to a grand scope.

Hendrickje's Summons

People were talking about Hendrickje as she passed through town with her big belly. So the brothers came to our house to say that God has revealed her sin. Three times! I received a summons too, but when they realized I was no longer an active member of the church, they dropped the charge. Hendrickje had to go before the council because she attends services regularly and sometimes brings Titus with her. Those wretched Calvinists, how dare they call her my whore! Though we cannot marry, she is my wife. After eight years, my wife!

The painter's lover, her face swollen and blotchy, enters the bedroom where her lover is waiting. The two sit on the bed, side by side. She slips off her mules, leaving her bare feet to dangle from the edge.

RVR: (*Aside*) Her feet look so vulnerable.

HS: *Takes a deep breath and begins.* They asked me if it were true that I was living in sin with the painter, Rembrandt, that I had committed unholy acts with you. At first, I said nothing. But they told me if I did not confess, they would announce my sin to everyone in the congregation. No one would speak with us any more, or even step into our house. So I had no choice. I told them I was five months pregnant with your child. *Buries her face in her hands.* I'm sorry.

RVR: No, it is not your fault, darling.

HS: There were twelve brothers, all in black. They sat down behind a table and I stood in front of them. But I was trembling so much I nearly couldn't speak! It was horrible, horrible! The eldest one, a white-bearded man, told me that I was depraved and wicked. He made me do penance . . .

RVR: Wicked? You're not, Hendrickje!

HS: I got down on my knees and apologized to the Lord while they raged at me with Scriptures, saying my body was a temple which I've desecrated, God will punish me for my sins if I continue to lie with you, fornicators will not inherit the Kingdom of the Heavens . . . *Lowers her voice.* Regent Tulp was one of them.

RVR: That ass?! What did he have to say?

HS: He sat there all lofty in his fancy clothes and bellowed at me, 'Hendrickje Jaghers, you are not to partake in the Lord's Supper!'

RVR: How dare he! Is that all?

HS: *Eyes widen.* What do you mean, is that all? I have always supped at the Lord's Table since I was a little girl. *Begins to cry.* I'm so ashamed!

RVR: *Caressing her back.* I meant, what else did Tulp say?

HS: Do you really want to know? He condemned us both to Hell! He said if I were penitent, I should leave you and return to my mother's house. And there I should have the baby.

RVR: That bloody puritan, I'll kill him! How will he feel when I turn his own tweezers on him, aye?! *Jumps off the bed and bangs his fist against the wall. (Aside)* Oh, wretched me! How have I become this evil, lurking animal?

HS: No, don't say that! I did not agree to it.

The painter kneels before his lover and lays his head on her thigh. The soft fabric of her skirt caresses his cheek.

RVR: We must stay strong for our child. I need you, Hendrickje. Please don't leave me. *(Aside)* Love has made me cowardly.

Apelles and Homer

My painting of Apelles has sailed for a long month on the Bartolomeo, all the way to Messina in a wooden crate packed with sacks and oilcloth. It survived the perils of the Strait: Scylla, the six-headed beast with twelve barking dogs for feet, whose maws devour every ship within reach; and Charybdis, the monster who sucks water in and out three times a day, sinking sailors in its wake. Don Antonio Ruffo Spadafora di Carlo, Lord of Nicosia, commissioned me to make a half-length figure for his gallery of scholars. In the end, I decided to unite the greatest poet and painter who have ever lived: Apelles and Homer. I used an arched canvas, six and a half feet long and five feet wide. A large painting for a large man in his large palazzo.

Apelles was the first painter to make a self-portrait, and depicted Alexander the Great when no other artist was permitted to do so. The most famous one showed Alexander holding a lightning bolt that emerged from the canvas. If only it had survived, these stationary legs would suddenly spring to life and run to Ephesus! According to legend, Alexander once said he did not think a portrait resembled him, but when his horse neighed at the sight of it, Apelles declared that the animal understood art better than its owner. He often showed his pictures to the public then, standing out of sight, and trying to overhear their remarks. When a shoemaker criticized Apelles for drawing a sandal with one loop too few, he rectified it. However, when the shoemaker then found fault with the subject's leg, Apelles looked out from behind his painting and rebuked him: 'A shoemaker should not go beyond his sandal.' We would have been great friends.

According to Pliny, Apelles had a simple style based on the beauty of line and the charm of expression. He was bold and progressive too. If he could make lightning protrude from the canvas, he must have used loose brushstrokes and worked his paints into a thick impasto. He achieved his effects by using only a limited palette, similar to mine: black, white, ochre and earth red. He, too, used a thin varnish to soften his colours and make them appear sombre. Most important of all, he knew when to take his hand from a picture, though some ignorant fools criticized him for his works appearing unfinished.

When Don Ruffo collected the wooden crate and unwrapped the cloth in the presence of his marbled Roman emperors, this is what he saw ... A tall, thin man with a heavy brown beard stands in the dark. The light shines from the left, falling on his gaunt face — slender nose and pronounced cheekbones. A wide-brimmed hat casts a shadow on his forehead, wrinkled in contemplation. His dark eyes glaze over with sadness. He wears a black brocade vest with gold shoulder clasps over a white gown, its sleeves billowing and puckered at the wrists. His left hand settles on his hip while one finger caresses the golden chain of being, hanging low across his breast, which boasts a medallion of the great Alexander. 'Better a short life of glory than a long life of obscurity!' I painted my hero the way he would have painted himself, down to the last detail. His left arm rests on the head of Homer, whose eyes are rounded and blank but pure in sight. The two men are joined in mind, thinking of their lost honour and passing fame.

Twelve sets of stony eyes stared back at Don Ruffo as he clapped his hands in surprise. Meanwhile, the Bartolomeo returned to the Provinces, hauling a load of Sicilian sugar and another request from Don Ruffo for two companion pieces, an Alexander the Great and a Homer. This time, I will charge an additional 123 guilders per piece for shipping, customs and insurance. With another child on the way, I will have three mouths to feed apart from mine.

The Great Thunderclap

In my printing room, amongst fresh ink and bubbling wax, I am running my latest etching of St Jerome. We are old friends, Jerome and I. This time he sits near a tree stump and some bushes, reading a book. A floppy sunhat shades his face. To the right, his lion stands on a rock, head turned to watch over his master. In the distance is a church on a hilltop nestling in the trees.

While I crank the wheel of the press, my muscles straining, I am interrupted by the sound of rumbling footfalls on the stairs. It must be another creditor coming to abuse me. They've been persecuting me for months, showing up at the house whenever they please. A brawny young man rushes in at me, his long, wavy brown hair flapping against his broad shoulders. I breathe a sigh of relief. It is Barent Fabritius, my former student and Carel's younger brother. Then I see the dark circles around his wide-set eyes: something is wrong.

BF: *Anguished.* Master, I have some terrible news.

RVR: *Hangs the wet paper on the line.* What is it?

BF: Hell has opened wide!

RVR: What, Barent?

BF: *Leans a hand against the worktable.* My brother, Carel, he's been killed.

RVR: *Staggers backward.* No, I don't believe it. I've only just heard from him!

BF: But it's true. Yesterday morning there was a huge explosion in Delft. Like a thunderclap! It came from the Clarissen, a former convent. The States-General was storing munitions there for the war. *Sniffles and rubs his nose.* The ground opened up, trees caught fire, bridges collapsed, canals burst. The whole town is ruined.

RVR: How could this be? What's happened to Carel?

BF: He lived close to the convent. His house went up in flames! The windows, doors, beams, bricks, dishes, pottery, all his tools and paintings gone, exploded into the sky. His mother-in-law Judith, his assistant Mathias Spoors and the verger Simon Decker were killed instantly. Someone found Carel stuck under the rubble, still breathing, and dug him out. He was taken to hospital, badly injured. Eyes fill with tears. *He died in less than an hour.*

RVR: I'm sorry, Barent. *Clasps his shoulder.* How did you hear?

BF: Carel's wife, Agatha. She'd gone to the market, and when the explosions went off – there were five of them – she managed to find shelter in the Nieuwe Kerk. But when she returned home . . . oh . . . my brother, he was so young!

RVR: *Eyes filling.* I know, I know . . . (*Aside*) The things he could have gone on to do!

BF: So many died, maybe hundreds. The streets are blocked with body parts, and people are trapped under fallen houses. Their friends and families are foraging with their hands to get them out, but the air is still thick with smoke and dust, and it's raining, so no one can keep their torches lit. People have arrived to help, doctors from Rotterdam, to amputate and bandage limbs. *Moves toward the door, shoulders sagging.* Carel's funeral is tomorrow. I thought you should know.

RVR: Should I accompany you?

BF: No, Master, stay here and work. Carel would've wanted that . . .

RVR: Well, please have a cup of tea before you go. Or a glass of ale?

BF: *Quietly.* Ale, if you don't mind.

The old painter leads the young painter into the parlour, then asks the maidservant to fetch the drinks along with a plate of cheese. The men sit opposite each other in two armchairs near the fire.

RVR: As I said, I had a letter from Carel a couple of months ago. I've been trying to arrange some work for him here. If only I had done something sooner.

BF: *Gazes out of the window.* I should've been with him.

The maidservant carries in a tray with two pints of ale and a plate of cheese. Before she can slip out of the room, the old painter asks her to put a candle in the window for the deceased.

BF: You know, he'd recently made a small painting of a view in Delft, in which you could see, in wide-angle, the road climbing over a humped bridge, a single leafy tree, some houses and the rear of the Nieuwe Kerk. In the foreground, a man sat in the shadows with a viola da gamba and a lute. Was he waiting for his lover? I was never able to ask him.

RVR: He mentioned a goldfinch to me.

BF: *Nods and leans forward in his seat.* Did he tell you about the *camera obscura*?

RVR: Ah, no.

BF: *Sits back.* Never mind.

RVR: Tell me.

BF: You know what it is?

RVR: Of course. Huygens showed it to me once, long ago.

BF: You never tried it?

RVR: *Slaps his thighs.* Absolutely not! That would be cheating. A painter must depend on his own eye, not a lens. Do you imagine Titian or Rubens resorting to such a ridiculous contraption?

BF: No, but apparently, Carel started using the camera in some of his work. The view in Delft was a miracle of perspective. The human eye could never capture such detail.

RVR: I'm disappointed.

BF: No, please, I think it was that Samuel Van Hoogstraten who coaxed him into it. Carel and another young artist, Johannes Vermeer.

RVR: (*Aside*) Just hearing Van Hoogstraten's name makes my skin crawl. In the first place, he attacks me, and then he tries to influence my prize pupil with his ignorant ideas! But a jealous former student is not worth my time. There is a more important issue at hand. (*To BF*) Barent, what has become of the true painter? Is he dying out?

BF: *Manages a small smile.* You seem to be the last of them, Master.

The young painter cracks his big knuckles and stands up. Reluctantly, the old painter escorts him to the door. At the threshold, their beefy arms embrace each other for several minutes. The young painter steps outside.

RVR: Please send my regards to your family, Barent.

BF: Likewise, Master. Thank you again.

Amsterdam, 1654

The young painter sets off down the path, a purse slung over his shoulder.

RVR: *Shouting.* Would you believe my time is almost up? It is your turn to carry on Apelles' legacy!

Fonteyn's Story

He doesn't know I can see him but I can. Through the slit in my eyes. He's looking at the crowd. Leaning over me with his dignified group of doctors. His tightly curled hair under that formal hat. His pointy beard. His pious black clothes and white lace collar. He's already taken my teeth with his bare hands. I wonder what he'll do next. Speaking in a mellow voice. His left hand in the air, the other gripping a shiny tool.

Ooh, that tingles. My belly looks strange from here, as if it belongs to somebody else. Maybe it does. Bulging but dark like a cave. I'm not easily frightened. Not when he uses the tweezers to pull up my innards, not even when he lets the blood out. A few hours ago, you could've seen me strung up by the neck with my arms hanging down. I faced the harbour to greet the arriving ships. Or stared at the horizon with a perfect view of the sea. Those nasty traders were sticking their noses inside crates. A handful of grain fit for profit in the sunlight. Then the body-snatchers spirited me up the spiral staircase and into this round room. This room made of bricks. A Meat Hall, no less.

The dome above is painted with coats of arms. The Death's Head is one of them. It has a strange glow. When I close my eyes and re-open them, blue spheres explode one after the other. It might be a comet. A skeleton of a man on a skeleton of a horse

338

gallops past me. At my side is an open book with pictures and drawings of cadavers like me. The doctors keep pointing to it. There are long white candles flickering in the mirrors and eyes following me. Hundreds of people jostle for space, even children. They pass around food and drink and scatter herbs on the floor. Look at those snooty ambassadors who sit in the front row. They clutch their handkerchiefs like women! Dr Deyman must be amusing because they keep shrieking *Ah!* or *Oh!* Is that someone sketching me? Don't mind me, I say. I'll just lie here with my feet in your face, perfectly happy to rest and dream. Free from my body and floating in the clouds. I'm thinking about my old life. They used to call me Joris Fonteyn van Diest.

Yesterday I was standing on the corner, my shoes full of water. It was a crisp winter day. I wore a pair of tattered breeches, a flimsy shirt, torn stockings and those shoes full of water. So parts of me hung out. It was very quiet, except for a bricklayer talking to his buddy. I ambled over and held out my frozen fingers. Could they spare some tobacco? Nice fellows. They plopped a pipeful in my palm, enough to last a few minutes. It burnt my chest and felt good. The morning's beer was wearing off. It would've been nice to go back inside the pub, sit near the fire. But I wasn't welcome any more. They kicked me out because I owed them money. My stomach rumbled. I hadn't eaten for two days. The air smelt of yeast and fresh bread and sweetmeats. The cats had already picked over yesterday's remains.

A blind pedlar shuffled by, selling nuts. Tap, tap, tap. His cane felt the ground. Ring, ring, ring. He tugged his bell. I grabbed a handful of cashews and stuffed them in my mouth. Nice and salty. He must've sensed my movement or smelt me, because he whacked me with his stick. *Keep your hands to yourself*, he mumbled. I was constantly hearing things like that, and sometimes it bothered me. But he was just a poor old man so I couldn't blame him. He moved along into the fog. I leant against the tavern wall and began whistling a tune called 'The Cabbage Salad'. A nervous habit of mine.

What a beautiful woman, with braided blonde hair and a face like a bird. I thought maybe I could take her purse, but she looked so kind. Instead, I smiled at her and asked if she had a room for the night. I was tired of sleeping in corners. *A room? You swine!* She slapped me across the cheek, then shuffled off towards the market. What an unlucky day. I was always misunderstood. In less than an hour I'd been hit twice. It was trying my patience, and like I said I was freezing cold. I jumped from foot to foot to keep warm. When that didn't work, I rolled around on the ground, to keep myself from stiffening up. I stayed away from the edge of the canal, a bog of mud and horse piss. It was still early in the day, others would be happening by.

Suddenly a beggar came out of nowhere, a bottle of wine sticking out of his pocket. I was dying for a swig and reached up for it. My fingers weren't quick enough. He bent down and burped in my face. Then two men I recognized came out of the pub. Bakers who worked nearby and had given me a handout in the past. I jumped up. *Spare a stuiver*, I said. They mocked me. *What's the matter, Fonteyn? Can't pay your debts? Get a job!* I grunted and spat at them, ready to rough them up. But I told myself to stay calm. They're just miserable bastards. Little do they know I used to work hard. Now it's too late for me.

The bricklayers, the blind pedlar, the blonde, the beggar, the bakers. Then finally a draper. A very respectable-looking man wearing pleats, ruffs, a doublet and a thick woollen cloak. When he came out of his fabric shop, I jumped up and walked bang into him. Nobody intimidated me. *Oh, sorry!* he said. What nerve to apologize when it was my fault. Still, I knew what I wanted and tugged at his coat. He struggled. I guess he didn't expect it. We wrestled about several times, but I was stronger and taller. And I had a knife. Even with the glistening blade at this neck, he wouldn't surrender. *Thief!* he squealed. The greedy bugger must've had a million in his shop just the same. I could see it in his face. He had no idea about need and had never suffered a hardship in his life. I tore at his clothes like an angry madman and finally got hold of his cloak. *Thief!* he shouted again. He stared at me with his judging eyes. That bloody Calvinist, I hated him. *Don't look at me like that, you old cock!* I yelled. Then I hit him with my fist, once or twice. Hit him hard in the mouth and drew blood. He fell down on his knees and cried. He held his face, weeping loud enough to stir the dogs. They came running down the street, growling and howling. Luckily they didn't go for me, but jumped on the burgher. Snapping, biting.

The noise roused a horde of men, who came after me with knives. I knocked them down, one by one, and left the draper to the dogs. I ran as fast as I could with the cloak in my hands. I didn't want to end up in prison to be beaten by a bull's penis. Or squeezed into a drowning cell with water up to my armpits. I followed this alleyway, ducked down this street and the next. But dashing round one corner, I headed straight into the authorities. They surrounded and battered me with their clubs from all sides. That's that, and my glory days began.

It's taken forty years to get some attention, I'll tell you. Now I'm worth something. The sum of body parts: bones, limbs, chords, organs. Laid out on a slab, I am the perfect example of a man gone wrong. What a dazzling spectacle it must be! The doc's just finished dissecting my brain, the ingenious mind that brought me here in the first place. How peculiar. He's used his knife to expose the bloody lobes. He pokes, fondles and grabs them in such a dreadful manner. His assistant admires my skullcap in his palm. Not a bad head, I think. A white mist rises from within, and the smoke drifts over me like a cloud. *There but for the grace of God go I.*

'Post tenebras spero lucem'

It so happened that without as much as a knock, my father entered my bedroom, ducking under the wooden frame to keep his hat intact, and found me seated at my desk, arched over my notebook replete with stories and secrets while thinking of my fair maiden. Then he glanced around in horror at the pictures hanging all over my walls, from ceiling to floor, leaving no space untouched. He stood near the fireplace, tugging on his starched cuffs in alternating rhythms.

'What is going on in here?' The tone of his voice suggested he had deliberately come in unannounced to catch me at some immoral act – for whatever I was doing must have been wrong or harmful – while he continued looking round as if he might find that last bit of evidence which would expose me as a criminal.

My heart beat wildly, and my first instinct was to slam the doors within me, making it impossible for him to penetrate my world any further. 'Nothing,' I said, shutting my notebook in a panic.

The stench of the room made him gag. 'How many pipes have you smoked today, and what is all this? I haven't been in here for months and – oh, my Lord – please explain this, Pieter. Pieter?'

I ran my fingers through what was left of my hair. If I explained that I was gratifying a simple curiosity about Rembrandt, or taking an aesthetic interest in his craft, he was sure to ridicule me then do everything in his power to rid me of my colossal compulsion. Besides, my room was clearly a shrine to the artist, and I had no way of explaining why I was hardly at home these days unless I was worshipping there — in other words, writing, though I had made no large advance. Another option was to tell him to leave me alone, but if I angered him he would make it impossible for me to engage in anything apart from my work at the foundry. I decided to feign ignorance, my usual tactic.

'What do you mean?'

He raised his eyebrows and puckered his lips as if to say, *You cannot fool me son, I know you better than you know yourself,* but what he really said was: 'Where are you going today?'

When I stood up to face him, I noticed that I had gained an inch on him: he had begun to stoop in his old age. 'I will not be at the foundry, if that is what you're asking. I have an appointment. With Titus van Rijn.'

When he rested an arm, with a billowing sleeve, on the mantelpiece, he knocked over my plaster bust of Aristotle and sent it flying in the air. I let out a large gasp, but instantly he caught it in one hand, and with a frown, returned it to its place as if nothing had happened. 'Well, I forbid you to go. This Rembrandt of yours is ridiculous. I should never have sent you there. Besides, that area has been quarantined. You will not bring any contagion into this house!'

I mopped my forehead with a handkerchief. 'To ruin our Garden of Eden?'

Not a fleeting shadow of emotion flitted across my father's sallow face. 'Steady now, son, or I'll cast you out. Your behaviour is a disgrace! Missing work, sneaking in and out of the house —

who knows where you've been going and whom you've been seeing – actually, I do, because I heard you were spotted in town, arm/in/arm with that Catholic dissident Clara de Geest. Don't think for a second that you can marry her! Oh, and you've been commiserating with that atheist friend of hers, that Jew. Have you once thought of your family in all this? You are marring our reputation.'

In silence I hardened my heart, letting the words spill over me, then made an attempt at honesty. 'Of course I think of my family, but my friends are very important to me.'

'More important than your family, I see. What about blood, Pieter? B/L/O/O/D . . .'

I crossed my arms over my chest and seethed with anger. With each letter he was telling me that my inheritance was at stake. The threat was serious – I needed that money for a secure future – yet I would not subject myself to his way of life or to his manner of thinking in order to attain it. 'I'm not getting married, Clara will never marry, but she is the most honourable and genial woman in the city. Furthermore, Espinoza is not an atheist, he only encourages religious tolerance, and there is nothing harmful in that!'

Although his suspicions were confirmed, he replied in a calm manner with the severity of a general, 'He denies the existence of God, the act of creation and the first principles of Christianity. That sounds like an atheist to me.'

I was startled by his professed acquaintance with Espinoza's ideas; his tract had been printed anonymously and was circulated only in underground meetings, the ones Clara attended. She had introduced me to Espinoza once, and his pamphlet made it into my hands, but I was only beginning to grasp his philosophy with its unexpected vistas, and in them I found the most passionate and comprehensive painting of life. 'Not necessarily, Father. He believes that God is immanent and indistinct from His creation, that all things have been predetermined by God, not from free will or pleasure, but from His absolute nature or infinite power.'

'Ah, it is too late, you have already been blinded by that most wretched of creatures, the prince of darkness. Where is your common sense?'

I had grown accustomed to my father's condescending manner, and responded in the habitual way: with a hangdog look and a self-deprecating shrug. As his judgement hung in the heavy air, I formulated a rational response. 'If we relied solely on common sense, we would still believe the earth is flat and the sun is a small object in the sky two hundred feet above us. Grandfather taught me that!'

When my father seemed stumped for a moment, I believed I had won the battle. Then he said, 'We can also be thoughtless and immature in our emotions and conduct our affairs foolishly without control and direction. If God did not punish wrongdoing as a judge does, what would prevent an imperfect man from rushing into wickedness?'

'When we understand the workings of the mind and all its causes, we can avoid vice not out of fear of punishment, but because it leads us astray from knowledge and wisdom.'

He let out a sardonic laugh. 'What is philosophy but a mere illusion, a chimera? Yet to it you entrust your peace of mind and the salvation of your soul . . . Is this my son, whom I raised to fear and love and worship God? I brought you to the straight and narrow, and now you abandon it for the broad road? You will find out soon enough, it leads to destruction.'

My eyes darted to and fro, avoiding his stare. I had defied him before on various occasions but always in a fuzzy way, and afterwards I had repented and returned to him with my tail between my legs. This was different, for I had crossed the final line. 'I still adhere to the morals you taught me, but I have come to believe that the way to God and happiness is through the intellect.'

He wagged his finger at me and sneered. 'You little worm, how dare you put yourself before the infinite wisdom of the Creator! Turn away from your sins and consider the arrogance of your reasoning. If you do not give ear to God, His wrath will be kindled against you and His mercy will abandon you for eternity!' With an eye of disdain, once more he took in the prints, etchings, paintings and *objets d'art* that smothered the room. 'You want to be free, eh? Then go. I doubt you will feel free after you've caught the plague and die a horrible death like your mother.'

How could he? I swivelled round to face the windows, threw my arms in the air and screamed at the top of my lungs, only no sound emerged. I swung back again and met his niggling gaze. This time my shouts rang loud and clear, but little tears formed in the corners of my eyes. 'You can jail me, torture me, kill me, shun me, label me as a heretic or a worm, but I am still your son!'

He made no overture to pity me. 'You will no longer be my son if you continue to see that disgraceful woman and her atheist friends. Consider that an order. If you cross me, I will revoke your inheritance.'

In an instant, I saw the flap of his coat tails, then the door shut with a bang, shaking my coffin and fluttering the pages on my desk. I dashed to the washing bowl, cupped it with two hands and thrust my face inside; then my stomach lurched and heaved up my breakfast. Afterwards I felt a great relief, but my brain had dug itself into a dark and sinister hole. While my father's final words made me hate him, then hate myself, they lured me towards the forbidden even more. I could not bear to stay inside his house for another second, and I desperately needed Clara. *Consider how strong your shoulders be; you must be a good swimmer, a Delian even, yet in this stormy sea swim not without a buoy.* So I quickly rinsed my mouth with anise before leaving the room with my trusty notebook – tiptoeing down the hallway, shoes in hand – and stepped into the street.

As planned, I headed for the Van Loo house, where Titus lived with Magdalena and his mother-in-law. Several months had passed since that night of their engagement dinner, enough time for them to get married and conceive a child, enough time for me to feel strange about returning, because I had had contact with neither Rembrandt nor Titus since, apart from the thank-you letter I sent the following day. When Clara mentioned she would like to bring the couple a belated wedding gift, she invited me to come along, and though it took me a minute to consider whether I would make a nuisance of myself, I did not think so; while I had regularly pestered their friends and family through the course of my research, I had shown great dignity with them.

I walked quickly in an effort to avoid thinking of my father; if I did not fend off the bitterness, it would plunge me into a desolate abyss. *We are the heirs of customs and traditions hallowed by age and handed down to us by our fathers. No quibbling logic can topple them, whatever subtleties this clever age invents.* There were hardly any people on the narrow alleyways, and the houses leant into one another to form a steeple that blocked out the sun, so it seemed as if I were walking through a cemetery yard between tilting tombstones; and these homes were crypts in the most literal sense of the word. I felt relieved when I broke out into the wider streets and open squares, which, during the day, were generally kept clear from dead bodies unless somebody dropped down unexpectedly, and even then they were immediately brought to the graveyard, where they were burnt along with their infected clothes. It was impossible to know who was infected unless they had already broken out with the Lord's tokens; they often did not realize it themselves, strolling through the square one minute and finding themselves dead in their homes the next. Some people wore antidotes or cordials around their necks (dried figs, nuts, rue and salt or sugar, pomegranate wine and vinegar) in case they encountered any danger because, apparently, the breath of an infected person could poison and instantly kill even a pigeon. However, others spoke of the air itself being corrupted with miasmas from God-sent flying dragons and snakes, which were impossible to avoid. None of these varying opinions could ever be supported, so I carried a viper's tail in my pocket and put my Fate in the hands of God: if I were meant to catch the disease I would, despite time, manner or place.

When I arrived at the Appelmarkt across from the Van Loos and their herring-boat facade, Clara was already there, pacing up and down the nearly bare stalls, which held the rejected remains of fruit, stripped of colour and life, ridden with worms, shrivelled in their skins. She smiled when she saw me, then raised a finger to grab my attention. I watched with amusement as she picked up a rotten apple, a brown peach, a pear full of holes, and began throwing them up in the air. Her tiny hands made perfect arches, a continuous flow of objects gliding past one another and never colliding, like swallows in flight . . . Initially, the fruits were blurred in movement, but then I began to see each one individually ripening in my imagination; their colours sharpened and their forms became whole again. When I drew closer, she lost her concentration and failed to catch a peach, which fell to the ground with a juicy splatter. She looked down at it sadly.

'Oh, never mind,' I said, taking and kissing her hand, the hand that disappointed her. At that moment I did not care if anyone spotted us together, even my father.

She recovered quickly and told me that only individual houses were under quarantine, and the Van Loos' was not one of them, but we should probably proceed in haste if we wanted to reach Titus at home, because he usually spent the day at his father's workshop. First, she wanted to give me something, she announced, and with an adept gesture, pulled a tall narrow book from her bag and handed it to me. I looked down in surprise at this mysterious heart-kernel: *Mr William Shakespeare's Comedies, Histories and Trage-dies*, published by Philip Chetwynde. Clara's eyes never stopped moving as she identified it as the third folio volume of his previously printed and unprinted dramas, including seven not found in the first two folios, for instance, *Pericles*; she had obtained it from a friend in London. I ran my fingers over the marbled brown leather then breathed in my favourite smell of bookbinder's glue. Inside, on the first page of thin parchment, she had written an inscription in English: *'Your face, my thane, is as a book where man may read strange matters', Yours ever, Clara.* Blushing, I thanked her with insufficient words – the book must have cost her a heavy guilder. It also seemed she had known about my difficult morning or had somehow overheard the debate with my father, and was wishing to reassure me. This is what love was supposed to be, I thought, as if you were experiencing a memory from long ago and at the same time feeling that everything was about to begin.

As we stood on the porch, awaiting an answer to our knock, I recalled my flight down the canal that night when I sought Rembrandt in the dusky air then found him slumped in the street instead. It seemed so far in the past, and did I know him any better now? Perhaps his son would offer some insight, I thought, while the housekeeper ushered us inside then left us alone in the parlour to wait for Titus and Magdalena. We were sitting quietly on the green velvet chairs that matched the heavy curtains pulled back from the windows, our feet planted on the shiny black and white marble floor, admiring the gilded hangings, portraits of ancestors and Flemish landscapes, when Titus peeked his head round the doorframe. As he entered the room – those intense brown eyes peering out over his round nose – he seemed thinner than I remembered him, especially in a pair of oversized breeches.

He kissed Clara warmly, then shook my hand firmly. 'Magdalena has morning sickness, so it is better if she rests. She sends her apologies.'

'Not to worry,' Clara said. 'We wanted to offer our congratulations and give you this.' She pulled a wrapped box out of her bag (the bottomless pouch of secrets), and handed it to him with two steady hands.

'You're in a generous humour today,' I whispered, partly to

tease her and partly out of jealousy – because it made me feel slightly less 'unique'.

She ignored me and gazed at Titus as he tore into the paper and opened the box. Pulling out the gift, he set it on the table between us, then inspected it carefully; a strand of his long auburn hair broke loose from his beret and fell across his face. The bell-shaped drinking bowl, placed upside-down on its rim, was chased with fruits and foliage. Mounted on the cup's bottom was a small cupola bearing three volutes that held the windmill. A miller descended a long stepladder at the back, other figures looked out of the door and windows, and a bird perched on the roof.

'A windmill cup!' Titus exclaimed. 'It's beautiful, but how do I use it?'

Clara laughed. 'I thought, as the grandson of a miller, you might already have one.'

He shook his head. 'I have seen them before, but no . . .'

'It's a game, you see. You blow through the pipe to set the arms in motion, then empty the cup before they stop turning. The clock on the back,' she said, pointing, 'will tell you how many cups you have to drink in order to atone for your sins.'

'Ah, this will be fun,' he said, sitting back in his chair. 'Wait until I show Magdalena! Thank you, Clara.'

'It's from the two of us,' she said, which was a lie: I had nothing to do with it.

His eyes sought mine. 'Thank you, Pieter, I never had the chance to tell you how much I valued your visit last year with Prince Cosimo. My father was very pleased too, and that is a rare occasion these days.'

'With pleasure,' I said with a swollen heart, hoping he was not just being polite. Rembrandt, happy? It seemed the perfect time to ask him a few questions. 'How is it, being your father's agent?'

Clara nudged me in stealth, but Titus seemed pleased to talk about it, even eager, as if he were waiting for someone to ask. 'Well, after nine years, I have learnt all there is to know about dealing, but it can be tiresome. The clients are demanding, never satisfied, not to mention the creditors, accountants and notaries . . . My father has been in some financial trouble, you see.'

I crossed my leg and gripped my ankle for support. 'Yes, I heard. How did that come about, if you don't mind my asking?'

He did not seem to mind, though he held his reply until after the maidservant brought in a pot of tea, poured three cups then left us in peace. 'He lost various investments on account of the war, and the sales of his paintings diminished because fashions changed, so his debts accumulated over the years. He does have the tendency to overspend, only it wasn't his fault. It's the fools who cannot recognize that he is the greatest artist alive. You know, I still curse those Regents who removed his Claudius Civilis from the Town Hall. The largest picture he ever painted, you know. Sixteen feet square!'

'Yes,' Clara piped in, 'and to replace it with such a timid picture? By a German, no less!'

'I saw his Civilis in the Hall, just before it was taken down, when I was a boy,' I said. 'At first the man frightened me, staring out with one enormous eye, the blind one sealed shut, but the longer I looked the more I wished to be one of them, his chief nobles, crossing their long glimmering swords . . .' Just as I wanted to cross swords in communion with its painter, I finished in my head as my companions silently sipped ther tea. I tried to bring the discussion back to Rembrandt's bankruptcy. 'How did you continue after the money troubles?'

He pursed his red lips in thought. 'Pa tried everything. He held auctions to sell his collection, but the proceeds never satisfied the creditors. By fifteen I had drawn up three different wills, so the house was transferred to me, but the creditors wouldn't warrant it. Eventually Pa applied for bankruptcy, so they stripped the house of everything and declared me an orphan. They even appointed me a guardian. It was awful, the shame was awful, Pa's friends abandoned him, even my mother's relatives, Uncle Hendrick and Aunt Hiskia, your cousins' – he nodded to Clara – 'as you know, he owed them money too.'

'Yes, it's terrible. I'm so sorry,' Clara said.

'No, all in the past.' He flicked his hair over his shoulders, as if bothered by its intrusion into such a serious matter, then tipped back his cup to drain the tea.

'How did you come to the Rosengracht?' I asked.

He picked at his fingernails, remembering. 'We sold the Breestraat house for two thousand less than Pa paid for it. He was left with a stove, some partitions for his shop and a few painting supplies. Hendrickje managed to save her big oak cupboard and packed it with linen, silver and other basic things to bring with us.' He paused, his eyes straining, his brow creasing. 'Do you really want to hear this?'

Clearly, he did not discuss these things with anyone, except possibly Magdalena, but I trusted he would unburden himself if he were confident in our interest. Clara and I exchanged glances then faced him with eager nods.

He shrugged. 'Well, in 1660, the three of us appeared before a notary and drew up an agreement that all of my father's property — from his painting supplies down to his pink stockings — would be transferred to Hendrickje and me, provided on the security of his work. The Commission cleared him, but he still owed sums to private individuals. As you can imagine, we have lived very simply since then.'

No, I could not imagine being my father's keeper, his owner; it seemed inappropriate and unnatural. No matter how much I wanted to find fault with Titus in order to tell myself I was Rembrandt's rightful son, I could not conjure up a single criticism. He had bravery, maturity, devotion — all those righteous qualities I could never possess or demonstrate, and my family was wealthy; how much worse it would have been if we had no means to pay for our next meal. 'How have you managed without Hendrickje?'

'It hasn't been easy.' He tugged his goatee. 'Apart from running the workshop, we've had to look after my sister Cornelia. She's thirteen now, but she was only seven when her mother died and she still misses her terribly. Pa hasn't been the same since. Hendrickje's death hit him very hard. It was unbearable for all of us. She raised me as her own, you know.'

'Hendrickje died of the plague,' Clara said to me, though obviously I already knew; she was prompting Titus into saying more, making it easier for him. I was torn between wanting to hear every detail and wishing he would stop at that, because his forthcoming confession was bound to unearth too many terrible memories of my own mother's death, which I had long suppressed in the black shadow of my soul. I twiddled my thumbs, searching for a way to escape or a place to hide, as he continued speaking with a horrified look on his face.

'She went very slowly. Pa locked Cornelia and me out of her room, afraid that we would catch the disease, but I wanted to be with her more than anything, so I used to peep through the keyhole, just to get a glimpse of her, and there she would be, writhing in the sheets, soaked in sweat, her teeth chattering. She called out all sorts of fanciful things, memories, I think, about flower-picking and dancing with Pa. She loved to dance! But I knew she sensed me there, because a couple of times when I was about to walk away, she cried out, "Please don't leave me! Don't leave me, my son!"' Titus stopped, blinking back tears. 'She thought of me as that, her natural son.' When his hand began to tremble, he set down his cup, though it had already been empty for a while. 'I slid little pictures under the door, ones I'd drawn of dogs, cats or tulips, and Pa hung them on the walls for her to see. If only she could see! He stayed at her bedside day and night through the fever and vomiting, even as she swelled with black blood and broke out in buboes, screaming at the top of her lungs. I don't think he cared if he caught the disease, he just wanted to be with her until the final second. Still, a day doesn't pass without him mentioning her.' He tapped his foot in embarrassment. 'Forgive me for . . .'

'No, you mustn't apologize,' Clara said.

We breathed heavily, side by side. Closing my eyes, I slipped into that deep abyss of the past, and found myself standing in the doorway of my parents' bedroom, where, inside, my mother is strapped to the bed, naked and splayed, her once pale skin broken and purple, and the doctor stands at her side, brandishing a burning rod, lowering it on to her sores as she howls in agony and begs me to stay, but I cannot protect her or ease her suffering or give her another breath, so I walk away, down the long, gloomy passage, past the portraits of my dead ancestors, one by one, following the glow of a soft and gentle light which seems to lead to a wondrous silence. When I re-opened my eyes, Clara's hand was on my shoulder.

Titus propped his chin on his palm. The little colour in his gaunt face had disappeared. 'Several years ago, my father sold my mother's grave for money. Did you hear that, Clara?'

'I heard something through the family, and assumed he needed the money.' She returned her slender hand to her lap and turned to me. 'Saskia was buried in the Oude Kerk, in the chancel behind the organ.'

'Pa and I would visit her together when I was a boy,' Titus went on. 'Then the men came to dig up her bones and carted them to the rubbish heap. Another woman, perhaps someone else's mother, is there now, so I cannot be angry, but I often wish that I could still visit her tomb, to know her.'

I bowed my head, feeling guilty for taking everything in my life for granted, even my father and especially my mother, who was privileged to have her own grave which would remain sacred and untouched for years to come while I never spared a moment to call on her, telling myself that the pain was too great, the grief too unbearable. I realized now it was merely an excuse, and the real reason could be nothing other than the fear of faith. *After the darkness I hope for the light.*

Amsterdam, 1655

Snorting Like a Horse

My grizzled face has the same value as a balled-up rag. The malice of my age has turned my skin to yellow wax. Everywhere it sags. My grey hairs shrink, my forehead swells, and its wrinkles spread like the waves of the sea. These two teary eyes can hardly see beyond my frowning brows. I have lost all my lashes, but there are so many whiskers sprouting from my ears! A dirty moustache lines my mouth, sinking inwardly in fear. If I were compelled to smile, it would reveal a few decayed teeth. I almost do not recognize my nose with these newly formed crags. There's another new mole, surrounded by red patches. Who is this bolting-hutch of a beast with a pudding in his belly? Here he is, coming closer into view. A look of surprise forms naturally. With my nose pressed to the glass, the mist of my stinking breath clouds up the mirror. Then I am a lost stranger. Oh well, patience, patience ... I go snorting like a horse as the clock ticks on.

Child to the Teat

Hendrickje sits at my desk amongst papers, books and tools, near the fireplace to keep warm. Her broad shoulders pushed forward, her chemise bunched round her waist, she grips the seat of the strutted chair. The lower shutters are closed for privacy because she has just finished feeding our newborn daughter, Cornelia. 'There is nothing an upright man would rather see than his dear wife bid the child to the teat,' says the old proverb. And there is nothing an artist would rather sketch. Hendrickje has the soft touch of a milkmaid and the determination of a hen. Heart in mouth, my pen scribbles on with wonder.

She looks after me, too, as if I were her child. People would laugh at my helplessness in her arms. While the net of Fate draws closer around me, I become more frightened of everything, especially fatherhood. How vulnerable a child seems, a baby girl ... All loving images of Saskia with my daughters have grown vaguer with memory, muted by sickness and death. In those pictures, the two girls lie lifeless and still in their mother's arms, and their father stands by unable to protect them. Even Saskia's once-smiling, pink face has broken down into mere bones. I wish I could hold on to that face, any of their faces. These are the strange workings of time. My only hope is that the nightmarish images will vanish too, or dim, or be replaced with ones of life and beauty. Perhaps my fear will lessen as the years go by; it will never completely abandon me. Now that Fate has dealt me a second chance, I will never neglect the opportunities I have to cherish my woman and child.

As parents, Hendrickje and I call on the Lord in love, faith and steadfastness. It helps that the field of medicine has advanced during the last fifteen or twenty years. First, Hendrickje did not fast after the seventh month of pregnancy, nor does she swaddle our baby as Saskia did. We feed her rosehip syrup, bathe her and regularly take her out for fresh air and sunshine. Each time Cornelia opens her eyes, she sees two pairs of hawk-eyes gazing down at her. Little does she know they are always there, even when she is asleep. Right now, though I am working, our two-month-old lambkin sleeps nearby in the bassinet. But Hendrickje assures me that

Cornelia is full and happy. She will be fine in Rebecca's care for the next few hours. I want Hendrickje to pose for me so I can make a record of my great love in a painting.

The Glorified Pig Trough

Dark is the basic tone of my paintings, but how full of life it is! Sometimes my figures stand sharply against oblivion, at other times they submit to it slowly or simply vanish in the half-light. My critics can shake their heads till the price of tulips goes down — no painter has attained this before.

What can I say? This is partly the result of my freer technique with spatula and brush, but the real harmony comes from my choice in pigments. I begin with the middle shades of brown and yellow, deepening them in gradations, yellow-grey, yellow-red, brown-red, and so on, then sparingly set in the more opaque colours, which are simply colder variants of the same tone, grey-blue, grey-green, etc. This contrast of warm and cool colours is the result of pure craftsmanship, a splendid handicraft which cannot be imitated. My sparkling lights could glorify a pig trough. If anyone says otherwise I'll shove this palette up his back passage!

A Woman Bathing

I have in mind a painting after the antique sculpture of the Mulier impudica or the unchaste woman. A bather, her hair pulled up and curls hanging down her neck, lifts her chemise above her thighs. Dat gaat 'er na toe, zei de meyd, en ze nam haar hembd tussen haar tanden *(This is the way, said the girl, and took her shirt between her teeth). The setting of my picture is a woodland in the evening as the sun is setting, during what my friend Menasseh would call 'the twilight of the dove'. There is a riverbank, a plinth draped with an embroidered dress of gold and red, and a stream, a low tub filled with water.*

The oak panel is covered with a muted yellow ochre and umber — the basis for everything. The left side shows brambles and leaves in a washed manner. To the right is a knotted, mossy tree with a winding branch creeping up to the sky and feathery leaves at the water's edge — both will frame the scene. I can just about hear the chorus of frogs in the distance. I crouch in silence, my eyes darting to and fro, watching for any signs of movement. My model should be ready by now, finished with her household chores. I have already prepared her for the role. My brush is raised in the air, ready to make quick motions when she steps into place.

In the retreats of the crag, in the concealed place of the steep way, show me your form, for your form is comely. *Ah, I hear footfalls. My bather emerges from the darkness into the wan glow of the moonlight. I hold my breath. Does she sense me stirring? Does she hear the bristles playing against the panel? Be still. Catch her unawares! She wades into the water from the steep bank, lifting the shift with both hands to expose her legs to the cool air. Her left shoulder cleaves the surrounding gloom.* Who is this woman that is looking down like the dawn, beautiful like the full moon, pure like the glowing sun? *She moves forward cautiously then stops, legs parted, leaning on her left foot. Everything is in full view: my Bathsheba, my Ruth, my Shulammite maiden. I take off with a frenzied energy, gesturing the lines of her figure.*

Look! You are beautiful, O girl companion of mine. There is no defect in you. *Her hair is gathered in waves, wispy along the temples like the plumed leaves on the tree. My round, sable brush paints a golden curl springing down then falling over her right shoulder. She perspires in the sultry heat. On her broad forehead, I make the oil glisten with beads and flounce another cascading curl. Her thin brows are swept by a tiny brush, framing her wide* eyes like those of doves. *I dapple the light on their upper lids. The dimples in her cheeks are just a few scratches of charcoal black, pinched in a small smile. She gazes down into the stream, a lukewarm bath.* Your lips are woven as a scarlet thread . . . *with* comb honey they keep dripping. *I spread a warm grey shadow under her chin, created by her bent head. Is she putting on a slight smile for me because she has become aware of my presence? Is she playing for her lover?*

Your skin is a paradise of pomegranates . . . *My eyes rediscover her secret curves and gestures. Her youthful skin frees itself, lucid and pale.* Your breasts, like date clusters. Between them I will spend the night. *At the cleavage of her bosom, my pigment, a warm red and yellow, plunges downward where her flesh is closer to the light, the blood is closer to her flesh. The shift of lead white and yellow ochre hangs off her shoulders — two rounded, hunched hills. My loaded brush makes its folds in quick, heavy strokes so that they catch the light. In the furrows I form shadows, only a few swipes of grey. A broad highlight on her left sleeve lifts it from the darkness. The fabric swings across her upper legs, and my brush slides along to mimic its valance.* The curvings of your thighs are like ornaments, the work of an artisan's hands. *I seek something private and buried in the deep shadows at her groin. They lead me back to the dark passage into the woodland.* A lily among thorny weeds! *The muscles in her thighs are flexed, her knees taut. I smear them with ashen pigment, traces of pink and blue. The water ripples at her rounded calves, half-exposed. Under the surface, they look blurred, and the opaque colours of her dress swirl in the reflection.*

You have made my heart beat, O my sister, my bride. *Her left hand is hidden from me, only stipples and dabs. The right one, closest to me, holds up her dress. Her index finger is curled back to clutch the fabric, and her thumb fades into the shift itself. Again, I seek her face.* Come back, come back! That I may behold you. Let us go forth to the field. *Her downcast eyes do not greet me but smile at her own nakedness. She is wholly absorbed, like Heraclitus, who saw the symbol of fleeting life in his river. Different and again different waters flow. Nothing is the same now as it was before, and nothing now will be the same tomorrow.* Place me as a seal upon your heart, as a seal upon your arm; because love is as strong as death is . . .

Here I am, concealed in a dark hollow. My bather arrived, my bather remains. As long as I am gazing she will never depart. When she steps out of the water, the shift falls over her knees. I hold up a clean towel, ready to pat her dry.

Only the Feet, Rembrandt!

I have just finished four completed etchings for Menasseh's latest work: Piedra Gloriosa o De la Estatua de Nebuchadnesar. *After months at the mercy of my hands, they are ready for his final approval. I have not read the entire book because my understanding of Spanish is limited, but the author himself describes his 'heroic' volume as a total history of the Hebrew people. Yet he wants his book to appeal to both Jews and Gentiles. Only one artist in Amsterdam can speak for both!*

The images are based on four passages in the Scriptures. The first comes from the Book of Daniel and Nebuchadnezzar's dream, in which he sees a statue with a head of gold, with its breast and arms of silver, its belly and thighs of bronze, its legs of iron, its feet of iron and clay. A stone is hewn from a mountain, not by human hands, and strikes the statue on its feet.

363

The precious metals are shattered and swept away until no trace remains, then the stone grows into a great mountain filling the whole earth. In my print, the statue is a man hovering above a plinth, wearing a headdress, a cape and a loincloth. His head bears the name Babel; his arms, Persia and Medes; his stomach, Greece; and his legs, the Roman and Mohammedan empires. Originally, my stone came rolling in from his right to shatter him from the hips down. When I showed the first state to Menasseh, he corrected me, saying, 'Only the feet, Rembrandt!' Now the stone sails in from his left, leaving his legs intact while his feet topple off the plinth. In this way, according to Menasseh, the other nations will give way when the Messiah arrives.

The second illustration is based on a passage in Genesis, when Jacob has stopped on his way to Harran for a rest. He makes a stone his pillow and sinks into a dream in which he sees a ladder reaching to Heaven, where Angels are climbing up and down. Later in the account, Jacob uses the stone to set up a sacred pillar. In my etching, he rests halfway up a wide ladder and the four Angels have stopped to minister to him. They stand for the rise and fall of nations.

The third illustration comes from the Book of Samuel, where David slays the Philistine by slinging a stone. The towering Goliath, dressed in his armour and bearing a circular shield, dominates my picture. He is on the brink of collapse, for David has just released his stone to hit the mark. The fall of the Philistine represents the toppling of other nations.

Finally, there is Daniel's vision of a great sea churned up by the winds of Heaven, from which four huge beasts emerge. In the lower regions of the picture, the winged lion stands on his hind legs like a man, arms raised in the air. The second creature is a crouching bear, holding three ribs in its mouth. The third resembles a leopard with four heads and birds' wings. The most terrible beast has iron teeth, bronze claws and ten horns. I have shown in the cloudy heavens 'one ancient in years', his robe as white as snow, his hair like cleanest wool. He floats in a beam of light, almost transparent, because Menasseh objected to my representation of God in the first state. He is surrounded by myriads of Angels and the Messiah reporting for duty. After the slaying of the fourth beast, the fifth sovereign will rule for ever.

Together, the four passages reinforce the message that when the Messiah arrives, his kingdom will be firmly established. For my friend, this means the political restoration of the Jewish homeland and the spiritual redemption of his people. It will lead to a period of judgement and bring true happiness for those who have led a virtuous life. I keep asking him, like a true disciple, 'When? When will these things occur?', to which he replies, 'After the people of Israel are completely dispersed from one end of the earth to the other.' That is why Menasseh has been trying to get to England for the last two years. The war has delayed him until now. Alas, he will sail across the Channel to meet the Lord Protector Oliver Cromwell. Perhaps he will even bring his book with my illustrations ... This mission is the great endeavour of Menasseh's life, so I pray that he succeeds, even if I am unconvinced about his interpretation. Every Church has a grasp on some small piece of the truth.

Conversations at the Synagogue

In the early morning, the streets are deserted. Not a human being is to be seen or heard. The clouds are on the move. A shaft of sunlight shoots down on to the canal and gleams over the water, a murky brown. Without a word, Titus and I make our way to the Synagogue, where I will give him a brief drawing lesson before he goes to school.

Here is my son, gawky in his coat, too small for his inordinately long

arms. Rapidly as his body grows, his face changes, narrowing and length-
ening. A sparse whisker is sprouting on his full, upper lip. A patch of
spots has broken out on his cleft chin. God has held a mirror to my face:
Titus resembles me almost exactly at that age. From a distance, we must
look like the same person separated by four decades, wearing our brown
cloaks and black berets tilted over one brow. My instinct is to take his hand,
but I know he does not want me to show affection in public any more, even
if no one else is around. I do not blame him. These are the most difficult
years: he is no longer a boy but not yet a man. Still, I have important
things to discuss with him. Nowadays we hardly ever have quiet, unimpeded
moments between us. The art lesson was not my only reason for bringing
him with me.

RVR: *Clearing his throat.* Titus, there is something we need to talk
about.

TVR: What? *Kicks a stone off the path, sending it to plunge into the canal*
with a splash.

RVR: Is it true, you're going to turn fourteen soon?

TVR: So? *Gives a shifty eye.* You know how old I am!

RVR: So, it seems the proper time for you to draw up a will.
(*Aside*) He has grown more precocious, too! Why is a simple
conversation so awkward for a father and son?

TVR: *Stops in his tracks, fiddling with the buttons of his coat.* A will?
Why would I want to do that?

RVR: You've seen all the creditors coming to the house lately? I'm
having financial trouble, you see. We are, as a family.

The painter's son stops under a tree. The sun trickles through its branches, making a shifting pattern of light on his face.

RVR: *Leans his weight against the tree, tucks a thumb into his sash.* I want to protect us for the future.

TVR: *Begins picking the leaves from a dangling branch.* You're not talking about something illegal, are you?

RVR: Don't be ridiculous, and please stop that for a second.

The painter's son drops an arm to his side, frowning.

RVR: I want to transfer my possessions to your name so the creditors cannot take them. Your will would state that I control all that property. You can also name Cornelia as your heir and ensure that Hendrickje is secure. Otherwise, everything will go to Aunt Hiskia. Your mother's family thinks we owe them a great deal, but at the time of her death we were a lot wealthier. If your mother were aware of the situation we are in today . . .

TVR: How bad is it?

RVR: I am going to hold a sale at the Emperor's Inn, to auction off some paintings and part of my collection, but the proceeds will go straight to my creditors. I may have to transfer ownership of the house to you, so the commission cannot take it. Even then, we will probably have to move, and I may have to apply to the High Court for a *cessio bonorum*.

TVR: A what?

RVR: A form of bankruptcy for people who are good citizens, for people like me who have lost a lot of money, not from their own doing.

TVR: I don't understand, Pa. How did you lose your money?

RVR: There's a decreased interest in paintings these days. I also invested some money overseas, all of which I lost. It is difficult to explain.

TVR: *Lowers his head, and digs his toe in the dirt.* You — you — can't go bankrupt.

RVR: It's too late for that, and anyway, that is why I need your help. You have to trust me, Titus. I am your father and I know what is best.

The painter's son steps away from the tree. Shoulders slumped, he sets off down the street into a crowd of pecking pigeons. They scatter around him, beating their wings. He picks up little treasures from the ground, examines them for a moment and then either stuffs them in his pockets or hurls them into the water.

RVR: (*Aside*) That's no answer. Still, I had better not push him. If he refuses my proposal, I will have no choice but to demand it. He will probably need a few days, so it is useless to go on worrying about this right now.

Father and son walk down the Houtgracht, where the floral and vegetable markets have yet to come into swing. When they reach the Synagogue, intent on making some sketches, a large group of Sephardim, well dressed in black, loiters on the front stoop and perches on the benches. The outside of the building resembles an Italian palazzo. The entranceway is flanked by tall pilasters with Corinthian capitals, topped with an ornate balcony.

RVR: (*Aside*) What are all these people doing here? I wanted Titus to see the Synagogue empty, with its simple interior — the wooden vaults over the nave, the Doric columns and chandeliers, the tevah at one end, the ark of the Torah at the other. I wonder why the men are wearing such solemn faces. Is it a special day in their calendar, or has something sinister happened? Are they putting one of their members under a cherem?

The painter's son loiters near the bank while his father surveys the scene, scratching his head. He notices one of his friends amongst the shrunken visages: the physician Ephraim Bueno, who wears a dark coat lined with buttons, a bleached collar and turned-back white cuffs. A tall black hat sits atop his straight, grey hair.

RVR: Ephraim! (*Aside*) I could pick his face out of any crowd. Years ago, he commissioned a portrait from me.

EB: *Raising his index finger with its heavy, bejewelled ring.* Rembrandt, what brings you here this morning? *Breaks away from the group and hobbles over.* Have you come for the funeral?

RVR: *Glances down at his long cloak, torn pink stockings and paint-stained boots.* What funeral?

EB: *His large, dark eyes examine the painter over his squat nose.* Oh, pardon me, I thought you would have heard. I'm afraid our brother, Miguel d'Espinoza, has passed away. We are just on our way to the cemetery in Ouderkerk.

RVR: How terrible, Ephraim. This is sad news, indeed. (*Aside*) The words sound so silly! I did not know Miguel very well, but I met him once or twice before to sample his sugar and spices. When his big, liverish eyes flash before my face, I feel on the brink of tears.

EB: *Tugs on his coarse beard.* Yes, he was a member of our mahamad. Sad to say, he has struggled with his health over the past few years. We buried his third wife, Esther, only last year.

RVR: *Nods solemnly.* Please pay my respects to his family.

EB: You are welcome to accompany us.

RVR: We hadn't expected this at all. *Caressing his stubbled face, he sees his son standing behind them, shifting his feet nervously.* You remember Titus, don't you?

The painter beckons his son, who then shuffles over to join them and shakes the physician's outstretched hand.

EB: Well, you've certainly grown since I last saw you. Such a handsome young man, and so tall! But your father's eyes . . .

TVR: *Blushes.* Thank you.

EB: *Laying a hand on the painter's shoulder.* Why don't you say hello to Miguel's son?

The physician points towards the shore. A handsome young man in a full-length camel coat is standing several paces away, near a low, flat boat. He has olive-coloured skin and large, shiny eyes. His face is gaunt, and all the skin is pulled into his protruding chin.

RVR: Perhaps I will ... (*Aside*) He could easily be the son of a successful merchant. Though he is small in stature, there is something confident and convincing about his manner, his head held high, his eyes pausing for nothing. Miguel, too, wore a mysterious, almost sarcastic, curl on his lips.

The painter dimisses himself from his son and the physician then approaches the dead man's son and offers his hand.

RVR: My sympathy to your family.

BE: Pleased to meet you at last, Master van Rijn. I am a great admirer of your paintings.

RVR: *Eyes light up.* How kind of you. But your name is?

BE: Baruch d'Espinoza. Miguel is my father, or *was* my father ...

RVR: I'm very sorry. A fine figure of a man! Please be assured that it was God's purpose for him at this time ...

BE: *Interrupting.* Do you really believe that? When someone dies, people always take refuge in the will of God, but that is merely the sanctity of ignorance.

RVR: No, you misunderstood me. I was simply suggesting that your father had a higher calling, or ...

BE: Forgive me for my abruptness, Master van Rijn. On these occasions people always seek the causes of the causes to offer comfort to those left behind; 'it was his time', they say, perhaps it was because he was walking down that certain road, or because the sea had begun to toss, or the moon was in motion from the meridian, and the wind was blowing this way or that way . . . I have heard all explanations.

The dead man's son turns away to peer at the boat, which the other Sephardim, their boots sinking in the mud, are beginning to board.

RVR: I understand. (*Aside*) I've really stuffed my foot in my mouth this time! Is he about to cry or is he checking to see how things have progressed? I cannot decide, though he seems utterly calm.

BE: *Turns back.* I am anxious to speak with you further. Unfortunately, it looks as if they are ready to set off without me.

RVR: We will meet again? (*Aside*) His gleaming eyes are so black they seem azure.

BE: *With one hand, brushes the collar of his camelhair jacket.* All my hours are usually spent over books; perhaps you could provide me with an excuse to leave the house? I would be honoured to visit your workshop.

RVR: *Raises a finger.* Rare is the man who sees my workshop and survives.

BE: *Smiles mischievously.* I'll hazard anything.

The dead man's son walks to the boat on graceful legs, taking his time although the Bikur Cholim are waiting. The men have assembled themselves on the benches in an orderly manner as they would sit in their pews. Stretched along the middle, the black wooden coffin is a daring contrast to the men's white starched collars. One space remains for the dead man's son. After he takes his seat, another rabbi begins to mutter in Hebrew. While the rest join in, the dead man's son extracts a pipe from his pocket and sets it askew in the corner of his mouth. The smoke eddies into the air and drifts towards the shore.

TVR: *Joining his father.* Is that Portuguese? What are they saying, Pa?

RVR: No, that's Hebrew. Listen, it sounds like a prayer. (*Aside*) Usually, on the rare occasions I meet a kindred spirit, they seem to vanish into the mist immediately afterwards.

The physician removes his tall hat to expose his kippah, then unties the rope from a hook and shoves the boat away. A dull slap of water hits the shore. The men take up their oars and lower them into the dirty, glinting water. Shoulder to shoulder, father and son look on as the boat passes under the bridge in a peculiar silence, as if carrying a cargo of ghosts, and dissolves into the fog.

RVR: Their cemetery is two hours down the Amstel, in Ouderkerk, a small farming village. Whenever I go there to make my sketches, I often peek through the iron gates. I will take you with me next time. (*Aside*) The yard is a dozen or so acres of lush greenery divided by trees and hedgerows, bordered by the river and a stream on the other side, surrounded by flat fields. The tombstones are beautifully illustrated with biblical scenes. This is where Menasseh will be buried with his books when he passes away, to wait until he rises again.

TVR: *Nudges his father.* I have to leave now. My Latin lesson starts in five minutes!

RVR: I suppose we'll hold our drawing lesson another day.

TVR: Oh, Pa? I've thought about what you said, and I'd like to help. I mean, if you want me to draw up a will.

RVR: Really? Thank you, Titus. (*Aside*) This is all I can say, because my eyes are welling up with tears.

Father and son say goodbye, then set off in opposite directions.

RVR: *Walking with his head lowered into his collar.* (*Aside*) No one must see my weakness, especially not Titus. After all, I am his father and I know what's best. But, on my way home, I can't stop thinking of Miguel d'Espinoza making his last, silent journey, and the freedom his son must feel as he smokes his first, true pipe.

Jacob Blessing the Sons of Joseph

When Joseph heard that his father was becoming weak, he brought to him his two sons Manasseh and Ephraim. Yet the eyes of Jacob were dull from old age; indeed, he was blind. 'I had no idea of seeing your face,' Jacob said, 'but here God has let me see also your offspring. Bring them, please to me, that I may bless them.' So Joseph brought the boys close to Jacob, putting Ephraim by his left hand and Manasseh by his right.

However, Jacob put his right hand on Ephraim's head, though he was the younger, and his left hand upon Manasseh's head, though he was the firstborn. He said, 'Let my name be called upon them and the name of my fathers, Abraham and Isaac, and let them increase to a multitude in the midst of the earth.' When Joseph saw that his father had placed his right hand on Ephraim's head, it displeased him, so he tried to move it to the other. 'Not so, my father,' he said, 'for this is the firstborn.' Still,

Jacob kept refusing — perhaps he was remembering the time when his own father, Isaac, was deceived into blessing himself as firstborn instead of his hairier brother, Esau. 'I know it, my son, I know it,' Jacob said. 'He also shall become a people, and he also shall be great. But truly his younger brother shall be greater than he, and his seed shall become a multitude of nations.'

With these two blessings, Jacob reconciled the earlier sin committed against his blind old father. That is why, in my painting, Joseph will not show dissatisfaction or defiance on his face, according to the pictorial tradition. He will stand near the old man's bed, gazing tenderly at his father's loving gestures toward his sons. And Asenath, his righteous wife, will look on as a reminder of the deceitful Rebecca. I may even place an animal's skin around Jacob's shoulders!

Portrait of Abraham Francen, the Apothecary

I have a good friend with little monies but a generous heart. Abraham promises to help me through my financial trouble and to testify for me if the need arises. I am repaying his kindness with a portrait etching, for he tightens his belt to indulge his love of prints.

On a summer's day, the apothecary's study is gloomy. His window is open, and the curtain is draped over the corner of his triptych of Christ to let in the sunlight and a soft breeze. Abraham has barely settled on a stool, far back from his desk, where rest a large open book, a Taoist sculpture, a human skull and a ceramic pot. His left hand holds the bottom of a print while his right hand is raised to hold the top, but is hidden behind the page.

No, no, no. That is all wrong! Let me begin again.

On a summer's day, the apothecary's study is gloomy. The window is open to a view of trees, and the curtain is pushed to one side to let in the sunlight and a soft breeze. Abraham sits in a leather chair close to his desk, where rest a large open book, a Taoist sculpture, a human skull and a ceramic pot. His left hand holds the bottom of the print while his right hand is raised to clutch the top, fingers curled round the paper. He gazes down at the picture of an old warrior, his face bathed in the light — the high forehead and pale green eyes, the trimmed little beard and fine hair curling over his white collar.

The Inventory

Hendricus Torquinis and his entourage of clerks have arrived. They open every window and shutter so that no corner lies in darkness. Then they disperse and scamper through the house like rats, clutching their notebooks and quills. They fling open the cabinets, turn over the chests, pull the drawers out of cupboards, rifle through my papers, flip through my albums of drawings and prints, examine every painting on the walls. My house is skinned from ceiling to floor, stripped of its warmth. As they assess and tally, I look on, scowling. Or I shout and spit:

Be careful!

Don't touch that!

You can't look in here!

Lord have mercy, let it go!

Damn, damn, damn you all!

When I raise my fists, they tell me I am their ward. The law entitles them to do whatever they want with my goods, furniture and linen, silver and jewellery, down to my socks and handkerchiefs. This time, they are only *looking. Next time, if they win the battle, heap after heap will be loaded up and carted away. Shame on you. Shame on you and your household.*

My entire life is a list:
1. Object
2. Description
3. Worth

When I awake in the middle of the night, my big toe is on fire. It is red, engorged, and so tender that the weight of the blanket is intolerable. Oh, MY BIG TOE hurts so badly!

The rats have infiltrated my kunstcaemer. They prowl through my coral and nautilus shells, lion skins, nose flutes, suits of armour, Indian guns, plumes and pipes, helmets and turbans, halberds and busts, Negro heads, Mogul miniatures, Venetian glass, rhino horns and fish jaws, porcupines and pelicans, bamboo and string instruments, a Blaeu globe, a catapult ... As each object is noted, my eyes fix on its inexorable end.

Deeds, quittances, injunctions;
Lawyers, syndics, magistrates;
Petitions, petitions, petitions.
I must surrender my property,
or go to debtors' prison.

Goose quill, hog bristle, fine sable, even those of badger backs and oxen ears.

The word spreads quickly through the city: Rembrandt van Rijn is insolvent. Strike him off the list! He is no longer fit to be a father. If Titus doesn't have a mother, he must be an orphan now. Call in a guardian, someone to protect him. His father is a worthless beggar.

Goodbye to . . .
The Figure of the Virgin by Raphael
A Dürer, a Holbein
Three Brouwers, three Lievens
Jan Six's Medea
The death-mask of Frederick Henry
One Van Eyck, my Michelangelo
The statues of Homer and Aristotle
Prints by Giorgione, Raphael and Rubens
A book bound in black leather with writings and sketches
>   *(What? No!*
>   *You mustn't take that.*
>   *Cross it off.*
>   *Give it back.*
>   *Oh, write it down, but leave it here with me.)*

Thomas Haringh, auctioneer, is set to orchestrate the sale of my life. Less than a year ago, the little runt was sitting in my chair in front of my window in my workshop. A cloud of dry white hair. A foolish little grin on his face.

1 Bible, worn and frayed

God has punished me for my sins. Something is coming down from my anus. I find a hard bulge there, the size of a grape. My ass is pink and swollen with ganglions. Lord, it itches. Oh, the pain! How can I even sit down? Hendrickje, help me — wretched beast that I am. Pass me a bottle of gin!

There is Socrates, gazing at me with his empty eyes.

A Black-cloaked Heretic

Demonstrated in four of his letters, which treat God, the Mind, Human Bondage and Freedom.

Dear Sir,

Your letter, which I received yesterday, was most welcome to me both because I wanted to hear news of you, following our discussions at the society's meetings, and because your queries were mysterious in nature. I might fail to give you the answers you deserve, for I do not know how to set about them, as most of my correspondence is generally spiritual or philosophical, but through my forthrightness I will attempt to repay you the warmest thanks for your courtesy and consideration.

To begin with, my shelves hold everything from Machiavelli to Bacon, Calvin to Hobbes, Cervantes to Gongora, the two Thomases, More and Browne, anatomy books and Descartes' writings in excess not to mention several Bibles and the Kabbalah. I live in Den Haag, on the wide Paviljoensgracht, in a house owned by the painter Hendrik van der Spijck, whose seven children usually stay out of my way unless seized with the mood to sit on my lap, so I may labour over my papers in seclusion for two or three days at a time, and have my meals brought up to me, or forget to eat altogether, whilst I attempt to finish the *Ethics*. My two rooms are on the third floor, up the tightly spiralled staircase: one room for sleep and thought, the other for my workshop. I spend long evenings there, grinding and polishing lenses with patience and constancy, for experience has sufficiently taught me that the free hand is better and surer than any machine. The glass reveals itself through my love of detail: transparent, smooth, fragile and sensitive, it desires perfection and responds to what it receives.

Yes, we have our roots in the same soil, though I studied with Van den Enden at an earlier time, primarily to learn Latin, which was not offered in the curriculum at Hebrew school, being tainted with suspicion as 'the priests' language'. Little did I know that mathematics, science and philosophy were in store for me! Towards the end of my studies, my father passed away, and my sister Rebekah endeavoured to deprive me of my share of the inheritance on the grounds that I was a heretic. In the end, I won the legal battles and bequeathed everything to her anyway. (I only wanted one special item: my ledikant, a wooden four-poster bed surrounded by heavy curtains, where I was conceived, where both my parents slept and died, where I can hide and live well. Even now, as I write, the smoke from my pipe curls up and spreads under the canopy.) When Van den Enden found that I had nothing definite for support, he provided me a room and all necessaries at his own house – an arrangement which, as you can imagine, entailed a complete breach with Jewish dietary laws; and because the school was suspected of being a centre of atheism, my reputation did not improve by my intimate connection with it. Furthermore, being too naive to appreciate the wisdom of discretion, I freely voiced my heterodox views and provoked the rabbis into disciplining me.

Thank you for your offer to print my treatise – your house is a prestigious one – yet I am determined to delay publishing due to the horrible circumstances of late. Today I have no choice to go outside or receive guests, as I like to do now and again, for Van der Spijck has locked me inside, and as a true republican, he is ready to confront the mob on my behalf. You have likely heard of the assailants who clubbed and knifed the De Witt brothers in my neighbourhood only a week ago: a mob broke into the prison whilst Jan was visiting Cornelis and killed my friends in the most brutal manner. They dragged them to the gallows, suspended them upside down, quartered them then sold their body parts as souvenirs, eaten raw or cooked. Because Jan supported the publication of my *Tractatus Theologico-Politicus*, which stirred a hornet's nest, I am thought to be a spy, worst of all, a traitor. This is my darkest hour.

People say my pamphlet endeavoured to show that there is no God, and various theologians took the opportunity to complain of me before the magistrates, including those wretched Cartesians. Most honourable writers have been treated this way, especially when they seek the true causes of miracles, not to wonder at them like a fool. My adversaries think I take away freedom from God and subject Him to Fate. This is flatly false, for I have expressly stated that God must be acknowledged as the highest good and must be loved with a free mind; that the reward of virtue is virtue itself whilst the punishment of folly and weakness is folly itself; and lastly, that every man ought to love his neighbour and to obey the commands of the supreme power. If my enemies read evil intent in my arguments, what do they think of their Descartes, who said that nothing is done by us which has not been preordained by God, that we are newly created at every moment though we act according to our own free will? This, as Descartes himself confessed, most minds cannot comprehend. However, minds are not conquered by arms but by love and nobility.

If hope is nothing but an inconstant joy, arising from the image of something future or past whose outcome to some extent we doubt, I must be grateful for this quiet time to sort my thoughts and memories. Forgive me for not expressing myself better in Latin; I would have written in my first language or even your native tongue if not for the need of discretion. Commit this letter to your prudence, and myself, who am, &c.

B. d'Espinoza

Worthy Sir,

I will speak about the subjects on which you desire me to disclose my sentiments; however, be forewarned that you must lend your ear for a great deal of time, as your queries about my history, my education and my subsequent dissent from the Jewish faith require a lengthy and serious answer.

It all began when I was six years old and my mother passed away, due to a problem with her lungs (still I choose to inhale glass dust all day long!). She was buried in the cemetery at Ouderkerk, where her tombstone was beautifully carved with her name, Hana Deborah, and a drawing of a rose, though it was not as elaborate as the other graves, which had menorahs or moons or spread-fingered hands to ward off the evil eye. Across the rushing stream was a dark tomb with a column on top, which, my father said, was the resting place of *o vehlo*, the old one, called Abraham Franco Mendes, the first Portuguese man to settle in Amsterdam and to become a successful merchant. I wanted to be a trader like my father, unless I became a rabbi like Menasseh ben Israel, who taught me the mourner's prayer for my mother. My uncles, who came all the way from Porto, said their prayers in Portuguese and stayed on with us, telling their stories, talking about God and science in the parlour. I remember one of them asking me; if the sun is more than six hundred diameters away from us on the earth, why do we think that it is near, only slightly above us? I don't know, I said, is it like a dream? No, he returned, think about it some more, and I did, but I could not come up with a definite answer. Each day I went to the Synagogue two or three times reciting aloud that prayer for my poor mother. Rabbi ben Israel told me she had gone to *olam ha-ba* to receive her everlasting reward for virtue. My father said that all things are indefinite, that I should not worry about rewards or punishments.

Upon commencing my studies at Hebrew school, I thought I had gone to heaven: it seemed to be a land flowing with milk and honey. During my years there, I completed seven classes altogether. First we were taught to say our prayers in Hebrew and to chant the Pentateuch, then we translated parts of the Bible into Spanish, and later we studied Rashi's Hebrew Commentary, written in the eleventh century but sober far beyond its age. During the hours I was at home, I received private tuition in secular subjects under the direction of Rabbi ben Israel, the most brilliant teacher in the Synagogue, who thought of me as his prize pupil. Soon enough, my keen interest in Moses Maimonides, in particular the *Guide of the Perplexed*, became equal to the rabbi's own, though it led me to discover certain inconsistencies in Biblical theology.

Laden with these doubts, I had no idea how to proceed, for I lacked the ability and strength of my teachers, who seemed to detach their theories from their everyday life. However advanced their views, they were conservative in feeling and practice like most orthodox followers of Calvinism or Catholicism. Whilst I felt that the Hebrew faith could appeal to an authority which no other religion equalled, I could not deny my own wider knowledge and altered spiritual needs. It was understandable that the congregation felt betrayed by my behaviour – breaching ritual observances, failing to attend the Synagogue while engaging in Christian prayer-meetings – as my father and grandfather had held prominent offices within, and I, myself, had shown promise as a rabbi. After all, my own name – Bento in the cradle, Baruch in the synagogue, Benedictus on the page – means 'one who is blessed and praised'. Yet, before I relate the events thereafter, let me share with you an early experience that caused me, at eight years old, to begin questioning tradition and superstition within my faith, which is, after all, the topic on which you inquired.

Everyone gathered in the Synagogue, both sitting and standing, waiting for the ceremony to begin. There was only the sound of our shoes grating against the sand grains on the floors when a middle-aged, bearded man was asked to come to the stage. He was the one we were supposed to shun, because he published a book to disprove the immortality of the soul, but I had never joined the other children in throwing rocks at him. The man cleared his throat and began reading aloud to the congregation a paper prepared by the rabbis. I have failed to observe the Sabbath and the Law, he said, I have prevented others from joining the faith, and so on, until he had confessed his every sin and had promised never to commit them again. After he stepped down, the rabbi directed him to the corner and ordered him to undress down to the waist. He also removed his shoes. The rabbi tied a red handkerchief over his eyes and told him to hug the column, then proceeded to wind a rope around his wrists. That is when the slashings began, leather straps against his bare back, our cue to begin singing a psalm. My mouth was open, only no sound emerged, for I was counting.

At thirty-nine, the beating ended – to exceed forty is against the Law. The man sat on the floor, holding back tears, and put his clothes back on. When the rabbi announced his reinstatement after seven years, we did not applaud. Then the man lay down at the threshold of the door, and the chamach clutched his hand tenderly. One by one, we left the temple, stepping over him on the way out. When it was my turn, I looked down at him and smiled weakly: his eyes were closed. Whilst everyone gathered outside in the street, I tried to peer into the Synagogue, but Father pulled me away from the door. Heresy is a sin worse than murder, he told me. Murder robs a man of his physical life, but that is only a short time. Heresy steals away his spiritual inheritance, an eternity of happiness; it murders the soul. Later, the man shot himself with a pistol. His name was Uriel da Costa.

Although I was deeply affected by this experience, it took sixteen years for me to understand the humiliation Da Costa had endured and why he had taken his own life. At that time, the congregation's distrust for me turned into apathy, and in July 1656, I was formally issued the high cherem *in absentia*: 'By decree of the Angels and by the command of the holy men, we excommunicate, expel, curse and damn Baruch d' Espinoza . . . Cursed be he by day and cursed be he by night. Cursed be he in sleeping and in waking; cursed in going out and in coming in . . .' Yet this compelled me to do nothing that I should not otherwise have done.

Shame is a sadness, accompanied by the idea of some action of ours which we imagine that others blame. Remorse is a sadness accompanied by the idea of a past thing which has turned out worse than we had hoped. However, Joy is a man's passage from lesser to greater perfection.

Your sincere servant,

B. d'Espinoza

Dear Friend and Sir,

I was very saddened to learn of the loss of your mother and, strange as it is, your recurrent vision of her, in dwarf size, dancing atop a candle flame – news of this nature has such heavy wings! Therefore, to answer your query: I cannot deny the existence of ghosts, but there are an infinity of things impossible to make out. What are spectres? Are they children, fools or madmen? Perhaps my own experience with one such mysterious figure will help you to draw your own conclusions.

One morning, after dawn, I woke up from a very unpleasant dream and the images presented to me in sleep remained vividly before my eyes, especially that of a certain man whom I had never seen before, coming at me from the shadows. This image disappeared for the most part when I cast my eyes on a book, but as soon as I lifted my eyes again without fixing my gaze on any particular object, the same man appeared again and again, lurking round me all through the morning until he gradually vanished.

That evening, as every other, I wore my black cloak and set

out into the city, threading my way through alleyways on a quest for mystery, as I like to do now and again. Whilst walking down a particularly grotesque and deserted passage, I suddenly heard footsteps behind me. When I turned round, I saw a man lurking in the shadows, the same man I had encountered in my dream. It was not his features revealing this fact to me for, indeed, he was unidentifiable through the shroud of mist; rather, it was his phantasmic aura that told me he was the one sent to kill me by my former teachers and friends. I tried to flee but it was too late; he lunged at me with a knife and tore into my back. I staggered like a drunken man over the stones, thinking I had been stabbed; fortunately, only my cloak had taken the wound, protecting me from the blade. When my assailant lifted his dagger a second time, to plunge it into my chest, I knocked it from his hands with my cane. As we struggled for a while, twisting in each other's arms, I still could not identify him for he moved too briskly. Finally, I wrestled myself from his grasp and broke into a run. My cloak, with its long tear down one side, flapped in the wind all the way home. I have saved it for some years as a remembrance of my fortunate escape from death.

A timely flight shows as much tenacity as fighting, for a free man avoids dangers by the same virtue of the mind in which he tries to overcome them. By tenacity I mean the desire with which each one strives, solely from the dictate of reason, to preserve his being. By danger I understand whatever can be the cause of some evil, such as sadness, hate and discord. I say with Descartes that if we cannot extend our will beyond the bounds of our limited understanding, we shall be most wretched — it will not be in our power to eat a crust of bread or walk a step or go on living, for all things are uncertain and full of peril. Nothing remains for me but to subscribe myself, &c.

B. d'Espinoza

Respected Friend,

Your letter has duly reached me, and I cannot refrain from expressing my astonishment that your latest question concerning Rembrandt van Rijn has only now been presented. Yes, I met him at my father's funeral and liked him immediately, for he struck me as a strange and legendary creature about whom endless stories should be told. We commiserated again at the house of Menasseh ben Israel, prior to the rabbi's departure for England — as you may know, he later returned from his mission broken-hearted and poor, having failed to convince Oliver Cromwell to accept the Jews, accompanied by the corpse of his young son. Shortly thereafter, the rabbi passed away in despair, and to my dismay I was not invited to his funeral, for the aforementioned reasons, but rest assured your friend Rembrandt was in attendance to mourn his loss.

Returning to my earlier point, good sir; when the great master expressed his desire to paint me, I accepted without reservation to pose for him as the young David playing his harp for Saul. It required lengthy days of sitting through a period of several months, but we spoke little during that time, often sharing a contemplative silence and infrequently launching into discussions on theology, when he proved himself well versed in the Scriptures. In the end, I had made little advance in understanding him through this personal interaction, and discovered far more upon my observations of him at work in his craft. Rembrandt seems to carry within himself a stage, for whilst he paints the scenes unfold as naturally in his mind as they do on the canvas. His dramatic spirit is manifest in his paintings, where there exists no boundary between the figures themselves and the atmosphere — that imponderable, intangible whole where neither space, still less time, exists. It is this atmosphere I like best, what the Italians call 'l'ambiente' and which is unique to Rembrandt's paintings, not to mention unrivalled. He allows his figures to mirror and seek and fortify one another, so the great and small are cancelled out and the near are as mysterious as the far. His light melts everywhere and his darkness exults. What harmony! There is no artist like him, excluding, perhaps, the English dramatist William Shakespeare.

In the instance that you have not lain eyes upon this picture of David and Saul; the broken king sits in a chair, wearing an embroidered gold costume and a long scarlet robe draped over his shoulders. The light strikes his ballooning red turban upon which sits a golden crown. He limply holds on to a spear with his right hand whilst, with his opposite hand, he wearily draws a brown velvet curtain over half his face to conceal his tears. His revealed eye has a faraway look; his cheek is weighed down by suffering. Outside this circle of misery, kneeling at Saul's feet, is the fragile figure of David, without his armour, attending to the King whom he loves. My back is gently bent over a harp as I pluck its strings with my hands. The light bounces off my white collar and cuffs to emphasize my face — the olive skin, the long nose with flared nostrils, the brown eyes and trimmed black beard. Absorbed by my music, I play with a closed smile on my lips.

Although I fancy myself as an amateur draftsman — indeed,

Rembrandt offered me counsel on my charcoal drawings — I am
not skilled in speaking about painting, but I hope to have
furnished you with enough material for your research until we
may speak face to face; that is, should you decide to visit the
society once more. If this little word may give you satisfaction,
I shall be glad as yours in all affection, sir,

Yours, &c. Benedictus

'Quis talia fando temperet a lacrimis?'

On 7 September 1668, the annual fair had begun, and the market in Dam Square brimmed with exotic delicacies while fire-eaters and sword-swallowers performed in the streets, and tightrope walkers stepped from steeple to steeple. It should have been the happiest time of year, but as I looked around me I saw aggrieved faces and tears of sorrow. Even the trees wept in the wan light of evening, for amidst the happy hubbub, a coffin was being carried upon the shoulders of eight pallbearers through muddy streets and over humpbacked bridges. A long procession of mourners clad in black, torches atremble in the wind, snaked in and out of sideshows and vendors, wove through jugglers and acrobats to keep pace with the shiny coffin hovering in the distance. Some observers, pointing or staring as we passed by, probably thought it was all part of the ceremonies, a joke no less cruel than the displays of freakish specimens: midgets and giants, savages and conjoined twins, while those who were taking part wished it were only a theatrical show, because even the most repulsive of monstrosities could not have stirred such pity, such grief, such fear. My heart was in my mouth as I followed the procession along the canal and saw the tip of the Westerkerk tower, a blue and yellow crown flashing above the storm clouds. When the crowd dwindled, just a few more steps would bring us to the cemetery, and once every person in the cortège had passed through the iron gates and beyond the merciless walls of stone, the bells tolled from the clock tower. *Who, on hearing this, can hold back his tears?* Titus van Rijn, at twenty-seven years old, had unexpectedly died of the plague.

Only a few weeks ago, Clara and I were sitting in Titus's parlour, sipping our tea and listening to his stories; he had trusted us with his secrets, and I, too, had confided in him, so when we left his house that day, we were sure our friendship would last for many years. Not long afterward we received Magdalena's thank-you for the windmill cup, and in the same letter she told us that Titus had caught the disease. Clara and I read the message in her study, and as soon as its gravity struck us – he would die in a matter of days; they had been married less than a year; she was five months pregnant – we collapsed into each other's arms, weeping. How could this be? It did not matter that I was competing for his place in life, seeking his father's attention; it did not matter that I, at times, had secretly hoped he would disappear – I never thought in my cruellest moments that I wanted Titus to die. I was beginning to love him. So Clara and I cursed ourselves, convinced that one of us had infected him, and that we would be visited by the Angel of Death ourselves; then we became inseparable, preparing to die together while seizing every opportunity to live in a world that had made us outcasts. I knew I would be happier suffering with her in Hell than living on this earth with anyone else.

Even as the fifty or more mourners collected near the shallow grave – huddling into their handkerchiefs, clutching one another's arms, placing flowers near the casket – Clara stood next to me, one finger clandestinely curled round mine like a little worm.

Rembrandt had rented an outside site where the dead were in the thousands and unable to rest at a decent distance from one another. Titus would have been welcome in the Van Loo tomb had there been space, but many of Magdalena's relatives had died during the last sweep of the disease, so his final resting place was pleasantly situated amongst a clump of willows, which provided shelter when the rain began to fall, trickling through the leaves. *That in sorrow we should eat our bread, till we return to the ground from whence we are taken.*

The pallbearers carefully lowered the coffin upon the planks laid over the empty grave. Rembrandt was one of the eight, but he could barely do his part, wobbling as if he might collapse at any second. Although I stood a dash away, I could not offer any help for my knees were as shaky as his, my feet at the mercy of the stinking mud. A shudder ran through the roots of my hair: who was I lamenting more, the deceased or the man left behind who should have gone first? Despite the care he had taken with his appearance – the crisp black suit, the white cravat, the tall hat (I had never seen him looking so formal) – Rembrandt resembled a broken-down animal with his moles and lumps, his beady eyes fixed in a suffering gaze. He did not wish to be here among us, I thought; he wished he were as dead as the son he loved. If only I could assure him that he had not been completely abandoned! Remembering his outburst at the engagement party, I tried to pull myself together and ducked under my cloak for a swig of gin from my flask; before the end of the service, he was bound to need my assistance in some way.

The pallbearer behind him was his old childhood friend, Jan Lievens, a tall, handsome, moustachioed man with grey hair and deep-set brown eyes. He had returned to Amsterdam almost twenty years ago, but this was probably their long-awaited reunion, for the word in the Cock & Bull was that they did not visit each other though they lived on the same street. So what if it were not 'long-awaited' at all? Funerals often unite people who would otherwise spend the rest of their lives estranged and embittered, and I could only hope that Lievens's presence was not another source of discomfort or sorrow for Rembrandt. At least there seemed to be an atmosphere of civility between them as they convened about the placement of the casket. Clara and I convened too, in whispers, identifying the others: Hendrick Uylenburgh's son, Gerrit; Abraham Francen; Lodewijck van Ludick, a friend of Rembrandt and art dealer; two of Magdalena's brothers and her uncle Gerrit Van Loo. Gerrit's wife, Hiskia, was the only one of Saskia's relatives in attendance.

After the men had bowed their heads for private prayers, they walked away from the grave to join their loved ones. Meanwhile, Rembrandt seemed afraid to let go and maintained a firm grip on the handle of the casket. Looking up, he realized he was the only one remaining, and pulled a brightly coloured feather out of his pocket then placed it on the coffin. I recognized it as the plumage of a Bird of Paradise because of its bright colours; I had seen one in my grandfather's collection, but I could not be sure why he had chosen this particular specimen. Did it have some personal significance for him or his son? Perhaps I would have a chance to ask him later. When he ambled across the grass to take his place beside Magdalena and her mother, Anna, directly across from me, his eyes met mine and understood me as a trusted soul; they seemed to say, 'Do not keep far off from me because distress is nearby.' My heartbeat slowed and my breathing relaxed, so if anything troublesome should happen, I would be able to act quickly.

Her full form sheathed in a long black dress, Magdalena came forward and tossed a garland of flowers on to the coffin. The banner on it read: *Titus van Rijn, florentibus occidit annis*, dead in the flower of his youth. Though I could not see her tears, because her pretty face was hidden behind a lace veil, her teeth chattered and her chest heaved with sobs. She could hardly tear herself away, hands crossed over her pregnant belly, feet immobile in the grass. The scent of wet leaves and earth saturated the air when, out of nowhere, a mangy dog came lolling down the mossy hummock, bounded through the wooden markers and sat next to the dead man's wife. She did not seem to notice it squatting there next to her, staring at the coffin, panting with its large red tongue. After a few minutes of silence broken only by the sad patter of the rain and an intermittent weeping, the mother took her lost child by the arm and led her back. Then the black dog dashed off through the yard and disappeared. When Clara dug her nails into my arm, I did not turn to comfort her, for I was finding it difficult enough to maintain my composure. My nose dripped tears: *What is your life? You are a mist that appears for a little while and then vanishes.*

A Calvinist elder emerged from the spreading fog to offer a few words before the coffin was lowered. The family had already expressed their sorrow in the privacy of their home before the procession began, and for once I approved of the Calvinist custom. What grieving person should subject himself to the critical eyes of those who cannot comprehend the pain which fills his heart? Unfortunately, I had missed Rembrandt's eulogy, but gazing at him now, surrounded by the rippling light of torches and sunk in deepest despair, I could not imagine him making even a paltry attempt to speak. The aged brother gazed down at the Holy Bible open on his palm, and the other hand shielded the pages from the rain as his breath made puffs in the cold air:

'Now when Jesus came, he found that Lazarus had already been in the tomb four days. Bethany was near Jerusalem, about two miles off, and many of the Jews had come to Martha and Mary to console them concerning their brother. When Martha heard that Jesus was coming, she went and met him, saying, "Lord, if you had been here, my brother would not have died. And even now I know that whatever you ask from God, God will give you." Jesus said to her, "Your brother will rise again." Martha said to him, "I know that he will rise again in the resurrection at the last day." Jesus said to her, "I am the resurrection and the life; he who believes in me, though he die, yet shall he live, and whoever lives and believes in me shall never die. Do you believe this?" She said to him, "Yes, Lord; I believe that you are the Christ, the Son of God, he who is coming into the world."'

Then the minister said, 'Let us pray,' and as everyone lowered their chins I kept one eye on Rembrandt, who seemed to be watching the raindrops that drummed upon the coffin, or the flower petals that slipped loose from Magdalena's garland and slid down its sides. 'Almighty God, we give thee hearty thanks, for that it hath pleased thee to deliver this our brother out of the miseries of this sinful world . . .' His hands were clenched firmly together and his head swayed as if, like a storm cloud, it were holding in an impending shower. '. . . that we, with all those that are departed in the true faith of thy holy Name, may have our perfect consummation and bliss both in body and soul . . .' His mouth compressed into deep folds and his nose dilated wildly. '. . . in thy eternal and everlasting glory through Jesus Christ our Lord. Amen.'

At that, three of the pallbearers returned to their places and took up the ropes holding the casket, but the fourth man, who was Rembrandt, did not step forward to offer himself. In fact, when Anna leant over to nudge him, he rocked back and forth, hands in pockets, his eyes wrinkled and sealed like two piecrusts. The other men called on Lievens to replace him, and when he did, they removed the planks from over the hole and began shuffling the cords through their palms to lower the casket inch by inch. Clara looked up at me with moist, glassy eyes, and I pressed my thumb into her soft palm as we said goodbye to Titus in our heads. But Rembrandt could not bid his final farewell: his hands shook pathetically at his sides while his facial features showed no sign of movement apart from his eyes, shedding silent tears. This was the moment I had anticipated: he was going to burst!

Just as I was about to go to him, Rembrandt rushed forward with a moaning sound of terror and lifted his hands above his head, striking them in the air like a ghoul. His swarthy face turned to the sky, his lips in a wild snarl, he hissed, 'This is my beloved Son, with whom I am well pleased!' Gasps of astonishment rolled through the crowd, but not a soul stirred apart from me. I dashed towards him, pumping my arms, moving as fast as my spindly legs would allow. He side-stepped me and ran to the grave, his long hair flapping, his coat tails lifting up like wings in the wind. I was too late to stop him and only prompt enough to catch his hat, which took flight as he hurled himself into the open hole, belly first, then disappeared from view. *You will go your way among dim shapes, having been breathed out.*

The coffin lurched downward with the force of his weight, and as the pallbearers strained to keep it from dropping further, I quickly got on all fours in the mud. With the rain trickling down my neck, I peered into the grave. Rembrandt was slumped like a man who had been stabbed in the back: he hugged the casket with two arms, his face buried into the wood. Around him, the walls of damp earth seethed with wriggling bugs. I extended an arm and called out, 'Rembrandt, take my hand!' His body surged as he sobbed loudly, but he did not answer. I yelled again, 'It's me, Pieter. I've come to take you home.' He craned his head to look at me over his shoulder with one dark eye. 'Save me from the mouth of the lion,' he groaned. 'Yes,' I said, 'give me your hand.' Glancing around for help, I saw that no one had come forward — perhaps they thought, mistakenly, that I had a handle on the situation — and the pallbearers were still desperately clutching the ropes, which had started to split and thin. In a matter of minutes, they would snap entirely. 'Rembrandt, please.' He slowly rolled on to one side and extended a limp arm. My two hands gripped his sweaty fingers, then, bracing myself, I yanked with all my strength to rescue him from the roaring pit. I pulled as he scrambled up the side of the grave and I pulled as he began to emerge from the mire. When I let go, we tumbled backward on to the wet grass, and Rembrandt landed on top of me with distressing force.

We blinked frantically, face to face, dripping with rain and sweat. His once cloudy hair was plastered to his head, his cheeks had fallen into his collar, and his breath stank like manure. When he snapped out of his trance, his eyes narrowed in embarrassment and avoided my confounded gaze. 'Pardon me,' he said nervously, then scrambled to untie himself from our despairing knot. Lievens, who was towering above us, assisted him to his feet. 'Are you all right?' he asked, pulling him to one side as the minister started shovelling dirt into the grave. Rembrandt nodded solemnly. I felt utterly ridiculous, splayed on the grass as Rembrandt and Lievens stared each other down in an awkward silence and the minister recited his last words: 'Forasmuch as it hath pleased Almighty God of his great mercy to take unto himself the soul of our dear brother, Titus van Rijn, here departed, we therefore commit his body to the ground; earth to earth; ashes to ashes; dust to dust . . .' Who was going to help me? Where was Clara? Heaven forbid she should come to the aid of such an oaf! When the pallbearers ambled away, I lifted myself up and began brushing the mud from my breeches. I heard Rembrandt say, 'You can go now. I don't need your help.' What? Surely he could not be speaking to me! When I turned round and glared at him, I realized he was talking to someone else.

'Why did you invite me?' Lievens asked.

Rembrandt threw him a sidelong glance. 'For my son.'

Lievens frowned. 'Not for yourself? I see you haven't grown any wiser with age.'

'Neither have you. If you weren't so petulant, it might have worked between us.'

'No,' Lievens said, shaking his head. 'Because you've always wanted to play centre-stage!'

'Well, see me now? A poor old man, full of grief and age. Wretched in both!'

'Just as I said!' Lievens spat, before stomping off.

I pretended not to have heard the conversation and handed Rembrandt his crumpled wet hat. 'Let's go home.'

He yanked it over his damp hair and grimaced. The bell tolled from the steeple of the church, bringing me to my senses: the sexton was filling the grave with dirt and the mourners were trickling out of the yard, lanterns bobbing, on their way to the Gilded Scales. I could not believe the service had ended so quickly, and not a single person had been courteous enough to approach Rembrandt. Magdalena had vanished too — if she had been well enough she might have come over — so the only remaining guest was my faithful Clara, loitering near the trees and shivering in a black velvet shawl. When she waved to us, Rembrandt bowed to her, one foot sliding backward, his hand rolling through the air. She giggled into her handkerchief.

'Just a moment,' I said to him with a scowl, then shot through the wet grass.

With her chin puckered, her hair loosened about her face, she said, 'I'm afraid for him, he's so helpless. But he is fortunate to have you, Pieter. Watch him carefully. I'm afraid he will . . .'

'I'm walking him home. Would you like to come along?'

Her green eyes darted to and fro. 'No, that would be . . .'

'What?'

She fidgeted, gazing down at my muddy boots. 'Disagreeable.'

'Why?' As I waited for her reply, my mind reversed, not for the first time, through every personal thing she had mysteriously known about Rembrandt, through his hand on her shoulder at the engagement party, through the way he had only just bowed to her — and all these thoughts made me uneasy and suspicious, especially when she did not return a word. 'Is there something between you that I don't know about?'

'What are you suggesting?'

I glanced over my shoulder to make sure that Rembrandt could not hear us; and thank the Lord he was a safe distance away, perched in the grass near the gate. 'Well, forgive me, but it has crossed my mind on more than one occasion, perhaps wrongly, I mean, you're a beautiful woman and he's a . . .'

'How dare you! I cannot believe what . . .' She shook her head. 'Absolutely not! Are you calling me a whore?'

'That's not what I said. Just tell me, Clara.'

She rolled her eyes. 'This is not appropriate.'

'But has he ever . . .?' My relentless stare told her I would not leave until she satisfied me with an answer.

She crossed her arms over her bosom. 'Very well, yes, one afternoon, though it's not what you think. We held each other and he cried, nothing more.'

'You went to his bed and he didn't touch you? That's worse than I imagined!'

'I didn't say I went to his bed! He confided in me. Death. He talked about dying.'

'You lied to me.'

'No, I didn't,' she returned, through clenched teeth. 'You never asked me, and it has nothing to do with you and him.'

'What about *us*? Oh, I suppose that's unimportant.'

'It was well before you came along,' she said, breathlessly. 'I lost my father, remember?'

I smirked. 'Everyone in the city has lost a father or a mother, that doesn't mean they fall into the arms of anyone who might replace them . . .'

'But that in no way denies their need for them, does it? You of all should understand.'

I examined her face – the porcelain skin framed by a neatly folded black bonnet. She was watching me very closely. Was it true, what she had just told me? Then she said, 'There's a bit of grass on your cheek.'

'There is?'

Clara stood on tiptoe, and with a delicate hand, wiped the blade from my face. We were standing very close, so close that I could kiss her. Though her lips were still and cold, I pressed them with as much force as I could muster. I wanted to show her they belonged to me and no one else, and I wanted to show Rembrandt the same. She pulled away, her eyes smarting while she dipped a hand into her pocket and pulled out a small letter closed with a red seal. As if hoping to rid herself of it, she flattened the note against my chest, though I then had to prise it from her tiny, tidy fingernails. When she turned round and set off through the cemetery in the direction of the rear gates, my heart raged with jealousy, and it required all of my dignity not to follow her, a little maiden in the grove.

I tucked the note into my pocket and faced my rival, who was slumped against the fence, patting the head of a stray dog crouched next to him – the black one we had seen earlier with the shaggy coat and patchy tail almost without hair. The sight of his sad face and his sullied garments quelled my anger and softened me, at least momentarily, while I hastened towards him. Man and mongrel stared at me with eyes wide open, as if I were disturbing an intimate moment. The dog barked furiously as I coaxed Rembrandt to his feet then he followed us out of the lonely churchyard, beyond those merciless walls of stone, all the way down to the canal.

The Ox's Story

A Sacred Utterance

To say, you who have smitten my father,
have killed one greater than he;
You are upon my back as if upon the back of an ox.
Though I walk in the shadows, I will not retreat from death,
The death that comes to all living things.

In my dark cave, an offering of the butcher;
How he is terrified!
Red are the eyes which are in his head;
White is the tongue which is in his mouth;
Orange is the flesh which is his covering.
A knife goes against him, carving a deep wound;
Fall, collapse!

Yes, I kill for you he who killed me;
I overpower for you he who overpowered me.
He who stretched me out as the stretched-out ox;
He who slaughtered me as the slaughtered ox;
He who humbled me as the humbled ox —

I lop off his head; I sever his tail;
I hack off his hands; I sunder his feet.
Woe to the muscles, viscera, hide and fat;
I flay them and splay them for all to see.

His front legs, which guided him through the pasture,
for Titian and Rubens;
His back shanks, which trampled the mud,
for Michelangelo and Giorgione;
His bloody rib cage, which protected his organs,
for Apelles;
His two fleshy flanks, which guided him left or right,
for Homer and Aristotle;
These I offer as an example of the capabilities of mortal man.

I sprinkle the blood for eternal life.
I purify the heart for a precious price.

Fatten the red ox for Worthiness
Slaughter the red ox for Communion
Offer the red ox for Immortality,
Eat the red ox for Repentance.

Come, come into the radiant light!

He rests in silence, the Prodigal Son.
Take him for yourself as much as the heart desires,
Enfold him in your embrace.

'Extremum umbræ solis tremere videtur'

The three of us walked slowly across the bridge and into the aftermath of celebration, through streets cleared of festival-goers but littered with reminders of their presence — tickets and paper hats, hay and food scraps skittering across the cobblestones in the wind. Rembrandt and I huddled together for warmth — even if it had stopped raining, the sun was setting — but despite my urge to say something to him, I was allowing Fate to guide us along the quiet, narrow lanes toward the Rosengracht. The mongrel trotted behind, picking about in corners for something to eat, then whined with joy over the smallest morsel. Although his breathing was troubled and heavy when we ducked through puddles, Rembrandt seemed calmer, even surprisingly lucid, and generally walked a straight line through the gathering dusk. He was not drunk at all; it must have been anguish that had overcome him earlier, driving him to such extreme conduct. I could not understand how I myself survived such a painful ordeal with only a small amount of gin sloshing in my head, but a violent pressure attacked my temples as I remembered Clara's confession. Then, without warning, while we passed the trinket shops and dark apothecaries, Rembrandt was in the mood to talk.

'I only saw him once in those last few days,' he said. 'At the beginning, before he broke out in buboes.'

'Were you able to say goodbye?'

He ambled along, his arms swinging at his sides. 'How could I? He was barely recognizable as my son.'

'I visited him a couple of weeks ago. Did he tell you?'

He shook his head. 'No, no.'

So Titus had not told him about my visit; this revelation leant more weight on what he had confided in me that day. Perhaps their relationship had not been so close after all, or perhaps there hadn't been time. 'How is Cornelia?'

'She stayed at home with Rebecca. I thought it best, she's only fourteen.' He looked apprehensively at me out of the corner of his eye while we continued walking, and just as I noticed the dog was no longer panting behind us, he began to pour out his heart with unusual candour.

'After we moved from the Breestraat house, I sent Titus to the Lommerd, the pawnbroker,' he said, 'to redeem some of my things with the little money I'd made from my etchings, particularly a mirror framed in ebony from Floris Soop's factory. That evening Titus – he must have been nineteen or twenty at the time – set off to repurchase the mirror with a pouch full of money, and when he got there, the transaction went well. He found a bargeman willing to carry the heavy piece back to our house for a small fee. They set it on top of the man's head so he could balance it with two hands, but the mirror was large and awkward. From the start the man walked uneasily, probably drunk, and it was getting dark. As they hurried through the heavy crowds, the bargeman started to perspire, and his hands became sweaty and slippery. Titus thought he was going to lose his grip, but he could do little more than lead the way. When they reached the Rusland bridge, the night lotteries were going on — you know how crowded it can be — so the man cried out something like, "Friends, please be careful, don't let anyone bump into me! I am carrying this expensive piece here."'

'What happened?' I asked, while pointing out the next turn; his storytelling had made him temporarily forget the route to his house.

'When the man stepped off the bridge, there was a loud cracking noise, and in an instant, the glass shattered into a thousand little shards and slivers. Titus said the man hadn't fallen or bumped into anything. But they were both so angry that they left the glass there, on the ground, and Titus had no choice but to pick up the empty frame and carry it back to me.' His voice balled up in his throat. 'When he got home, and I saw the state of my mirror, you know what I did?'

Rembrandt stopped in his tracks, so I stopped too, but when he spoke his voice emerged from the back of his throat and his eyes looked beyond me toward the canal. 'I raged at him. I told him he was a lazy, good-for-nothing son. Why didn't he help? Why didn't he carry it himself? Why didn't he save it? I called him a filthy liar. That is what I'm really like . . .' His eyelids dropped in reflection as he went on, as if talking to himself or thinking aloud. 'But Titus was the most devoted boy in the world, and I was angry at myself for expecting so much of him, for spending his mother's legacy on paintings when the money was needed for more important things . . . He'd been asking me for his own painter's smock, and did I buy it for him? No, I made him wear my old grubby one . . . He felt terrible about what happened, he begged me to forgive him, and yet I did not retract what I said, not even the next day when I had come to my senses, not even when he was lying on his deathbed in torment.' He was silent for a moment, his face worn and hollow, then he set off down the street, his feet dragging behind him like stalking spectres. *The extremity of the shadow caused by the sun seems to tremble.*

I caught up with him and took his arm. 'When someone dies we can always think of things we didn't say, or things we said and didn't intend to say, we can blame ourselves for a flood of words or a dearth of words, loving them too much or not enough, and it is probably all true, or at least it seems so, but we can't stop living because of what did or didn't happen long ago in the past.'

He hobbled along, scratching his belly. 'When I was younger I was able to live in the present very happily, but in old age there is only my memory. Now Titus is gone, I feel guilty for everything I inflicted on him from the time he was born, my only son! How can I go back to such infamy?'

I pitied him and wanted to help, but how could I give him a reason to live? How could I convince him that my friendship was worth suffering for? We reached his canal, and trudged through piles of fallen yellow leaves. To our left a blind man sat on a doorstep, his head tilted toward the clouds as if forming them into rose-gardens. I watched in disbelief as Rembrandt tossed a generous guilder into his cup, without stopping or even looking at his intended goal; he must have done it all the time though practically destitute himself. When had he last eaten? I watched him in profile and saw his face in patches of colour – greens, blues and yellows bubbling to the surface. He began talking again.

'I have lost so many people, first there was my father then Saskia, my Rombertus and two Cornelias, my mother, my friends, poor Menasseh, then Hendrickje and Titus . . .' His lips quivered as if he might cry. 'I have hoarded numerous things over the years to fill up my life and yet, in the end, I am left alone in emptiness. I understand now that my art has not kept me alive but the people I have loved, and without them I still have to carry on though I don't have the slightest hope of survival. No matter how many paintings I make! I used to create my faces and figures with a compulsive fever, hoping they would long surivive me, but even if they last for eternity their world is not real – they do not answer back when you ask them a question! – it's the darkest place on earth.' He straggled his sleeve across his mouth. 'I've tried to live by remembering, and now my reality is made up of only dead faces, ghosts, and the new faces make no lasting impression unless I can follow their lines towards someone who has been but is no longer. Most of the time, I cannot be sure whether I am awake or dreaming. Even now.'

His voice muffled against the frayed collar of his coat as he peeked at me with one green eye. 'She seemed to vanish overnight. One day she was standing there in my studio, posing for me in furs, the next she was gone like a shadow, deep in the grave with no name or date, no words to indicate her personality or achieve‑ ments, as if she never existed, Hendrickje Stoffels, the sergeant's daughter from Bredevoort. So when I stand there in the cemetery I feel nothing, sometimes I just roll about the grass in order to tickle my skin. It is only when I walk away and return home and sleep alone that I feel the horror of her having left me. I never captured her face in paint, her true face, but it is still here inside my head, so why not live there, I think, why not sleep for ever? It will be the same with Titus.' He stopped and looked around, realizing we were only a few trudges from his door.

We terme sleep a death, and yet it is the waking that kills us, and destroys those spirits which are the house of life, I quoted to myself then, as if he had heard me, made a pathetic attempt to console him. 'But you've painted her spirit, and the spirit is eternal!'

He shrugged. Perhaps he had said more than he had wanted to and regretted it, or perhaps he felt a great relief at having purged himself and was ready to move on to something else, for his face lifted into shape and he changed the subject. 'Who was that woman back there?'

I glanced over my shoulder. 'What woman?'

'The little fair-haired one you were talking to.'

'Oh, Clara de Geest . . .' I frowned. 'But you know her!' My mind flashed up the image of her tiny body in this wasted man's arms, smothered against his bosom. It made me want to retch. When I stuck my hand inside my pocket to feel the smooth edges of my flask, I felt the sharp edges of her letter instead.

My companion feigned ignorance. 'Good stock. I knew her father, a very interesting painter.'

'Yes.' I debated about whether to mention the incident and decided against it, because I did not want to betray Clara, even if she had done so to me, or to embarrass Rembrandt, either. I told myself to quell my rising temper, that he was simply being a father to a lost orphan. Perhaps there was a way to find out for sure? 'She wrote me a letter. I have it here.'

'Aren't you going to open it?'

'I'm afraid of what it might say.'

He put his hands on his hips. 'Don't be a coward. It's probably a confession of her love.'

We stood near a grey, disorderly willow, our feet wading in water. The sun had sunk lower to cast ominous shadows around us, which might either conceal or reveal the truth. Was that a glimmer of intrigue in Rembrandt's eyes? How much did he know? *Light that makes things seen, makes some things invisible.* I yanked the paper from my pocket and removed the seal.

'Should I read it aloud?'

His shoulders perked up. 'Yes!'

I scooted him towards the bridge, nearer the torch light, then unfolded the corners of the letter to encounter Clara's beautiful script and her smell, the sweet vanilla which faintly scented the page.

Taking a deep breath, I began. 'It says, "Dearest Pieter, I do not know what has overcome me, but I cannot bear it any more."'

He piped in. 'Honest at least.'

When I glared at him over the top of the paper, he flashed his palms at me.

'"We've vowed to be honest with one another always . . ."'

'Ha, I told you.' He hopped from foot to foot like a child. Didn't he know how serious this was? My heart was on fire!

'". . . and so here I am, standing before you, with the fear that I am becoming a woman I do not admire or wish to be. Please understand that you have not done anything wrong — if only I could be happy as your wife it would be my greatest wish — but the time for parting has come, lest I slip into a life that does not suit me. Please trust that I have always behaved honourably and with the kindest of intentions towards you. I will grieve for the memories and think of you often with plume in hand. Yours ever, Clara."'

My hands fell to my sides, and the letter dropped into a puddle. I watched the ink bleed and spread in veins across the paper until the water swallowed it entirely. I had expected her to reject me eventually, but never so soon in a letter like this, never today. Why now? The previous weeks had been bliss for us, at least for me.

'What are you going to do?' Rembrandt asked softly.

'Nothing,' I mumbled. 'If that is her wish, I must grant it.'

He grabbed my arm. 'Are you in love with her?'

I nodded, my throat pulsing, my temples beating.

'I'm glad. Love cures you of the spleen and harmonizes the soul. She is a proud lady, but she loves you too. Show courage, Pieter. Bring colour to her pale cheek.'

She loves me? I could hardly believe it, though he seemed sincere. If he had confided in her, perhaps she had confided in him. 'But how?'

'You've never had a woman before?'

I blushed. 'No.'

'Not even a whore?'

I shook my head. 'Well, one, but I was fourteen and she was sixty-four . . .'

He laughed. 'You'll learn how to please them soon enough, by the time you reach my age. Oh, if only I could return to those young girls with what I know now!'

Just an old man being boastful, I thought, my hands fluttering like broken wings against my trousers. 'Mustn't I win her heart first?'

He gestured frantically, as if overcome by some madness, his eyes rolling in their reddened rims. 'Ask her to run away with you. Take her out of this dreadful city! It is my one regret in life, that I didn't travel to Italy when I had the chance. Even if she refuses, go alone. Why not make a poor man proud?'

My neck swallowed my chin as I smiled weakly; it sounded like good advice, but was he reasoning clearly? Was it all part of some sinister scheme? While I was willing to do anything Rembrandt suggested, he was expecting something out of my character. The events of the day had clearly muddled him. Once I made sense of the sparrows swimming round my head, I saw the canal melting into soft shadow and his vague figure walking the gloomy path towards a decrepit house. I dashed after him, then stayed at his heels as we stepped into the cavernous entranceway. Almost a year had passed since I last set foot there, and while I had changed dramatically the room was the same, a strange hollow with the faintest illusory glimmer of an oak press and stool, Spanish leather chairs and paintings on the walls. The house was so still it seemed not a living soul could be found, and a ghastly chill arose from the hallway, carrying the foreboding of my hasty dismissal.

At once, Cornelia rushed out of the shadows — she must have been sitting on that dark chair in the dark corner — threw her arms around her father and buried her face in his chest.

'Don't you worry, Neeltgen,' he said, stroking her long brown hair.

When they finally separated, the girl ogled me with wide, watery eyes that told me she had been crying for hours. Their flickering reminded me of her father though her pupils were steady, and the rest of her belonged to Hendrickje — a slender nose and arched forehead, fair skin set off by heavy brows. Utterly dazed by her beauty, I wanted to console her too, and imagined running my hand over her silky hair.

'This is Pieter Blaeu,' Rembrandt said, turning to me. 'My daughter, Cornelia.'

She frowned at the stranger in her house.

'I'm sorry about your brother,' I said.

She straightened up and held out her hand, but her eyes did not leave my face and seemed to divine everything going on inside me, for instance, the wanton idea that if Clara would not have me perhaps she would. Imagine if I married Rembrandt's daughter! I blushed so furiously that a haze blurred my eyes and my hand closed around hers with force. Her soft and pudgy fingers reminded me that she was not yet a woman though she looked like one. Stabbed with guilt, my lascivious thoughts went no further.

'Did you see him go?' she asked.

Her directness did not ruffle me, but Rembrandt's inspection made me nervous. 'Titus went very peacefully and comfortably. Your father could not have chosen a more perfect place for him, near a clump of trees.'

'I wish I could've been there,' she said dejectedly. 'Why couldn't I, Pa? It's not fair.'

'Tomorrow.'

She blinked furiously. 'Tell me about the funeral. I've been waiting all night.'

'Well—' Rembrandt began.

I interrupted. 'Your father put a feather on his grave, from a Bird of Paradise.'

Cornelia raised a thick brow. 'Really?'

'Yes,' he said, nodding, as if he had long forgotten. 'It came from Pieter's grandfather. He gave it to me years ago.'

'I thought it looked familiar,' I said, my chest expanding. I wondered if he was ever going to tell me that, but it did not matter because everything made sense to me then. If my grandfather had given Rembrandt a valuable part of his collection, they must have been great friends. Kindred spirits, even! At last, the lines of my life seemed to converge into a sensible point.

Rembrandt loosened his cravat and tossed it at the nearest chair. 'Neeltgen, I want to show Pieter my latest painting. Then I'll come upstairs and tell you everything.'

'I'm tired.'

He nudged her playfully, trying to cheer her up. 'But we promised to play a game of cribbage, remember?'

She cracked a slight smile. 'Maybe I'll let you win this time.'

He crinkled his nose at her. 'Just you wait – I'll get you!'

Dissatisfied, she nodded and turned round. 'Goodbye, Pieter.'

As I watched her walking towards the staircase and admired her womanly saunter, my heart felt sorry for her but yearned for Clara, her lean limbs and the way she stepped on her tiptoes to make herself taller. Rembrandt's call to action seemed more pertinent in retrospect, even imperative.

He removed his hat, revealing a web of yellowy-white hair, and held it to his belly as he led me down the hallway towards his workshop. Although a cloud of distress hummed around him, it could not blunt my excitement over seeing his latest painting. When we entered the faintly lit room, I gagged from the strong scent of paint and mildew which seemed to have been trapped there for decades. An oil lamp burnt against the dusty windows and drawn shutters, making this room, too, appear the same with its clutter of objects in those strange and indistinct forms – pots, jars, swords, feathers, shells, arrows. There were greasy rags balled up over every surface and unsized canvases leaning against the walls. A few pieces of shiny armour stood in one corner, which I

417

had not noticed before, and the easel sat in the other, covered by a faded red cloth. As Rembrandt slipped on his rumpled, dirty smock, my eyes were drawn to the worktable, which held a palette caked with crusty paint and a black leather book closed to the world, the very book I had coveted for some time. This was my chance, I thought; what if I picked it up accidentally? Then he noticed me looking, and I knew there was no way I could steal it under his nose.

He picked up the book and slapped it against his palm. 'What would you most like to write, Pieter?'

Was he taunting me? I wondered where this conversation was leading, but thought for a moment and answered truthfully, 'A story about a great man who suffers a lifetime of misfortunes.'

'One of Homer's men, or someone closer to home? Your grandfather, for instance?'

I was ready to test him as he was testing me. 'A magnificent painter even.'

He cackled. 'An artist's life is nothing but vanity, greed and falsehood. Substitutes for living! Such an undertaking would require tremendous judgement and understanding.'

'Which you think I do not have?'

'From time to time even Homer nods.' He smiled, then waved his hand in the air as he continued. 'Let me offer a word of advice. That is, never write about a good man passing from happiness to misery, because it is not inspiring, nor a bad man passing from misery to happiness, because that kind of story is not a tragedy and does not arouse any feeling. You should also avoid writing about an extremely bad man falling from happiness into misery, because the reader will not be moved to either pity or fear. There remains, then, the perfect plot, about a man not pre-eminently virtuous and just, such as Oedipus or Thyestes, who passes from happiness to misfortune, brought upon him not by vice and depravity but by some error of judgement.'

I stood with my mouth agape as he put into words what I had intended to do in writing my story about him, though I had not realized it myself until then, and he knew nothing about it at all. Or did he?

Rembrandt tossed his book on to the table and ambled across the wooden planks to remove the cloth from his easel. 'Stand at a distance. Remember it's not finished.'

I fell silent and gazed intensely from several paces away. The painting showed an old, grey-bearded man with crinkled eyes, shut as if he were blind. He hunched over, a red cloak draped on his shoulders. His arms stretched out to a young man kneeling before him in contrition, his wrinkled hands gently resting on his back as he cradled him to his bosom. The young man was gaunt and thin, obviously weary from a long journey, his dingy brown clothing so tattered it almost crumbled to the floor in threads. One of his slippers had fallen off, exposing the worn blistered sole of his foot. His shorn head rested against the old man's chest, revealing his face in profile.

Though the young man's features were lightly painted, they seemed familiar to me: the slender shape of his face, the tiny ears, the high cheekbones and jutting chin. My heart fluttered, for in every aspect apart from his closed eyes, which hid their colour, I resembled him. In fact, the more I looked the more I became convinced that it was a portrait of me as the Prodigal Son, that Rembrandt was sending me a message in paint. My hands seized the edges of the worktable to steady myself: what was he trying to tell me?

Rembrandt sidled up to me, holding the candle. The orange light struck his drowsy face as he said, 'This my son was dead and is alive again. He was lost and is found.'

Amsterdam, 1668

A Final Bow?

Hallo? hallooo, halloo ... *Is anybody out there?* Out there, out there
... *Someone must hear me. I squint my eyes like a bat. The gallery is full
of shadows. Did my audience abandon me? You who claimed to admire me
so much! Without you, there is no reason to perform. No money, honour
or fame. Unless you are hiding under your seats, waiting to spring out with
applause when my back is turned. Or triumphing secretly while I suffer in
silence. The orchestra has stopped playing, too. Where is my spinet, where
is my lute? Don't snicker. I will not stop after forty-five years ... Encore,
encore!*

The Foliage Is Dropping Fast

*I sit in my worn leather armchair, smoothing my hands over its carved arms.
The rest of the room is almost empty: my ordinary bed with bolsters, the
upright armoir, a side-table next to me, with oil saucer and wick, the hearth
behind. Near the window, I can see everything I want to see and everything
is the same.*

*The foliage is dropping fast from lindens and chestnuts stretching along
the canal bank. Yellow and brown leaves scurry along the cobblestones and*

pile near the bridge. My milkman lumbers down the street, pushing a wooden cart at his belly. With the tinny sound of that rattling metal, I always think he is about to forget us, and pass by. But he never does, labouring up my path. With a swift hand, he ladles out two measures and pours them into jugs that Rebecca holds out for him. Then he carries on. In his wake, a rubbish cart releases its butterflies of food and paper, fluttering in the wind.

Along comes a trio of girls, laughing and teasing one another, tossing their hair. Such odd gestures! If I were younger I might feel the urge to yell out of my window and engage them in a flirtatious exchange. Oh, at sixty-three my spirit is weak. I can't even take pride in the size of my cock! The worst thing is — I am rather content to feel this way. In the blink of an eye, these girls will be married, squeeze out a dozen babies between them, grow old and wrinkled, lose their passion. Some of their children, if not all, will get sick and perish in their very arms. Through my eyes, they are already pale and suffering creatures, plagued by the melancholy memory of things. They will never laugh or shout or tease each other this way again. Life is absurd.

Magdalena's Visit

Trailed by a fat-footed dog, Magdalena walks up the path. The light of the sun plays on her face as she looks about her, pushing the cart which holds my newborn granddaughter, Titia. In my head I bound to the door and take the baby in my arms. She hardly ever comes to visit. My body waits for Rebecca to answer the call, for I hardly have the strength to move around today. There is no desire to clean these blackened hands or even smooth my unruly hair. I haven't changed my clothes in weeks — the crumpled brown breeches, yellowed shirt and woollen coat full of moth holes. The window is shut when it should be open, letting in some fresh air. The smoke of my pipe clogs the sticky room. Through the open doorway, I see my workshop across the hall. A large canvas stands on my easel, practically blank. I wonder if a figure will ever emerge there. What good is genius without energy? I can ruminate here for hours, breathing in the fumes of paint and tobacco. There is no daytime or night-time, only a silence broken by the continuous shuffling of feet. Then I put my ear to my palm and fall asleep. Sliding into that sombre dream, I wish it would last for ever. This is my solitary life, in a maze of mirrors and echoes.

A muffled mewing drifts up the stairway, then the daughter-in-law enters the room, beautiful and plump, with large brown eyes and crimson cheeks. She is in mourning, wearing her black garb. On her hat, the feathers curl backwards like dying birds. The low-cut neck of her lacy chemise shows off her prominent collarbone.

RVR: (*Aside*) I can see why Titus was violently in love with her.

MVL: *Pecks him on the cheek.* I've just fed her, so she might need to burp.

The daughter-in-law hands the grandfather a tiny bundle of white linen, then settles herself in the chair next to him. His hands tremble as he holds the baby on his shoulder to hear a light clucking at his ear, followed by a burp, then another. That familiar sweet scent, unique to a newborn, wafts into his nose.

RVR: Has she finished?

MVL: *Eyes him with unease.* Give her a minute.

The baby babbles in its unintelligible language then burps again very loudly. A moist, oozing sensation spreads through the grandfather's shirt. He lifts the baby up in the air, her feet dangling, as vomit drips over his shoulder.

MVL: *Frowns.* Oh, she's spit up.

RVR: I can see that.

The baby's eyes crinkle up and she begins to cry, her face as red as a crab.

MVL: Do you want me to take her?

RVR: I've had five children of my own, you know. (*Aside*) Look at the tears dropping from Titia's tiny eyes. How can such a little thing make so much noise? She sounds like an unhappy kitten. *Shhhh.* I hold my face close and tell her she's beautiful, but she continues bleating. I try my old technique, which always worked for Titus. I make faces for her, smiling, frowning, wagging my brows. When I dilate my nostrils then wriggle my ears, she begins to quiet down. I take off my beret to cover my face then peek out with one eye, slowly. Her hand clasps my finger like a delightful torture, a hope. Finally, her tears stop, and her glistening brown eyes examine me, a near-stranger. *It's all over.* Her mouth stretches into something like a smile. Is she smiling at me? When she drools, her lips pucker just like Titus's. The spitting image of her father! When she closes her eyes, little veins dance on her eyelids. Oh, my dear Saskia. If only she could be here to see our granddaughter . . . (*To MVL*) She's looking more like Titus.

MVL: *Fiddles with her sleeves, watching him.* Yes, but she resembles my side of the family too.

RVR: (*Aside*) That might be true, but she seems to be avoiding something. Perhaps that is why she does not visit me often, because I remind her of her dead husband. There is something else: when she looks at me, I get an odd feeling that she is seeing me through my son's eyes.

MVL: Sir, I don't mean to be disrespectful, but you smell to high heaven and you look unwell. I hope you've been looking after yourself.

RVR: Of course, and Neeltgen is good to me. *His dirty fingers play with Titia's toes.*

MVL: Sir, I want to come to an understanding with you. Please, I need the money for Titia and for the funeral.

RVR: (*Aside*) She calls me Sir instead of Pa! I suspected there was an alternative reason for her visit. She wants her half of Titus's money from Saskia. If it were possible I would give it to her, but there is so little left, and I have my Cornelia to think about. (*To MVL*) I understand your situation, but please try to understand mine. Neeltgen will need a dowry.

MVL: I've waited for months. Look at your granddaughter . . .

The grandfather removes the baby's bonnet and smoothes his palm over her head, as if she could overhear.

MVL: How much money is there?

RVR: Hardly any. (*Aside*) Why do we have to talk about this now? My head is spinning like a crazed top.

MVL: Are you dipping into Titia's share to keep the house?

RVR: What a ridiculous accusation!

MVL: Your son had every right to that money, and now you want to withhold the rest from his daughter? It's inconceivable.

RVR: Titus legally signed it over to me, that's what he chose to do. I never said that I wouldn't give Titia her fair share. (*Aside*) All this unhappiness is making me ill.

MVL: *Sighing.* Titus was too young. Even when he got older, he could never understand . . .

RVR: (*Aside*) What is going on? The room is swimming with confused reflections. I shake my head, and the furniture takes flight. My eyes focus on the table, but it is not there — at least, it has no depth. Light plays on the surface — it seems transparent, almost like a lake. The candle flickers in broad sweeps. Only a glimmer of shapes all around me. The curtains are a falling haze, a suggestion of green, and outside the window, the houses and rooftops hover in mid-air. The few meagre trees resemble trees but they are not trees: they have no substance or life. Brown spots float before me instead of passing clouds, instead of seagulls swooping over the canal. The sun is in fragments, surrounded by a filmy halo. Below me, even Titia's face is veiled. Her eyes like two milky moons! Magdalena's features are undefined, abuzz in the air. Could this really be happening? Something has poisoned me. What did I eat this morning? Oh, my blasted, diseased eyes!

MVL: Sir, did you hear what I said?

RVR: Magdalena, take the baby.

MVL: What?

RVR: *Raising his voice.* I said, take the baby!

The daughter-in-law jumps in front of the grandfather and pulls the baby from his arms. He rises from his chair and takes a few steps towards the door.

RVR: (*Aside*) I have to get to my workshop. Look at one of my paintings. Then I will know . . .

MVL: *Behind his back.* What's happened? Are you ill?

RVR: You should go. (*Aside*) I move across the hallway one step at a time. Where the hell is the door? My toe catches the edge of a board and pulls off my slipper. I must look like poor old Tobit! My hands are outstretched, guiding me as if through a fog. Thank the Lord they know the way.

A Creeping Infection

When I reach the door of my workshop and look in, everything is blurry. I recognize that pungent smell — and the atmosphere is familiar, but the room resembles a skewed box, all its walls misaligned. Which way is right and which is left? Trying to skirt round the furniture, I stumble against my easel. It floods the room with a sinister creaking. My leg buckles under me. Grabbing the table, I send a jar flying — it hits the floor with a crash. Not important; I'll leave it for later. I fumble round for a canvas in the corner and grab the edges with both hands. As I heave it over the table, my brushes and trinkets crash to the floor. I stand in front of the painting and look at it squarely: my Lucretia. At least, it seems like my Lucretia . . .

While I know there is only one figure, I cannot make her out. I see her white shift like a veil, but where is the dagger she has plunged into her heart? What was once a crimson lake of blood is only a blur, restless and crude. I tell myself that the red patch is red only in relation to the shadow lying across it. Focus on the play of light there! But the colour runs away in a pale pink stream, losing its saturation. What is happening to my painting?

Half-closing my eyes, I try to find the vermilion and gold in her gown, but there are no variations, no intermediate shades. I know they are there! What about the light ochre in her face and throat? The terre verte in her hands, one clutching the knife, the other raised to open the curtains of her bed? No matter how hard I try, rubbing my lids then squinting or opening wide and staring, I cannot conjure up my colours. There is only her brown hair and beaded hat hovering in the distance. A hat with no head. Then I am left with a single teardrop, a pearl, dangling from her earlobe. All I see is a cloudy, macabre shade, not like any I have witnessed before. How could this be? The disease has spread like a pool of turpentine, erasing the rest of the picture. My canvas is blank!

Reality hits me: I am going blind. I must be! This is what I have most feared for my entire life . . . my father's weakness, his eyes of death. Oh, my poor father! Perhaps the fear has brought me here, or Fortuna, who allures me with false good fortunes, smiles upon me then turns away. I am overcome with nausea and drowsiness. My teeth chatter. Sleep, that's all I want to do. Sleep.

I walk my hands along the walls, skirting toward the parlour. When I reach the door, the opening jumps from place to place. Trying to slip through, I bang against the frame. My head throbs and drums. Where was I going? Oh yes, back to my chair. Magdalena looms in front of me, a smudgy outline enveloped in ghost rings. I hold up my palms, blinded by the brightness of her form. Falling to my knees, I sink into obscurity, an abyss of darkness.

INTERLUDE

Clip-clop, clip-clop.

Sir, can you hear me?

A rustle of fabrics, clipped breathing.

The scent of breast milk.

Rebecca, come quickly!

A firm hand pressing my arm.

Here, let me help you into your chair.

Heavy footfalls on the stairs.

A gasp then a high voice, Gracious me!

Beef brisket? Stewed pork?

A baby's cry fills the room, an echo.

Shhh, hush now. Look! Grandpa's just playing.

Master! Are you ill?

Pat, pat, pat. A gurgle.

No, I'm blind.

That cracked jar: linseed oil.

Are you certain? Master, look about you. Who goes there, ha?

Muffled squealing in the walls, the cry of roaches.

I hold my eyes tight.

Rub on the egg yolks. Then fetch the doctor.

Clip-clop, clip-clop.

Is someone speaking?
The odour of raw eggs.
Warm sap on my eyes and temples, trickling down my cheeks.
Listen to the rain.

Nothing but a Mist

The doctor enters the parlour and extracts his shiny utensils from a leather satchel. He yanks open the blind man's eyes with two fingers and shines a light in them.

RVR: *Struggling from his grasp.* Don't touch me! Get away from me, you old goat!

As the blind man grunts and groans, the maidservant and the doctor hold him down and tie his arms to the chair with leather straps.

THE DOCTOR: *Tugs at his lids, prods his pupils.* What do you see now?

RVR: *Shouts.* Nothing but a mist!

THE DOCTOR: *Holds up card after card of pictures — mostly red and green circles.* Look closely.

RVR: There's nothing. Didn't you hear me?

THE DOCTOR: Very mysterious, indeed.

The doctor unbuckles the straps round the patient's forearms.

RVR: Thank heavens!

THE DOCTOR: *Pinches on his fine spectacles.* There is no explanation for your blindness, Master van Rijn. Your eyes seem perfectly normal, despite a slight deficiency in the left one. But you already knew that, didn't you? I can only suppose you must resign yourself to being blind for the rest of your days.

The doctor bends down and scoops up his leather bag.

RVR: *Grabbing handfuls of air.* Is that all? No, please, wait! (*Aside*) I hear the fabric of his trousers crackling, leather brushing against wool. How can he leave me here?

The maidservant and the doctor shuffle down the stairs, their mules scraping against the grainy floor.

The Old Blind Man Wasting Like a Candle

For the next few hours, I stumble round my house, colliding with objects. I scoot up and down the stairs, my hands caressing the walls to feel their bumpy texture, or lean out of the window to catch any passing sounds: the cackle of an old whore, the chickens in the coop, the flies buzzing on the canal. How I long to see my old territory! I blink. Never again. All I see is the windmill perched on the riverbank and a desolate plain in the distance. Where am I? Let me listen. I can hear the steps of those heading home, their exhalations after work. The sound of a flute calls up the bluish-green colour of the sky. When the evening wind rustles delicate leaves, I see the waning light in trees and bushes. By the rattle of a carriage and the rhythm of horses' hooves, my eyes sense the unevenness of the cobbles. I coast among the people coasting by. They carry on with their lives, no questions asked.

I try to convince Rebecca to let me cook or at least chop the vegetables — to feel the cold colours under my fingers — but she refuses. What if I cut myself? I should stay in bed, where it is safer. She is probably right, considering that I was old and clumsy even when I could see. Yet I refuse to become my father! In the process of going blind, he abandoned his habits and made himself into an invalid. I never understood how he could resort to such immobility, such nothingness from the very start. He did not try to see, even in his mind's eye. He left the world too soon. From early on I vowed that, if ever I were blind, I would not change my life or my conduct in it. Now, here I am.

When Cornelia returns from school, she does not come to me immediately. She whispers downstairs with Rebecca for what seems like hours. Oh, even time is blurry! Afterwards, my daughter rushes into the room and finds her invalid father, cane in hand, walking wall-to-wall across the shabby floorboards. I am thinking of Descartes. What did he say? The hand is affected by probing with a stick just as the eye is affected by light carried in the air. I must resemble a blind beggar, shattered and grey-headed, irritable and mistrustful.

My daughter stands before me, her liquorice breath on my face. It does not feel like indifference or scorn. Is she scared? As her nose hovers before my nose, her voice is extremely solemn, telling me not to worry. She vows to stay by my side and be my eyes. She wipes my rheumy eyes with her handkerchief. I stutter like someone unfamiliar with speech, telling her about my day — Magdalena's visit, Titia's sweet face and how I lost my sight. Then, devout like her mother, she holds my hand and recites her prayers aloud. I wish I could see her face, the soft down on her cheek. I have no desire to eat, but she feeds me a plate of beetroot and sprats with horseradish.

With this, I renounce myself once and for all. No one has spoon-fed me since I was a boy in the arms of my mother. I am in the arms of my daughter, wasting like a candle, the better part of which has already gone. Like Job, my soul is weary of my life.

Deception and Defeat

Pliny tells the story of two rivalling Greek painters, Zeuxis and Parrhasius, who participated in a competition. Zeuxis was bound to win after he made a painting of grapes so lifelike that the birds flew up to peck at them. Then Parrhasius produced such a realistic picture of a curtain that Zeuxis requested the curtain be drawn so he could see the painting displayed. When Zeuxis realized his mistake, he yielded the prize to his rival for a greater achievement. Whereas he himself had deceived the birds, Parrhasius had deceived him, an artist. Perhaps it is time I admit my defeat.

The Company of Captain Frans Banning Cocq

Cornelia and I scud through the rain arm-in-arm. The edges of my grubby smock flap in the wind, sending up an odour of rancid paint and sour milk. I am taking her to see my most accomplished work in the Kloveniersdoelen, but she is escorting me because, after two days, I am still blind. This is the irony of my old age. It does not matter, for I can see everything in my mind's eye. The back of the ramparts of the militia, with its U-shaped medieval tower, rises into the clouds. The old, crumbling fortification is known as Zwijg-Utrecht – 'Be Silent, Utrecht' – and surrounded by water. The two of us head for the front of the building, set back from the road behind an iron gate — rusty now, I imagine.

Father and daughter pass a hurdy-gurdy player pumping out a few pitiful notes, trying to make his day's earnings despite the poor weather.

RVR: Saskia and I used to live here, two doors down the Doelenstraat. Did you know Rubens's garden backed on to the yard of the Antwerp militia guild? (*Aside*) Perhaps she doesn't find me interesting, a fifteen-year-old girl with no end of admirers. After all, there are almost fifty years between us. I must seem ancient to her, a shoddy antique. Not only am I blind, my two legs can hardly hold me.

Father and daughter cross the bridge over the choppy river, then scoot across the white stones near the entranceway. When they pass under the massive archway decorated with fancy plaques, and into the gloomy courtyard, the father stops in his tracks, letting the rain trickle down his face.

RVR: *Shouting and blinking through the rain.* Do you see what I see, Neeltgen? This was the setting for my painting. There — right there (*he points*), my venerable party forged ahead on its watch. Imagine them emerging from the dark underpass into the blinding sunlight! You'll recognize all this when you look for yourself. (*Aside*) Her father is a bore, always talking about his work. Sometimes I forget that she is not Titus, not my son, and ramble on for hours. At least she has been learning more about art. That is why I am anxious for her to see my picture, an emblem of my glory days. There are bound to be disappointments, but I want her to know that I was once an important man in the city, not the insignificant fool she has always known.

The guard, wearing a shining waistcoat of blue and gold, waves to them: the public is most welcome. As the daughter assists her father up the grand staircase, each step makes his knees buckle. They enter the handsome classical addition of the original fortification, which holds one of the most spacious interiors in the city. The palatial room is sixty feet long with high ceilings and chandeliers. The six tall windows, separated by pilasters, overlook the boggy Amstel. A shiny walnut table with matching chairs stretches down the middle.

RVR: What do you think, Neeltgen? Isn't it beautiful? Until the new Town Hall was built, this was the most elaborate chamber in the city, used by the kloveniers for feasts.

CVR: It is impressive, Pa. Oh, I wish you could see it!

RVR: No need to worry, my memory is perfect. Take me to the first wall, just there. We'll save my painting for last.

The father clings to his daughter as she leads the way to the short wall. Together they gaze up at a painting of four regents by Govert Flinck.

RVR: Flinck was once my assistant. He took over in Van Uylenburgh's workshop after I left. This was his first group portrait and, as you can see, he used to copy my style. He should have stuck with it, in my opinion. This was his best work yet.

CVR: You speak about him as if he's dead.

RVR: Well, he is. Eight or nine years ago. He had just secured a contract to decorate the Town Hall when he dropped down suddenly . . .

CVR: That's sad.

RVR: Yes, I suppose it is. (*Aside*) I feel no sadness for Flinck, just a competitor I would rather forget.

The daughter guides her father towards Joachim von Sandrart's two compact pictures of the companies of Bicker and Bas, hanging on either side of the fireplace. For a moment, she rests her head on his shoulder.

RVR: (*Aside*) Those small gestures always make me feel another day is worth living. (*To CVR*) A German, Rubens's travelling companion, but you'd never know it, would you? Where is the unity between these figures? Where is the reality? He tried to combine a horizontal setting with the effect of depth by placing symmetrical groups at various distances, but the picture fails by its stiffness. The subjects are standing in front of a classical palace, no less.

CVR: I don't like it either. Why would a table with a bust be out in the street?

RVR: *Mutters.* Good girl.

The daughter leads him to Bartholomeus van der Helst's painting, fitted into a narrow area above the fireplace on the entry wall. Painted in a slickly brilliant manner, it shows an elongated line of military figures accompanied by a big, hairy dog lying down.

RVR: This should be Van der Helst's piece. He did well with this cramped space, don't you agree? Tell me what you see.

CVR: I like the dog. He's very shaggy. The colours aren't poor either, nice and bright.

RVR: But the style is rigid and improbable. (*Aside*) I'd better not correct her about the colours; we are just warming up. Besides, she is barely a woman. I will ease her in slowly.

The pair approach the long wall facing the second-storey windows, the prime position in the room because of the sufficiency of light. There are three paintings on this side, the first of which is nearest the door: Jacob Backer's Company of Cornelis de Graeff. While the two others follow the conventional practice of lining up the figures on a horizon, Backer's figures are arranged in a semicircle, below and on a staircase.

RVR: Are we at Jacob Backer's painting?

CVR: Yes, Pa, I believe so.

RVR: For years, he did so many portraits of regents of old-age homes and orphanages that he just wasn't capable of such a high-calibre commission. The result is not very satisfactory, even with the velvety lustre of the colouring. Am I correct?

CVR: I don't know. The men seem more natural in this one, lazing around on the stairs, talking with one another or looking up at the sky.

RVR: Yes, but they're still posing, aren't they? *Pause.* Let's move on. My skin is starting to itch.

The daughter walks her father towards the second painting in this section by Nicolaes Eliasz Pickenoy.

RVR: Pickenoy used to live nearby, when your mother and I were on the Breestraat. Fancies himself as a portrait painter. What a lush! He even tried to outbid me at auctions. *With his elbow, he pokes her in the ribs.* Neeltgen, these group portraits are all static. I haven't seen them in years, but I still think of them as packs of playing cards. Do you see how the subjects are standing, kneeling or sitting in orderly rows? The artists probably asked one member to come to the workshop each day then, in the end, joined them together in a rigid way. The light, shadow and perspective should be harmonious. The scene is flat and doesn't seem real at all. Do you understand?

CVR: *Giggles.* I suppose . . .

RVR: This is important! Think hard! (*Aside*) Isn't she listening? It makes me so angry! I want her to learn.

Father and daughter step up to the final picture in the room. There, on the left, is an enormous painting — three strips of cloth totalling about 12 feet in height, fifteen feet in width — which seems to advance across the room and through the windows.

RVR: *Speaks into her ear.* Now look at mine. Notice the forward action of the company? The figures march out as a single body with energy and order. Everything is in constant motion, as if taking place in real time. This is great drama!

CVR: *Gasps.* You're right!

RVR: Tell me what you see.

CVR: Well, I see the bridge we only just crossed, over the canal in front. A powder monkey runs along the railing on the left, and the edges of the flagstones lead to the centre of the arched doorway.

The company comes out from a shadowy place, sixteen in all, but the light shines on two figures . . .

RVR: *Interrupting.* Captain Banning Cocq and Lieutenant Ruytenburgh. Go on . . .

CVR: *Excitedly.* The captain wears a black costume with a large lacy ruff and fiery red sash. He is a dark figure, and doesn't seem to pause for anyone. Yes, he's the centre of attention, and he has a bright white cuff which surrounds his outstretched hand . . . Let's see . . . his hand puts a shadow on his lieutenant as he moves in front of him. But the other man is dazzling, too. I love his costume! A coat in canary-yellow hide, with fancy bows and striped sleeves . . .

RVR: Not to mention his cavalier boots and plumed hat. The tassel on his partisan is blue and gold, the colours of the kloveniers and the war council. He's announcing his station and fortune, you see? (*Aside*) Did I really paint this astonishing piece?

CVR: But what does it say on his collar? G-i-j-s-b . . .

RVR: Short for Gijsbreght. The arquebusiers are descendants of the famous Gijsbreght van Aemstel. The two sergeants at the extreme right and left are Rombout Kemp and Reijnier Engelen. They were very important men in the cloth business, and each of them paid to be in my picture. Kemp is on the right with the silver helmet and red collar. He was deacon of the Calvinist Church and governor of the poorhouse. Engelen is seated on the parapet, wearing my antique golden helmet – oh, I miss that helmet! – and holding a halberd. I remember something shady in his past. Then there's Ensign Jan Claesz. Vischer, the one in the centre with the moustache, wearing the silvery-green costume, waving the flag.

CVR: He's very handsome, and he seems brave.

RVR: Yes, but it's most unfortunate. He died from the plague eight years after I finished this, before marrying or fighting in combat.

CVR: He did? I like how the light hits his face and costume, how he is looking away as if thinking about something else.

RVR: Well, he loved paintings and music, so perhaps he is imagining a wonderful landscape in his head or hearing a symphony . . .

CVR: Was he that tall or is he standing on something?

RVR: Ha, wouldn't you like to know! Sometimes I partially conceal something, in this case his lower body, to arrest the eye's attention. See the drummer peeking out from the right? You might guess that he's a member of the company, but that's Jacob Jorisz, a musician who often beat his drum for the marches. All but his face and hands are hidden. It makes you want to follow him off the picture, doesn't it?

CVR: *Takes a few steps forward to peer closer.* Maybe, but he's old and ugly. The ensign's more for me. I like the little girl in yellow the best. Who is she? Why is she carrying a chicken?

RVR: Oh, she's not really part of the company, just a daughter of one of the arquebusiers. The chicken that hangs from her girdle is holding on by its claws – the emblem of the kloveniers. There's even another girl behind her, harder to make out . . . See the man in front of her, with oak leaves on his helmet? That's a motif of the guild.

CVR: You never forget anything, Pa.

RVR: Every tiny thing must be in harmony, even if no one else notices. Why, I even lined up the picture as a St Andrew's cross. Three black crosses on a red field form the arms of Amsterdam, and that same cross appears in the pattern of spikes on the right and on Ruytenburgh's lapel.

CVR: But how did you do it? I mean, how'd you actually make it? Because the men look like they're walking right off the canvas and the captain's hand seems to come right out at me!

RVR: If you look closely, you'll find that I worked from the back forwards. See the way the paint overlaps in the front sections? When I painted the girl in yellow, I had to work around Banning Cocq's glove, the leg of the marksman in the purple trousers, and the butt of the musket of the red schutter.

CVR: Oh, yes.

RVR: Evenness makes objects appear distant, so I painted the foreground in a rough manner. The light bounces off the bumps of the paint surface to reach your eye. The heavy brushwork on Ruytenburgh and Banning Cocq leads to a gradual smoothing of the paint towards the background. Every inch counts! With some elements in focus and others blurry, there is an illusion of space. The highest-lit areas are the most important, Neeltgen. Notice how the painting sparkles? (*Aside*) My head is reeling: perhaps I rambled on too long. I want to kiss her dimpled cheek and thank her for being so devoted to me, in spite of my ignorance and insanity.

CVR: Wait a moment. Is that you, the nose, hat and eye looking over the ensign's shoulder?

RVR: Perhaps.

CVR: *Laughs*. How amusing! I've discovered something else, too.

RVR: What?

CVR: The schutter in red velvet? His pose is wrong. The way his left hand holds the butt of the musket, no trained musketeer would do it that way.

RVR: I don't believe it! How do you know?

CVR: I learnt it in school.

RVR: Really?

CVR: It's true, Pa.

RVR: I know that, but I copied the pose from another shooting portrait by Jan Tengnagel. Well-cooked pickings make a good stew! He must have made the mistake. Oh, it does not matter in the end. Isn't it wonderful how I built up his shoulder with that shiny glaze of red lake? That was my master stroke! I meant to flatter my patrons and sweep them off their feet, and I succeeded, Neeltgen. Even if my picture wasn't what they imagined when they saw it, they were so dazzled they believed it was their original desire.

CVR: No, it doesn't really matter. No one else would notice you got it wrong. But I thought that Grandpa was in the civic guard, surely you must have seen him hold his musket . . .

A Radiant Light

My workshop has never felt so still and dead. Three days of immobility! For hours I've been sitting here, fingering my brushes — coarse hog hairs and soft badger bristles. Suddenly, my lids are flooded with a radiant light. What could this be? Madness! When I open my eyes, my pupils sting but the glare remains. My lids feel heavy, crusted over. A nebulous cloud floats overhead. Then it disappears like a vapour. Every object around me slowly penetrates my vision. Black and white, with no definition. They swirl in the air, all jumbled together. What a strange sensation! Is this real or a hallucination? Slowly the other colours begin to act on me, one after the other — red, green, blue, yellow — in no determinate form. All shades and tones follow suit. Circles and lines buzz in the air, confused. I try to join up the pieces, reversing and forwarding them until they are recognizable to my eyes. I run my gaze around outlines and try to take hold of the figures before me. These things are definitely there — yes, I can feel their shape — but I cannot wholly perceive them. I blink again and rub my eyes. What is it that I see precisely, if anything?

When I open my window to the outside, green and gold flutter in the grass and flowers across the canal. White clouds stretch out like cats. Spiky chestnuts dangle from the ochre trees. A peasant girl carries a basket of vegetables in gorgeous yellow and red heaps. The wind sweeps a mulberry along the ground, a crimson red. I laugh to myself until my cheeks hurt. Is it possible? How does one find the words? The truth is, I can see more clearly than ever before!

The blinding cannot be undone, Athena said to the mother of Teiresias. But I have proven her wrong. The Lord has opened my eyes to revelation just like the faithful apostle. He must have forgiven me. There is no other reason for this coincidence. Paul was blinded for three days, too, after breathing out threatenings against the disciples of the Lord. As he approached Damascus, there suddenly shone round about him a light from heaven. Falling to the earth, he heard a voice saying, 'Saul, Saul, why persecutest thou me?' Saul rose from the ground, but when he opened his eyes he could not see. Three days later, a disciple named Ananias ministered to him, and he regained his sight. Saul was baptized in Damascus by Ananias and became Paul, a great defender of the new faith.

Now that I can see again, I must live in devotion to God and show my appreciation for his forgiving love. Never shall I take my sight for granted. 'Strip off the old and put on the new.' With this reformed pair of eyes, a familiar energy surges through my blood. I cannot wait to take up my palette and brush. I will paint again!

Simeon and the Christ Child

There was a righteous man in Jerusalem named Simeon, who, in old age, was awaiting Israel's consolation. The Holy Spirit divinely revealed to him that he would not meet death before he had seen Christ. Under the power of the Spirit, he came into the temple. As Joseph and Mary brought the young Jesus inside, Simeon received the child into his arms and said, 'Now,

Sovereign Lord, you are letting your slave go free in peace because my eyes have seen your means of saving, that you have made ready in the sight of all the peoples, a light for removing the veil from the nations and a glory for Israel.' Joseph and Mary wondered at the things spoken. Yet Simeon blessed them and said to Mary, 'Look! This one is laid for the falling and the rising of many in Israel and for a sign to be talked against — yes, a long sword will be run through the soul of you, yourself — in order that the reasonings of many hearts may be uncovered.'

Simeon with the Christ child is a subject from my early etchings, but the story is different after losing my sight. In my head, Simeon is no longer my father but me. In my latest painting, Simeon's eyes are almost entirely closed, shrunken in their cavities. Their slits are dark strokes of umber. His face glimmers around his cloudy beard like falling snow. Behind him, the face of Mary is alight, and the rest of her sinks into shadow. The two seemed joined, shoulder to shoulder. The old man cradles the baby as if to draw strength from her. The child looks up at him — his arms are warm — with pudgy cheeks and puckered lips. My very own Titia as the Christ child! Simeon's oversized hands stretch out in prayer. His eyes may be concealed from the world, but inside, they are aglow with spiritual truth.

Fragments of Clara

7.

three cakes flipping in a flat-bottomed pan
and the woman —
hair long-turned white
fans her fire to keep it ablaze

a lad fishes for his coins
a baby whines
two others in horseplay
under this flapping tent
hungry

17.

Dark streaks of sunlight
a charging cloud
three sturdy elms

and a clear patch of sky
the fishermen cast their lines
oblivious to the lovers
playing in the growth
as the storm recedes
beyond the dyke
towards the sea

20.

    Eve hoards the apple
    Adam wants the apple
    The elephant wants the apple

23.

    axe and cambrel
    the tools of his trade
    a butcher binds the sow
    plump for the kill

    his son cradles the bladder
    and pokes it with a straw
    with tiny breaths, up and up
            (this little life, up and up)
    over his shoulder

                            he grins

28.

    as winter draws near
    this man has forgotten
    her face —
                        infinitely dark or absent of dark
    the country girl on a stroll in June
                        (daisies in her hair)
    the young wife on a *danse macabre*
                        (with hourglass and scythe)
    honoured bridegroom,
    do you love her still?

447

32.

a little boy you seem to me
fair-haired and clumsy
when your eyes look through me
like grass under snow
      the fire under my skin

        angry
        golden
              I bite my barking tongue

Amsterdam, 1669

The Laughing Philosopher

Ha, ha, ha, ha, ha ... *Hear me laughing in the face of human folly. Watch me spit my joy at the watchers and their calumny. This is me as Democritus!*

Amongst his people, he was called 'The Maker'. He could predict the future. Others called him 'Wisdom'. There was no subject on which he couldn't notably contribute ...

1 *To live badly is not to live badly but to spend a long time dying.*
2 *People are fools who hate life yet wish to live through fear of death. Men who shun death pursue it.*
3 *One must not respect the opinion of other men more than one's own, which must stand as the law of one's soul.*
4 *You should consider the lives of those in distress, reflecting on their intense sufferings, in order that your own possession and condition may seem great and enviable.*

In order to master his intellect, Democritus blinded himself with burning glass. He lived well past a hundred years, but spent the end of his life in caverns and sepulchres. Those same vile caves in which I now dwell.

I Pass Entirely into My Canvas, Calmly

The lustre of my mirror is dimming. I am waiting for God, who is everywhere. In the pale sphere, a man appears instead. I see him from the waist up, his right shoulder pressed to the glass. A face takes form, a final face. It is me in truth.

My skin is dreadfully pale, pitted and thick. A creature could walk round in its grooves. The dim lights bring out my two black orbs in a steady gaze. When I blink, the curled lashes scratch my pupils. The whites of my eyes are yellow, their corners watery. The frowning flaps on my lids speak of many sorrows. Above them, my brows are sparse, straining to meet. One displaced wrinkle trails across my left cheek, forming a saccule. Wet scribbles and scratches plague my jowls. A badly trimmed, grey moustache tickles my nose, swollen and shiny with open pores. The veins break across it like a cracked eggshell, making me smirk. My lips purse together and form deep dimples.

This gown, pulled over my big belly, is a muddy brown with hook-and-eye fastenings down the front. My bare neck peeks above its fur collar. A rusty cap rests on my head, over my unruly hair, snowy about the temples. A white band crosses my high forehead. My hands are clasped together, pleading, 'Do not throw me away in the time of old age; just when my power is failing, do not leave me.' At sixty-three, all my desires and vanities have gone away. The world stands behind me. Silence rushes into my ears like water breaking against the riverbank. I pass entirely into my canvas, calmly.

A Guardian Angel

The maidservant brings in a plate of pickled cod. It smells disgusting, but she forces me to eat it. She wipes my face with a cold towel, dipping it into her bowl, wringing it out and pressing it against my hot skin. She drops a tincture on my tongue, a special remedy from my apothecary Francen. It keeps the ghosts away and calms my fever, she says. Ah, that feels better. After a time I can see her more clearly. It is not Rebecca, after all, but the sweet angel who watches over me now and again. My little guardian nymph. Her hair is the most lustrous strawberry colour! I reach out and stroke it. She plants a little kiss on my forehead and tells me she loves me. What else do you need? Are you comfortable? Would you like to sit up? No, I'll stay here, I say, my eyes peeking from the blanket. The pillow swallows my head and sends up a puff of goose feathers. She totters off, two hands round my chamber pot, brimming with vomit, piss and phlegm. I watch her rear wriggle out of the room. On her way to the canal, I know she will not spill a drop.

I Never Painted Tulips

The dim lamp gleams, and a motionless spot of light reflects in the distance near the door. When it opens, a tall man who resembles the Prodigal Son walks into the room. He approaches the bed and towers over the old painter lying in bed.

RVR: (*Aside*) I wonder who wants to see me in this pathetic state. A debt collector, perhaps. An old mistress from my days in the brothel? Someone else to haunt me from the dead? Oh, I do not recognize him. He walks limberly on his long legs. Is it Titus?

PB: *A vague smile.* Master, can you see me?

RVR: It's six o'clock, boy, I am hardly awake. But I recognize the voice. Pieter Blaeu?

PB: Yes, that's me. Only, it's afternoon!

RVR: What are you doing here? I thought you'd gone abroad. (*Aside*) He has a lot of nerve, bursting in here and invading my privacy. If I could stand up, I would boot him out the door!

PB: *Perches on the edge of the bed.* I wanted to hear your story first.

RVR: What story?

PB: *Speaks softly in his ear.* About Elsje Christiaens.

RVR: *Groans feebly.* Have you no manners? Can't you see I'm within a few hours of giving my enemies the slip for ever?

PB: *Eyes dart over his face.* You don't look bad. Why do you think you are . . .?

RVR: Look again. A regurgitated ostrich would be more appealing. My sorrow has destroyed my face!

PB: Don't be ridiculous! There is still time! The play has yet to end.

RVR: Leave me be. What makes you think I'm unfinished, eh? (*Aside*) The fetid air clogs my nose. My tongue scratches against the roof of my mouth. I need to spit.

PB: Someone like you can't pass quietly. You need a perfect ending, a dramatic exit.

RVR: *Raises a weak brow.* For once, my boy, you are quite right. (*Aside*) I suppose I have nothing to lose. An old story might distract me from my misery. If only I could remember. (*To PB*) I will tell you the story on one condition.

PB: As you wish.

RVR: That you don't get too close, and watch out for that dog. He bites.

PB: *Glances about him but sees nothing.* What's his name?

RVR: Crab. He's the sourest-natured dog that lives.

PB: Don't worry. I've brought sausages.

After rising from the bed, the Prodigal Son takes the wing chair from the corner and pulls it to the bedside. Sitting down, he gazes at the old painter's limp hand on the blanket.

RVR: *Raises his head and lowers it again.* (*Aside*) The bedsprings creak like splintering wood. The fresh, green scent of timber. The salty sea air. My eyes look fixedly at the ceiling as time rolls back. My memory rushes me towards a spring day. If this is a dream, let me sleep!

PB: I'm waiting, Master.

RVR: Shhh, can't you hear the lapping water, the plashing oars? My boat creaking? I am rowing through the motionless air. Grey clouds pile up on the horizon, near the windmills. Dark waters, thick clouds, and nothing but the heavy sky . . . *Speaks in a faraway whisper, in a delirium.* It is early morning when I reach Volewijk. I step from the boat and walk up the steep bank into the potter's field. Not a soul is there apart from me. The moving shadows remind me of ghosts. The headland grasses sway in the breeze, and seagulls swoop overhead. Look at them, cloud-bound! I see, in the distance, two corpses hanging on the gallows, two men dangling on posts above a large stone gibbet that resembles a monument to a warrior. Or a great king! One has an impaled body and an iron spade next to him, the other is a murderer broken on the wheel, a pistol nailed above his head. To my right, more posts like decrepit trees melting in a mist. They seem empty, but on drawing closer, I catch sight of a young girl trussed up on the far side. Her hatchet dangles in front of her, upside down. She has been dead for several hours, and is already beginning to rot away.

PB: And then?

RVR: I am taking out my sketchbook. I draw her looking very serene, as if asleep. A rope runs under her armpits, so her body slumps with dead weight, and her arms droop from their sockets. Her lifeless hands dangle from the tattered sleeves of her grey coat. Her feet stick out from her red skirt, which trembles like a leaf in the wind. And her head is strangely awry. There are contusions on her neck. She has been strangled! But I can see her face, the wet hair over her high forehead, those youthful cheeks devoid of colour, her lopsided lips stretched tautly back.

PB: *With a gasp.* Do you know her?

RVR: She seems familiar, yes, and a distinct moan escapes her lips.

Soft as it is, I know she is trying to tell me something. When I stand on tiptoe and strain my ears, I hear a definite sound, and the word she says is 'Escape'.

PB: Escape?

A sputtering in the old painter's throat interrupts him. The sweats come out on his forehead. Waving his hand helplessly, he falls into a terrible fit of coughing that lasts for several minutes. While he hacks into his palm, the Prodigal Son offers him a handkerchief. Coughing some more, the old painter spits up blood. His chest winces in pain as he scrutinizes the discharge.

RVR: *Curls the silk into his hand.* Ah, here my candle dies. Only darkness and rottenness.

PB: I will light it again. Stay a little while longer!

The young man reaches out and touches the painter's hand.

RVR: You are impetuous.

The Prodigal Son scowls and retracts his hand.

RVR: *Cranes his head to see his companion.* (*Aside*) That face of his I remember well. The handsome brow, the pointed features and plump lips. At first glance, he seems just another mawkish youth, thin as a stick, cowardly in his skin. Yet look at the way he leans with devotion over his lap, thrusting out his honourable chin, the eyes aglow with dreams and desire. What a whimsical fellow, and what a mind! This is admiration I see . . . and here I am, just an old man, conquered and wasted. How kind of him to ignore my fits of flatulence. That awful stench! How he yearns to please me, to expel my demons, at least for the moment. What can I give him in exchange for his zeal?

Sensing the old painter's discomfort, the Prodigal Son stands up and offers him a sip of water from the glass on the side-table, and when a few drops dribble down the old painter's chin, he wipes them away with his sleeve.

RVR: Take my hand again, boy. Thaw this block of ice! I must tell you the beginning of the story. Then you can decide for yourself whether the sentence was a cruel or a just one.

PB: *Sits down on the bed, takes his hand.* Here I am, Master!

RVR: *In a rasp.* A month before her death, Elsje travelled from Jutland and procured work as a servant here in the city. She acquired a temporary room on the Damrak, hoping to pay for lodging from her first wages. After two weeks, the landlady was already demanding the money from her, and of course she did not have it, so the landlady threatened to take away her few possessions. When Elsje refused to give them up, the landlady beat her with a broomstick. In a fit of anger, or perhaps it was defence, Elsje took the hatchet from the nearby chair and hit her attacker. From the force of the blow, the woman fell down a flight of stairs, and at the bottom, she met her death.

PB: It was an accident?

RVR: Do not be too hasty! Elsje then got a hammer and broke open the travelling chest of a fellow lodger. She took out some linen for herself, then went to another lodger's chest and did the same thing, this time taking a coat to keep warm. Meeting the neighbours on the way out, she told them she had a nosebleed, for her hands were bloody. After she fled, the neighbours discovered the corpse in the house and pursued her through the streets. Elsje jumped into the Damrak, but soon they found her and led to court. At her trial, she confessed to everything and insisted that the death was accidental. Nonetheless, this was the verdict: she was to be hit with the same hatchet with which she killed the woman and hung on the pole until death, to be eaten up by the air and the birds in the sky. Your father was among the men who sentenced her.

PB: *Slaps the bed.* What a dog! She wasn't guilty at all! Now I know what I have to do . . .

RVR: What?

PB: As you said, escape! My father, it's unforgivable what he's done.

RVR: In spite of his faults, you must honour him.

PB: If only you could understand. He's threatened to revoke my inheritance.

RVR: Dear boy, listen. You cannot trifle with Fate. From birth until death, you are subject to all your father's weaknesses, his stupidity and vices and big ideas. Even if you are able to escape from his house, you cannot change your blood. Though you want to be free, you will inevitably act at his behest. In old age, you will look at yourself and see him in your reflection. You will inherit his lines, frown his frown, feel his agonies, speak his words. As long as you are alive you can never escape him, because you can never escape yourself. That is the truth, you must accept it.

PB: I must submit?

RVR: No! Do not become a slave to anything, not an old man, a ghost, a woman or even your art, for it will only deceive you with tales. Seek to be master of yourself, let discretion be your tutor, serve your youth well, for the more it is wasted the sooner it wears. Play not to the gallery but the stalls and boxes, and some day people will say of you, 'He is better by far than his father!'

PB: *Stammers.* Despise me for saying so, but somehow I feel it is my duty to follow you, if not my duty, then desire. We have only just met and . . .

RVR: A worthless fool such as myself? Where I am going you cannot follow. Prove yourself in deeds. Set me packing and finish the play.

PB: I promise you, Master, I will not sleep until I have told the world a tale, just as you advised, of an honourable man who suffers misfortune late in life, not through vice or depravity but from an error in judgement. It will send the hearers weeping to their beds!

RVR: Do not flatter me. No one loves me, and when I die, no soul will pity me. Why should they, since I feel no pity for myself?

PB: What about me?

RVR: *Eyes struggling to stay open.* Lord, have mercy on me. All the devils are here . . .

The Prodigal Son kisses the old painter's hand and rises from the bed. He slinks towards the door, hands thrust in his pockets.

RVR: Boy?

PB: Yes?

RVR: I never painted tulips.

The old painter turns his head on the soft pillow and falls asleep.

The Fever Rages, Shaking Me with Sweats

Samson lies on the ground, his eye spurting blood, his teeth clenched and toes curling in pain. Someone has spiked him with a shiny kris. Danae's golden mules rise before my eyes then fall again. Are they Hendrickje's? She is always forgetting to put her things away. When I reach over to touch them, they vanish in the mist. Between my eyes, where my nose should be, a dead bittern dangles upside down, feet bound together with string. My pupils roll back-'n'-forth, following it like a pendulum until that old lady, Aechje Claesdr., nudges her way in. She purses her lips at me and growls under her breath. I yell at her to go away, let me sleep. Her brows droop over her fleshy lids, and her face wrinkles as if she smells something bad. Perhaps it's the dead bittern. I could always eat it. Oh, but my stomach aches. The heat swallows my forehead. Spasms, thirst, shakes, sweats.

A young man wearing a red fur cap gallops straight past me on his white horse with a severed tail. What a racket! His black hooves trample my duvet. Where did he come from? How he rides with a proud hand on his hip! He is here and then he is gone. The fog grows thicker. A group of officials lean over their red-carpeted table. Six men dressed in black, leaning and looking. The one with the white beard has an eagle's eye. He wants to check the quality of my cloth, to pass it for inspection. I hope he can't detect all the holes from there. Who is that sitting in my chair? She resembles Margaretha de Geer, dignified and severe. With a gnarled hand, she waves her white tassled handkerchief at me. Is she trying to tell me something? I cannot hear her over the barking. That mangy grey poodle wants to play again. Always pestering me. His yelping becomes laughter, ringing through the room. It sounds like one of my students ... Flinck or Van Hoogstraten? Give me my brush, you rogues; give me my brush and be hanged!

Here is Mother, kissing my hands. Wait a moment. A handsome man stands at the far end of my room, watching me in the half-light. His pale face bears the traces of a long journey, but it is a young face. He smiles a sad smile. I cough discreetly into my collar, so as not to disturb the apparition. His eyes fix upon me.

Stay, illusion! Speak to me!

As he creeps closer, the room fills with the smell of grain. I see my father in his youth, before his accident with the musket, before his blindness.

What do you want me to say, dear boy? I have only come to see you one last time.

But you left me when you were still alive. Why did you leave me?

I had seen my final sunset! Don't you understand? There, in the dark, was a new world, an infinity of yesterdays. My reality was beyond my sight. I had begun my voyage to the other side. Like you, like you today. Why are you ready to die, son? You still have your eyes.

I can finally look at things around me with calm.

Now you understand, son. The man in the mirror, do you know him well?

Alas, I do.

Then, when you die, you will become him. Are you prepared to go?

What should I do, Father?

Close your eyes and remember a lifetime of beautiful things. The windmills rotating their arms, the pastures edged with blossoms, the farmsteads nestled in the oaks, the sparrows perching on a thatched roof, the warmth of your mother's hand, the look on your child's face while crying, the eyelids of your lover who has fallen asleep, the tear of a beggar receiving his alms, the play of moonlight on the canal ... Did I die smiling?

Yes, you did, Father.

Do you know why?

No, tell me.

Because I knew you would carry on my sight. You were my eyes, my footsteps, my tongue and my voice.

I have no such person, Father.

Look again. Out there in the distance, a sea of eyes! Do not be afraid. Follow the black river through the cold blue haze, past the grove of thickets and brambles, over the moss-covered stones, then beyond the muddy bend and across the rickety bridge. You will find the way.

With that, he raises a sigh that shatters his bulk. He vanishes through the chink in my door.

Goodbye, dear father. Remember me!

Deep Shadows Erase Me

The old painter lies in bed, eyes rolled upwards. The room is in shadow, apart from a taper flickering in the window. Outside, the snow keeps sadly falling.

RVR: (*Soliloquy*) This is the final moment. I am no longer wary.

Dust settles over my form and gradually creeps into my crevices. *See how I lay the dust with my tears!* My colour fades too, less cool, less warm. The greens become blue and grey, the reds lower into brown and yellow, the black turns dull as ash. Everything is sombre, deeply bruised. I no longer sparkle. *Give me a taper! Light, more light!* My skin is sallow and jaundiced. A fluttering current runs inside my veins. The damp warps from within and makes me bubble. My face curdles and clots into a field of faeces. A river of oil meanders through these festering wounds. There, on my nose, a blister has erupted, then it bursts. The destruction spreads, a malignant boiling from sole to crown. *My tears do not keep silent; put them in your bottle. Are they still in your book?* A furrow runs through my forehead and starts its descent. Once it reaches my spine, it will rend me in half. *O Lord, I am afflicted and poor. Do not conceal your face from your servant. Come near to my soul and reclaim it. On account of my enemies, redeem me.* Suddenly, all is quiet. My very roots dry up. My hair bristles and breaks. My eyelids chip and flake off. My ears swallow my neck. My lips harden into crust then rot away. *I have grown numb and crushed to an extreme degree. I have roared due to the groaning of my heart.* These hands, which hold each other tightly, become simply a blur. Of what use are they to me? In them, my vigour has perished. *O, that I had wings like a dove! I would fly away and be at rest.* Thread after thread of my smock unravels and crumbles into dust. The creaking begins in my limbs, rotting slabs. My flesh wastes away from sight, shedding a mouldy peel. *He has brought me down to clay, so that I show myself like dust and ashes, to be remembered no more.* Once my frame bows and breaks, my four corners curl and roll inwardly. I grope in the darkness. The outline of my figure dissolves slowly, as if it had never been. My heart becomes like wax, melting in its inward parts. The deep shadows erase me, all but my eyes. *Let us now relieve the Romans of their fears by the death of a feeble old man.*

[*Exit Rembrandt.*]

'Stultorum infinitus est numerus'

I was standing at the top of the stairs that descended two storeys to the ground floor of the foundry, after having swallowed an entire bottle of gin, when the message from Clara, containing the horrific news and nothing else, no terms of endearment or consolation ('Rembrandt is dead'), slipped out of my hands and flitted across the landing, and so I turned, knowing I had to escape – run, go somewhere – but getting hold of the paper, stepped down and lost my balance then stumbled over my very own foot at the top of the stairs – *the number of fools is infinite* – and clutching the parchment tightly, crumpling it in my palm, tumbled headfirst, down – down two flights, while remembering all the moments between us, Rembrandt and I, in a *one, two, three* second-flash of memories – I smelt, touched, tasted, heard and saw the strangest things: my first glimpse of his workshop when he told me about his carmine red and the kermes insect, and I, in turn, told him the story of Pyramus and Thisbe while perched on a stool ('Sit down'), then later, seeing his weary face *through a glass, darkly,* his white cloud of hair, his dark green eyes and sardonic grin ('To live well, you must live unseen'), an image which materialized into the dead features of a slaughtered ox on the side of the canal, a creature flayed and splayed for all to see, and I touched his shoulder, breathing in the rancid odour of paint and tobacco on his musty coat – indeed, I carried him home through the long, dark, dismal corridor ('My God, look at the gathering clouds!'), and he told me about his friendship with my late grandfather ('Prove it to me') – then, beyond that, the funeral, when I saved him from the pit of lions, the jaws of death, only to bring him home again and feel him open to me like a sliced pomegranate ('My art has not kept me alive but the people I have loved'), and best of all our final farewell, the story of Elsje ('The word she said was escape'), his parting words ('Set me packing and finish the play'), his hand in mine or mine in his – the friends, hands clasped; the lovers, hands clasped – it did not matter, they were one and the same, he and I were one and the same, for my senses played tricks on me as I tumbled headfirst, down – down two flights; I smelt, touched, tasted, heard and saw the strangest things, his pictures, too, in great flashes of colour as if I had walked round in them, as if I had lived them: Flora offering me a sprig of flowers, her cheeks blushed red; Susanna resisting my lustful stare, fleeing in her plain white shift; Mary Magdalene gazing up at me in disbelief, her face in the sunlight, astonished that I, the gardener, could really be the Christ; my old wife, Anna, offering me a goat as my mangy dog prowls round a wood fire, though I cannot really see them, my beloved ones, because I am blind or he is blind, it did not matter they were one and the same, he and I were one and the same, for my senses played tricks on me as I tumbled headfirst, down – down two flights, while remembering all the moments between us, Rembrandt and I, in a *one, two, three* second-flash of memories, until I hit the ground with a quake then sprawled there, twisted up in the silence of the hallway, all the while crying out through tears, so that no one could hear me – I wish they could hear me – Alas, poor Rembrandt!

The Ghost's Story

They don't know I can see them but I can. Through the open door of my room. Their dresses break into ripples. They flit around the house, draping black ribbons over landscapes, portraits and fruits of the field. My soul must find its way to the Promised Land. A warm gust of air rustles the drawn curtains. Neeltgen pauses in the doorway to look at me, spread along the bed in milky serenity. The candlelight shines on my frayed gown and my chest, rising in rigor mortis. She can see my eyes, withered in their cavities, my open mouth and the shadow there. I seem to be alive. My precious girl kisses me in tears. If only I could feel her soft, young skin.

There is a knock on the front door. The visitor introduces himself as a shopkeeper and genealogist who likes to haunt graveyards. Pieter van Brederode's the name. He heard that the deceased painter actually had a helmet once worn by a knight named Gerard van Velsen. Is it true? May he poke about? Rebecca nods twice, then shows him into my *kunstcaemer*. He scrambles amongst my things, the few things I carried through fame and misfortune: Roman heads, a bust of Caligula, the death mask of Prince Maurice. He tries to untie my Gordian knot. That greedy bastard, how dare he rifle through my chaos of memory! The collection takes revenge. My shells shrink from his large eyeball. My feathers make him sneeze. Oh, but he finds what he came for:

a medieval helm with eyelets, so narrow a sword could hardly pierce them. He fingers the cold metal in delight. His desire does not stop there. He also wants my helmet of a Roman commander, my bust of Democritus and my four arms and legs flayed by Vesalius. He offers Magdalena a few coins, a pittance. This is the cross I bear.

The other cabinets are open in mourning. Steeman, the notary, crawls inside. These are the instruments of my survival, the things that held me here. Ten nightcaps, eight cravats old and new, four tablecloths and handkerchiefs, three snuffers, a big lantern and a Bible. I would give anything to tie that cravat once more, feeling it pinch my wattle, or to finger the oily leather of my books. He checks my socks for holes, examines the stains under the arms of my shirt. Sweats from yesterday or a week ago. This is time taking its revenge. Oh, for ever let me weep.

In haste, he opens the workshop to all the things I created by my capable hands. The very ones that lay stiff at my sides! He tries to restore purpose to each item, but without me they are nothing. No reason, feeling, action. His feeble script records everything that saved and failed me. Thirty finished and unfinished pictures; Simeon still on the easel; a rusty mirror; piles of dirty cloths; palettes caked with paint; etchings stacked up in albums. As he touches them, one by one, he erases faces and hands, fields and bridges, barns and temples. I wait for my final amnesia.

Christiaen Dusart charges through the door like an overexcited bull, ready to cart off my daughter. I see his hand on the small of her back. My heart splits. Do not stand there torturing me . . . Go! He huddles with Magdalena, making plans. They must take care of matters. Her mules clip the boards in panic. How will we pay for his burial? The poor beggar had no money, or did he? Did he hide any silver in the house? No, Rebecca says, he took money from Hendrickje's legacy just for housekeeping. Magdalena asks for the key to Hendrickje's cupboard. Something must be in there! Dusart's hungry eyes peer over her shoulder. She unlocks the cabinet door. Dipping in a desperate hand, she finds my two moneybags and some gold. Half of this is mine, she says. Cornelia will receive her half in silver. That ungrateful hussy – I will haunt her for life! Where is Abraham Francen and his faithful heart? Dusart and Magdalena agree before Steeman that, by the mercy of God, the dead belong to the earth. They will accept money from the sale of my possessions only if it is free of all debt. They will also pay for my burial. Thanks be to God.

When it is over, Magdalena and Dusart lock the rooms one by one. Mine is the last, but they do not look in or bid farewell. Neeltgen stands in the doorway and bows her head in a sob. My eyes glimpse the faint curve of her neck, trapping a few wet strands of her hair. At that moment, she could be her mother. I wait for her to show me her face, her final face. She closes the door and leaves me behind in the bluish tinge of evening. A beautiful memory, even in death. Steeman locks the front door, sealing me inside. He takes the keys with him. The blue spark grows long in the flame. I shudder at the sight of my own shadow.

Three days pass, days of dust and long-suffering. I laze in a deep stupor until sixteen ruffians burst into my room and encircle me. I do not recognize these burly men outlined against the glow. They wear long coats and tall hats. Where are my friends? Where are my admirers? Before I can protest, they hoist me up and dump me into a rotten wooden box. Closing the lid over me, they nail it shut. Through the thin walls, I overhear those stockfish laughing at me. The gravedigger from the Westerkerk hired them for twenty guilders a piece. Monies for ale too, perfect after a hard day's work.

With a peculiar bump, I am in the air. Their boots click on the floorboards, and the front door bangs behind us. My coffin jostles and jangles as the stones cry out under their dragging feet. Only a short journey to my dear Hendrickje and the Promised Land. What did my father say? Out there in the distance, a sea of eyes! Follow the black river through the cold blue haze, past the grove of thickets and brambles, over the moss-covered stones, then beyond the muddy bend and across the rickety bridge. Do not be afraid.

I am not afraid. The hazy evening sun filters through the gaps in the planks, making little points of light on the ceiling. I would peek out for one last sight, but my rigid limbs are at the mercy of this accursed box. I imagine a lifetime of beautiful things. A dirty back-alley and its shadowy corner. A blind man outside a jeweller's shop, his decrepit eyes raised to a mercury sky. Two stray cats fighting over rubbish. A rascal crying out, ''Tis bitterly cold!' The clouds, tattered and black, smothering the light. Splatters, rivulets, swirls, blotches, tendrils, beads, bubbles, pearls, strokes, notches, torrents, dribbles, blobs, lumps, tears . . . Then I hear the murmur of water. It seems we are crossing the bridge. Gliding soundlessly along, I wait for the church bells. Only, there are no bells or knells tolling a dirge, no eulogies, poems, chants or prayers. They lower me under the stone floor into a cold silence. The winds and terrors carry away my eyes.

Upon the Surface of the Watery Deep

You find a stagnant quiet, a long-hidden secret. Listen closely and you will hear his name in one syllable. He visits you on lonely nights, during hours of anguish or hours of peace, when your destiny is unknown. He overtakes you as would thieves, greedy and insensitive, and makes you none the wiser. He shows you no faces, not a single star.

Why, even your hand is invisible before your eyes!

In the whispering gusts, you feel weary and alone. It seems you will never find a way out of the labyrinth, this frozen cave. As you wander in blindness, thousands of feelings spread themselves out: guilt, grief, shame, desire, revenge, lust. They make you shudder deep inside. What will become of you?

Such is Time's monotony.

Remember, all of this is his intention, for he teaches you to walk by Faith and not by Sight. He reminds you that all things desire to endure in their being: ashes are ashes, dust is dust, stone is stone. In the absence of the world, you must reside inside your mind, in its places, years and faces. Everything is eternal, for he shows you three months ago or ten thousand years past.

Remember your ancestors, fairies, angels and spectres.

Yet beware that you do not stray or follow him to the Cimmerian shore. While death is at work in him, there is life in you. The gloom will shatter in the instant of daybreak. Tell yourself, then tell yourself again: the end is nigh. He will call you out of blindness and open your eyes to hope. There is no greater miracle.

Here is your blank canvas, take it.

Epilogue

Perhaps it does not matter to anyone what happened to me in the five years since Rembrandt died, though I shall tell you nonetheless and so end my story. I recovered from the injuries taken by my tragic fall down the stairs – a concussion and a broken hand – in a matter of a few months (though at times my fingers still tingle and my head still swims: whether fevered or not, I have a recurrent vision of my mother, in dwarf size, dancing atop a candle flame). Then I plunged myself into an inconsolable, exacerbated kind of sadness that would have nearly annihilated me if not for the command to 'set me packing and finish the play', which would have seemed a crazy, unrealizable idea if not for my sustained drunken stupor. So, for those three years I put everything but my gin aside for our beloved painter, even my growing love for Clara de Geest, who no longer graced my presence wearing a dress the shade of poppy juice, or indeed, any other colour. I also managed to visit Rembrandt's tiny unmarked stone in the Westerkerk every day, sometimes with the gift of an exotic shell or a stuffed creature, in order to make him feel that his long, hard-working life had not been a waste nor indeed forgotten.

Then, in 1672, most likely you have heard, a tremendous fire razed our printing works with its famed collection of maps, globes, books and tracts, but the fire brigade never attributed the cause or source of the spark. When Jan van der Heyden, station general, suggested the old type of boilers revolted against the cold, he was wrong, you see — *that cause or source was me*, though guilt over the consequences has prevented me from making this confession until now. The sad truth is, not a year afterwards my father, Joan Blaeu, died from lung complications due to smoke inhalation. It was not part of a sinister plan as one might think; rather, it was an accident that occurred late one night when I was writing my pages by candlelight and, admittedly, just a little the worse for wear. I had only penned my final word before falling asleep with lazy limbs, and the taper happened to topple from the desk, igniting the Turkish rug and the silk curtains. Yes, I could have saved the house and the foundry from burning to the ground lest I did not save myself, and more importantly my book, which I secreted under my coat before leaping from the second-storey window and landing in the pig trough.

I never discovered how my father managed to escape that roaring pit of flames, nor why he would want to (he had already given up on life inwardly), and not because I did not care but because I fled the pit of destruction immediately afterwards. The newspapers reported that some witnesses had seen me upon my departure from Amsterdam in a carriage burdened with paintings and other curiosity items, accompanied by a fair-haired woman with downy cheeks and a crescent-shaped scar near her right eye, who was later suspected to be Clara de Geest, the wealthy daughter of a deceased portrait painter. There were also rumours that we, the unlikely pair, fled to Rome, where we started our own publishing company, specializing in poetry, philosophy and the odd piece of fiction. Well, those speculations are true, for on the eve of the fire, I showed up on her doorstep, a homeless vagrant in tattered rags howling at her to let me in, and soon enough she called down from her window, confessing that she, too, had been suffering without me. Together we live in married bliss (alas, I have learnt to bring colour to a woman's pale cheek!) in a palazzo surrounded by cypress trees, and as the sun sets every evening, the two of us – her with silver sprigs, me with a receding hairline – huddle together in our parlour, reading our books and silently sharing our disappointments as the crickets chirp in the distance. *Vieni a veder la tua Roma che piange.*

Which brings me to my next revelation. This very morning, I received a letter from the sweet Cornelia van Rijn, who at sixteen years old, married the painter Cornelis van Suythof and sailed with him to Batavia, on Java, where they established themselves in an artisan's house amongst vagabonds and pirates. Her hus-band earns additional monies as a jailer when he has few com-missions, she wrote, because they have three instead of two mouths to feed now. She has just given birth to a son, a lusty crying boy, and they have christened him Rembrandt. Along with this won-derful news, Cornelia's parcel contained a faded black leather tab-let – rounded in form from intensive use, some of its pages torn or uneven – which, she told me, had come into her hands from Abraham Francen after a long battle over her father's legacy. In his final moments, Rembrandt had requested that she bequeath his book to me.

I laid my hand on the cover, feeling the bulge of its contents, then picked it up and ran my fingers along the two rusty clasps engraved with leaves and the worn metal needle. I suspected it was a sketchbook or journal or both; in any case, it appeared valuable, and I thought that, alas, after all this time, I possessed a small token of my experience, like Atalanta with her head and hide from the slain beast, a small token ... Perhaps it would contain a scrap of the mysterious man I believed to have known for a short time. My hand trembled on the cover, feeling the bulge of its contents, *and the great ocean of truth lay undiscovered before me.* Then again, I thought, too often the prospect of happiness is sacrificed to one's own impatience for instant gratification.

Pieter Blaeu
Rome, 1674

My deepest thanks

to the experts on Rembrandt, his art and/or his times: Svetlana Alpers, Anthony Bailey, John Berger, Edwin Curley, Antonio Damasio, S. A. C. Dudok van Heel, Victoria Finlay, Steven Nadler, Geert Mak, Simon Schama, Gary Schwartz, Christopher White, Ernst van de Wetering

to the translators of the following editions: *The Correspondence of Spinoza* (NY, The Dial Press, 1927); *If not, winter (fragments of Sappho)* (Virago, 2003); *Don Quixote* by Miguel Cervantes (Secker & Warburg, 2004); *The Philosophical Writings of Descartes* (Cambridge University Press, 1984–1991); *Seven Letters by Rembrandt* (L. J. C. Boucher, The Hague, 1961); *Old Masters* by Thomas Bernhard (University of Chicago Press, 1989)

to those who helped me loosen the Gordian knot: Hans Jürgen Balmes, Patricia Duncker, Jacqueline de Jong, Sjaak de Jong, Andrew Kidd, Malcolm McNeill, David Miller, Enrique Murillo, Michael Nyman, Marijke Versluys

to those who paint in the spirit of the old master: my brother, Charles Miano, for giving me the idea for this book and painting my portrait; my best friend, Nina Gehl, for her strokes of brilliance and bottomless cups of coffee

to the Arts Council, for their generosity & support

SEM

Visit **www.picador.com** to read more about all our books and to buy them. You will also find features, author interviews and news of any author events, and you can sign up for e-newsletters so that you're always first to hear about our new releases.